TORCHWOOD
ANOTHER LIFE

Belongs to Kathryn White

TORCHWOOD

ANOTHER LIFE

Peter Anghelides

2 4 6 8 10 9 7 5 3 1

Published in 2007 by BBC Books, an imprint of Ebury Publishing.
Ebury Publishing is a division of the Random House Group Ltd.

The Random House Group Ltd Reg. No. 954009.
Addresses for companies within the Random House Group can be found
at www.randomhouse.co.uk.

A CIP catalogue record for this book is available from the British Library.

ISBN 978 0 563 48653 4

The Random House Group Ltd makes every effort to ensure that the papers
used in our books are made from trees that have been legally sourced from
well-managed credibly certified forests. Our paper procurement policy can be found at
www.randomhouse.co.uk.

Torchwood is a BBC Wales production for BBC Three
Executive Producers: Russell T Davies and Julie Gardner
Producer: Richard Stokes

Project Editor: Steve Tribe
Production Controller: Peter Hunt

Cover design by Lee Binding @ Tea Lady © BBC 2007
Typeset in Albertina and Century Gothic
Printed and bound in Germany by GGP Media GmbH, Poessneck

For Anne Summerfield
I can't imagine another life without her

ONE

You've never been the kind of soldier who would disobey a direct order. That's about to change right now. Because here you are gripping the cold and pitted plastic of the steering wheel in a stolen Wolf Land-Rover. The Wolf is loaded with equipment, and you are staring into the barrels of two SA80 rifles. Those L85 individual weapons are what have stopped you driving the Wolf through the barracks' exit barrier. In the bright midday sunlight, the barrier's tattered candy-stripe is still the most colourful thing among a swathe of brown earth, the dirty grey guard post, and the sentries' khaki uniforms.

You recognise both the soldiers who are aiming those rifles at you, of course. Privates Foxton and Kandahal. It's only a few months since you first saw them in training, at the start of their twenty-four weeks. Ross Foxton looks the more nervous, with none of the cocksure swagger of his first days at Caregan training camp. His pale face is flushed, threatening to match his cropped ginger hair.

Sujit Kandahal is shorter, stockier, dark in appearance and demeanour. He is bracing his feet in the dirt to steady his stance. He's got a good grip on the weapon, he's balanced well, and he's positioned himself to your right with a clear view of you beyond the bonnet of the Wolf. In other circumstances, you'd tell him you were impressed. 'Turn the engine off and step out of the vehicle with your hands raised. Sir,' he adds, like an afterthought. Not used to giving orders. Especially to you.

You can feel the hunger rising again. So soon, much sooner than you'd thought possible. You try to swallow it down, and then watch for the reaction that this provokes in the sentries. Maybe Foxton interprets it as nerves, because he steps calmly to your left, some of that old confidence returning. 'Sergeant Bee, you have to step out where we can see you.' A clear, shouted statement. No hesitation in his Scots accent. You stare at the weapons, and don't make eye contact with the soldiers. Your face is impassive. You'll give them no more clues.

'All right,' you say, calm and loud. 'I'm coming out.' You reach down. slowly, and kill the Wolf's Rover V8 engine as easily as you're going to kill one of these sentries.

As you step from the vehicle, you scoop up your Browning and slip it into the rear of your waistband. At nearly two pounds weight, it's not comfortable or safe to hide the pistol there, but it's out of Foxton and Kandahal's line of sight.

The light wind wafts the sound of church bells to you from the local village, heralding the afternoon service as usual. You think: Time of death, twelve thirty.

No point in running. Just time for a quick smile. 'See you again,' you tell them brightly. 'Soon.'

The muscles in Kandahal's forearm twitch. 'I said hands in the air, Sergeant—'

Even before he's finished speaking, you've brought the Browning around in a double-handed grip and loosed off two shells in quick succession. The first takes Kandahal in the forehead, just below the badge on his beret, and he sprawls in an ugly pile on the tarmac.

Foxton still has you cold. You let him fire the killing shot, and hope for better luck in another life.

TWO

'People live here,' Jack Harkness said to Gwen as they stepped out of the Torchwood SUV.

'Yeah. Awful, isn't it?' she answered. 'Even when it's gone eight o'clock in the rest of Wales, it'll still be 1955 in Splott.'

Jack looked at her sideways. 'No, I mean they *live* here.' He gestured around the alley, at the concrete walls of the flats that stretched nine storeys above them on both sides. 'They don't just exist. They breathe. They love. Play, decide, plan, laugh, screw. It has the smell of life.'

'It has the smell of something else, if you ask me. Vomit and piss.'

'And just a dash of dog shit,' conceded Jack. 'Labrador, I'd say.'

'Now you're just showing off.'

'Well, watch your step. And you wanna take a look at *him* while I check out the victim?' Jack pointed to a hunched figure opposite, and then strode off down the alleyway into the crime scene, his long military coat flapping around him.

Police Constable Jimmy Mitchell had his head in his hands when Gwen went over to him. She didn't recognise him immediately. She only saw the burly policeman sitting on the kerb, where he clutched one leg of the nearby road sign as though he was frightened to let go. The uniform, the fluorescent jacket, should have given him an air of authority. Instead, he was like a lost child. His posture looked defeated and his peaked cap was discarded on the pavement beside him. There was a fresh pool of vomit near his feet. He looked up, and she almost didn't know him then either, because his face was grey with shock. She'd worked for a while with Mitchell on late patrols, weeks ago, the usual boring driving tour of night-time Cardiff, enlivened only by the chance to break up a bottle fight in a dingy pub at closing time.

'Mitch?' Gwen asked him. 'Oh God, what's happened to you?'

Mitch opened his mouth, but for a moment couldn't speak. There were flecks of vomit in his moustache. He gestured wordlessly back down the alley. Should she leave him to take a look, or stay with him to make sure he wasn't injured or badly in shock? An angry shout from Jack decided the matter, and she hurried down the alley to join him.

Jack stood by the corpse, his hands on his hips. He tilted his head up towards the blue afternoon sky and screwed up his eyes, whether from the bright sun or from sheer exasperation it wasn't clear to Gwen. 'What do you see?'

She studied the body. It lay supine, half on the pavement and half in the gutter. Legs folded over to one side, arms splayed out at shoulder height. The back of the head had leaked blood and brains into the roadway, and wetted the otherwise dried mud that caked the nearby drain. 'Looks like the same cause of death as the others' she said.

'Look again.'

Gwen took a broader view of the alley. 'This is a new location. Still out of the way. Secluded. But further into town.'

He dropped his gaze and his pale blue eyes stared directly at her. 'Look again.'

'Time of death must be early this morning.'

He clucked his tongue. 'Let's leave that for Owen to decide at the autopsy. Now, look again.'

Gwen stooped for a closer examination. The corpse's lower face and chest were spattered with fresh vomit. Gwen coughed and gagged abruptly. 'This is too recent. It wasn't him.'

'It wasn't him, right,' agreed Jack. He raised his voice to a shout. 'It was *someone else* who barfed over the evidence!' Gwen could see Mitch further up the alleyway, still staring silently at his own feet. 'It was someone,' Jack continued, 'who had two corned beef sandwiches and a Tango Orange before he came on duty.'

Gwen arched her eyebrows at him. 'I don't believe you can work that out from just looking at that pile of sick.'

'It's the smell,' he told her.

'Dog shit, vomit… Now *I* feel sick.' She hunkered down to examine the corpse again, unsure whether to breathe through her nose or her mouth

10

in the process. The face seemed familiar. And why did she associate that face with the smell of fish and raw meat? Not from the stench of Mitch's acid vomit, that was certain. She could see that the victim had been a tatty-haired vagrant who looked much more than his teenage years. 'The previous victims were older than this guy.'

Gwen remembered where she'd seen this kid before. He'd been selling magazines by the covered market. He was one of the badged vendors who cheerfully cajoled shoppers to part with their money, and who didn't scowl even when the passers-by gave him the finger instead of cash. And now here he lay, dead in a grubby back alley in Splott. Someone or something had extinguished that lively look in his eyes by crushing the back of his skull. Crushing it so completely, Gwen already knew, that when they turned him over they would be able to see the cracked remains of his top vertebrae.

'Youngster.' Jack nodded, satisfied. 'Won't be so hard for Tosh to cover up, 'cause he won't be missed.'

'He will be missed.' Gwen was surprised how angry she felt about it. 'He'll be missed by me. I've seen him selling the *Big Issue* in town.'

'So, what's his name?'

'I don't know what his—' She bit off the rest of her sentence. 'That's not what I meant, and you know it.'

Jack smiled at her. Now she'd been working with him for a while, Gwen knew that he was trying to encourage her, not mock her. That still didn't stop her feeling like he was patronising her. 'It's all relative,' Jack said. 'Which of us will be missed? And when? Next year? Ten years? A century? When they're building the next Millennium Stadium, in Cardiff or whatever Cardiff has become by then, who will miss any of us?'

Gwen stood up again. 'Don't give me that "the universe is an atom in a giant's fingernail" bollocks. If you exaggerate the context, of course nothing's significant. What we *do* is important. What Mitch does is important.' She saw Jack puzzling over this. 'Him, that poor policeman down there, staring at his own spew, he's significant.' As if to prove it, she began walking back to Mitch's beaten figure.

'Name any famous cop from two hundred years ago,' Jack called after her.

'Robert Peel,' she snapped back without having to think.

'Wrong. He was the Home Secretary. Go on, name anyone from his police force.'

She faltered in her step, reconsidered, and kept walking.

'Joseph Grantham,' Jack told her. 'Who remembers him? He was the first officer killed on duty. People have moved on, many times over. They don't care. They're all living their own lives. Existing, breathing, screwing, remember? But see, that's why I like you, Gwen Cooper. You do care. It's at the heart of you. It motivates you. And it makes people see they can be better themselves.'

'Sometimes I don't think you care about anyone,' she muttered. She was standing by Mitch again, helped him to his feet. She mimed 'moustache' to him by waggling her finger under her own nose, and offered him a tissue to wipe away the vomit.

'C'mon, Gwen.' Jack was calling her back.

'Have you radioed in?' she asked Mitch. He nodded mutely. 'OK, I've got to go now. Sorry.'

Jack was angling his mobile phone at the dead youngster. He had the mobile on speaker, so that he could talk to Toshiko at the same time as transmitting a crime-scene image back to her at the Torchwood Hub.

'… second one within a one-kilometre radius of his apartment. Starting to look like we've got our man, Tosh. So, where is he?'

'Working on it, Jack,' Toshiko's voice told him from the radio.

'Are these pictures any good? I mean for analysis, I wasn't gonna get them printed up and framed for my desk back at the office. People hated that last time.'

'They're ideal,' enthused Toshiko. 'I can cross-reference the upload with structured information in pictures and captions from the Police National Database. Smart stuff they've got – a multimedia setup that integrates the text, image, video and audio data at the level of the bit-stream so that they can be stored, accessed and processed by the same system.'

Jack rolled his eyes. 'I was interested right up to the point where you said "upload".'

Gwen tutted. 'All the SOCOs I know would love that kind of system. Something that could identify patterns that link directly to individuals. Like persistent offenders whose patterns of offence haven't been obvious to investigators.'

Jack grinned at her. 'Oh, you and Tosh were just made for each other.'

A breeze was starting to lift litter down the narrow alley, and swirl it around their feet and onto the corpse. Sweet wrappers stuck in the blood and vomit.

Gwen studied the sky. Dark grey clouds were obscuring most of the blue now. 'Weather's deteriorating.'

'Yeah,' said Toshiko's voice. 'There's a strange cold front over the city. Not what we'd expected from the forecast. Plenty of rain on its way, and the temperature's unusual for this time of year. Low 60s. Like Owen's IQ.'

Jack pulled his collar up as the breeze stiffened. 'OK, Tosh, your smart system has had plenty of time now. So where's our killer?'

'Already left his office. Office mates said they thought he was going into the city centre, not back home. Then we lost his trail behind a lorry on the M4, and missed his exit junction.'

'Options?'

'I'm trying to get to his secretary,' said Toshiko. 'And we're still scanning for his car.'

Jack considered the corpse at his feet. 'All right, Gwen and I are going into the centre. Tosh and Owen, we need clean-up here for the corpse. Location…'

'Got it from your GPS signal,' Toshiko said. 'Post code CF24 9XZ. You're in Gwion Lane, Splott.'

Jack broke the connection, and started back towards the SUV. Mitch had got to his feet now, and stood to an awkward kind of attention as Jack and Gwen approached. This meant he stood between them and the Torchwood car.

'I radioed for back-up, and they're on the way. Until then, anything I can do to help, sir?'

'Radio them again and cancel,' Jack told him, 'Torchwood will handle this now.' Gwen saw Mitch's face flush with embarrassment. 'Go ahead,' Jack urged him. Mitch fumbled for his radio and did what he was told.

'You know,' Jack said to Gwen, 'I was kind of worried that we'd never find a big-boned policeman to vomit copiously on our victim and then cower on the pavement. But I was wrong. Here was Constable Mitchell, ready to fill that vacancy.'

Gwen prodded Jack in his side with an angry finger.

'All right,' grumbled Jack. 'Constable, keep any arriving bystanders away from the body until the Torchwood clean-up team arrive. And here…' From one of the flapped pockets in his greatcoat he pulled an evidence bag, transparent plastic with a coloured seal. He thrust it at the baffled policeman.

'Try not to throw up on anyone else.'

All Gwen could do was smile an apology to Mitch as she climbed into the SUV. Jack swiftly dropped the car into reverse and the SUV's tyres squealed their way back up through the trash-strewn alley. In the reflection of the side-mirror, Gwen watched Jimmy Mitchell sink slowly back to the pavement, still clutching the plastic bag.

THREE

They sat in the Casa Celi café and watched the street outside. Jack had previously brought the whole team here for what they'd all thought was an evening jolly, recognition for the hard work they'd put in during the Cyclops business, or maybe a bonding exercise. Fat chance, Gwen had realised afterwards – it was just that Casa Celi afforded a clear view of The Hays shopping area, and it had been ideal for spotting a vagrant Weevil that Jack was hunting that evening. They should probably have guessed when they saw Jack was carrying the defensive spray and the hand-clamps, because they obviously weren't designed for a fun night on the town. In the end, Gwen hadn't even got to finish her antipasto.

Now they both took the same pavement table as that earlier night. A couple of city types – striped shirts, pint glasses, clouded intellects – sprawled at an adjacent table and leered at Gwen. Jack propped himself in a metal chair, still wearing his greatcoat but draping it so that the chair back was between his body and the coat.

By sitting next to him, Gwen got the same clear view of the street, ideal on a sunny day and still acceptable as the sky became more overcast and early evening began to draw in. There was a pre-storm smell in the air, 'the ozone tang of unspent lightning' Jack had called it as they'd sat down. The tarmac released the day's earlier heat. Shoppers bustled past with too little time and too many bags on their race back to the car parks against the coming rain.

A small knot of Merryhill pupils, still in school uniform, jostled past another group from Roath High. The early evening concert at the Millennium Centre must just have finished, thought Gwen, spilling a brawling crowd of secondary-school kids into the area on their way home. God, it was bad enough keeping them apart when they got older and got bladdered and went on the town. She hoped they weren't going to have to keep them apart when they were in their early teens as well.

Then she remembered that wasn't her job any more. And wasn't sure whether to be sorry or just relieved.

She and Jack were served by the same good-looking waiter who had served Gwen on their last visit. Her mental notebook told her he was Enrico 'Rico' Celi, early thirties, second-generation Welsh Italian, with almost stereotypical Latin looks but an incongruous South Coast accent. He'd inherited the café from his dad. Jack teased him that his tan was fading the longer he stayed in South Wales. Rico could swear in Welsh, Gwen discovered. But he didn't seem to mind Jack slapping his backside as he stooped to deliver their drinks.

Gwen had a lemonade, ice and lemon, tall glass. Jack ordered a still water in a plastic cup. He paid for it as soon as it arrived by dropping money into the ashtray on the metal table. 'Means I can get up and go whenever I need to. Rico's too cute for me to rip him off,' Jack explained to her when she asked. 'Or steal one of his glasses.'

Gwen fingered the coins in the ashtray. 'Exact change,' she noted. 'No tip?'

'He's not that cute.'

Throughout this, Jack's eyes never left the street. He obviously wasn't going to let their target slip past unnoticed while Gwen was making polite conversation.

Gwen let her eyes linger on him for a while instead of the street. Jack had told her once that he drank water because it kept him hydrated, ready to leave at a moment's notice. Apart from what he wore, and a few minor and rather odd artefacts back at the Hub, Jack didn't seem to own anything. He was tall and broad, a big presence physically and personally. And yet if he disappeared he would leave little evidence behind. Though he would leave a large gap in her life.

A couple of months had passed since she'd first become aware of Torchwood, but it might as well have been a lifetime. Jack was like the ideal boss she'd imagined back in the force. When she did the right thing, he told her. When she screwed up, he told her that too. That didn't make it comfortable, but it meant she knew what was expected, understood it, accepted it. No soft soaping, no bullshit. None of the fast-track bollocks she got from Inspector Morrison, no discussions about structured career paths for officers who showed 'flair and potential'. No courses on assertiveness without aggression. And no listening to fellow officers like Andy, bleating about the inadequacies of the system, giving her grief about being overtaken by smartarse graduates who wouldn't know an arrest form from their arsehole.

She had no idea where this job with Torchwood was taking her. The more important thing was, she didn't give a toss about that either. She only knew that she loved it. When had she last had to give evidence in court, escort a scumbag to the cells, go through the rigmarole of writing up a witness statement?

She loved every day. She loved working with Owen and Toshiko and Ianto and Jack. Just now, she couldn't conceive of leaving them. Couldn't imagine Jack disappearing. Losing him.

Jack sneaked a quick look at his watch, then at Gwen, then straight back to the street. 'I don't know whether to be flattered or irritated. Shouldn't you be watching for our guy instead of watching me?'

Gwen snapped her eyes back to the street, suddenly self-conscious. 'Yeah.' She fumbled for her palmtop computer, and called up the image that Toshiko had sent them earlier. The screen showed her a badly lit, flat-featured picture – a face with the rictus grin that characterised any security photo. Guy Wildman, early forties, grey suit collar to match his hair. What made him the killer of four vagrants in Cardiff?

What made anyone?

She and Jack observed the pedestrians flowing through the street. An old lady in a patterned headscarf hobbled along, a Tesco bag in each hand. A pinstripe suit beside her flicked a finger at the city types on the next table, who jeered a boozy chorus in response as he joined them. A blue one-man dustcart paused outside the café to empty a waste bin. Jack was on his feet immediately, getting an unobstructed view, shooing the driver on, watching the street beyond. Watching a tired woman struggle with a squealing preschool child along the opposite pavement. Watching two teenagers as they idly peered through a newsagent's window, their shirt tails stuck out below their school pullovers and each with their backpacks slung low over one shoulder. Watching a bleach-blonde woman in a too-tight skirt and fuck-me shoes totter in the opposite direction with a supermarket trolley full of groceries. Watching a crumpled man thread his way through the thinning crowds on his way north. Watching him shoot looks to left and right. Watching him clasp his briefcase firmly in one hand, and clutch his collar tightly to his throat with the other.

The man's demeanour drew attention to him. He was short, maybe five foot six, broad rather than athletic. He was in a hurry, but trying not to look it. He was grey-haired, dishevelled, on a mission. The way he grasped his beige raincoat collar, it was as though the weather had already worsened and he was walking through a non-existent rainstorm. He was Guy Wildman.

'That's our boy,' said Jack. He swerved around the dustcart, and manoeuvred into the street thirty metres behind the target. Gwen fumbled her palmtop computer into her jacket, and started after him. As she did, her sleeve caught the half-empty glass of lemonade. The glass fell, rolled across the table, and smashed on the pavement. The city types at the next table cheered and clapped sarcastically.

Wildman heard the noise. Turned and saw Gwen.

She flicked a look at Jack. Immediately cursed at her own tactlessness.

Wildman was already looking back at Jack. Seeing Jack's hand reach beneath his greatcoat for a weapon. A panicky look of disbelief. And Wildman darted into a side street and away.

Jack was after him in an instant. Pedestrians scattered like a flock of startled pigeons as he burst through their midst.

Gwen launched herself after him, half-colliding with the woman pushing the supermarket trolley. She ignored the woman's stream of obscenities, resisted the temptation to stop and give her a hard slap, and chased down the narrow side street after Jack. She could see the tail of his grey greatcoat twisting behind him as he shimmied between a couple of shoppers. Far ahead of them, Wildman was rounding the next corner.

As she approached it at a run, Gwen could hear angry shouts and swearing. She turned into the alleyway, and found half a dozen school kids gesticulating after the disappearing Jack. A ginger-haired lad had been knocked down in the rush. One of his friends was helping him to his feet again, and another was recovering his scattered ciggies from the gutter.

'Watch where you're fucking going,' bellowed the ginger lad.

Gwen hopped around them, still staring down the alley at Jack who was about to turn another corner. 'Smoking can seriously damage your vocabulary,' she told them before haring off down the alley.

She had dropped well behind now, fifty metres at least. It was obvious from the way Jack was running that he'd taken out his revolver, a curiously old-fashioned pistol that he seemed to prefer to anything modern. And it was also apparent that he was unable to take clear aim at the fleeing figure of Wildman. Too many early evening pedestrians were wandering these side streets. A group of girls from a private school, incongruous in their expensive blazers, formed a buzzing crowd outside a clothes shop. Two business men walked in parallel but were oblivious to each other in their separate mobile phone calls.

A couple of dusty construction workers laughed as they began to secure a makeshift door in the chipboard wall around a building site. Their appearance and manner told Gwen that it was the end of their shift. Their yellow hard hats were clipped to their belts and their fluorescent jackets were off their shoulders and hanging behind them from the waist. So they were unprepared for Wildman to barge straight at them. One he smacked with his shoulder, and the other caught a solid blow when Wildman swung the side of his briefcase into the man's head. They stumbled aside, and Wildman pulled the door open again.

The workmen staggered back to their feet and cursed him with the fluency of long practice. The younger man, a crew-cut teenager with a cauliflower ear, had taken the blow from the briefcase. He was attempting to seize Wildman by grabbing onto his beige raincoat when Jack approached at full pelt and yelled at him to step aside.

Wildman struggled at the door, fumbling with the latch and open padlock. He glared at Jack, and seemed to convulse. From her perspective, still halfway down the alleyway from him, it looked to Gwen as though Wildman was going to be violently sick. She heard a plopping sound, and Wildman regurgitated a green-grey bolus at Jack. Jack stepped aside with a surprised yell, bumping into the two construction workers. Wildman took his chance in the confusion. He almost wrenched the door off its rusty hinges, and dived into the building site.

The construction workers were staring at whatever Wildman had sicked up. It hadn't splattered as it hit the ground. It just lay there, pulsing slightly. Jack reached out one foot, trod the thing into the dusty pavement. Then he kicked it through the door. He was briefly prevented from following it, as the two workmen grasped him by the arms. Jack shucked them off with a swift, violent shake of his shoulders. That's when they saw his pistol, and they backed off, raising their hands.

'Good choice,' said Jack, and disappeared into the building site, still in pursuit of Wildman.

Gwen pounded up the street to the door, and brandished her ID card.

The older of the two workers stared at her. His wide round eyes were pale in the dirty brown leather of his face. Now he'd seen the ID, his manner was wary, less confrontational. 'What's going on here? That bloke's not well. He was throwing up… what was that thing?' The door was slightly ajar, and he was about to open it for a look, but Gwen pushed it shut again.

'Well, this site isn't safe to go wandering around in,' persisted the workman. 'I'll have to let the gaffer know about—'

Gwen dismissed his objections. 'I don't need your gaffer's permission. I just need you to get out of the way. Anyone else in there? Anyone else arriving for another shift?'

'We're the last. All done for the day. Just locking up,' said the younger man, eager to sound helpful.

'But the floors aren't all in yet,' protested his older mate. 'Not beyond the fifth, at any rate. And the external sheeting doesn't go beyond that, either.'

Gwen leaned right back, and stared up into the early evening sky. The building construction loomed over her, a vertiginous cliff of scaffolding and grey concrete. Far above, a dirty orange crane poked out above the top floor. Green fabric netting flapped in the breeze around the unfinished office block, a rippling sign announcing that it was a Levall-Mellon development.

'The site manager'll have my guts. I can't be blamed if you lot get yourselves killed.' The construction worker's tone had changed completely now. Gwen recognised it from a dozen similar encounters with her new team. The people you encountered started out superior, arrogant. And when faced down by anonymous authority, they were cowed into submission. Or, like now, they started looking to offload the responsibility they'd made such a fuss about to start with. That's when you knew they weren't going to be a problem, because they no longer wanted that authority.

She pointed to the yellow hard hat clipped to his waist. 'I'll need that,' she said. He hesitated. 'Come on, we haven't got all day.' She pulled the door open again. 'Lock this behind me.'

Beyond the chipboard barrier, it was gloomier than in the street outside. Gwen paused for a moment to let her eyes adjust. She tried the hard hat and found that the guy's head was much bigger than hers. She gave up trying to adjust it, and placed the hat on the edge of a rusting yellow skip. The skip was half-full of rubble, grey chunks of broken wall and spiral scraps of concrete reinforcement steel.

The thing Jack had kicked through the door had fetched up against the angled side of the skip. How had Wildman been able to spit that out, Gwen wondered. It had unfurled now, like a snot-coloured starfish with four legs. The thing quivered for a moment before it went stiff, leaking yellow bile into the grey dust.

Gwen flipped open her palmtop computer, thumbed a fastkey, and dialled Toshiko at the Hub. 'We've pursued Wildman down Blackfriar Way. Into the construction site. Wildman's covered some distance since we spotted him.'

'Interesting,' Toshiko replied. 'He must have made a miracle recovery. The reason we couldn't get his secretary earlier was that she drove him home, because he wasn't feeling well.'

'Just an excuse, d'you think?' asked Gwen. 'A reason for them to sneak off for an afternoon shag?'

'Unlikely,' said Toshiko. 'From what I can make out, Wildman is a bit of a sad bachelor. No suggestion that he's got a girlfriend. Or a boyfriend. Or a close relationship with an animal.'

'I'm not sure about that.' Gwen eyed the dead starfish thing that Wildman had spat out at Jack. 'There's certainly something that's not quite right with him,' she said. 'I'm going in to support Jack. Can you get police back-up to close off this whole area, and then get here yourselves?'

'OK,' confirmed Toshiko.

'Was Mitch all right?'

'Mitch?' asked Toshiko.

'The policeman at the pick-up.'

'When did you start worrying about the police?'

'I never stopped,' Gwen told her. 'So, was he OK?'

'Didn't notice,' admitted Toshiko. 'We were too busy scraping up bits of victim. Talk to you later.' And she ended the call.

Gwen could hear running on the floor above her. Shoes pounding and scraping on dusty concrete. She scanned this floor, and saw where they must have gone. She stepped through a gap in the wall where emergency doors would later be fitted, and looked up into the stairwell. Concrete stairs made a four-sided spiral up into the building. There were no rails in place, so she hugged the wall, staying well away from the edge where, flight by flight, the drop became sheerer and more disorienting.

Her lungs were starting to burn as she approached the eighth floor. Beyond the next landing was the scuffling sound of shoes on concrete. Gwen she slowed her progress and peered out carefully.

The early evening sun fell in a brilliant shaft of light, angled through the whole area. Concrete reinforcement wire poked out of blocks in the centre. Gwen blinked in astonishment. She could see through the unfinished floor, and again through the next three floors below that. On a cross-beam in the centre stood Jack. He was balanced, apparently unconcerned by the dizzying gap below him, with his pistol trained on the far side of this shell of a room.

Wildman had picked his own way carefully over the fretwork of connecting girders, and now scrambled over the partly constructed exterior wall and onto the raised wooden and metal framework that surrounded the building. He had to use both hands to balance, and then to grasp the weathered steel of the scaffolding and hoist himself out onto the ledge. His beige coat no longer clung tightly to him. It rippled in the breeze that whistled through the carcass of the building. Gwen could see that the raincoat was actually too small for Wildman, and the arms had ridden up above his wrists to reveal the soiled cuffs of his grey suit.

Wildman stood on the pale brown scaffolding platform. He turned to face Jack. The race up the building and the subsequent scramble across this floor had exhausted him. He took deep, desperate breaths of air. Several metres to his left a stretch of the zigzag laddering straddled the side of the building, an even more precarious route down than the unfinished emergency stairs. To Wildman's right, the battered plastic opening of a long debris chute yawned ominously, ready to devour whatever was dropped in and to regurgitate it many floors below into another, unseen yellow skip. Wildman couldn't seriously be considering either of those exits, thought Gwen.

Jack must have been thinking exactly the same thing. 'C'mon, Wildman,' he called across to him. 'Where are you gonna go from here?'

Wildman peered behind himself, out across the city. While he did this, Gwen shuffled carefully into the room. She could now see through the skeleton of the building at this height, and a momentary nausea washed over her. She clutched at the wall to steady herself.

When she looked up, she could see that Wildman was still staring out. The green fabric netting outlined this part of the building beyond the frame of scaffold poles, but through a gap in one section it was possible to see right out over Cardiff. They were high enough now to have a clear view, uninterrupted by nearby buildings. Streets criss-crossed their way towards the waterfront. There was the bronzed hump of the Millennium Centre. The glittering Bay reflected light between the moorings, and stretched out towards the barrage. Clouds were starting to roll in across the Bay, threatening rain from beyond the barrage and out into Môr Hafren.

Wildman swivelled back around to consider Jack again, careful not to overbalance on the scaffold platform. Gwen could see now that the top of Wildman's grey jacket was wet and dark. The vivid red splash on his white shirt indicated that this was blood. Wildman's neck and face didn't seem to be marked. Maybe he had somehow scraped himself in the chase up through the building. The coat wasn't his either, it was now apparent. The position of the buttons were for a woman's raincoat, and that explained why the sleeves were too short. Wildman was breathing more easily now, and smiling broadly. His smile wavered a little when he saw Gwen at the rear of the room, but he soon refocused on Jack.

Jack had not moved from his precarious position in the centre. He held the pistol in a one-handed grip, unwaveringly pointed at Wildman. Jack's other hand was at his side, the outside of his wrist against his hip. He knew Gwen was twenty metres behind him, even though she hadn't spoken, had barely made a sound. He was waggling his fingers slightly, unseen by Wildman, to indicate that Gwen should stay back,

'OK, so you checked out the view,' Jack called to Wildman. 'And you know you're going nowhere.'

Wildman cocked his head to one side, contemplating Jack. 'That weapon is a fascinating item,' he said. His voice betrayed no worry, just amused interest. 'Is it an antique?'

'It's a Webley,' Jack replied calmly. 'Mark IV. Point three-eight calibre, and a five-inch barrel. More than enough to pick you off where you stand.'

'Interesting. Where do you get the cartridges?'

Jack's aim didn't falter. 'What matters is where you might be getting one. Any moment now. Step back into the building. Away from the edge. Carefully.'

'I think I'm safer where I am. Why don't we just continue our chat right here?'

Jack moved his head to one side, and Gwen could see him smiling grimly. 'OK. So maybe we start with the obvious stuff. Like, what's your connection to the deaths of four vagrants. The ones that were found within a few minutes walking distance from the offices of the Blaidd Drwg nuclear research facility?'

Wildman tutted. 'Shocking. I saw that on the news. We were all warned about it at the facility, of course. Wouldn't want the staff to be harmed.'

'No,' snapped Jack. 'No you weren't warned. The murder of the vagrants didn't make it to the media. We made sure of that. So you're unusually well informed.'

'I suppose I am.'

'And their deaths match the times that you were just about to enter work, or you'd just left. We checked your ID badge accesses at Blaidd Drwg. They all match.'

Wildman's smile didn't change. 'Do they?'

'You even snuck out one lunchtime. What was that about? Hadn't taken a packed lunch that day? No, that wouldn't be it, because your access badge shows that you take lunch in the works canteen every day, 12.15 on the dot. Except for that day. The day the third victim died.'

'It's no crime to take a walk at lunchtime,' observed Wildman mildly. 'You could say it's my constitutional right.'

'You were killing people, not killing time…'

'I don't think so.'

'… attacking defenceless victims and splitting open their heads.'

'How dreadful,' said Wildman.

'It's hard to believe, looking at you now. But you murdered them by biting into the backs of their necks.'

Wildman laughed in disbelief.

'In fact,' persisted Jack, 'isn't that spinal fluid now? There, down your chin? All over your shirt collar.'

Wildman raised his hands to his face, an almost involuntary reaction. His face clouded with anger.

Jack laughed. 'Made ya look.'

The breeze through the building had begun to stiffen now. Jack's greatcoat wafted out behind him, though his stance and his aim remained rock steady. The melancholy wail of a police siren carried up to them from the street as it drew nearer.

Wildman took another look backwards into the street far below. Returned his gaze to Jack. He didn't look angry any more. He was calm.

'C'mon, Wildman.' Jack had adopted a cajoling note now. 'There's no escape from this. Gwen here, behind me, you've seen her. She's called the police. So even if you get past me – and you won't – you wouldn't beat the cordon around this building. Come away from the edge now, carefully.'

'Are you going to read me my rights?' smiled Wildman.

'You're in the custody of Torchwood now. We're not the police. We do things differently. But you'd know that already, from your work at Blaidd Drwg, wouldn't you? And that means you know we can help you, Wildman. Whatever the problem is.'

Wildman raised his left arm, slowly so that it wouldn't alarm his captor. Studied the chunky watch that poked out beyond his soiled cuffs. 'Time of death…' he murmured to himself. He lowered his arm, and studied his feet with a look that suggested he had never seen them before, or perhaps that they were the most fascinating things in the whole room.

Gwen thought she saw Jack's arm tense up. 'Don't fool around, Wildman. I can take you out from here.'

Wildman looked up from his shoes. He stared past Jack, at Gwen. He was grinning now, like it was all a huge joke. He switched the grin back to Jack.

'See you again,' he said cheerfully.

Wildman allowed himself to fall. His feet didn't move. His arms remained calmly by his side. He just dropped backwards, as though it was a trust exercise and someone was going to catch him.

But no one could catch him. The green netting parted soundlessly behind him. Guy Wildman was still smiling as he plunged backwards, head first, and tumbled to his death.

FOUR

Gwen pushed her way through the police cordon. Her words were 'excuse me' and 'sorry' as she moved the police constables aside, but her tone was 'get out of my way'. She knew that coppers responded to the sound of authority, were less likely to question her seniority because they were accustomed to simply obeying orders that were spoken clearly and unambiguously. It was a technique she'd seen the other Torchwood members use, even the more reserved Toshiko. Gwen was still trying to be polite about it. Unlike Owen, who was more likely to wave his ID, shout 'Coming through!' and then barge his way past. Sounding more assertive meant that Gwen got things done faster, got to her destination sooner. Not that Wildman was likely to be going anywhere in a hurry, mind. His last journey had come to an abrupt end after only a few seconds.

'Sorry... Excuse me... Thanks... Keep those pedestrians back there, please...'

The only time it was awkward was when she came across her former colleagues. Like now. The blue flashing light of the nearby police car strobed over the chubby features of Andy Davidson. Once upon a time, he'd been showing her the ropes. Today, she was asking him to stay behind them.

'We've got to stop meeting like this,' Andy said to her. But she noticed that he still held the yellow-and-black cordon tape up for her. 'People will start to talk.'

'Thanks,' she said, stooping under the tape. 'I imagine people are talking anyway, aren't they Andy?'

'Special Ops?' he said. 'Bound to have tongues wagging, isn't it?'

Gwen chose not to answer his next, unspoken, question: *What is your job now, Gwen?* She let Andy guide her down the road, and along the length of a bendy bus that seemed to have stalled in the middle of the carriageway.

'Can this be moved?' she asked him.

'Wait and see,' he replied.

They rounded the front end of the bus. The windscreen was a crazed spider's web of splintered glass, with a long smear of blood down its full height. The diesel engine was still chattering away. And the crumpled remains of Guy Wildman lay sprawled under the front wheels.

'He was determined, this bloke.' Andy pushed his cap further back on his head, so that he could stare up at the building site and point. 'Eight floors down. Smacks into the top of the bus. Slides down the front. Bus doesn't stop in time. Finishes the job.'

A dark pool was spreading beneath the bumper, like a target that had Wildman's head in its dead centre under the front of the bus.

'Scraped him along the tarmac for several metres.' Andy sucked air through his teeth, like a plumber appraising a quotation. 'I suppose we'll be left to shovel up the bits, as usual.' He shook his head. 'Anyway, high-rise suicide isn't very Special Ops, is it? I'd have thought you'd be more involved investigating all these vagrant murders. Serial killer, is it?' He obviously wasn't deterred by her silence. 'Can't you tell us anything, Gwen? Or aren't we a part of the team any more?'

'I would tell every one of you,' she said gently. 'Except then I'd have to become a serial killer myself.'

Andy studied her thoughtfully. 'I'm starting to believe that you're not joking when you say things like that.' He concealed his disappointment badly. 'Ah well, I'll get the forensics team out here.'

'Not this time, Andy.' Gwen felt that keen awkwardness again, the sense that she was clumsily rejecting her friends on the force, and couldn't yet find a graceful way to do it.

As if to underline this, Owen brusquely charged up to them. 'Are you coming, Gwen?' He had stopped right in front of Andy, like he didn't exist. 'Tosh is snapping on her rubber gloves, and you're not gonna want to miss this one.' Owen strode off around the bus.

Gwen shrugged a kind of apology at Andy. 'While we're on the subject,' she said as she turned to go, 'you don't want to talk about cleaning up if my boss is listening.'

Andy had the grace to look embarrassed at this. 'Mitch? Yes, I heard about him chucking up at the scene.'

'I hope he'll be all right.'

'Not after the lads find out, he won't be. I reckon that he'll be over it by about... ooh, eight months? But you know what Mitch is like, he's a bit of a...' Andy trailed off, aware that Gwen was giving him a tight smile while looking meaningfully over his shoulder to the cordon. 'Ah, all right then. Well... Be seeing you.'

He turned on his heel and retreated, away from the scene of crime. Gwen wasn't sure whether she heard correctly, but she suspected he'd sarcastically added a murmured 'ma'am' before he went.

'Whoa! Whoa!' yelled Owen as Gwen reappeared at the front of the bus. 'No, not you, darlin'.' He stood up and banged on one of the unmarked parts of the windscreen. 'Tosh, what are you doing with that bus driver?'

Toshiko's head appeared through the driver's side window. 'He's in no fit state to drive.'

'You can bloody talk. Try reverse gear, would you? I want some of him left for the autopsy.'

There was a horrendous grinding of gears, and the whole bus seemed to shudder. With a further reluctant groan and a startling hiss of air brakes, the vehicle slowly moved backwards. From beneath the front of it emerged the gory mess of Guy Wildman. He must have hit the bus head first before crunching into the roadway and then being dragged along underneath for some distance before it stopped. Wildman's limbs were twisted into impossible angles. The shattered remnants of his head lay in a bloody pool that encircled it like a gruesome halo. There was so much blood that it created a reflective surface, in which Gwen could see the streetlights that had started to come on around the scene of the accident.

Owen considered the brutalised remains. 'This is going to bugger up the tourist trade again. They're only just getting over the death of Gene Pitney in that hotel across the way. Remember that? He was on tour in Cardiff, and dropped dead in his hotel room.'

'How awful,' said Gwen.

'I think something got a hold of his heart,' said Owen, still poking at the corpse. 'Not what the manageress had in mind when she told him that checkout was before 10 a.m.' He positioned a small daylight lamp beside the fresh corpse, and began snapping photographs on a digital camera.

Gwen had seen Owen at so many scenes of crime now, yet was still amazed by his detached view. She wondered if his disparaging attitude was part of his training as a doctor, something that kept him separate from patients and relatives in the face of death, and now kept him sane amid the madness of what they did.

Toshiko joined them by the body. She'd given up trying to park the bus neatly, and had left it jack-knifed with two wheels across the opposite pavement. 'Nasty,' she said. 'Did he jump or was he pushed?'

'Suicide.' Gwen remembered Wildman's demeanour beforehand. So different from the panic he'd shown when fleeing from them in the street. 'He was absolutely calm,' she said. 'Smiling at us. He was ready when he finally jumped.'

'Jumped?' Toshiko was surprised.

'No,' Gwen corrected herself. 'He didn't jump. I've seen people jump before, it's a kind of last desperate act, once they've screwed up the... yeah, the *courage* to do it, I suppose. Wildman here, he simply let himself fall. Dropped off the eighth floor like he was collapsing backwards onto a bed.'

'Not what it looked like from down here,' Toshiko said. 'He screamed. Threw his arms about like he was trying to grab the air and hold on.'

'Flailing,' offered Owen. 'Thrashing about he was. Desperate.'

'It was only a few seconds, I suppose, but it sounded like...' Toshiko's eyes looked haunted as she recalled it. 'Well, like despair, I suppose.'

'Not straight away. He didn't start screaming until about halfway down.' Owen tucked the digital camera back in his jacket pocket. He stared at the corpse. 'Maybe you changed your mind, eh? No going back on that decision, mate. What got into you?'

Gwen didn't understand. 'How could you have noticed that? It must have been over in seconds.'

Toshiko pointed to their car. 'We'd located you with the heat sensor array in the SUV. So we knew that he was on the edge.' She indicated the protective shroud of material that protected the middle section of the Levall-Mellon site. 'Just as well. With all that green stuff covering the outside, we couldn't see into the building. And there's no CCTV in operation up there, either.'

'Nice explanation,' Owen told her. 'Refreshingly free from the technobollocks you usually give us.'

Toshiko scowled. 'Don't parade your ignorance, Owen, just because you don't understand the language.'

'I thought you preferred to speak C-minus.'

'That's C++,' she chided. 'I also know that Java is more than coffee. And that Assembler has nothing to do with IKEA furniture.'

'All those languages, Tosh, and you still don't include English.' Owen put his arm around Gwen's shoulders and steered her so that they were looking up at the point from which Wildman had fallen. 'He was just there. We noticed you were further away. Jack was obviously the tall bloke in the middle, and you were the one with boobs on the far side of the area. But never fear, freckles. If it had been you on the edge, I'd have been there to catch you. Falling for me, eh?'

She disengaged his arm from her shoulder. 'As if.'

'All the pretty girls do, y'know. Before they know it, I've swept 'em off their feet and they're lying next to me…'

Gwen rolled her eyes. 'The only way you'll end up lying next to a "pretty girl", Owen Harper, is if you're both knocked down by the same bus.'

Far from being disappointed, Owen leered at her. A moment later, it was like he'd already forgotten. He drew back the smeared raincoat to reach into the corpse's jacket pockets. This brief search produced a crushed wallet and an ID badge for the Blaidd Drwg nuclear research facility. 'We got the right bloke then.'

'I think "got" is putting a positive spin on it,' Jack called out from above them.

Gwen had left Jack back on the eighth floor when she'd hurried down to see what had happened to Wildman. Who knew what Jack had been doing up there since then. She remembered he liked to look out across the city at night from high vantage points, so maybe he'd been taking in the view up there while he had the chance. He must have decided to descend in style, because he was using the builders' lift down the side of the building. As it started to vanish slowly behind the chipboard barrier that surrounded the lower floor, he jumped onto the top of the wooden partition and then leaped the remaining seven feet to street level, agile as a cat.

'As interrogations go,' Jack concluded, 'it wasn't one of my best. Hey, who parked that bus there?' He cast a glance past it at the gathering crowd of rubberneckers. Further would-be eye witnesses were leaning out of upper-storey windows in adjacent buildings. 'I guess we could try and continue this here, but clearing this bunch of ghouls away is gonna be like trying to keep flies away from shit. Get him back to the Hub and do the autopsy there.'

'Oh great,' moaned Owen. 'We've got one corpse in the SUV already, and now we have to fit us and this carcass in there too.'

'Quit griping. That car's deceptively spacious,' Jack told him. 'Gwen and I will take the other vehicle.'

'Let me think,' Owen said, as though talking to himself out loud. 'Whose conversation will I enjoy more on the journey – a dead guy's or Jack's?'

'See you back home,' Jack told him.

Gwen watched Owen's face darken as he twisted to watch Jack walk away. Maybe it was just a trick of the light.

She started after Jack Owen was still complaining to Toshiko. 'Let's get this stiff shifted. What I need is a really big spatula. And gloves. I hate it when I get bits of brain under my fingernails.'

Toshiko's attention flitted from monitor to monitor. The display frame on her desk in the Hub held six of them, each illustrating some aspect of her analysis or showing the results of a search she'd initiated.

Gwen stood behind her, quietly watching. Toshiko didn't like to be studied, Gwen had discovered early on. She said it reminded her too much of her father supervising her homework. All that study didn't seem to have been wasted, Gwen wanted to tell her. This was Toshiko absolutely in her element, despite Owen's occasional disparaging remark about her 'geek chic'. Toshiko was a composer, with data as her music. She coordinated all the elements of her orchestral score, pulling them together until they made sense, so that everyone else heard the symphony and not a cacophony of unrecognisable noise. And, as with an orchestral performance, it was usually only when Toshiko presented the completed piece to them that they were able to recognise it. A masterpiece from the disorderly mass of information.

Toshiko's work station in the Hub appeared the same, a mass of random junk that seemed to make sense to her alone. 'Creative chaos' was how Jack had once described Toshiko's methodology, in an admiring tone that suggested the others could take a leaf out of her book. Not that he was any different – on the desk in his office, amid the paperwork and old TV sets and bowls of fruit, she'd seen a dish containing fragments of coral, as though he was trying to grow it.

Toshiko's was the first station you saw when you entered the Hub – a jumble of display screens, scribbled piles of paperwork, and assorted electronic parts. There was even a Rubik's cube that she could complete within a minute. Owen kept messing it up and dropping it back on her desk when she wasn't looking. She would infuriate him by somehow completing it each time, even when he'd peeled off and replaced several of the stickers. 'Teenage bedroom' was Owen's alternative description of Toshiko's desk.

Gwen cast a look over at Owen now, and saw him locating his keyboard amid the piled mess of his own desk, which was the next station along. He had the keyboard on his lap and was thumping at the keys. So unlike Toshiko's elegant touch typing.

Toshiko used a data pen now to annotate a couple of her displays. On the two screens to her left, a long list of names and dates scrolled past, almost too quickly to read, and certainly too fast to remember. On the right, the displays revealed Wildman's journey through the centre of the city, in the jerky stop-frame animation format of stolen CCTV images. The two smaller screens in the centre showed a combined satellite image of the area around the Blaidd Drwg office complex. Toshiko overlaid the local roads as a grid of white lines, and picked out the scene-of-crime locations as red dots. Gwen remembered the spreading pool of red in the roadway earlier, with Wildman's smashed head at its centre. These blood splashes on Toshiko's displays revealed the locations of his victims over the past week.

Gwen eased forward to get a closer look. Toshiko let out a little sigh of exasperation. 'You're dripping on me. Do you mind?'

'Sorry.' Gwen stepped back again. 'The rain started before we got back to the car. Took us a bit by surprise. It had looked so nice earlier in the day. Wasn't in the forecast.'

Toshiko spun around on her stool. 'Look, why don't you get settled in the Boardroom? I'll pipe the results up there in a few minutes.'

Gwen nodded. 'OK.' Better leave Toshiko to it, she thought. She made her way down the short flight of steps that led to the walkway across the shallow basin. She was still amazed by the way the Hub was aligned with the surrounding area above ground. A clue was the tall stainless-steel pillar that reached from the basin up to the distant ceiling, where it continued up another seventy feet beyond the pavement of Roald Dahl Plass opposite the Millennium Centre. Constantly flowing water cascaded like a shimmering curtain on all sides of the pillar. The base had started to turn green with algae, yet the Hub neither felt nor smelled damp. The basin itself seemed to rise and fall with the tide. Once they had found a bream flapping about in

33

there, lost and forlorn until Owen had caught it, analysed it, pronounced it fit to eat, and cooked it in the Hub's kitchen on the upper level. This had briefly earned him the nickname 'Harry Ramsden'.

Gwen met Jack at the top of the spiral staircase that led up to the Boardroom. He was still wearing his greatcoat. Rainbow spots of rain stood out on the collar and shoulders, strangely illuminated in the irregular light of the Hub. He stared out over the main area, evidently enjoying the sight of his team busy at work.

'Saw you talking back there with the policeman…'

'Andy?'

'Yeah. He giving you a hard time?'

'No, not at all.' Gwen considered how she'd felt talking to Andy in the alleyway. Or not talking to him, more like. 'Sometimes I just hate keeping secrets. Sometimes I wish people wouldn't tell me them, then there's no pressure. Know what I mean?'

'Part of the job,' he told her.

'My mum used to say you shouldn't keep secrets from your friends. If you can't trust your friends, who can you trust?'

'No point wrapping your birthday presents then!'

Gwen laughed. 'Ah, that wouldn't be a secret. She'd say that counted as a "surprise".'

'And the difference would be…?'

'A surprise is something you tell everyone about. In the end. You can't have a surprise party if no one turns up.'

Jack laughed too. 'And a secret is something that you tell people about one friend at a time?' He watched her thoughtfully. He scratched his forehead with his forefinger, and his pale eyes never left hers. 'Do you share your secrets?'

Gwen knew what he meant. She'd seen him shot through the head and survive it. Heard him talk about some unexplained incident that meant that he *could not* die. He could feel pain, that was for sure – he'd had one hell of a headache for days after that shooting incident, even though there wasn't a mark on him now. She didn't know how safe he was; whether a disease or a catastrophic accident or being consumed by fire would be enough to carry him off for good. But more than that, only she knew about this. Ianto, Toshiko and Owen had no idea. Jack hadn't explicitly asked her to keep his secret – he simply seemed to know that she would. An unspoken understanding.

Jack was still studying her reaction. 'And what about Rhys?'

What about him, she thought. Every day she was keeping things from her boyfriend. She couldn't tell him the truth about Torchwood. He didn't understand why she was always on call, day and night. And he never asked her about it. Another unspoken understanding. Or was it? By not talking, how could she be sure?

'Don't lose track of your own life,' Jack told her. 'You mustn't let it drift away. Torchwood can consume everything. Everyone…'

His voice trailed off. He'd seen Ianto, their receptionist, walking up the spiral staircase. Ianto was about her age, maybe a few years younger, and not bad-looking, she decided. She hadn't worked him out yet. He seemed happy to do the more mundane work in Torchwood – the fetch-and-carry stuff, whether that was a Tesco bag full of shopping or body bag full of Weevil.

He was headed for the coffee machine, and smiled in recognition as he spotted them leaning against the balcony rail. 'Sorry, didn't see you there.' He waggled a freshly rinsed coffee pot at them. 'I was about to get fresh.'

Jack smiled at this comment. He shrugged off his coat, and draped it over the rail. 'Ianto, you've anticipated my need for something warm and wet.'

Ianto rolled his eyes theatrically. 'Very amusing, sir. I should have guessed that, whatever I say, you'll always want to top me.'

'You wish,' Jack told him. He gestured for Gwen to follow him through the glass doors into the Boardroom. 'We'll take it in here, Ianto. Thanks.'

They tripped the motion detectors as they went in, and the strip lights blinked on. Gwen looked down across the Hub, past the steel column and its sheen of flowing water, to where Toshiko and Owen were completing their initial work. The flicker of the lights had attracted Toshiko's attention, and she gave Gwen a cheery thumbs-up to indicate that she was almost ready.

At the same moment, there was a buzz of power as the wall-mounted plasma screen behind Gwen faded into life. The big screen was quartered, and Gwen recognised several of the images as being those that Toshiko had been analysing.

She and Jack spent a few minutes considering the images. Again, the red blobs on the map recalled the spatters of Wildman's blood on the bus at the most recent SOC.

Toshiko joined them and sat quietly at the opposite end of the oval conference table. Her elfin eyes blinked through her glasses at the PDA she'd carried in with her.

A minute later, Owen was clattering up the metal stairs to join them, late as usual. He was still wearing his white lab coat over his crumpled t-shirt. Seeming to realise this, he peeled off the coat, spotted that there was nowhere to hang it, and bundled it under the table before taking his seat.

They settled into their places around the table, while Ianto delivered the fresh, steaming coffee to murmured thanks from everyone.

'So I think I've completed the movement analysis that pinpoints Wildman,' Toshiko began.

'Round of applause for Dr Toshiko Sato,' Jack told the room. 'You know what "completed" means to her. Sometimes I think you'll never stop polishing the apple, Tosh.'

Gwen and Owen grinned in appreciation. Toshiko blushed prettily.

'I cross-correlated the locations for the deaths of all the vagrants.' She displayed a list of names on the main screen. A substantial minority showed only as 'A. N. Other'. She continued: 'Now, it's not unusual for vagrants to drop down dead, even at this time of year when the weather's still quite warm. So I obviously eliminated the less dubious cases.'

'Any of them that hadn't had the backs of their neck and skull chewed off,' Owen said.

Toshiko frowned at him. 'Not exactly. These victims aren't exactly missed and mourned. No one's looking for them. They're already missing, so they can drop down dead and nobody cares. That means that foraging wildlife might predate the bodies.'

'Eww,' said Gwen. 'Predate? Like predatory? You mean, eat them?'

'Of course.' Toshiko tapped at her PDA screen with a stylus. The main screen in the room flashed up a shorter list of the names. 'The victims we're interested in have had their heads chewed by human teeth. There's no connection with where they live. Or used to live, I should say. Some of these addresses are from many years ago.'

Owen stood up to look at the screen more closely. 'Bloody hell! Look at all these Welsh place names.' He wrinkled his nose at Gwen. 'Don't you people use vowels? It's like the English town planners finished naming all our places, and your lot had to use all the left-over letters in the box.'

'*Gwirionyn*,' Gwen told him. 'As my nan would say.'

'Bless you,' retorted Owen. 'I mean, look at this. How do you even pronounce this one?'

'That's Ystradgynlais,' Gwen said. 'It's up north somewhere, I think. How have you got all this, Tosh?'

Toshiko looked pleased to be asked. 'Cross-match of the DNA analysis with their NHS record.' She called up another screen of information, this time a map of the whole Cardiff area. There were two clusters of red dots, and one solitary dot at a distance from them. She indicated the largest cluster. 'As you can see, these are all within easy access of the Blaidd Drwg offices. There's one isolated similar case out in the Wetlands Nature Reserve, from some days previously. And then there's a smaller cluster here. The nearest things to that are a tourist centre, an army training camp, and the market town of Cowbridge.'

'Excellent work, Tosh.' Jack was clearly pleased. 'The larger cluster is pretty conclusive: Wildman is our guy.'

Gwen said: 'Couldn't someone else have been using his security card to badge in and out? Set him up for this?'

Toshiko shook her head. 'It was a card-plus-thumbprint system.'

'He still has both thumbs,' said Owen. 'Nobody borrowed one from him.'

'Wouldn't matter,' rejoined Toshiko. 'Contour of the skin distorts once a digit gets severed. Print would be imperfect.'

Gwen saw Jack smile indulgently at this competitive exchange. 'OK,' he said loudly. 'We need to see if anything ties Wildman in with the other cluster. Mr Harper, what have ya got?'

'Doctor Harper, if you don't mind.' Owen sat up straighter in his chair, as though the teacher had picked him out to answer a particularly tricky question in class. He flipped open the top of his laptop and thumped at the keys to get his information displayed on the plasma screen. He seemed to be directing his explanation at Gwen now. 'Done some prep work for Wildman's autopsy. No knife work yet, but a load of scans to be going on with. They show evidence of osseous tissue in the upper gastrointestinal tract, but nothing much beyond the pyloric antrum.'

Gwen was amused to hear Jack and Toshiko both start to fake a coughing attack. Owen scowled at them, and resumed his explanation to Gwen. 'Or, to put it simply…'

'He swallowed a whole load of bony bits,' interjected Jack.

'Well, yeah,' said Owen.

'I'm betting,' continued Jack, 'that Wildman's stomach will contain blood and skull fragments and brain fluid from at least three different DNA sources.'

'The clue will be what was most recently ingested.' Owen pummelled some more keys on his computer. Fresh images expanded on the wall display. The photos showed Wildman's bloody remains, somehow starker and more brutal when laid out on the cold metal of the examination slab. The face was a pinkish-grey mush.

'I may never eat strawberry yoghurt again,' Gwen said.

Owen seemed to be enjoying her discomfort. 'You should see him when I've sliced him open. Then we'll see if his stomach contains DNA evidence from the other vagrant victims. The one's who were... what was the word again Tosh? Predated.'

Jack leaned forward on the conference table. He poured himself another slug of Ianto's coffee. 'Think there's gonna be a more recent victim's DNA in Wildman's stomach. One that isn't on your chart yet, Tosh. I saw Wildman's face before he bounced it off that bus. Before he took the drop. Looked to me like spinal fluid all down his clothes. Messy eater.' He took a big slurp of his coffee. 'Y'know, the worst thing about being bitten to death like that? It's not a clean death, because the Welsh have such terrible teeth.'

Gwen defied this slur with a big, insincere smile. 'Where's the latest victim?'

Jack shook his head. 'Dunno. Looked like Wildman had been snacking pretty recently. Probably another vagrant, but in the city centre. Any news on the police frequency, Tosh?'

Toshiko performed a staccato rhythm with the stylus on her PDA. 'I've put a trace on.'

'A vagrant would be good,' nodded Owen. 'No need to provide a cover story for their disappearance.'

His casual tone enraged Gwen. She felt her neck and face flush with anger, and heard her own words almost before she knew she was saying them. 'Vagrants are people too, Owen.'

'Hark at her.'

'Don't patronise me! For all we know, another poor lad is lying dead in a gutter. Unfound at the moment. Unnoticed, certainly. Real people like you would just walk past him, even when he was alive. Maybe he was selling the *Big Issue* in town. Or maybe he was just wandering around trying to find somewhere to kip for the night, and the first time it looked like anyone was showing him any attention was when Wildman approached him, and that was the last thing he ever knew.'

'I'm just saying,' insisted Owen, 'it's not like Tosh is gonna struggle to conceal the death of some chewed up pikey when he turns up in a gutter somewhere in Grangetown.'

Gwen slapped both hands on the table, an alarming sound that echoed off the glass walls of the Boardroom. 'How can we know what made him come to Cardiff, this poor bastard we've not even seen yet? How can we say that his family aren't somewhere out there, somewhere else in Wales, or further out? Wondering if he's all right. Not knowing if he's alive, but praying that he is. Not knowing that he died today.' She blinked hard, and looked up at the strip lights in the ceiling to stop the tears. She wouldn't give Owen that satisfaction. 'Unfound? Unnoticed? Yeah. But unmissed? I don't think so.'

Owen leaned across the table to her, uncowed. 'When you've been here a while longer, you'll see it differently. I mean it. I'll ask you again in a couple of months' time, you'll have changed your tune. I mean, I honestly hope I'm wrong about that…'

'No you don't,' Toshiko said quietly.

'No,' admitted Owen after barely a pause. 'I don't.'

Jack stood up. It was a casual gesture, and he made it look as though he was pulling together their cups and putting them back on the tray. But by doing so, he leaned over the table towards each of them. It was an elegant gesture of control, reasserting his authority. Calming the room.

He smiled across the table at Owen. 'Good job on the initial scan.'

Toshiko's PDA interrupted him with a beeping alarm. 'Search result,' she said, and put it up on the main screen. 'Police report that matches our interest profile.'

'Result indeed,' Jack observed. 'They've found Wildman's car. Now where did I put my coat?' Gwen pointed through the glass door to where she could see it on the railing outside. 'OK, good, thanks. Tosh, here's another search I'd like you to run.' He slipped a folded piece of paper across the table to her. She looked at it briefly, nodded, and put the paper in a pocket alongside her PDA. 'Owen, let us know what else you find after you've opened Wildman up.'

And with this, Jack was off through the Boardroom door, beckoning for Gwen to join him.

She caught up with him at the foot of the spiral staircase. 'What's the rush?'

'The car wasn't empty,' he told her as they approached a solitary paving stone that lay incongruously in the floor of the Hub. 'It pains me to tell you this, Gwen, but I don't trust your former colleagues to handle this well.'

'You can feel pain then,' she said to him.

He stood on the slab, and held out his hand to her. 'Not according to my exes.'

Owen retrieved his coffee from the table. It was just warm enough. He took it over to the glass window of the Boardroom, where he could stare down and watch Jack cross the floor of the Hub. Gwen was skipping down the stairs after him, like an eager puppy.

She'll learn, thought Owen. The magic wears off eventually. It's a great job – the best he could imagine. But it was never quite the same after the first six months.

Toshiko was still busy at the table, tapping away on her PDA with that pen device. She was eager too, keen to complete Jack's latest request.

Owen thought about Wildman's corpse, ready for him over in the pathology room. He sipped at his lukewarm coffee, and decided that the stiff could wait.

He pushed open the far door of the Boardroom and strolled out onto the balcony. The noticeboard on the back wall had a cluttered collection of yellowing newspaper clippings pinned to it, along with cartoons, photos and leaflets. One polaroid showed him and Toshiko, grinning at the lens held at arm's length. It was from outside the Castle. He'd got bored of having the photo stuck to the front of his dishwasher by a magnet, so he'd brought it in and half-hidden it on the board behind some money-off coupons for Jubilee Pizza. Toshiko hadn't noticed yet.

By sitting in one of the metal chairs on the balcony, Owen could see Jack making his way to the exit platform. With a grinding sound far above them, a corresponding flagstone slid out of its place to create a square opening.. A handful of lights in the Plass twinkled on the steel tower, visible through the distant gap.

With a thrum of power, the hydraulics began to power the platform upwards. He could see Jack holding Gwen's waist to balance her on the square stone podium. She was staring up into his eyes, engrossed in whatever he was telling her, favouring him with that gap-toothed smile of hers. The two of them were so preoccupied that they were both oblivious to Owen observing them, even when the lift drew level with him at the height of the balcony. It was like he was invisible.

Owen watched them draw further away from him, disappearing, leaving him behind. He saw them duck briefly, and laugh together. For a moment, he wondered why.

Then the first fat blobs of rain dropped from the open portal, blew over the balcony, and splashed into Owen's upturned face. It felt like he'd been spat on. He shook the drops off.

Toshiko joined him on the balcony. 'Design fault,' she tutted. 'I mean, have you seen the leaves that get blown through there? Not so many birds flying in these days. Not since Jack uncaged the pterodactyl.' She was laughing, pointing to where the raindrops had spattered on Owen's shirt. 'Nasty weather tonight. There's a storm brewing.'

Owen narrowed his eyes at her. 'Yeah, and I'm starving. Not going out in that lot, so I think we get something delivered.'

He towelled his hair with his hand, tousling it, and studied Toshiko for a reaction.

'I fancy a pizza,' he told her. 'How about you? We've got some money-off coupons somewhere, haven't we?'

It was a miserable alley on a miserable night. They'd started off walking through the initial spots of rain in the optimistic brightness of Mermaid Quay, laughing even as the weather started to deteriorate. By the time they'd reached this grimy backstreet further over in Butetown, a steady drizzle had killed their high spirits stone dead.

Stone dead conveniently described the occupant of Wildman's car. Gwen knew before she reached it that the scene wasn't going to be pretty. She could deduce that from the dazed expression on the face of the police constable, a young woman who stood, trembling, twenty metres from the vehicle. Gwen touched her on the shoulder, a gesture of reassurance or solidarity, and then trailed in Jack's wake as he cut through the police cordon to where Wildman's car had been abandoned.

Jack waived the polite introductions, but didn't immediately wave away the scene of crime officer in his usual manner. Gwen knew this was because there had been no information radioed in yet, otherwise Toshiko would have overheard it and passed it on to them. She gestured wordlessly to the other police officers at the scene to stay back.

'Passer-by thought the woman had fallen asleep in the driver's seat,' the SOCO started. No preamble. Efficient, to-the-point. English accent, with a downward intonation that suggested Birmingham. A Brummie that Gwen didn't recognise, so he must be fairly new. Only a few months out of the force, and already she was losing track of the team on her patch. Well, on her old patch.

'Then the witness noticed the mess down the window, and called it in,' the

Brummie explained. 'We forced the rear door to obtain access, in the unlikely event that the victim was still alive and needed urgent medical attention. Didn't want to move the body, obviously. Photographers aren't here yet.'

Jack scanned the area quickly, left to right. The car was a four-door Vectra estate, parked midway under the only streetlamp in the alley that wasn't working. Jack played his torch through the windows into the car's interior. A middle-aged woman was sitting upright in the front seat, though her head had drooped against the driver's window. Her eyes were closed, and where her dyed blonde hair fell over her shoulder it was matted with blood.

'OK, thanks. You can clear the area now,' Jack told him.

The Brummie didn't seem to understand this. Perhaps he thought Jack was talking to someone else. 'Nasty wound. Gunshot from the seat behind, perhaps? The spray pattern across the roof of the car might suggest that.'

'Thanks,' repeated Jack.

The Brummie seemed to relax a little, now that he'd delivered his brief report. His attitude had changed, and he was chatting comfortably, despite the falling drizzle. 'This reminds me of that woman in Tesco car park on a hot sunny day, who dialled 999 on her mobile,' he laughed. 'Heard a gunshot, felt a blow above the base of her neck. Sat for thirty minutes with her hand cupped behind her head to stop her brains from spilling out. Until we arrived and told her that the heat had exploded a canister in the back seat, and she was only holding a lump of ready-mix dough.'

Gwen watched Jack's brow furrow. She stepped smartly between the two men. 'We'll take it from here,' she told the Brummie before he dug himself into deeper trouble. 'You can secure the perimeter, and keep the photographers back when they arrive.'

The Brummie opened his mouth to object, saw her raised eyebrows, and slunk away.

Despite the way he had spoken to the SOCO, Jack actually showed a great deal of respect for scene-of-crime protocols. He slipped on a glove, then eased open the Vectra's rear door. He reached in to pop up the front lock, and opened the driver's side. By swiftly positioning his hand in the gap, he was able to prop up the corpse and gently push it back into the car to prevent it from falling out into the road.

The dead body was still strapped into the seat. With the door now open, the upper torso lolled over onto the steering wheel, head dropped, right cheek downwards so that the face pointed back towards the passenger seat.

Jack's torch played over the back of the corpse. She had been a thin woman in late middle age, wearing a knitted green cardigan over a patterned dress that was now stained heavily with dried blood and gory fragments. The head was only half-attached to the shoulders. Blonde hair had been torn out in lumps or wrenched away from the nape of the neck.

Not that there was much of the nape still visible. The flesh was ripped almost down to the clavicle. Further up into what had been the hairline was a ghastly hole, filled with clotted blood and with clumps of greyish matter visible in the mess. The curdled mess reminded Gwen once more, horribly, of strawberry yoghurt. It was too unbearably apt an image. She shivered because she knew that something had killed this woman by gnawing into the back of her skull.

The woman's handbag was on the back seat. Her purse contained a name and address, plus an ID card from Blaidd Drwg. 'Jennifer Fallon,' Gwen read aloud. 'Now we know why Tosh couldn't reach Wildman's secretary. She was with him in the car. Drove him here from the facility.'

No need to crouch over looking at the dead woman any longer, Gwen decided. She straightened, and a trickle of cold rainwater ran from her hair down her neck. All the fancy equipment at Torchwood's disposal, she thought sourly, and they never had any umbrellas. She hunted her mobile out from her coat pocket, thumbed a fastkey and dialled the Hub. When Toshiko answered, Gwen briefed her on their discovery in the alleyway.

'That fits,' Toshiko told her. 'Jennifer Fallon finished work early today…' Gwen could hear the rattling sound of Toshiko's typing. 'Yes, the logout details confirm that they left at the same time. Her desktop machine was powered down a few minutes before she badged out of the building with Wildman. But she sent a couple of e-mails immediately before that…' More tapping of keys. 'OK, the last one is a quick message to her boss that Mr Wildman is still feeling ill, and that she's insisted on driving him home.'

Gwen considered the ravaged remains of the secretary ruefully. An act of kindness had been repaid by a fierce, merciless assault. The savage attacks on the vagrants around Blaidd Drwg were disgusting enough, but on this occasion Wildman had brutalised someone he knew from work. Maybe even someone he once cared about. She suddenly realised how tired she was, unsure whether it was all the chasing around or something else – the numbing horror of the crime scenes today. She stifled a small yawn. Gwen angled her face into the night sky, letting the rain fall onto her.

Even with her eyes closed, she still had the image of Jennifer Fallon's broken, brutalised body in her mind. 'What could drive a man to that?' she asked Jack.

Jack grimaced. 'She drove herself, here, to her death. With Wildman. Unwittingly, that's probably obvious. How do we know it's Wildman?' He studied her, expecting an answer.

'The raincoat,' Gwen remembered. 'He took it with him, to cover the blood and remains that would have spilled on him. She'd have put the coat on the back seat, with her bag, because it wasn't raining or dark when they left Blaidd Drwg.'

Jack gently pushed the Vectra's door shut. Jennifer Fallon's corpse rocked slightly with the car and was still again.

'Oh, great.' Jack threw his head back in disgust. 'I've trodden in more dog shit.' He bent his knee and twisted his foot out, illuminating the underside of his shoe with the torch. There was a large irregular gap in the sole.

'Dog shit didn't do that,' said Gwen. 'It's like something's eaten right through it.'

'Consumed it,' pondered Jack. 'These are my favourite boots. Standard issue for 1940s non-jumping personnel. Ankle-bracing, leather soles, good laces, instep support. Where am I gonna find another pair?'

'Army surplus?' suggested Gwen.

'Look at that.' He balanced against the side of the car and removed the shoe so that he could waggle it at Gwen. 'Whatever it is, it's eaten through the sole and then stopped.'

'Leather soles,' mused Gwen. 'Eaten could be the right word. What's the inner sole made of? Sponge rubber?'

Jack nodded. Sniffed the sole of the removed boot experimentally. Coughed in disgust, and propped the boot on the Vectra's roof amid the bouncing rain. 'Yeah, you're right, it's been digested. Still being digested, too. See there?' He pointed carefully with his forefinger.

'That thing you trod on. The thing Wildman coughed up outside the building site?'

Jack cracked a huge smile. 'Smart girl.'

'Still here,' said Toshiko's voice from Gwen's mobile.

'OK, I think we're done,' Gwen told her.

'Thanks, Tosh.' Jack raised his voice so that the mobile would pick up his words. 'End of your shift for the day.'

Gwen let Toshiko say goodnight before ending the call. She pocketed the mobile.

'I'm starting to worry where else I may have trodden this stuff,' Jack grumbled. He scrunched up his face in dismay, because he'd just absentmindedly put his unshod foot down on to the rainy pavement. 'All right. Not looking so cool, now. Time to call it a night.'

'What about this lot?' Gwen jerked her head at the corpse. There was so much left to do here, and yet she knew she was exhausted. She felt the sides of her face tighten, but subdued the tired reaction.

Jack peered into the Vectra. 'I'll take her back to the Hub. You get our police friends over there to disperse, and then you can go home.'

Gwen couldn't stifle the yawn any longer.

'There you go,' Jack smiled. 'An honest opinion, openly expressed. I'm boring you. Go home. It's past nine.'

She checked her watch and was dismayed to find he was right. Where had the day gone?

He was still looking into the car, probably wondering how he was going to move the body. Or maybe move the whole car. The obvious problem was that the unfortunate Jennifer Fallon was still in the driver's seat.

'Go home,' Jack urged Gwen once more. He angled his head to look up at her. 'Rhys is waiting. You promised me that you'd keep hold of your life, remember? You may even have promised him. Don't let it drift.'

'What about you?'

Jack straightened up, and pushed his shoulders back to release the tension. 'Think I'm going swimming. I'm wet enough already. And it's time to reconnect with life after all this death today.'

'Sounds like fun,' Gwen smiled.

She walked back over to the police cordon, to let them know they were no longer required. The police photographer repacked his camera case with bad grace. The Brummie was trying to object, but Gwen cut short his protests, more snappishly than she would normally.

In the distance, Jack was opening the nearside door of the Vectra and reaching into the passenger seat. Gwen could see the thick woollen sock on his shoeless foot, sodden from his journey through the puddles. He'd still be working long after the rest of the team had finished, as usual.

She dialled home. Told Rhys she was sorry to be late. Again.

Should she be ashamed, or relieved, or grateful that he reacted so calmly?

Again. Was he being calm, she wondered, or did he really not care? Or maybe he was watching *Matrix Reloaded* on the DVD. Again.

Rhys told her that he'd saved her some tea, and he promised not to eat it if she got a shift on. 'Get a shift on' was what he told the drivers at his office when they were running late. She told him thank you. And yes, he could eat the final strawberry yoghurt if it was reaching its use-by date – she didn't fancy it tonight.

She listened again for clues in his voice, to anticipate how he might be when she got back to the flat. Tired? Irritated? She let his words wash over her for a while, until she abruptly realised that he'd fallen silent. Asked her a question and was waiting for an answer. She'd let her mind wander, hadn't been listening properly to him.

She told him sorry, she was a bit tired, and they could have a proper talk when she got home. But as she hung up, she knew that she'd said that to herself every night for the past two months. That's what their evenings had become. Chit-chat, usually from him about office intrigue, or Banana Boat's road warrior stories, or Sonja the Secretary's latest emotional crisis. Telly often. Eating off a tray, some quick meal that Rhys usually cooked. Maybe some perfunctory lovemaking if they weren't too tired before bedtime.

She was going to walk home now. She gave Jack one last look, then turned towards the main road. The drizzling rain that had clung to her all evening was now a steady stream, splashing in the growing puddles all around her.

Was this her life now? Was this what you expected, she asked herself. Can you continue to keep this from Rhys, from whom you never had secrets before? Or is this something new? Another life that you never expected, never knew existed. Do you have any idea how you got here?

SEVEN

You have no idea how you come to be lounging in the back room of a hairdressing salon called the Lunatic Fringe. But that's where you find yourself this Saturday night, watching the sunny day fade into memory as a sinuous teenager called Penny Pasteur pours your *piña colada* into a frosted martini glass.

Through the shop window a pair of neon curling tongs rotates and flashes. In the street there's a bustle of pedestrians heading home. Even from the back room, you can hear their scabbards clank against their leg armour as they stagger off to the stables to saddle up their steeds and gallop away. Penny kisses you, her tongue flicking briefly over your lips and teeth, before she withdraws to the kitchenette to rinse out the empty cocktail shaker. To get there, she has to step over the corpse of an awkward customer, the Norse demigod called Kvasir whose neck you earlier snapped like a brittle branch after that altercation. He should never have insulted your dwarf assistants. And spitting in your eye was the final straw.

You are not the kind of guy who stares at danger with fear in your eyes. The strongest and brightest of your lineage, at six feet ten and fifteen stone you tower over your family physically and intellectually. Your stocky frame belies your litheness, and your twelve years of battle knowledge as a Brandywine dragoon places you in the marksman's upper quartile for accuracy, speed, and dexterity. Your strongest asset remains your hand-to-hand combat experience, and there are few who can match you in an unarmed close-quarters brawl. Especially tall Scandinavians with long hair who can't tell the difference between a fiver and a tenner.

The sky outside darkens, presaging a storm. Beware the coming night, for agents of Chaos ride and you may be consumed by their powers.

You consider your clothes. The black leather jerkin covers a thin vest of meshed steel over a pure cotton chemise. The ends of your dark cotton trousers are stuffed into your sturdy black boots. A dragon motif emblazons your left breast.

You have stamina, you have drive. Your overriding ambition is an assault on the Wrestling League, to top it within three months, and to turn professional before year-end.

Beyond the shop window, off into the distance, the shimmering buildings of the Millennium Capitol beckon you. Though first you will need to make your way through the shadowed alleyways that surround Apzugard Bay. Beware the aerial beasts that swoop through the bruising purple sky, the predatory creatures from within the Bay, and the crazed, half-forgotten denizens of the Capitol slums who stand between you and your dream.

The door is ajar. Go forward now! Your destiny awaits!

You are Glendower Broadsword!

Continue? Y/N

'Glendower Broadsword?' laughed Toshiko. 'Put your weapon back in its scabbard, Owen. No one's impressed.'

Engrossed in the display on his terminal, Owen hadn't realised she was standing behind him. He clicked an icon at the top of the screen, and the text window minimised to reveal an image of the Lunatic Fringe. A row of barbershop chairs angled off into the distance, distinct shapes in primary colours. Through an inner door, a cartoon image of Penny Pasteur stood paused in a kitchen area, her back to a sink full of washing-up. Penny's character wore a fluffy pink bikini that barely covered what even Owen would admit were implausibly large breasts. She'd be rubbish at doing the dishes, he decided. How could she see the crockery as she washed it?

Toshiko interrupted these idle thoughts when she took the mouse off him and maximised the text window. 'No point hiding it, Owen. I read most of it already.' She scrolled down the words. 'What's this, you miserable sexist? A serving wench attending to your every need. In a *hairdressing* salon?' She made a half-hearted attempt to stifle her amusement and retreated back to her own work station.

Toshiko sat at her desk, surrounded by an accumulation of computer spares, alien artefacts, and stacked coffee cups. She eventually lifted her pretty almond eyes to look back at him through the piles of stuff. When she spotted Owen scowling at her, she fell into a new bout of giggling, and covered her mouth modestly with a raised hand.

Owen tried not to rise to this. 'I thought you'd been working on improvements to this game?'

'Keep your hair on, "Glendower".' She tapped a few more keystrokes at her terminal. 'I've got your enhancements here, as promised.' Toshiko came back over to Owen. She brought a DVD case and what looked like a motorcycle helmet with an opaque visor at the front. 'Before we get started, you should log off your Internet connection.'

'Because…?'

'Because you're only going to do this within the confines of Torchwood's firewall. At the moment, that low-resolution graphics version runs from the *Second Reality* company's server machines in Palo Alto. Many thousands of people around the world, all simultaneously connected to a shared system. That's why they call it a "Massively Multiplayer Online Game".'

Owen clattered away at his keyboard until the screen told him: '*Second Reality* – do you really wish to disconnect (Y/N)?' He pressed Y. 'See you next time, Glendower Broadsword!' it announced cheerfully.

Toshiko slotted the disc into the DVD drive of Owen's machine. The screen flashed up a series of messages, and the hard disk chattered as her software installed itself.

She hefted the helmet into Owen's lap, and proceeded to plug one of the attached cables into his computer. 'OK, this should do for now. Put these gloves on first.' She offered him a pair of bright blue items in a thin material, which Owen immediately recognised as the non-sterile disposable nitrile gloves he used for examinations and autopsies. Only these were now covered in wires and sensors, at the rear, along the side, even on the fingertips. 'Prototype data-gloves,' Toshiko told him, 'adjusted to allow haptic feedback.'

Owen screwed up his face into his 'what the hell?' look.

'Reacts to touch,'

'So do I.'

'Careful not to get the wires tangled up,' sighed Toshiko. 'All right, put that on now. It's a head-mounted display system. There are two emissive electroluminescent screens embedded in the visor to give you a stereoscopic image. No, the other way round…' She helped him pull the helmet on correctly, and he thought that perhaps her fingertips lingered on the nape of his neck for just too long.

'It's very dark in here.' Owen's own voice reverberated in the helmet.

Toshiko's voice was muffled now. 'It's not switched on yet. Here, pull the microphone up so it's just level with your chin. That's for the speech-to-text translation – no need to do any more typing on your keyboard.'

'Just as well, I can't see a bloody thing! And what's that smell?'

'Cheese and onion crisps, I think. Just be patient, Owen. Right…'

A kaleidoscopic flare of colours made Owen flinch. Even with his eyes closed, he could see the flicker of light on his lids. When he opened them tentatively, a grid of bright green lines on a grey background vanished off into the distance. He moved his head tentatively to one side, and the field of lines whirled around him. When he leaned forward, the nearest lines got closer.

'Steady,' Toshiko told him. Her voice was perfectly clear now, playing through the speakers in either side of the helmet. 'It has six-axis position sensing, so it'll translate any movements you make into the virtual world. Careful if you twist around, because it's plugged into your computer.'

'I think I may be sick.'

Her muffled voice sounded worried. 'That shouldn't happen. It's calibrated to keep in sync with your head movements.'

'No,' Owen teased her, 'I mean that I hate cheese and onion. Ouch!'

Toshiko had rapped hard on the top of the helmet with her knuckles. 'Pay attention, this is the science bit.' As she spoke, Owen could tell exactly where she was in the room from the way her voice moved between the two speakers. 'This is my early prototype. It should keep you happy while I try to sort out my stress test harness for the main implementation without the attached input devices.'

'Sounds kinky.'

'Software test harness, you perv.' He could hear her typing away at his computer keyboard while she set things up. 'The next stage will be to use projectors so that the user's not encumbered by the headgear and gloves. A proper, 3-D immersive environment, with natural interaction gestures. So you'll be able to touch objects, physically sculpt the world to make things.'

Owen nodded, and the green grid nodded with him. 'You mean I could make things happen by doing stuff, not just by describing stuff?'

'Exactly. Hang on, nearly there. Yes, there you go. As it is, what you're wearing there is a thousand times better than the commercially available version of *Second Reality*. I've debugged a lot of their stuff, so you'll get fewer system crashes.'

'Smartarse.'

'And as you can see, with the processing power we've got available through the Hub, the user environment is more photo-realistic too.'

Owen knew how Toshiko loved to talk technogeek. He was letting her chatter away without trying to understand it, but that last bit begged a question. 'What do you mean, photo-realistic?'

There was a pause. 'Ah. Sorry. Let me plug your helmet into the grid.'

Owen could hear her looking for a connection, scrabbling around between his knees. This looked promising...

And then he didn't need an explanation about this new system any more. He could see what she meant. He could experience it, right now. Because the world had come to life.

He was in the Lunatic Fringe. Sitting in one of the barber's chairs. Only they weren't the blocky shapes in primary colours that he'd last seen on his flatscreen display. These looked like cracked red leather, the machine stitching clearly visible, some of it fraying on the arms where a thousand previous customers had levered themselves in and out of position for a haircut.

The chipped linoleum floor was strewn with hair clippings, patches of black and brown, blond and ginger that bore witness to previous customers. One of the previous customers, Kvasir, was still there, also on the linoleum, his body and limbs spread out clumsily in the scattered hair. His severed head, still implausibly in its horned helmet, lay against the bottom of the panelled wall, with black blood coagulated around the base of the neck. 'Change for a tenner,' remembered Owen. The realism of the dead body in front of him somehow made the earlier fracas more embarrassing.

He turned at the sound of horses clopping by the shop window. A neon sign flashed beside the entrance door, weirdly illuminating the armour of the passing pedestrians. Something alarmed a passing horse. The animal gave a shrill whinny, and it half-reared up. The mounted rider attempted to rein it in, but the horse's nostrils flared and it reared again. A nearby maid in a mob cap shrieked in surprise – 'Oh my Lord!' – and dropped her bundle of provisions.

'What do you think?' asked Toshiko's voice.

He considered for a moment. 'Nice tits. You look good in pink.'

Penny Pasteur was standing in front of him, talking in Toshiko's voice. She tutted and sighed. She held out her bare arms and waggled her fingers in the air. The bangles on her wrists jingled as she moved, but Owen could also hear keys clicking, as though she was using an invisible typewriter. Penny spun on her heel like dancing a pirouette, and was instantly transformed.

Now she looked more like Toshiko Sato, down to the skin tone and short, black hair. Instead of a fluffy pink bikini she wore a smart black trouser suit, with a Nehru jacket buttoned up to the neck. Owen pouted, and pointed to a martini glass and cocktail shaker on the kitchen counter beside her. 'I see you haven't finished the washing-up either.'

'Don't make me slap you,' she warned him. 'This was the nearest character I could use to interact with you. Unless you count him.' She indicated the headless corpse. 'I think I'd better tidy him up, don't you? Nothing stays dead for very long in here.' She typed in mid-air again, and Kvasir's corpse snapped silently out of existence. 'There, I've even mopped the floor. I'll leave the dishwashing for you.'

'This is just amazing, Tosh.'

'Tell me I'm a genius.'

'You've made your bum smaller, I notice. Are you glamming yourself up?'

'You can talk,' she retorted. 'Have you seen yourself? I think you may have issues. "Glendower", indeed!'

He squared his broad virtual shoulders. 'So what? It's a computer game, not a psychology session. I have to admit, I am gobsmacked. This is fantastic, even for you.'

'Did I mention that I'm a genius?'

'You're a genius.' He stood up and stepped towards her, but banged his knee on an invisible desk. He could hear pencils and DVD cases scattering onto the floor, though he couldn't see them.

'Stop, stop,' urged Toshiko. 'You have to stay sitting at your desk. Don't go wandering off! You're still attached to your computer.'

Owen fumbled behind himself for his office chair in the real world, and settled back into it as though it was the leather barber's seat.

Toshiko glided over to him with an unfamiliar sinuous grace. 'Try gesturing with your data-gloves. They can move you about as though you're using your keyboard.'

Owen tried a few movements. At first he managed to upend himself, which had the disorienting effect of giving him an inverted view of the barber-shop while his body told him he was still the right way up. Soon he'd mastered the gestures, and was striding around the Lunatic Fringe as though he owned the place. Which, virtually speaking, he did.

'When I get it sorted out,' Toshiko explained, 'it'll be able to use positional info from the cameras and sensors here in the Hub. The tracking devices in our mobile phones. That kind of thing. And the resolution will be good enough to be close to real life.'

'Fleshspace,' he told her.

'Eww. What?'

'That's what players of *Second Reality* call the real world.'

'One day, I'll be glad to welcome you to the real world, Owen.'

'I don't imagine I could do this in fleshspace.' He reached out and fondled virtual Toshiko's breast through the material of her Nehru jacket. The sensors in his gloves pressed softly against his fingers and the palm of his hand. A series of smacks on his real-world head made his ears ring. 'Ouch! Come on Tosh! Stop slapping my helmet.'

Toshiko's attack ceased. 'I bet you wouldn't say that to Penny Pasteur if you made contact in fleshspace.'

From outside the shop came the sound of a shrill whinnying. Owen wafted a gesture, and his virtual self walked to the front of the shop. A hunter was half-rearing up, snorting nervously, startled by something. A maid in a mob cap and a dusty overcoat was shying away from the creature.

Owen grabbed for the door handle, in the hope of rushing out and pulling the maid to safety. Before he could seize it, the door wrenched itself open, and he was in the street. The maid leapt to one side with a cry of 'Oh my Lord!' and dropped her bundle of shopping. A large ham bounced out of its wrapping and onto the pavement. By the time the hunter's rider had calmed the creature, the maid had recovered her composure and her ham. Owen watched her scurry away down the street.

Toshiko peered at him through the shop doorway. 'You must be Prince Charming,' she told him. 'Go on, slap your thigh for me.'

Owen re-entered the shop. The door closed, and the shop bell tinkled prettily behind him.

Toshiko tutted. 'Glendower Broadsword. You've tried to create an avatar for the game with no weaknesses or flaws. People aren't like that in real life.

No one's a fairy-tale character, all good or all evil. And neither are characters in the game.'

Owen growled at her. 'Well, my character is. Like I said, this isn't a psychology session.'

'You're in denial.'

'Very good,' smiled Owen. 'I can hardly dispute that statement.'

'Well, be careful what you wish for, Prince Charming.'

'I'm glad you're not my Cinderella.'

Toshiko wiggled her typing fingers, and looked out of the window expectantly.

Owen followed her gaze. A huge sphere of metal and glass crashed out of the sky and onto the pavement, crumpling and distorting as it came to rest. Owen nearly leapt out of his real-life office chair with shock.

For a second, he thought the whole thing had dropped onto a couple of white horses in the street, before he saw that they were shackled to the tangled remains of the shape. They were apparently unharmed, but still attached to the wreckage by golden reins. Two coachmen in pink waistcoats staggered back to their feet, and helped a beautiful young woman to step gingerly from the strewn debris of her coach. As she brushed gingerly at the shards of glass on her iridescent ball gown, the coachmen spun on their heels and transformed into rodents before scurrying off. The coach was now merely the remains of a large pumpkin splattered on the pavement. The woman's ball gown had dissolved into smutted rags. When she saw them, she gave a little cry of despair and proceeded to limp off down the street through the uncaring pedestrians.

'All right, Tosh. Do you think I could have a go now?'

'I'll leave you to it, Owen.'

'I certainly prefer the real Penny Pasteur. I'd love to see what she'd make of this.'

Toshiko threw him a disapproving look. 'Her graphics wouldn't be this good, for a start. She'd only have her current computer. Assuming it is a she, and not some hairy-arsed fifty-year-old bloke taking you for a virtual ride while he secretly plays with himself in a late-night Internet cafe.'

'You paint a lovely picture.'

'For some of these game-players, *Second Reality* is just an escape from the dull reality of their daily routine. They can be brave confident characters, instead of sad antisocial losers. They can visit places they can't afford.

They can even have sex with complete strangers. Lots of them. It's literally a different life for them, Owen. It's an addiction. Who knows who Penny Pasteur really is?'

'I think I know her pretty well by now.'

A horse whinnied in the street outside. A woman's voice shrieked, 'Oh my Lord!'

Owen offered Toshiko his most winning smile. 'So let me find Penny on *Second Reality*. Really get to know her with these fantastic new... what did you call them? These fantastic new interaction gestures.' He waved his hands at her, and for a moment found himself floating in mid-air.

Toshiko shook her virtual head. 'No way. I have downloaded a broad selection of different avatar profiles from *Second Reality*'s main server on the West Coast. You can have fun interacting with them while I finish off the freestanding version of this. So there is no need to connect this to the Internet, Owen. We want to keep this well away from the black-hats and the hackers. This version of *Second Reality* should not make *any* kind of connection through the Torchwood firewall.'

'What's your problem with hackers?' grumbled Owen. 'You're a genius, you can handle them.'

'It's not me I'm worried about,' she retorted, 'it's you. You're a security liability because you have no idea what you're doing on a computer. I mean, you haven't even got the hang of creating your own avatar. Do you realise that you originally based yours on a female wrestler?'

'Female? What, with these shoulders?' Owen flexed them for effect.

'Yes,' replied Toshiko. 'Take a look – you have nice tits of your own.' She gave him a little wave and melted away into nothing.

Owen jutted his chin down awkwardly. The helmet wouldn't let him bend that far. So he gestured towards the far side of the barber-shop, and positioned himself in front of the wall-mounted mirror to get a full-length view.

Well, from the reflection, it was undeniable. Glendower Broadsword was broad, tall, golden-haired and very good-looking. And for the first time it was apparent that, within that stout leather jerkin, she possessed a very impressive pair of breasts.

Once he'd got the hang of flying, Owen was able to zoom around to several locations he remembered from his previous visits to *Second Reality*. Only now he was totally immersed in the world, and the images and sounds that surrounded him were almost overwhelming. He spent time on a beach, swinging on a tyre suspended from nothing. A giant eye, called Harold, floated unblinking next to him and together they watched the sun set orange over the sea horizon, before baby turtles fought their way across the sand into the surf.

He visited a slum area adjacent to a bright commercial district, where gun battles raged. Grubby dispossessed zombies stared blankly at their reflections in the smoked glass of passing stretch limos, before succumbing to a vigilante attack. Indifferent law enforcement officers looked on from the corner. Owen watched the same zombie consumed by flame twice before he moved on. The commercial district was a Chicago-inspired cityscape. The streets were covered in stylised flower motifs like giant asterisks, and the trams chattered their way down the hills to the sound of 'Chasing Cars' by Snow Patrol.

He watched a tennis match played on top of a skyscraper. Andy Murray was losing the first set to an unnamed and unranked hippopotamus who had startling white tennis shorts and a savage backhand. Owen eventually moved on in disappointment when he spotted that Murray's repeated inability to read the hippo's limited repertoire of passing shots was evidence that they were playing the same four games over and over again.

Owen also recognised several characters from his previous visits. A tavern owner called Jeremy Cross. Molly, a schoolgirl on a tricycle. Belle and Alexei, twin explorers in pith helmets, who appeared from a caravan in the desert. It was like seeing cartoon characters brought to life as living people. A pirate called Cap'n Ian Sharkchum leapt at him from some overhanging trees in the shadows of a London park, trying to unseat him from a horse he'd borrowed from the Coldstream Guards. He managed to shake Sharkchum off. When the Cap'n had tried the same thing from the same tree on two further occasions, Owen got bored and decided to experiment with mortality.

He'd located a Russian roulette game in an abandoned snooker hall. He took one of the four seats around a dusty blue pool table, and surveyed the other players. Their faces were lit by the reflected illumination of the shaded strip light overhead. Opposite, Brad Kominsky was a GI, his tight khaki T-shirt half-covered by the empty bandolier across his chest. Brenda Simone looked like a fortune teller, wreathed in the smoke from her fat cigar. And seated next to Owen was Walter Pendulum, a barrel-chested man in a tuxedo but with the head of a giraffe. Walter seemed very impressed with Owen, and batted his long eyelashes suggestively. As a cruel distraction, Owen pointed to the double-action revolver on the table. The gun they would each be using in turn.

They placed their initial bets, notes fluttering down on the blue baize. Owen could feel his heart starting to race. What was it about putting a virtual revolver to his character's head that could cause such anxiety? When he picked up the weapon, he knew. In the greater realism of Toshiko's version of *Second Reality*, he was actually raising his hand to his own head

Spin the cylinder. Pull the trigger.

Click. No shot.

Owen felt himself relax. He started to breathe again, and tried not to make his relief obvious to the other players.

Walter Pendulum picked up the revolver. It was obvious at once that his arm was not long enough to reach up and place the barrel against his giraffe-head. Kominsky offered to aim and fire for him, and this started a debate with Simone about whether a killing shot would constitute murder rather than suicide. In the end, Pendulum cranked his neck down and pulled the trigger himself. No shot.

Kominsky snatched up the gun, spun the cylinder. Hesitated with the barrel to his head. Opened his eyes to stare straight at Owen.

Pulled the trigger.

The gun exploded into life. Kominsky's head dissolved in a mist of blood, and his body was flung back from the table to land in a crumpled pile.

Brenda Simone recovered the gun. Calmly reloaded from a box of shells on the table. Spun the cylinder. Squeezed the trigger.

No shot.

'Round's over,' she observed coldly. 'Let's raise the stakes.' She stacked up more notes on the table. 'Call the ante, or take a hike,' she said to Pendulum.

Owen watched a huge gulp work its way down Pendulum's long throat. He was looking at Kominsky's dead body where it lay in a heap on the snooker hall's stained floorboards. Pendulum stood up, terrified. Banged his head on the lampshade. Ran for the door, his little giraffe's tail waggling fearfully through a hole in the back of his tuxedo trousers. They could hear his hoofbeats clank down the metal stairs as he fled.

Simone transferred her basilisk stare to Owen without blinking. 'Call the ante, or take a hike.'

'Or bid up the pot,' replied Owen, and slid all his remaining cash across the table.

He was surprised again at how breathless he felt. He picked up the revolver, spun the cylinder. His chest tightened as he lifted the gun to his temple. Heard the greased click as it revolved. For a split second before he pulled the trigger, he wondered: 'What if…?'

The long trigger pull cocked the hammer. Owen continued to apply pressure.

The hammer released. Struck the round in the chamber.

The bullet exploded into his head.

EIGHT

The third time that he shot himself through the head, Owen began to suspect something was not quite right. He would find his way to the snooker hall, sit down with the three other people, and play Russian roulette. The outcome was always identical, no matter what he did – using a different route to the hall, sitting in a different seat, firing with his left hand, not raising the final stake. The others survived or died in the same sequence. And he always copped it after Walter Pendulum abandoned the contest.

This version of *Second Reality* was more realistic in many ways, but that was only on the surface – the quality of the graphics, the fidelity of the sound, his total immersion in the sensory experience. In the most important way it was less real. Because the whole thing seemed predetermined. The other players had the same backgrounds and experience every time they played. They were just programmed, they didn't seem to learn. It was so unlike the Internet-connected version, where the advantage of playing with real people was their unpredictability, and the opportunity to riff off their ideas as they participated.

Owen struggled with the clasp on his helmet and managed to unlatch it and free himself. The Torchwood Hub reappeared around him. He discovered that he'd twisted his chair around several times during his game-play, and now needed to disentangle himself from the wires attached to the helmet.

Once he'd carefully peeled off the data-gloves, he located his old-fashioned keyboard and typed in a search request. The computer revealed where the locator in Toshiko's mobile placed her at the moment.

'Did you have fun?' she asked him when he walked in to find her in the R&R area. Toshiko was lounging on the far side by the 1980s *Asteroids* machine. A couple of other figures played pinball just behind her. Owen hadn't been expecting them to come back in this evening.

'Quite impressive,' Owen admitted. 'Hi guys. I thought you'd all gone home for the night?'

As he stepped through the door into the area, he was aware of a shimmering effect around him. He rotated his hands in front of him, examining the front and back of each. He wore a pair of backless gloves in pale deerskin. Glendower Broadsword's gloves. And now he came to look, he was also clothed in Glendower's black leather jerkin.

He backed out of the room, and the clothes faded silently out of existence. Stepped back into the room, and they soundlessly reappeared on him. He saw the deerskin gloves again, but when he rubbed his palms together he could not feel them.

'I got the projectors working,' Toshiko explained. 'So now I have a 3-D rendering of the *Second Reality* characters in here.' She stood up and twirled around to reveal she was wearing Penny Pasteur's smart Nehru jacket again.

'Now that's even more impressive,' he admitted. They both appeared in character clothing, but the R&R area was the same familiar jumble of play consoles, arcade terminals and trip-hazard wiring.

Toshiko smiled proudly. 'It works out positional information for the characters, but it doesn't have to paint in the backgrounds any more, so everything is displayed much faster. If I wanted to, I could create a virtual Hub, using the construction data in our systems.'

'What would be the point, Tosh? We can already walk around the real thing.' He strode into the room to demonstrate his point.

She pouted. 'I've introduced new characters. Recognise anyone?'

The two people in the corner turned to look at Owen. They were not Jack or Gwen, as he had originally assumed. Immediately behind Toshiko was Cap'n Ian Sharkchum, who doffed his pirate hat in a sweeping gesture and called out 'Ahoy, matey!' Next to him, Walter Pendulum straightened up from playing the pinball machine. He fluttered his long eyelashes and blew Owen a kiss, or at least he made the best effort that a giraffe-headed man can afford. Pendulum cast a last lingering glance over his shoulder before swinging his long neck back to his pinball game.

'The point is,' Toshiko said, oblivious to all this, 'we could use this set-up for training purposes. Imagine being able to practise patterns and moves, only without the danger of doing it out in the field for the first time. I've been experimenting with projectors here to demonstrate that you can interact with generated images within a 3-D space. Next stage is to create a virtual Cardiff. There's all sorts of data sources I can use. Positional data from US military satellites, Google Earth, the Land Registry, Public Private Partnership databases, various engineering companies...'

'Interesting,' admitted Owen. He took a slightly nervous look at Walter Pendulum, but that giraffe neck was still arched over the pinball game. Owen sat down next to Toshiko, smiling. 'Do you remember the training sessions we had with Jack? God, the bruises and the blood, every day! I thought I'd seen plenty of brutal stuff from my days in A&E. But that was something else.'

'I remember the exercise we did on that freezing day out in the Gower,' shivered Toshiko. 'Treasure hunt, he said it was!'

'Treasure hunt, my arse!' The memory made Owen laugh out loud. 'Still, it wasn't as bad as that couple of nights in the Rhondda. I've seen frostbite before, but I thought at the end that I'd be carrying my toes home in a box.'

'And Operation Goldenrod,' recalled Toshiko quietly.

Owen's laughter faltered. 'I saw Jack in a whole different light after that one.'

Toshiko nodded. Her expression suggested she couldn't decide whether to relish or regret the whole training experience. 'That all seems ages ago, and yet...' Her voice trailed off wistfully.

Owen watched her eyes. They seemed to be focused on something a long distance away. 'Before I came here,' she said eventually, 'I'd never killed anyone before. Never even thought about it. Oh, I mean, I got angry with people.'

'I'd pay money to see you get angry, Tosh.'

'No, the sort of thing you just say and don't mean. "I'll kill that guy if I get my hands on him," you know. But I'd never even used a gun before. Not a real one.' Another long pause.

Abruptly, behind them, the pirate captain loudly cheered on the giraffe-man in his pinball game. 'Avast behind!' yelled Sharkchum.

'I think he's talking about you, Tosh.' Owen nudged her conspiratorially, and added in an undertone: 'Can these guys overhear us? I mean, does Cap'n Birdseye understand what we're talking about?'

'No, he's just an avatar generated by the game.' She rattled off a few keystrokes on the console in front of her, and the pirate captain dissolved in a shower of white noise, like a TV being detuned and switched off. The giraffe man continued with the final pull of his pinball game, apparently unconcerned by his noisy friend's abrupt disappearance.

'Something I noticed in the *Second Reality*, when I was wearing that helmet thing. It was a big disappointment... Don't get me wrong, it's a *fantastic* achievement, Tosh,' Owen added hurriedly as he watched her eyebrows rise. 'But it was obvious that the other avatars were just running through a script. Responding to pre-programmed computer instructions. They weren't real people.'

'In fleshspace, you mean.'

Her sarcasm irritated him, but he persevered anyway. 'Yeah. You know, unreliable, erratic. Unpredictable. With the usual foibles and weaknesses that human beings have and robots don't.' He pondered this assertion for a moment. 'Apart from that robot we trashed in Pontypridd, obviously.'

'Too bad,' said Toshiko firmly. 'It's more secure that way. If you're that disappointed, I can download a larger amount of game-play data from the server and that will show more options.'

'No, I'm saying I had the same thought that you did, Tosh. *Second Reality* tests real people's potential. The more you play it, the better you get, because you start to understand the conventions of the game. So alien monsters in a virtual world won't freak game-players out like in real life.'

She was still looking at him blankly. Regular exposure to Toshiko's non-verbal repertoire had made Owen immune to such obviously faked incomprehension.

'You said it yourself, Torchwood could use this for training. Go that next step, Tosh. Why not use *Second Reality* for recruitment too? Connect it to the gaming community on the Internet! Find out who's good at this kind of thing, and approach them to join when they've shown enough aptitude? Test out their real-life skills against the kinds of situations we face in our daily lives but that they never would – until one day when it's too late for them?'

'No, no, no,' insisted Toshiko.

Owen was getting into his stride now. Why couldn't Toshiko accept this? Why was she even working on these enhancements if she didn't see the potential? 'Come on! There are all sorts of people we'd never contact normally. Loads of people play *Second Reality*. Bright kids, CEOs, programmers, surfers, accountants, soldiers, stay-at-home mums… You wouldn't believe the imagination that everyday people have. There's one guy who's created a game that the avatars inside *Second Reality* play, and it's so popular he's licensed it to a publisher. In the real world. They're gonna release it on video game-players and mobile phones. There was a fashion show using the design sketches and model avatars for the catwalk event in a virtual Paris. Last week I saw a competition to design a new mousetrap, where the mice were the size of donkeys. Where else can you find such a range of skills and abilities and aptitude all in one place? It's a scouting trip to die for. But only if you plug it in.'

'Not if you value your personal fleshspace,' warned Toshiko. Her manner was adamant. 'I won't hear of this version being connected outside the Torchwood firewall, under any circumstances. And I will chop off your scabbard if I find you trying to.'

Owen threw up his hands, fake gloves and all, in a gesture of frustration and despair.

'Look,' she continued. She was doing that earnest voice of hers, the one that she used when she wanted to sound so reasonable that you couldn't then go and bite her head off. 'There's another head-mounted display helmet available, and you could manage with just one data-glove. So if you want some unpredictable interaction with a real human being, give the other glove and the spare helmet to Ianto, and play with him.'

'Ianto?' Owen blew out a great long exasperated sigh. 'Unpredictable? I suppose we could make virtual coffee together.'

'I heard that,' said Ianto, 'and I think I may resent it.'

Owen's heart sank a little. Ianto's voice was coming from near the pinball machine. Like Owen and Toshiko, he was wearing a virtual costume. Owen hadn't recognised him inside the giraffe's head.

Walter Pendulum eased his portly frame around the pinball machine and retrieved a tray containing empty cups and a cafetière. 'Unfortunate timing, I accept,' said the giraffe with Ianto's voice. 'But don't let the coincidence of me doing this suggest otherwise.'

Walter waddled off across the games area. As he left the room, his shimmering image transformed back into Ianto. The last thing to vanish as he departed through the doorway was his little giraffe's tail.

Owen slumped into his seat, now embarrassed and dejected at the same time. 'Don't you ever take a risk, Tosh?'

'When it comes to system security,' she told him primly, 'I'm conservative. With a small "c".'

'Chicken starts with a small "c" too, you know.'

'Don't be an idiot with a big "i".'

'That Cyclops we found in Pontprennau last month. Now, he *was* an idiot with a big "i".'

Toshiko stood up and loomed over him. She fixed him to his chair with her scowl. 'Owen. I gave up my social evening to get this thing finished tonight, and all I get is abuse from you? Look at the time. I'm going to go home.'

'Social evening?' That didn't sound much like the Toshiko Sato he knew. Dr Sato the programming whizz-kid, first into the office and last to leave every day. This had potential. He grinned at her. 'You mean… you had a date? What would keep you here if you had a date?'

She stopped staring at him. Looked away. Blushed a little. 'If you must know, I've joined a chess club. We meet on Saturday evenings.' She was shutting down the computer system. Owen's leather jerkin, gloves and boots all glittered and faded. Toshiko was wearing her usual black top and trousers again.

Owen watched her leave the R&R area.

Chess, he thought. Right. Ideal for Toshiko. The only pairing where she was ever likely to make the first move.

He listened to her footsteps disappearing into the distance. Then he just sat for several minutes and let the night-time sounds of the Hub echo around him. The 50 hertz hum of the machinery. The tick-splash sound of a drip. The occasional creak of a board somewhere in the older fittings.

There was no sign of Toshiko returning. He went out to the main area, and satisfied himself that Ianto had also left for the evening. The helmet-mounted display and data-gloves were at his desk where he'd left them.

Owen powered up the computer again, and began to type. His logon screen appeared, and he tapped in his user id: *harpo@swalesonline.net*, followed by his password.

'This is *Second Reality*,' the screen told him. 'Connect to the Internet? Y/N'

He slipped on the data-gloves, flexing his fingers and feeling the touch-sensitive pads against his skin. He carefully strapped on the helmet. The screen image was already displayed on the stereoscopic screens, and the text seemed to leap out at him in three dimensions.

He reached out his right hand and pushed against the Y.

'*Second Reality*,' said the mellow voice of the game, all around him. 'Welcome back, Glendower Broadsword.'

NINE

The chlorine stink caught in her nose and throat. A child screamed from the far end of the swimming pool in alarm or delight; it wasn't clear to Gwen. She swung around, lurching, swaying, unsure of her footing on the bleached blue tiling.

Swimmers thronged the pool. A flotilla of inflatables carried a procession of whooping children and indulgent parents diagonally across the main race lanes and towards the lazy river, where water jets urged the tide of people onwards, onwards.

That man on the balcony was still watching her. He peered nonchalantly over the top of his newspaper. She knew him from somewhere, didn't she?

Gwen grabbed the stainless-steel rail at the edge of the deep end. Held on to it fiercely as the room snapped back into focus. In the dead centre of the pool, ignored by the endless stream of swimmers, one man churned the green-blue water. Floundering. Gasping. Going under for the third time.

It was Jack. Gwen recognised the black Speedos. (How did she recognise the black Speedos? She couldn't say. It didn't matter.)

Jack's face broke the surface again. Another huge gasp for air. His hair was slicked close to his head by the water. His eyes made contact with hers, past the kids on floats, past their attentive fathers, past the boisterous teenage lads who ducked their girlfriends or did handstands underwater. Unseen by them, Jack's mouth opened in a wide 'o' of surprise and horror before his mouth, his nose, his terrified blue eyes submerged beneath the churning water.

'Someone help him!' screamed Gwen. She looked wildly around. From the other side of the pool, a lifeguard sauntered slowly towards her. The lad was about twenty, absurdly good-looking, with short-cropped brown hair and startling green eyes. He peeled off his yellow T-shirt languorously, to reveal a smooth, muscular chest and a fuse of hair that circled his navel and ran down into his baggy red shorts. 'Leave him,' he told her, his voice warm and dark and calm. 'He's mine.'

The lifeguard slipped into the water, and the kids and parents and teens parted before him. He pulled himself towards the floundering Jack with slow, powerful strokes. Gwen felt the frustration build in her, a tensing of the muscles in her upper arms and shoulders. 'Hurry hurry hurry,' she chanted, like a mantra.

Just as the lad was about to reach Jack, a long-legged girl collided with him. Her blonde hair coiled like snakes around her in the water. Her tight red one-piece swimsuit was the same colour as the boy's shorts, and Gwen knew suddenly that she was another lifeguard.

'Leave him,' said the girl in red. Her tone was deliberate and her voice was breathy, yet clearly audible above the sound of the pool. She lifted one hand out of the water and pushed down on the other lifeguard's head. 'Leave him. He's mine.'

The young male lifeguard shook her off and pushed his head back to the surface, blowing air through his pursed lips and scattering water with a rapid shake of his head. He pressed up against the woman, forcing her away so that she slowly fell backwards, the swimsuit material stretched tight over her breasts.

The two guards continued to jostle together in the pool, a leisurely exchange of shoves and nudges that was more like a ballet than a fight. Beside them, Jack's face floated just below the surface, his eyes and mouth wide.

Gwen choked. She couldn't draw breath. It was as though she was underwater, unable or afraid to breathe in. She wanted to plunge into the pool, drag herself across to the middle and bring Jack to the surface. But her legs were leaden; she could not even slide her bare feet over the cracked blue tiles. Her hands spasmed, and her fingers locked, immovable around the barrier rail.

The thin-faced man stared down from the balcony. He had stood to watch the commotion in the pool. No, Gwen realised, his eyes were fixed on her. 'Owen Harper,' she said.

'It's *Doctor* Owen Harper, the thin-faced man called to her. 'Actually.'

Gwen cursed her paralysed legs, and tried to lunge over the barrier into the water. Her arms had no strength. The crowds continued their unheeding passage around the drowning man. Gwen screamed wildly at the lifeguards. They paused to study her incuriously.

'Save him!' Her shrill cry echoed around the swimming pool.

She woke up abruptly, surfacing from beneath her sheets with a wail of misery and fear.

'Bloody hell!' Rhys fumbled around on the bedside cabinet, and scattered books and pens on the floor before he managed to locate the light switch. He propped himself up on his elbows. 'What's the matter, love?'

Gwen found that her arms weren't paralysed any more, so she threw them around her boyfriend and started to sob.

She let him clasp her tightly, quietly, until she slowly calmed down. He was good like that, Rhys. He knew when to talk and when to shut up and just say nothing.

She knew she couldn't explain it, so she lied to him that she'd already forgotten what the nightmare was.

Rhys squeezed her again. 'It must have been the rain rattling the window. Sorry, love, I know I should've fixed it, and now with the storm and everything…'

'No, no,' she mumbled. 'S'all right.'

Rhys held her at arm's length to look at her. Jerked his head towards the window. 'And it's boiling in here, isn't it? Maybe that rain's not so bad, I can open the thing a bit and let some air in?' He slipped out of bed and ambled over to the window. When he cracked open the top pane, Gwen could hear the steady susurration of rain on the pavement below.

Rhys padded through to the bathroom. He left the door ajar, and raised his voice so that she could hear him over the sound of the running tap. He spoke in short bursts as he brushed his teeth. 'Every time my gran knew a storm was coming in. She'd cover up all the mirrors in the house with bed-sheets. White bedsheets. It was like her terrace house was going into storage. Wouldn't get unwrapped until the lightning had gone away.'

Gwen smiled to herself, not quite sure if she was amused or sad. She knew Rhys was just talking cheerful nonsense to cajole her out of the fearful mood, to help her completely forget whatever it was that had upset her. But his anecdote reminded her of that alien radiance sprite Torchwood had trapped a few weeks ago in a mirrored box. Toshiko had folded up the reflective surfaces and thrown a dark cloth over it. Would nothing be simple any more, Gwen thought to herself. Maybe she'd never again have normal points of reference for the stories that Rhys told about his family, or about what had happened to him at the office, or something that he and Banana Boat had laughed at in the pub. She could never talk about her own work, and lovely Rhys just didn't question it because he accepted 'Special Ops' was something she could never discuss. He could tell her about Barry's latest computer cock-up, or the naivety of the young secretary he'd just hired, or the latest crazy diet theory expounded by Lucy in his office. But Gwen never made up any of her own stories to exchange about Special Ops colleagues. She knew from her own police work that it was too easy to get lost in those kinds of fabrications, once you got started.

'Look at you!' Rhys was standing in the doorway. 'You're on the wrong side of the bed. I got up a bit earlier for a wee and a glass of water – all that Tiger we had with dinner, it just went right through me. When I got back, you'd rolled over onto my side. That's why I had a bit of trouble with your lamp there. Sorry, couldn't quite see what was what.' He stooped down by her side of the bed and started to pick up the books and pens and papers he'd accidentally scattered on the floor. 'You've had quite a few restless nights, haven't you? Since starting this new job. What's all that about?' He laughed. 'Guilty conscience?'

'Oh, hark at you,' Gwen retorted. 'Guilty conscience about my new job? That's your mate Gaz talking, that is. Like you never have nightmares?'

'I always sleep well. The sleep of the just.'

'The sleep of the shagged, more like,' she told him. 'Your post-coital coma is what you mean, Rhys.'

He dumped some of the papers on the bedside cabinet, leaned over, and attempted to snog her.

'Not fair!' she protested, laughing, as she smelled the Colgate. 'You've brushed your teeth, and I bet I've got bog breath.'

'I don't care.'

'Well I do,' she told him. 'And besides, I need the loo now.'

Rhys stood up to let her out of the bed. 'I'll tidy up the rest of this mess I've made while you have your wee, then.'

Gwen tiptoed over the cold bathroom lino and left him to sort out the strewn papers. Since joining Torchwood, she'd had restless nights because she woke up with thoughts and ideas and then stayed awake fretting that she wouldn't remember them the next day. She'd taken to scribbling them on shop receipts and envelopes, and eventually in a small notebook. She trusted Rhys not to nosey around in her stuff, but didn't trust herself not to lose it, so it was written in abbreviations and codes. Inevitably, that meant her night-time jottings were either in indecipherable handwriting or, when examined in the cold light of morning, just tired rambling nonsense.

'Is this a new mobile number?' Rhys called through to her.

She emerged back into their room, still clutching her toothbrush. She wiped one wet hand on her nightie, and took the Post-it note from him.

'Scribbled out in a bit of a hurry,' he observed, 'and not your handwriting. That says "Gwen", and a number… is that a zero or a six?'

Gwen knew that the scrawled word was "Owen". He'd shoved his mobile number at her, while giving her some half-hearted cheesy chat-up line. She'd told him to piss off. It was a joke anyway, a gesture, because all the Torchwood phones had everyone's number programmed in on speed dial. Even so, when she'd emptied the pockets that evening before hanging her jacket in the wardrobe, she'd found the Post-it note still there.

'Message from the office,' she told Rhys. Gwen took it with her back to the bathroom, sticking it on the mirror while she had a pee. As she sat, she thought about the dream. Jack in the pool. Owen watching from the balcony.

She got back to the bed, and stooped close to Rhys to get a proper snog. He was sprawled comfortably across his own side, mouth wide open, taking regular breaths.

Gwen listened to Rhys breathing. She went back and retrieved the Post-it from the bathroom mirror. Tucked it into her notebook. Put the notebook on the bedside cabinet. Slipped back into bed with Rhys, and switched off the lamp. Lay in the dark, listening to the ceaseless rain.

TEN

Russian roulette was definitely more interesting with real people, decided Owen. And playing it in the Torchwood Hub gave it an added frisson of excitement. There was the danger of being caught by Jack or Gwen or Toshiko, which was just as exhilarating as knowing that he risked getting his brains splattered across his own desk. Though that would be harder to explain than it would be to clear up afterwards.

He sniffed the air in the room, expecting his nostrils to fill with the scent of cordite and freshly sprayed blood. Beside him, slumped against the base of the *Asteroids* arcade game, the latest gun victim stared sightlessly at the Hub's high ceiling. It was Kvasir the Viking. One way or another, at someone else's hand or his own, that dumb Scandinavian was always going to wind up dead.

Owen kicked the dead man's fur-clad leg. 'Get up, Kvasir,' he told him. 'You're not as smart as they told me you were. Try again with your next life. I bet you can't lose four times in a row.'

The corpse blinked twice, rolled over and returned to the table.

After another couple of games, the novelty of combining elements of the *Second Reality* game with the physical contents of the Hub started to pall for Owen. For the first hour, it had amused him to run the 3-D projectors in the Hub's games area, but he soon found it distracting to navigate around the solid real-life objects, and a lot duller than exploring the unlimited, uninhibited worlds created by other people inside *Second Reality*. At one stage, he checked his watch to see that it was already approaching 1 a.m. on Sunday morning. After that, he put the helmet-mounted display back on his head and immersed himself once more in the startling clarity of the images on the stereoscopic screens.

He was keen to meet new characters, in the hope that they were also new people in the real world. You could never tell, because one person might have several avatars in the game. Penny Pasteur had already proved a disappointment. Remembering Toshiko's words earlier, he'd gone to the Wumpaam district where a Mage called Candlesmith had sold him a pair of sunglasses that showed you what the person's fleshspace name was. Perhaps unsurprisingly, they didn't work on Candlesmith, but when Owen used them on Penny Pasteur it revealed her in real life to be Donald McGurk Jr., logged in to the game from Minneapolis. And while Donald wasn't the hairy-arsed fifty-year-old that Toshiko had speculated about, when confronted with his true identity he confessed that he was a thirty-two-year-old *Star Trek* fan who secretly wanted to be Lieutenant Uhura.

Owen abandoned 'Penny' back at the Lunatic Fringe, making good use of an unfortunate accident when she had fallen into a huge pile of rotting fruit that had mysteriously appeared in the street outside the barber-shop. Within seconds, Owen had vanished around the corner and lost himself amid the glittering skyscrapers of the uptown Millennium Capitol, heedless to the wails from Penny and the screeches of the pteranodons that had swooped down from nowhere to peck at her where she lay in the street like a tempting hors d'oeuvre.

More promising was Egg Magnet. In his guise as Glendower Broadsword, Owen picked him up outside the Surer Square, a tapas bar near the centre of Millennium Capitol. He decided that Egg was the most stylish person in the place, because he was dancing on the table-top, and eating fire rather than the *queso con anchoas*. This endeared him to Owen, if not to the waiters, so he intercepted Egg as he was being thrown out into the street.

They danced diagonally across the cobbled streets of the food district. Owen considered the newcomer's brilliant white trouser suit and startlingly bright silver hair.

'What kind of name is "Egg Magnet"?' he asked.

'Name of a band,' Egg replied. 'How about you? Did your parents read a lot of Tolkien?'

Owen considered his Glendower Broadsword outfit. 'I've always wanted to visit New Zealand. But I never got further than dressing like this. It's a hobbit I find hard to break.'

Egg Magnet pulled a face. Literally. He seized hold of his cheeks and stretched them like putty into an exaggerated expression of dismay.

'Sorry,' grinned Owen. He reached over and smoothed out Egg's distorted features with soft pressure on the skin. Left his hands in position, gently holding the other man's cheeks and considering the possibilities. He'd experimented with *Second Reality* sex sessions in the past, though that was just getting other characters on the screen to snog and shag. He wondered what the possibilities were with his sight and hearing totally immersed in the game like this. Or with the tangible feedback from the sensors in the data-gloves. A recent copy of *The Lancet* had included a joke article about cybersex, and involved some equipment described as 'technodildonics'. He doubted Toshiko would think that was research worth pursuing for Torchwood. Though he imagined he'd have enjoyed describing the hardware interface to her.

'Do you want to get a drink somewhere?' he asked Egg. 'Or do you prefer to curl up with a nice cup of tea?'

Egg gently pulled his face away from Owen, chuckling. The movement scattered his silver hair around his shoulders. 'I had a boyfriend who always said that. I'd tell him, "No, I'll tell you what, I'll have a really *average* cup of tea, thanks. Unless you can do me a crappy cup of tea. " I do love a crappy cup of tea, don't you?'

Owen laughed too. It was something he'd said himself in the past.

Egg danced off across the street and up a connecting flight of steps to a raised area of shops and restaurants. He peered over his shoulder, checking that Owen wasn't left behind. Owen chased up the steps after Egg, taking two or three at a time to catch up.

'You have a lovely laugh,' Owen told him. 'What else did your boyfriend say that made you laugh like that?'

Egg sat on a low wall outside a restaurant, and patted it to indicate Owen should join him. 'Like you, he said he wanted to travel. But he'd never go to the North Pacific, because he didn't trust Hawaiians…'

Owen broke in, laughing again: '…because the "i"s are too close together!' He looked at Egg thoughtfully for a moment. There was something very familiar about him. Owen closed his eyes and listened to Egg talk, trying to concentrate on the words and not his appearance.

'When we met outside the Surer Square, I thought that you'd be S.I.T.'

'What's that?' asked Owen, knowing already.

'Safe in taxis,' Egg said. He indicated Owen's clothing. 'The whole medieval thing going on here, I didn't think you were looking to pick anyone up. And then I started to think you might be a gay man. Dressed up like that, with the false-looking boobs and everything. Not that that's a problem,' Egg added hurriedly. There was a pause which felt like he was pondering this. 'Though I did meet one strange woman earlier who kept asking me to open hailing frequencies. Do you think that's some sort of code?'

'Don't even go there,' said Owen. He had taken the Mage's sunglasses out of his pocket, and put them on to look at Egg.

Egg chose exactly the same moment to leap abruptly to his feet. He stared at his watch. 'Oh God, no! My shift's due to start. Sorry, gotta go.' He offered Owen a theatrical shrug. 'Laters, mate.' And with this, he twisted on the spot and spiralled out of existence.

Owen stared at the empty space where Egg had been. Only it wasn't Egg, he now knew. The sunglasses had confirmed his growing suspicion. The text floating in the air around the avatar's head had revealed him to be *m.tegg@caerdyddnet.net*, connected to *Second Reality* with an IP address in Cardiff.

The name should have given it away earlier, even before the coincidences of what had been said. Egg Magnet. Megan Tegg.

She was the girlfriend he'd walked out on in London six years ago. What was Dr Megan Tegg doing in Cardiff?

ELEVEN

Someone was shaking him, pushing on his shoulder. The instinct was to lash out with his elbow. He resisted that temptation while he tried to orient himself.

Owen was still wearing the helmet-mounted display, and his head rested on the keyboard of his work station. When he lifted his head, the image displayed by the helmet didn't change: it was the two-dimensional screensaver, which told him in stark digital numbers that the time was 05.58.

Oh shit. He'd dozed off while playing *Second Reality*. After a period of inaction, the game had obviously disconnected him and then his computer screensaver had kicked in on timer.

He struggled out of the helmet. The same screensaver on his desktop computer screen clicked over to 05.59. The rest of the room was in shadows, the main lights not lit and most of the other terminal screens still switched off.

When Owen's eyes adjusted to the contrast, he realised it was Ianto who'd woken him by pushing his shoulder. It wasn't like him to touch Owen, to touch any of them really. The lad could throw the Torchwood SUV into a hairpin turn, knock a Weevil down with a well-placed blow, and run a hundred metres like Christian Malcolm. But he wasn't the sort to put a comforting arm around someone or punch them playfully on the arm, and he'd die rather than hug you. Ianto never gave a second look to Gwen or Toshiko. And Jack was always hitting on him, so he was probably gay, hiding in the closet with the lights off and hoping no one could hear him breathing.

Ianto looked at Owen sheepishly. 'I didn't think anyone was in this early. I thought I'd better wake you before…' He trailed off and looked over his shoulder. From elsewhere, in the R&R area, came the distinctive sound of Jack whooping with delight to the sound-effect noises of a handgun.

'Yeah, right. Sorry,' Owen muttered.

Ianto gave him his serious look. 'You don't want to get addicted to this, do you?'

'Don't you start,' mumbled Owen. 'You're as bad as Tosh. No, I was… um… testing some new software for her.'

'I understand,' Ianto nodded solemnly. 'Are those breasts part of the test, then?'

Owen looked down at his hands. Instead of seeing the blue data-gloves, he could see Glendower Broadsword's deerskin gloves. *Second Reality* had logged him out, but Toshiko's 3-D rendering software and projectors were still active. And so Owen still sported a magnificent pair of tits. Ianto's smile looked like it might split his face in half.

'All right, yeah,' Owen warned. Ianto had obviously rumbled that he'd not been working hard all night. Perhaps he could brazen his way out of this. 'So what? I met someone online who was interested in cybersex.'

Ianto's smile evaporated in an instant, and a fleeting look of panic flashed over his features. This was a more extreme reaction than Owen had anticipated, but it was pleasing nonetheless to wipe that smirk off his face. Perhaps Ianto was more prudish than he thought. One of those valley boy Welsh Presbyterians, no doubt. Chapel every Sunday. They wouldn't like him being gay, would they? Churchgoer… yeah, that would explain why he was wearing his smart suit at this time on a Sunday, at the crack of dawn. 'What are you doing here so early, Ianto?'

Ianto looked shifty. 'I might ask you the same thing, Dr Harper.' There was another big whoop from the R&R area that suggested Jack had reached another level. 'But perhaps I won't.'

With a swipe of his hand, Owen disconnected Toshiko's equipment. Glendower's costume dissolved into the ether around him. 'If at first you don't succeed, destroy all evidence that you tried.' He gestured towards Jack. 'Has he been here all night?'

'No,' replied Ianto. 'He got back about thirty minutes ago.'

Owen nodded and moved off.

In the R&R area, he found Jack was enthusiastically engaged in a shooting game. It had amused him some months previously to install *Zombie Death* alongside the other twenty-year-old arcade titles like *Asteroids* and a pinball machine themed around *Bat Out Of Hell*.

'Jack!' Owen adopted a tone of breezy familiarity. Better to try and blag it at this stage. 'How are you getting on?'

'I'm wiping you off the scoreboard buddy,' Jack replied. 'All those high scores you had? Not any more!' He hefted a plastic gun, designed like an old-style revolver and attached by a stout cable to the base of the arcade game. On the display screen, a phalanx of the slavering undead menaced a cowering crowd of hospital patients and nurses. 'Tosh told me about her 3D game technology. But you know, I'm kinda traditional about these things. Prefer the classic look. Retro.'

You're telling me, thought Owen as he studied Jack's collarless shirt and braces.

'I thought I'd try it left-handed today,' continued Jack nonchalantly, 'to give you a chance.' He loosed off a brisk string of shots. The machine pinged in approval as the zombies exploded into dusty pixels on the screen. Jack gave another great whoop of celebration. 'Oh yeah! See that?' He pulled Owen closer to the machine and tapped the screen with his finger. 'That means I get an extra life. But…' He affected to look forlorn. '… I can't stay here all day. OK, you take it from here.' He tossed the gun in a short arc through the air so that Owen could catch it. Owen decided he wasn't going to be fazed by this challenge, and took up position in front of *Zombie Death*.

Jack stopped at the door on his way out, and considered Owen's posture. 'Have you done something to your tits?'

Owen couldn't stop himself touching his chest self-consciously. 'No. I switched the game off.'

'Well, you gotta start working harder on those pecs, buddy. I can recommend a good gym. Is the Wildman autopsy done?'

Owen tried not to let his 'Oh, shit!' feeling show on his face. He still had to complete that, because he'd got sidetracked by *Second Reality*. 'Sure, I'll finish up shortly,' he lied. While Owen was looking at Jack, in the *Zombie Death* game his character was dragged to the ground by the attacking monsters and devoured.

Jack laughed. 'Bring the results to the Boardroom in an hour.' He turned his back on Owen as he left the area. 'Or sooner if you run out of lives.'

* * *

The walk in from Riverside normally took less than half an hour. But today, there were repeated delays. The night-time thunderstorm had not eased off so, after kissing Rhys goodbye over his cornflakes, Gwen grabbed a taxi outside their flat in the hope of staying dry. A two-mile walk turned into a five-mile drive, but she was held up as even the normally light Sunday morning traffic ground to a halt along the drenched Penarth Road. Finally, she stood for a few moments on the paving stone by the stainless-steel water tower, waiting to descend into the Hub. Through the rain, she studied the armadillo shape of the Millennium Centre. '*Creu Gwir fel gwydr o ffwrnais awen,*' the text read. 'Creating truth like glass from the furnace of inspiration.' It always amused her to read these words while she was concealed in the deceptive invisibility of the paving stone that led into the even more secret underground facility of the Torchwood Hub.

Jack waved away her apologies for lateness as she entered the Boardroom, and then indicated her seat. Toshiko returned to studying her laptop, where she was making notes in one window, studying some calculations in another, and displaying live video feeds in two more.

Owen stared at Gwen from where he stood at the plasma screen, bristling with ill-concealed irritation at having his presentation interrupted.

'Death rejoices,' Jack said. 'Why was he so happy about it?'

'I don't understand,' Gwen said.

'It's what you see in some mortuaries,' Owen told her. '*Hic locus est ubi mors gaudet succurrere vitae.*' The Latin words sounded strange in his London accent. 'It means "This is the place where death rejoices to teach those who live." You know, to cheer them up that they're cutting into dead people.'

'Only this guy...' Jack's casual gesture encompassed several images of the dead Wildman before them. '... he didn't look worried about dying at all, last I saw of him.'

'He changed his mind about that, after the first fifty feet,' observed Owen.

Gwen frowned at this. 'Well, who really wants to die, eh? Like that programme about smoking last night on Channel 4, eh Tosh?'

Toshiko didn't look up from her laptop computer. 'I wouldn't know. I don't watch TV.'

'No TV at night?' Gwen affected astonishment. 'God, I don't know what me and Rhys would do without watching telly.'

'Talk to each other, maybe,' suggested Toshiko.

Owen coughed. 'Shall I start this all over again, then?' He was asking Gwen, rather than Jack. Jack was just smiling, amused by Owen's reaction.

'I'll catch up,' Gwen reassured him. Owen was looking pretty rough this morning. She'd seen him roll into the Hub before, looking like he'd slept in his clothes, lost his razor, and come straight in without changing. But this morning the circles under his eyes were almost as dark as the stubble on his chin. At least he looked a bit better than Wildman's corpse in the autopsy pictures.

It was only a few months now since Gwen had seen her first autopsy. She'd never had reason to attend one as a police officer, and she'd always dreaded the day that she'd have to. She'd heard the stories of strapping lads from her station who'd collapsed onto the scrubbed mortuary floor on first witnessing the clinical dissection of a dead body. Lads like Jimmy Mitchell, throwing up their canteen lunch. So her first autopsy had been here at the Hub, when she'd watched Owen dissect a woman of sixty-five who'd managed to get on the wrong side of a Weevil.

Owen had delighted in making Gwen help him, testing the new girl, trying to make her collapse or weep or throw up or just run from the mortuary. She'd determinedly refused to give him that pleasure. She'd approached the whole thing with the detachment she brought to bear when examining a scene of crime. Observing the hanging scale for weighing removed organs, with a round clock-face marked off in kilos and a stainless-steel pan underneath – that was like the one she weighed her fruit in at Tesco. A Bunsen burner on a counter was the same as she'd used at school. The severed grey remains of brain, heart, bowels in jars around the room were harder to dismiss. OK, they were like the specimens in GCSE Biology. She had survived the ordeal and been pleased by her own calmness and by Owen's obvious disappointment.

That night, back home, when the normality of the sofa and the chicken chow mein and *EastEnders* on the telly had calmed her, she'd suddenly remembered the old woman's pale grey eyes, revealed when Owen had casually peeled back the lids. And to Rhys's surprise, Gwen had rushed to their bathroom and vomited so hard and so long that she'd ended up dry-retching, nothing left to spew into the toilet bowl.

That was then. Now, she was hardened to it. Or was she simply harder?

'I used that Bekaran deep-tissue scanner for some of these,' Owen was explaining, 'so I could get some initial snaps without any invasive procedures.' The images were displayed on the wall screen, bright red and cream images of flesh and blood and bone. 'Amazing, innit? It's like it peels away the outer layers, or makes them invisible, or something.'

Toshiko looked up idly from her laptop screen. 'So why bother with the autopsy, then? Even without that, you've got MRI scans, ultrasound, nuclear medicine, molecular testing… It's not hard to work out how he died, is it? His head hit the pavement at thirty miles an hour. Case closed.'

'Wait and see,' Owen admonished her.

He ran through the images on the display. Many of the pictures showed Wildman's corpse with its arms spread, skin flayed back, the chest exposed and the abdomen open. The traditional Y-shaped incision had been made from shoulders to mid-chest and on down to the pubic region. Wildman's head had struck the bus, and then he had landed on his front. His face was smashed into an unrecognisable pulp, even after it had been cleaned up. Owen explained that he'd considered removing the brain through the big hole in the front of the skull, rather than the more conventional second incision across the head just below and behind the ears. 'He's not gonna end up in an open casket, that's for damned sure,' agreed Jack.

There were more pictures. Owen had cut the cartilages to separate the ribs from the breastbone. 'They were smashed up on landing,' he explained, 'and when I entered the abdominal cavity you could see that the large intestine had been lacerated by a penetrating injury sustained on impact. So freeing up the intestine took some time. Nothing of great interest for most of the organs. No bacteria in the blood. No interesting results from the bile and urine analysis. Non-smoker, slightly enlarged liver suggests he enjoyed a drink. No indication of drug use, prescription medicines or poisons.'

Jack drummed on the table. 'You're saving up the best bits for last, aren't you?'

'Yeah,' said Owen with relish. He put up some new images. 'Examination of the oesophagus, stomach, pancreas, duodenum, and spleen. Non-human elements there…'

'That creature that he threw up at Jack,' interrupted Gwen.

'Genius,' said Owen laconically, and continued as if nothing had been said. 'There's also an alien device inserted in his spine. Attached to the spinal column, actually, quite near the top. And here it is.'

He produced the thing with a flourish. It was spherical, about the size of a large marble, but with a dull chrome finish. There were three short spiked attachments to one side of it, which Gwen assumed were how it had been fixed in place. Toshiko took it from Owen, and placed it into a small black container about the size of a box of matches. She that to her laptop, and started to scan its contents. 'Is that round thing what killed Wildman, then?'

Owen rolled his eyes. 'He died of concrete poisoning. What do you think killed him?' To make his point, he flashed back to a SOC picture that showed the mangled remains of Wildman, sprawled in the street. 'Technically, you know, we'd call that a depressed skull fracture and cerebral bleeding.'

'What about that stuff you were saying yesterday about the spinal fluid?'

Owen flicked back to his notes. 'Confirmed what you thought, Jack. The blood and skull fragments and brain fluid were from three different DNA sources, including that smelly bag of shit we found yesterday.'

Gwen stiffened in her chair, and felt her face flush with anger again. 'That bag of shit was a person.'

'Not any more,' Owen replied.

'All right,' interrupted Jack. 'Good work on the autopsies, Owen. Tosh, what have you got?'

Toshiko smiled. 'Search results are coming through.' She touched her keyboard and her screen replaced Owen's on the huge plasma display on the wall.

Owen sat down and stared at the screen with envious eyes. 'Look at that,' he said. 'She gets the jobs that take her a couple of minutes and then this whizz-bang technology does the grunt work for her while she sits back and does her nails. Why do I get all the jobs that mean spending two hours up to me elbows in someone else's cold dead guts?'

Toshiko patted his arm on the table to make him shut up. 'It'll take a while, because it has to do a content search on multimedia databases around the UK. Oh, and Jack, I had no luck with that search you asked about yesterday. No UK hospital examinations or autopsies contain info about binary vascular system. Negative for overseas hospitals too. I did the last three years, like you suggested. Shall I extend to five?'

Jack shook his head. 'Never mind. Stay focused on the current problem.' But Gwen could see Jack was trying to hide his disappointment. That wasn't like him, he preferred to encourage and support his team. 'What else have you got?'

'I checked out the security reports from the place Wildman worked, the Blaidd Drwg nuclear facility. Do you think it's too much of a coincidence that a number of their new, experimental nuclear power packs have gone missing?'

Jack's eyes widened. 'Didn't see that on the evening news.'

'Well, it's not something they've made public, obviously,' admitted Toshiko. 'I wonder what…'

Her voiced trailed off as an extraordinary figure entered the room. The inflated white suit and cumbersome cylindrical helmet made it difficult for him to get through the doorframe. When he managed this small feat, he waddled across the meeting room towards them. Gwen could hear his breath hissing through a speaker to one side of the helmet. It took her a moment to see through the visor that it was Ianto.

'It's the Michelin Man!' laughed Owen.

Jack seemed unsurprised by the new arrival. 'The cut of that suit does nothing for you. It doesn't even look comfortable.'

'It's comfortably protecting my testicles,' responded Ianto's voice from the speaker.

Jack considered this unexpected news. 'I could talk to you about your testicles all day, Ianto,' he said. 'But I imagine you have something even more important to tell us.'

The helmet speaker coughed apologetically. Ianto brandished a Geiger counter at them. It was already clicking alarmingly. Gwen wondered fleetingly about where she could go to escape the radiation. But what was the source?

'I took the liberty of scanning the corpses in the mortuary,' Ianto began. 'And I regret to say that one of them is highly radioactive.'

'OK,' said Jack calmly. 'Not too much of a coincidence after all, Tosh.'

Ianto was quickly scanning them each in turn. The ratcheting sound of the Geiger counter didn't increase when it ran over Jack or Toshiko. It stayed the same when Ianto motioned it against Gwen, too, and she released a rush of air from her lungs that she hadn't consciously been holding. She stepped out of the way to let Ianto waddle further into the room alongside the table.

The Geiger counter crackled and spat violently when Ianto placed it against Owen. From the look on his face, Owen wasn't entirely surprised. 'Up to me elbows in the corpse,' he shrugged. 'For two hours. What did you expect?'

'The rest of you are within safe limits,' Ianto confirmed.

Gwen was faintly ashamed to discover that she'd unconsciously positioned herself at the end of the table, as far away from Owen as possible. Toshiko bumped up close to her, she noticed. Owen glared at them accusingly from the other side of the room. But where had Jack gone?

Ianto was still explaining. 'I'm afraid that Owen's close proximity to the irradiated cadaver means that he will need decontaminating.'

Jack reappeared through the door. He carried a wooden box, teak with brass hinges and an elaborate clasp. He placed it on the table, unfastened the clasp, and from the velvet-lined interior of the box withdrew what looked like a squat loofah.

Owen eyed this novel new item. 'If you think I'm going to scrub it all off with that…'

Jack held out the loofah, and waggled it at Owen until he took it from him. 'This will soak up six types of radiation.'

'Six?' Owen looked impressed. 'I can only remember three types.'

'Well, I got a deal on that thing,' Jack explained.

Owen was considering the radiation sponge more closely. He was starting to look less enthusiastic. 'This is it? Shall I just stare at it until the vomiting and intestinal bleeding starts, or should I wait until all my hair's dropped out?'

Jack gave Owen one of his disconcerting grins. 'That thing is so effective, I have to store it in this lead-lined box most of the time. Keep it with you, probably for the rest of the day.' He took the Geiger counter off Ianto, and handed it to Owen. 'You should stay in the Hub until the rem count for your absorbed dose gets down to here…' Jack indicated a reading on the counter. It looked as though Owen was going to complain bitterly about this, but Jack quashed his unspoken protest with a look. 'Tosh, you can keep him company while you complete the search for that thing in Wildman's spine. Gwen, you're coming with me to search Wildman's apartment for the source of this radiation. I think we can guess what that is, but if it's as radioactive as Wildman, we should make it safe. Ah, thank you, Ianto…'

Ianto had brought two more Geiger counters, each the size of pocket calculators. Jack put one in his jacket, and handed the other to Gwen.

Gwen held it at arm's length across the table, towards Owen. The dial flicked up into the danger zone. 'You should have said we were going to Wildman's, Jack. I could have met you there in the first place, saved myself a journey in here.'

'What?' asked Jack, leaving the Boardroom and strolling out into the Hub main area. 'And missed seeing Owen glow in the dark? Not to mention the pleasure of my company?' He stopped beside the stainless-steel fountain that stood so incongruously in the middle of the area. Jack pressed a button and Gwen could see, far above them, a piston pushing aside a paving stone in the ceiling. It was immediately obvious that the weather had worsened since she'd arrived. A sprinkling of rain started to spatter down on them, and water began to flow over the sides of the hole.

Jack leapt out of the way of the downpour, and immediately closed the gap again. 'OK, that's not gonna work for me. Let's go out through reception.'

TWELVE

You're not the kind of woman who stands out in a crowd. Not the kind who wants to. Your hair has never been too bright, your shoes have always been sensible, your lipstick was never too vivid.

Even as you ponder this, you can hear your father's voice commending you on your safe, uncontroversial choices. Science subjects for A level: 'Quite right, Sandra, none of that arty nonsense for you, you'll want a career.' A university close to your parents: 'So much more financially convenient to live at home, Sandra.' Regular attendance at church, sitting between your parents, trying to look inconspicuous although you're excruciatingly aware of your father's fluting voice rising above the standard murmur of the congregation during the Lord's Prayer: *'Ein Tad, yr hwn wyt yn y nefoedd, sancteiddier dy Enw…'*

Dad's mantra was that you should get stuck in, and not stick out. And yet his own insistence on being the most conventional, the most ordinary, the most outspokenly moderate man in Lisvane meant that he himself stuck out in the community more than anyone. 'Don't embarrass us,' he'd tell his family at the restaurant or the cinema. He'd rather die than be embarrassed in public.

Two weeks after he died, you abandoned the second year of your Physics course and signed up for the Royal South Regiment. It was only when, one night in bed with Tony Bee, you were discussing your father's idiosyncrasies that Tony had reminded you of the irony in your regimental motto. *'Gwell Angau na Chywilydd,'* he whispered as he moved his hands slowly over the moist curves of your body. 'Better Death than Dishonour.'

Your affair with Tony has been the most uncharacteristic thing you've ever done. You're still content to just to be another face in the crowd. Guy Wildman wasn't like that, of course, he always aspired to be more. But, by trying harder, he just seemed to become more insignificant, easier for people to ignore, more invisible. With you, it's the opposite. You're content if you appear to be saying to the world: 'I'm just average; there's nothing special about me.' Maybe that's why you persuaded Tony to bring Wildman on the sub-aqua trips, maybe it provided cover for your relationship with Tony.

You know from living with your father all those years that the best way to avoid getting noticed is to take time to get the little details correct. The Army catches people who do things wrong, not those who do things right. Same thing in life. You never park in the disabled bays at Sainsbury's in Thornhill, and you always take your trolley back to the shop to collect your pound coin.

Since your return, you've been home and chosen sensible clothing for a wet, dark night. That also gave you the opportunity to shower, to remove all the traces of blood and bone that you inadvertently smeared down your face and clothes when you killed and devoured that vagrant. You did that discreetly, of course, in a back alley. And with compassion, too – you snapped his neck first, so that he would feel no pain.

And now the deep hunger in you has been assuaged, here you are in Splott, confident that your walk up to Wildman's apartment block will draw no attention from anyone. You wear a green A-line dress, mid-length, no stockings, and a pale green cardigan in thin cotton. You chose flat-heeled, patent leather shoes, round toe, sturdy enough to keep out this rain. You're wearing a fitted boned coat, your favourite, in a soft navy-coloured material that keeps you half-hidden in the dark; you could see the weather was deteriorating before you set out, and didn't want to risk drawing attention by struggling with an umbrella in the wind and rain.

Not that there are many people around to see you, as the rain sets in. The few that you see in these side streets are scurrying for cover, watching out for puddles not people. You move up the steps to Wildman's apartment unseen, and even the sound of your footsteps is masked by the persistent hiss of rain and the hoot of a train further to the east in the direction of Tremorfa.

Once inside, it's different. The hallway is large and the clanking radiator is set too high, so that the windows are steaming up. The octagonal green and yellow tiles on the floor are even louder than the radiator.

You don't need a photographic memory to remember things. All it takes is practice. Your dad used to remind you: 'You've got two ears and one mouth, Sandra. Use them in that ratio.' And that's been true since you joined the Army, whether it's in weapons briefings at Caregan, open water training for sub-aqua, or just the lads' drunken conversations down the Feathers about fast cars, slow flankers, and easy women. Wildman has told you in the past all about the area where he lives, the way he's equipped his flat, the peculiarities of his neighbours. Of course, there's nothing you don't know about Wildman now.

Wildman's apartment is two floors up. The stairs beneath the worn carpet creak under your weight, but there's no sign of anyone else, and the only indication of any other life is the sound behind one of the doors of *Sunday Worship* on Radio 4 played too loud. Wildman's immediate neighbours on the same landing are John and Marcus who work at Club X, and Betty Jenkins who resolutely does not. You know all about Wildman's recent meetings, conversations and disagreements with them. You're ready for anything, if you meet them. It's only since Wildman died that you've realised how lonely he really was, and understood his protective instinct for Betty Jenkins, his frustration with John's casual indifference to commitment, and his never-articulated fantasies about Marcus.

You can be calm, logical, reasonable, without being unemotional. That was true of your relationship with Tony, as he used to tell you. Now that he is dead, you've moved on – literally. And what should be your grief is no longer helpful, no longer appropriate. It's still there, in the background. A curious feeling, buried deep, sublimated. Unnecessary. Do you really understand it any more? These people have a bewildering array of loose social constructs, half-formed affections, unspoken desires and occasional passions. It's only since he died that you realise how much Tony Bee loved you. You can examine those feelings dispassionately too – the ache in him when he was away from you, when he surfaced again, when he returned to the Caregan Barracks. Until the newer, primal ache in him had overwhelmed that.

Set that aside, now. You're here for a reason. Being distracted by those memories is a very human thing to do. And in your current circumstances, you find that amusing.

The key clicks and turns in the lock of Wildman's apartment, and your search begins.

THIRTEEN

Jack let Gwen drive. She enjoyed the chance to take the Torchwood SUV out. It was very different to her own Saab. The first time you drove it, you felt like you were steering from the top deck of a bus. You got a sense that the suspension was soft enough to let you mount the pavement and run down a flight of steps without spilling a drop from whatever drink you'd jammed into the passenger-side cup holders. You could probably drive over a crowd of pedestrians and not feel a bump. That was usually worth remembering when she was racing through the city centre, trying to beat the press to some scene or other.

Rain rattled on the SUV's roof. No matter how fast the windscreen cleared with a contemptuous flick of the wipers, more water immediately smeared their view of the road ahead. It was the middle of Sunday morning, and yet the downpour and the clouds made it seem like dawn was only just breaking. No danger of unwittingly thumping a crowd of pedestrians today, because the streets were almost empty. They would all still be in bed, well out of this lot if they had any sense. That's where Rhys would be.

Jack had programmed Wildman's address into the SUV's direction-finder. Toshiko had designed it as an upgrade to the usual passive satellite positioning. This could use local information about roadworks, police incident reports and judgements about traffic flow from analysis of CCTV images. It offered turn-by-turn directions in an infuriatingly calm schoolmistress voice. Gwen didn't need her help, and it amused her to take alternatives to the spoken directions, if only to hear it say 'Recalculating route' in a reproving tone, and Jack's accompanying chuckle.

Frequent mind-numbing patrols of the area when she was a police constable had made Gwen an expert in the urban geography here. She turned the vehicle into the next road along from Wildman's apartment block. The area was a set of parallel roads between the two railway lines, so it was possible to cut across through a walkway, and thus not draw attention to themselves by parking a monster vehicle with blacked out windows slap bang outside their target's residence.

The SUV easily negotiated the traffic-calming measures that straddled the width of the carriageway. 'They put these in a couple of years back, after the Wales Rally came through Cardiff.'

'Was it a rally or an obstacle course?' asked Jack.

'No,' she laughed. 'Bunch of local kids thought it was all right to run their own version of the rally through these streets. There was this rash of teenage TWoCs.'

'That's not what I'd call them.'

'Taking Without Consent,' she tutted. 'Worked out to be cheaper to discourage it. So they put these sleeping policemen here rather than put real policemen on the beat.'

Jack was unbuckling his seat belt as the car came to a halt. 'Sleeping policemen?' He followed her pointing finger that indicated the humps in the roadway. 'Oh, right. Y'know, I kinda like the idea that they actually buried some lazy cop in the tarmac.'

'Buried in paperwork, more like.' Gwen reached into the storage compartment, and took out two portable Geiger counters. She handed one to Jack. Then she buttoned her jacket, pulled her collar up tight, and stepped down from the car.

They ran through the hissing rain, managing to avoid the worst of the puddles. Scrawny hedges drooped over the pavement. The overcast sky was dark enough that the automated streetlamps had not been extinguished. A Tesco mini-supermarket smeared a patch of orange light across the cracked paving stones.

Wildman's apartment was in a three-storey building. Gwen huddled next to Jack under the concrete awning that was failing to provide much shelter from the rain. The unblinking eye of a video camera watched them from above. The main doors were stout, green-painted metal, Chubb-locked, and with artless graffiti scrawled in marker pen. Residents' names were written, more tidily than the graffiti, on plastic-covered scraps of paper next to illuminated push buttons. One or two had faded to illegibility, but one of them had neatly stencilled capitals in green ink that showed 'WILDMAN, G' on the second floor. A video lens peered at them from behind a glass plate.

'He's obviously not home.' Jack stepped back into the rain. He seemed to be squaring himself to barge the door.

'No!' snapped Gwen. 'You'll wake up the whole neighbourhood.'

'And your point would be…?'

'Where are his keys? They must have been on the body.'

'Oh yeah,' Jack told her. 'I'm really gonna slip a handful of irradiated metal into the pocket of my pants.'

'Well, you can't go barging in, not round here. You don't want any fuss, or to draw a crowd. Especially if he's left a tidy pile of nuclear materials in his kitchenette.'

He gave her a tight smile, and reached into the pocket of his jacket. 'OK, you're my local expert. We'll use ID.'

She shook her head. 'Not even if we were in uniform. They're suspicious. There's curtains twitching across the road already. No! Don't turn round! Think of it. You wouldn't want wet bobbies traipsing their flat feet through your hallway. We have to make them *want* us to come in. So…'

Gwen rummaged in her pockets, but couldn't remember where she'd left her purse. She held out one wet hand towards him. 'Lend me a fiver, will you? I've got no cash.'

He handed over a crumpled ten pound note. 'What are you, a member of the Royal Family?'

'Back in two minutes,' she promised him. She stared directly into his eyes. 'Promise you won't make a scene?'

She ran back down the street, and could hear him shout after her: 'I expect change!'

The weather was killing business at the Tesco mini-supermarket. The shopkeeper's badge told Gwen that she was Rasika. And Rasika looked grateful for her first and possibly only visitor of the morning, if surprised at what her customer bought.

Gwen showed Jack the four bags of groceries, holding them up like trophies. 'OK, press the button for the flat below Wildman's.'

He considered her shopping. 'You got hungry?'

'Six loaves of cheap bread and four jumbo boxes of cornflakes,' she scowled. 'Cheap and bulky. Looks like a lot, not too heavy, and cost nearly nothing.'

'Don't think I've forgotten about the change.'

'Press the button, Jack.'

A querulous woman's voice answered the call. 'Yes?'

'Tesco Direct,' Gwen shouted at the speaker, and held up the shopping bags in front of herself so that the video camera could see them. 'Bell's bust for number nine. I could leave this lot on the step, but I'd rather bring it up out of this rain.'

The speaker made the sound of someone clattering a handset back into its cradle. Almost immediately, the door buzzer sounded.

Jack leaned against the green metal. The doors opened into a dingy hallway of grimy linoleum. There were two doors to the left, with two more opposite. A flight of steep steps rose into the darkness further down on the right. The hall was flanked by two scratched side tables, one covered in free newspapers and uncollected mail. Jack scanned the letters but found nothing for Wildman. He took a reading from the Geiger counter, but it ticked softly in the safe zone.

Gwen made her way up the concrete stairs. A detector registered her arrival and activated a bare bulb on the half-landing above. Through the big picture window she saw the rain drumming down on a back yard containing dustbins and a half-filled rusty yellow skip.

By the time she and Jack had reached the top of the next flight of stairs, an old woman had appeared around one of the doors on the landing. She had long, grizzled grey hair and a face to match. Gwen held up the bags and nodded in the direction of the next flight of stairs. 'Thanks,' she told the old woman cheerfully.

She looked Jack and Gwen up and down, considering their casual black attire and the water running off them on to the floor. Gwen watched where the drips were falling, and was aware that the gaudy linoleum on this landing outside the old woman's apartment was scrubbed clean.

'I can remember,' replied the old woman in a measured tone, 'when delivery drivers wore a uniform. But it's all gone to hell these days, hasn't it?' And with this, she retreated into her apartment. Several security chains rattled as she secured them behind the closed door.

Gwen abandoned the four bags of cheap groceries at the top of the stairs, propping the bags against the railings. Jack scanned again for radiation, and was satisfied when he found the area uncontaminated.

Wildman's apartment was one of two on this second floor. The door to number seven was painted in a cherry red that made a cheerful contrast to the other apartments that they'd seen so far.

'Yale lock,' Gwen told Jack. 'Might be double-locked. But we know he's not in anyway.' She kept a look-out, watching for movement up and down the stairs, while Jack attempted to slip the lock.

'Oh.'

Something had surprised Jack. Gwen looked over to see that he was pocketing his Geiger counter but drawing his revolver from its holster in his great coat. He mouthed 'Door's already open' to her.

She reached for her own concealed weapon. Unlike Jack's Webley, hers was a standard-issue Torchwood weapon. That meant non-standard anywhere else in the world, because their armoury issue was almost certainly augmented by alien technology. Jack was never particularly keen to explain to her exactly how, and she'd discovered that asking Toshiko about it was like requesting an invitation to a lecture on particle physics.

Jack pushed the apartment door open with his toe, and they both flattened themselves against the wall either side of the outer frame. There was no response from inside. Jack swung around, his legs braced and his Webley held in a double-handed grip.

From inside the apartment came a shrill scream and the sound of glass breaking.

'All right, ma'am,' Jack said, and stepped slowly through the doorway. 'Stay calm. No cause for alarm.'

Gwen followed him into the apartment, noting that Jack did not lower his weapon.

A woman had pressed herself up against the striped wallpaper just inside the main room. Her brown eyes were wide, scared, unblinking. She couldn't take them off Jack's revolver. 'Please don't shoot,' she begged in the voice of a schoolgirl, though she must have been in her mid thirties. 'Please. Don't hurt me.'

At her feet were fragments of a small, glass-topped table and the ornaments that had stood on it. The woman had overturned them in her fright when she first saw Jack. She was wearing sensible shoes, no tights, just tanned bare skin.

'Room's clear.' Jack raised his voice so that Gwen could hear from her position in the narrow hallway behind him. 'Stay back for a moment while I sweep the place.'

From her position in the hallway, Gwen could see Jack kick open doors to places off the main room. Bedroom, bathroom, saloon doors through to a kitchen area. Eventually he called to her that the apartment was secure.

Gwen moved into the room and holstered her weapon. The whole room looked like it had last been decorated in the 1970s. The same brown shag pile carpet appeared to have been fitted throughout, trampled to death over many years.

'It's OK,' Gwen reassured the frightened woman. 'We're police. Special operations.' She showed the woman her ID. 'What's your name, love?'

The woman seemed to slide down the wall as she relaxed a little. 'Betty,' she said, 'Betty Jenkins.' She had a South Wales accent. Swansea, maybe.

Jack was openly scanning the room with the Geiger counter. 'I thought Tosh said Wildman was a sad bachelor with no life?' He was examining items in the room. A *Men's Health* magazine, with a black and white cover of a strapping male model and a headline: 'Six Simple Steps to a Six-Pack Like His'. Next to it, a thumbed copy of *Radio Times* from three weeks earlier. On the scratched coffee table was a single dirty coffee mug with a small plate of crumbs beside it. Cushions on the battered settee were all squashed together at one end, as though someone had piled them there when propped up watching the TV. The gas fire's dusty back-plate suggested it hadn't been lit for months, an impression confirmed by the positioning of a two-bar electric fire propped on a pile of books and attached to the wall socket by a long extension cable. By the door was a sideboard that must have been the height of fashion forty years ago, its formica top covered in old magazines, junk mail, and a battered letter opener.

Like any newly seen room, it offered a useful insight into its occupier. Gwen sometimes tried to look at things in a similar way when she got home to Rhys and their flat. Whenever she did, though, she just found she got an overpowering urge to tidy up and throw things away.

Wildman's apartment walls held photo enlargements in A4 clip-frames. Most showed images of colourful tropical fish, clearly focused underwater near a sandy seabed or against the startling grandeur of a coral reef. One showed a trio of people, ready to dive, on a boat that floated in azure water beneath a cloudless blue sky. They were in wetsuits, masked up, thumbs raised, and their brightly coloured scuba gear made them seem as exotic as the fish. On a stand by the window was a rack of barbell weights. The whole apartment was stale, unaired, cold. It had that smell you got on the first day when you returned home from a fortnight's holiday.

Gwen helped Betty to the nearest armchair, an ugly, oversized thing in green Dralon. The frightened woman sank into it gratefully. She pulled the tails of her navy-coloured coat into her lap, and smoothed it over her knees.

'I'm Gwen, by the way. Now, what are you doing here, Betty? Do you know Mr Wildman?'

Betty took a deep, shuddering breath in. She seemed terrified still.

'It's OK. We're concerned about Mr Wildman and his whereabouts. We want to help him.' After a while, Gwen knew, the half-truths and misrepresentations came more easily. Wildman was stone-cold dead, glowing slightly on a slab back in the Hub's mortuary. But they didn't know all his movements before this suicide. Perhaps the woman could help. 'Do you know where he might be, Betty?'

'He's in Egypt. Said he was going on a dive with some tour firm in… Dahab? In the Red Sea. I joked with him that he'd never get below the surface, because of all the salt, and he laughed because he said I was mixing it up with the Dead Sea…' She trailed off, her voice failing. 'The Dead Sea,' she repeated, and her liquid brown eyes stared into Gwen's. 'Oh God. Tell me he's all right. He's not dead, is he? What's happened to him?'

Gwen shushed her, and held her shoulders to calm her. She was trembling in Gwen's arms now. 'We don't know. It's all right, don't worry.'

Wildman can't have been thinking things through properly, Gwen thought. Because he'd been going to work for the past week – Toshiko had deduced that much from the badge-in records. It was uniquely Wildman's thumbs that proved he'd been in Wales and not Egypt. So why had he told Betty he was going to be in Egypt? In fact, why had he told Betty anything?

Gwen kept her voice soft. 'What's your connection with Mr Wildman, love?'

'Neighbour,' sniffed Betty. She plucked a hankie from her cardigan sleeve, wriggling awkwardly where she sat in the large chair. 'I've been feeding his plants for him while he's been away. The succulents don't need much, of course.' She pointed to a pot across the room that contained a plant with pointed pale green leaves. It was the only plant that Gwen could see, so presumably there were more in the other rooms. 'That's his *Amyris elemifera*. Can't neglect that one.'

Betty was constantly watching Jack, warily considering his moves around the apartment as he continued to scan his Geiger counter. The clicking noise never got much higher than a steady 'tut-tut' noise of disapproval, even when he ran it over the unwisely chosen leopard-skin rug in front of the gas fire. He must have sensed her gaze, because he turned away from the kitchen area and treated her to one of his unexpected, dazzling smiles.

'Cap'n Jack Harkness,' he told her smoothly. 'Do I know you from somewhere?'

Betty broke away from his gaze abruptly.

'Sorry,' Jack said. 'Thought from the way you were looking at me that you think you recognise me from somewhere. I get that a lot.' Gwen wondered if he was hitting on Betty. She was a conspicuously handsome woman, slim and fit with short-cut blonde hair and striking cheekbones. Her smart A-line dress fell to just above her knee, revealing shapely calves and firm, smooth skin. So Gwen was childishly pleased to see the grin falter on Jack's face as he held it just too long without getting any sort of encouraging response from Betty.

'OK,' said Jack firmly. He scuffed his way across the shag pile, and motioned Gwen to stand up. 'There's nothing surprising here,' he murmured to her.

Gwen cast a glance around the room. 'Except for the decor that time forgot.'

He clicked his tongue, in a way that reminded her of the Geiger counter. 'No readings above the sort of background radiation there would be if Wildman had visited the apartment. Nothing to suggest the fuel packs are in here.'

'Wildman probably just came in for a shit, shower and shave,' suggested Gwen.

'Yeah,' Jack agreed. 'Then hid the power packs elsewhere. So someone elsewhere in Cardiff could be getting a *really* big dose of radiation. Get on to Tosh and see if she's got any way of detecting that.' He indicated the bathroom door. 'One more room to check.'

Gwen smiled apologetically at Betty, and hunkered back down next to her to continue their conversation. She got no further because, just as she was about to inquire further about the absent Wildman, she was interrupted by a yell from Jack.

It was a cry of shock and anger.

Gwen bounced back to her feet, and rushed into the bathroom after Jack. He was struggling with a long beige towel that he'd got draped over his arm. But she knew that people didn't wrestle with wet towels.

It was the limb of some monstrous creature in the bath tub. There was no visible head or torso. The thing looked like it was just a collection of long, coarse-skinned arms emerging from the water in the bath. Two of them stretched up across the off-white tiles opposite, and made a soft popping sound as their suckers detached and reattached themselves to the smooth surface of the wall and shower screen. The other two draped over the edge of the tub, a metre long apiece. Gwen steadied herself on the linoleum, which was soaked in water that had splashed over the edge of the bath. The nearest of the monster's limbs had seized Jack's right forearm. It was wrapped firmly around the sleeve of his greatcoat and was dragging him, skidding him, across the floor. He must have struggled to draw his revolver with his left hand, because it was lying in a pool of water beside the bath panel.

Gwen stared, appalled. She went cold with fear as she recognised what it was. 'It's like that thing you trod on when you confronted Wildman!'

'I don't care how pissed its big brother is with me,' Jack yelled back, 'get it off!'

Gwen recovered her composure, and drew her weapon. She stepped sideways to avoid Jack's back, straddled the toilet bowl to place her feet firmly, and held the pistol steadily in a two-handed grip, the way Jack had shown her in the Torchwood shooting range. Took a deep breath. Released it slowly and, while she exhaled, squeezed the trigger gently but firmly.

Four shots in swift succession, deafeningly loud in the tiny bathroom. Four shots into the creature that writhed in the bathwater. Four shots that barely made it twitch.

Just above the edge of the bath now she could see where the limbs joined the creature's body. Underneath it a dark hole was opening up, and a tube began to extrude itself like some ghastly proboscis.

No it wasn't its nose, she realised with a thrill of horror. It was its mouth.

Jack was being dragged helplessly across the room towards the creature's maw, and Gwen couldn't stop it.

FOURTEEN

'Still need some help here, Gwen!' yelled Jack. His boots skittered on the wet surface of the bathroom floor. A grubby bathmat was crumpling up beneath one of his boots. The bizarre starfish creature itself made no noise, save for the slap of its arms against the wall tiles and the plastic side of the bath and into the water surrounding it.

Jack tried to throw himself away from the creature, using the strength of his upper body to propel himself violently sideways. He smashed brutally into a flimsy bathroom cabinet on the wall. The mirror shattered, and the chipboard carcass disintegrated and disgorged its contents on top of Jack as he slumped to the floor. Shampoo bottles, a packet of razors, a plastic basket of individually wrapped soaps. Several boxes of plasters and Paracetamol struck his shoulder, and two bottles of aftershave rolled off his back. A packet of individual haemorrhoidal towelettes scattered around him like a dropped deck of cards.

Gwen seized a bottle of pink aftershave – 'Espèce! pour homme', it told her. The revolting tentacle had now writhed its way twice around Jack's sleeve. Gwen twisted the cap off the aftershave and tipped up the bottle so that the astringent pink liquid glugged out onto the bizarre starfish's limb. The coarse skin bubbled and fizzed, but the tentacle did not withdraw. It didn't even flinch.

'Stop!' Jack yelled.

She pointed. 'It's starting to burn through it!'

'Unless you got another twenty bottles, it ain't gonna make a heap of difference.'

Gwen stared desperately around the room. A hairdryer had fallen from the cupboard, and she picked it up as though it might give her some inspiration.

'What the hell are you gonna do?' bellowed Jack. 'Backcomb it to death?'

'Nowhere to plug it in,' she admitted. It's a bathroom, she thought. No plugs.

Gwen cast the hairdryer aside, and it bounced off the sink and clattered to the floor, where it landed next to two empty tins of dog food that had been incongruously abandoned by the far wall. She scrambled over the toilet and back out through the door to the lounge area.

Betty was still sitting in the armchair, staring towards the bathroom with a curious, strangely calm air about her. Gwen could understand that she might be in shock. 'Get out!' she shrieked at Betty. 'Get out of here now!'

The blonde woman didn't need any more encouragement. She struggled up out of the armchair, pulled her coat around herself and fled through the hallway and out of the apartment. The sound of her flat heels trip-tripping their way down the concrete stairs in a flurry of noise quickly faded.

Gwen shoved the armchair savagely to one side. She ran to the socket by the TV to ensure it was switched on. She seized the two-bar fire, flicked it on, and raced back towards the bathroom. The extension lead snaked and coiled behind her. For a second she thought it was going to tangle around the coffee table, but she freed it with a sharp tug that caused the dirty crockery to clatter onto the carpet.

Jack was now lying lengthways on the soaked bathroom floor, parallel to the bath. His right arm was almost engulfed by the tentacle. Worse still, the second nearest limb was starting to slide out of the bath towards his leg.

Gwen could feel the heat from the two-bar fire on her face now. She clambered up onto the toilet seat, hefted the fire above her head, and lobbed it over Jack and into the centre of the bath.

The fire looped overhead, snaking its electrical lead behind it. It splashed into the water.

Immediately the room was illuminated by a huge flash. Blue-white sparks arced over the surface of the water. The repellent creature didn't make a sound, but its three unattached limbs flailed and thrashed. They slapped repeatedly against the wall tiles, and cracked the shower screen from top to bottom. Water slopped over the edge of the bath and onto the linoleum.

The tentacle that had wound its way around Jack's arm whipped away with a slurping sound as the suckers detached themselves. Jack sat up abruptly. 'Don't touch the water!' Gwen yelled at him, and he held his hands high up above his head in acknowledgement. He was able to shuffle out of the room and into the living area.

After a few seconds, the blue sparks disappeared and the starfish ceased its thrashing motion. The limbs slid lifelessly down the wall, and the entire creature slid under what remained of the water in the bath.

'Power's off,' Jack shouted from the other room.

Gwen slumped in relief. She stepped down from the toilet, and picked her way carefully out of the drenched bathroom.

'What the hell is it?' she asked him.

His expression confirmed that he was as baffled as her. 'Sure looked like the daddy of whatever Wildman puked, didn't it? And what was the deal with that aftershave?'

'You're right,' confessed Gwen, 'it would have taken too long to break its hold with that.'

'No, I mean who wears that crap? It smells disgusting. Wildman is a sad single guy. Well, hel-lo. He'd get luckier if he wiped his face with his haemorrhoidal towelettes. Ow!' Jack started shrugging his greatcoat off. 'Ow! Ow!'

He continued to struggle with the coat. Once he had shucked it onto the floor, he hurried back into the bathroom, still yelling in pain. He pulled off his sleeveless jacket, and slipped his braces off his shoulders so that they hung to either side of him. He wrenched his shirt off so quickly and violently that its buttons pinged off across the room. Jack plunged his right arm into the washbasin, and spun the top of the cold tap around with his left hand. He sluiced down his right arm, rubbing at his flesh with a towel that he'd seized from the nearby rail.

Gwen picked up the blue cotton shirt from where Jack had thrown it. 'Careful,' he warned her. 'The thing was digesting it.' Jack finished patting at his skin with the towel. He snatched a second one from the rail, soaked it in fresh water, and carefully wound it around his forearm. Then he turned to face Gwen.

'God,' she said. 'That really is a horrible smell.'

'Told ya,' said Jack. 'The great smell of Lonely Bachelor for five dollars a pint.'

'Not the aftershave,' she smiled. 'That thing in the bath.'

In the aftermath of her rescue, Gwen had not looked again at the creature.

Now she could see that the thing had shrivelled up in the bath. It looked like a grey, pulpy mass, slowly disintegrating and clouding the water. There were four plastic plant pots floating at one end of the bath, and under the shower were three more empty tins of dog food and a can opener. A small metal watering can was propped at the other end of the bath, as though abandoned.

'I usually like fried fish,' sniffed Jack from behind her. The room still stank of burning flesh. 'Calamari, mmm.'

'I thought that was octopus,' Gwen said. 'Or maybe squid?'

'Get me some vinegar and a fork. We can do a taste test.'

'No thanks,' replied Gwen. She pointed into the bath. In the scum forming on the water's surface she could make out silver slivers of plant spikes. 'No point in Betty feeding his plants. He was feeding them to the starfish. That and a regular diet of Pedigree Chum.'

Jack had slipped his jacket back on now, and was examining the arm of his greatcoat. 'It was secreting digestive juices that can dissolve organic matter. It's eaten through my sleeves, look.' There was a large patch in the forearm of his coat and, when she checked, Gwen found a smaller matching hole in his shirt. 'Pure cotton," sighed Jack. 'I'm never gonna get a replacement shirt that good.' He winced again.

Gwen helped him unpeel the towel from around his arm. There was a raw red patch, an irregular circle about five centimetres across, oozing blood.

Jack gestured to the remnants of the bathroom cabinet scattered around their feet. 'Reckon there's a big enough sticking plaster somewhere?'

'Er…' Gwen hesitated, half-considering his request. 'We've got a first aid box in the car.'

'Nah. Give it half an hour,' said Jack. 'These flesh wounds sting like hell, but they heal up if I leave them uncovered. Made the mistake of putting a shirt back on over a knife wound once, and had to have the material cut out again. That was hard to explain to the nurse in triage.'

The smell of burnt flesh was less noticeable in the living room. The apartment was eerily quiet, with only the patter of rain against the window to break the silence.

'Betty's safely out of the way,' observed Jack.

'Will she go to the police, d'you think?' pondered Gwen. 'Or to the press?'

'Or to the pub for a stiff drink and a chat with the locals,' Jack suggested. 'If you think kicking the street door down would get the curtains twitching, imagine what this will do for the neighbourhood.' He gave a disappointed little groan as he examined the hole that now penetrated his coat sleeve. 'Better get this place sealed until Owen can get across here and examine that… starfish corpse in situ. Let's give the local cops a call, have them post a guy on the front door.'

Gwen made the call to the local police. Like all the Torchwood mobiles, hers had a direct line. It connected them immediately to the major crime investigation team, whether the police wanted it or not. She was impressed the way that Torchwood not only had the technology to break into the police systems, but also that it was smart enough to accommodate the hierarchy and the standard admin procedures of incident teams. There was the right balance to strike between the need to get officers involved at all and the need to avoid getting the police crawling all over something they could not properly handle.

'OK,' she explained to Jack, 'they have officers on the way to stand guard. Just in case Betty gets enough courage to come back to water the plants again.'

They stepped out onto the apartment's landing. Jack pulled the front door shut, and pushed it to ensure it was locked again. 'Watering the plants,' he mused as they started down the stairs. 'How? She was there when we arrived. The watering can was in the bathroom, along with the remains of most of the plants. And she'd obviously not met the calamari when we got there.'

The rain had got even heavier outside. Gwen buttoned her jacket, and Jack pulled his damaged coat over his shoulders like a cloak. They hurried back down the side road, the only people on foot in the whole area.

Jack took the driver's seat this time. Gwen's mobile was ringing as they climbed into the SUV. She slotted it into the speaker attachment by the passenger seat.

Toshiko's calm voice filled the car from sixteen stereo speakers. 'Do you fancy a drive out into the countryside?'

'In this weather, what could be nicer? Why do you suggest that?'

'Because I got an interesting match on that artefact in Wildman's neck, Jack. I did a cubic search that gave a ninety per cent correlation—'

'Cubic?' puzzled Jack. 'What does that mean?'

'Q.B.I.C.' Toshiko's tone of voice revealed how pleased she was to explain. 'Query By Image Content. It's content-based visual information retrieval, really good for fast multi-resolution image search—'

'Very impressive, Tosh,' said Jack indulgently. 'Try again. What does that *mean*?'

'Oh, I see.' Toshiko sounded more abashed now. 'Well, the thing in Wildman's neck matches another one. And that was found in the corpse of a soldier at the Caregan Barracks. Sergeant Anthony Bee. He was shot dead in an attempted armed robbery recently at the barracks itself. I was just going out there to interview the senior officer.'

'OK. Taking Owen, too?'

'He'll have to stay here at the Hub. Still decontaminating.'

'We'll meet you at Caregan, Tosh. Thanks.'

Jack moved to disconnect the phone, but Gwen reached out and put her hand on his arm. 'Hang on a moment, Jack.' It was intended as casual gesture of polite restraint, but when her fingers touched the bare skin of his arm she noticed that his wound was less raw, and surrounded by new, pink skin. The whole thing was now only the size of a ten pence piece.

'Don't worry,' he said softly. 'Stings a little. Stings a *lot*, actually. Always does when the flesh heals.'

'Can't hear you,' said Toshiko over the phone.

'Nothing to worry about, Tosh.' Jack had raised his voice again. 'Bring me a clean shirt, will ya? I got a bit of a scratch, and this one's ripped.'

Gwen smiled at him. 'If you're OK, then I think I'd like to check on Betty Jenkins. Let her know that the police are on their way, and to stay away from Wildman's apartment. She's probably cowering under the duvet in her own place.' She spoke slightly louder so that Toshiko would hear her. 'Tosh? Can you tell me which apartment in this block Betty Jenkins is in?'

'Hang on.' They waited, imagining Toshiko initiating a search on her computer. 'There you go, I'm sending it through to you now.'

The small display screen in front of Jack flickered into life. It showed an aerial view of Splott, which zoomed in to a street-level image. This changed into a schematic of the apartment block, and finally a wireframe image of the building with one of the apartments picked out in red. 'Elizabeth Mary Jenkins, flat number four.'

'See you at the barracks, Tosh,' said Jack. 'Thanks.' He disconnected the phone, and handed it back to Gwen. 'I should drive you round to the apartment block. No point running through the streets in this rain again.'

'And the curtain-twitchers?' asked Gwen.

'They'll have plenty to look at once the police arrive.' He started the engine, and steered off into the rain. The SUV's lights flared on the wet roadway. 'How is it you get to check up on the good-looking blonde with legs all the way up to her ears?'

'You're not her type,' Gwen admonished him as the car drew up by the apartment block. 'I'll see you back down here. See if you can get the direction-finder programmed for Caregan Barracks. I promise not to take too long with Betty.'

It was a short dash across the pavement to the door of the apartment building. Gwen wasn't sure what the first thing she'd say to Betty would be, or how she'd persuade the terrified woman to let her back in to the building. As it turned out, she didn't need to use the buzzer, because another resident was just leaving. He was distracted in a fumbling attempt to put up his golf umbrella before he stepped out into the downpour, so Gwen was able to catch the front door before it locked in the closed position.

On the first landing, Gwen rapped the brass door knocker of number four. There was a long pause, so she rapped again more firmly.

'All right,' said a petulant voice from the other side. 'Keep your hair on.'

The door opened a crack, and a wrinkled face peered out past the security chain. The mouth puckered in censure. 'I don't want any groceries,' said the face. 'I've got someone from the Social who gets mine in for me, you know.'

It was the old woman who had let them in, and then looked so disapprovingly at them as they'd dripped on her clean linoleum.

'Is Ms Jenkins in?' Gwen was aware that she'd inadvertently raised her voice.

'I'm Miss Jenkins,' retorted the woman. 'And I'm not deaf.'

'No, I mean Betty Jenkins.' Gwen offered the old woman her most winning smile, the one she used to try out on suspicious witnesses during door-to-door inquiries. 'Is your daughter in?'

The old woman breathed out sharply in irritation. 'I told you. I'm Betty Jenkins. Miss Betty Jenkins. I don't have a daughter. Who are you?'

It was apparent that this was the real Betty Jenkins. Not a scared mid-thirties blonde, but a somewhat scary spinster in her mid eighties, determined to guard her privacy.

'I'm sorry,' said Gwen. She took a step back from the door to reassure the woman. 'I've made a mistake. I'm sorry to have disturbed you Miss Jenkins.'

'I should think so,' said the old lady, closing the door. 'All gone to hell these days.'

The SUV's engine was still running. Jack was drumming his fingers on the steering wheel when Gwen got back into the passenger seat. 'How's the good-looking blonde?'

'The experience has aged her,' said Gwen. She told him about the real Betty Jenkins in flat four. 'Should have noticed,' she concluded. 'Strange that she wore that big blue coat while she was in Wildman's flat. If she lived in the flat downstairs, why would she need to put a coat on to go up and water his plants?'

'Because she doesn't live downstairs,' agreed Jack. 'Any way we can trace where she went?'

'Not a chance. Streets are empty in this rain. House-to-house would be a long shot, on the off-chance anyone saw which way she went. And that'll only give us a general direction. No CCTV round here, so she's impossible to track.'

'All right.' Jack had reached a firm decision. He revved the engine. 'Let's go with what we know. I've told the direction-finder we want to go to Caregan Barracks.'

'Make a legal U-turn,' the machine told him in its prim schoolmistress tones. 'And then a slight left turn in…' It paused thoughtfully. '… seventeen miles.'

Jack reached into the back and passed an RAC road map to Gwen. 'I don't think Tosh got all the glitches outta this thing yet.' He slammed the SUV into gear, swerved it around in the street, and put his foot down, oblivious to the twitching of curtains all along the street.

FIFTEEN

Glendower Broadsword waited patiently with his feet up on a table at the Pork Barrel Arms and sipped his virtual cocktail. Vodka, tequila and lime. He couldn't taste it, but he liked the idea of it. He'd waited like this for an hour, and he'd wait another three if he had to. Glendower was expecting Egg Magnet to turn up. Owen Harper was looking for Megan Tegg.

An earlier search of the food district had turned up nothing. He wondered initially if he'd spotted her outside the Surer Square again, when one of the occupants had thrown someone through a window, but the figure had gone by the time he checked out the venue. She wasn't in any of the streets nearby, nor by the balcony where they'd last talked.

Owen knew she could reconfigure her avatar, but he'd kept looking for that distinctive white trouser suit and the sparkling silver hair. He knew also that she might have more than one persona in *Second Reality*, so he had worn the Mage's sunglasses to check out everyone's true identity. It was hard to guess how many people he should expect online right now because, although it was late on a Sunday morning for him now in Wales, it could be any time of the day or night for the other participants all round the world. Their IP addresses told him they were mostly from North America, predominantly East Coast, with a handful from elsewhere around the world. And it was somehow disheartening, a let-down to be honest, to discover that the multi-talented 'Harley Hydrurga' was actually only Colin Townsend from Wichita, Kansas, and not the juggling seal he appeared to be.

Owen smoothed his hand over the nearby table-top, and it transformed into a display screen. The results of a conventional web search rippled into view on the surface, information from his real world shown to him in *Second Reality*. It told him that Dr Megan Tegg had worked as a Senior House Officer at Cardiff Royal for the past six months. She lived in Whitchurch, over in the north-west of Cardiff. There were a couple of published papers, no criminal history, and no evidence that she was married or divorced or had kids.

What was he expecting after all this time?

A couple of albino twins peered across at his display screen from across the table. He extinguished it with a flick of his fingers and then threw the remains of his cocktail over the twins. They spluttered with indignation, rose stiffly from their chairs and walked quickly away to a nearby phone booth. They were probably trying to phone their mum to have a good cry, decided Owen – the sunglasses told him they were Jane Lawson and Tricia Lawson, using the same IP address in Timperley, Cheshire.

A cheering row of flame-haired midgets wiggled past Owen in a conga, stopping briefly only to light an Eskimo's cigar with their heads before snaking off into the nearest bar. Everyone around Owen was laughing or dancing or entertaining other enthusiasts. Owen wriggled lower in his chair, frustrated and powerless. This was so stupid. He could drive out to Megan's place in Whitchurch now. Her real place. Knock on her real door and say, 'Hi, remember me? I'm the boyfriend who abandoned you in London six years ago. You wanted to get married, I wanted to get away. So, how's it worked out for you, then, eh?'

His jaw clenched, and the tension rose in his neck and shoulders. He jumped out of his chair and stalked over to where a crowd had gathered to watch Harley Hydrurga. The seal was balancing a stack of chairs on his whiskery leather nose. Owen strode around the back of him, made a little jump into the air and landed as heavily as he could on the seal's tail. Harley gave a yelp, the chairs all tumbled, and the crowd scattered out of the way.

He wanted to laugh at the reaction and attempted a sarcastic wave at the furious Harley. But his Glendower avatar refused to move. It was as though the figure was locked – like the screen had frozen, except that everyone else was able to move around him.

A stern-looking policeman marched across to him. He looked like one of the Keystone Cops with a handlebar moustache and a comedy truncheon. When he reached Owen, a blue light on his helmet started flashing. 'Time out!' said the policeman, and everything started to fade away around Owen.

A couple of seconds later, he found himself standing on an endless square stairway atop a tall brickwork turret. Each leg of the walkway was two metres wide and formed an open square that vanished into a mist far below. It was just like an Escher engraving, except there was some sort of additional, invisible wall that prevented him from leaning over the edge to peer down. A blue sky with fluffy white cirrus clouds stretched in every direction. And on the opposite side of the square stood the distinctively brilliant outline of Egg Magnet.

'Busted, huh?' Egg Magnet called. 'Me too.'

Owen took a few of the steps on his side of the turret, and found he was going uphill. So he turned round and took the steps in the other direction instead. They were uphill, too, so he stopped trying.

'Where is this?'

Egg Magnet laughed. 'Hey! First-time offender, nice one! This is the Sin Bin. A place for reflection on your misdemeanours in *Second Reality*. Got to pay the penance before they'll let you back in.'

'Pah!' said Owen. 'I'll just log out and log back in again somewhere else.'

'Nuh-uh,' Egg told him. 'You'll end up here every time you log in, until they decide otherwise. So, whatcha here for, mate?'

'You first.'

Egg puffed out his chest grandly. 'Started a fight in the Surer Square. Again,' he added with perhaps a new note of regret. 'Now, what's your crime?'

Owen shuffled his feet. 'I trod on a seal.'

This amused Egg hugely. The silver-haired figure giggled and giggled. Energised by this hilarity, Egg hared up the steps around two sides of the tower until he stood next to Owen. 'Nice job! That's a new one on me.'

'I suppose I may have upset a couple of twins, too.'

Egg was delighted by this information. He offered his hand. Owen attempted to shake it and realised he was still holding his empty cocktail glass. After swapping hands, he was able to return Egg's firm grip.

'You're Glendower, aren'tcha mate?' said Egg. 'I remember you from the other day.'

'And you,' said Owen, 'are Dr Megan Tegg.'

Egg Magnet looked shocked. He tried to take a couple of steps away from Owen. This was more difficult than he'd expected, because it was a movement up the stairs, and Owen was still tightly holding his hand. 'Says who?' Egg said feebly.

'Megan Tegg. It's an anagram of Egg Magnet.'

'So what?' insisted Egg Magnet. 'So is…' There was a distinct pause while he worked it out. 'So is "Get Egg Man".' Owen sat down on the stairway, and patted the step next to him. It was wide enough for them both to sit side by side. 'I know you in fleshspace. In the real world, I mean,' he corrected himself hurriedly. 'Er… in the flesh. So to speak.' Egg seemed to be giving up the pretence now. Or rather, Megan was not pretending any more. 'How do you know? I haven't told you anything.'

'You've told me more than you think,' he replied. 'Remember what you said about preferring a nice cup of tea to a crappy cup of tea? And what else… oh yeah, that thing about "safe in taxis"? You might as well have suggested we have a kebab-throwing competition in Woodrow Road. Nearest to the late-night postbox wins?'

'OMG,' said Egg, oddly.

'You what?'

'Oh my God,' said Megan. 'You can't be!'

'I am,' he said. 'I'm Owen Harper. Dr Owen Harper, actually. But you'd remember that…' He showed her the empty cocktail glass. 'You know what this is? Vodka, tequila and lime. A Hawaiian Seduction. We bought these in the Kington Club. That's when I told you that joke about Hawaiians.'

'So you're trying to seduce me?' Megan asked.

'I'm trying to convince you.'

'What's the difference, Owen?'

'So it's Owen now, is it?'

'This could be a trick. I've read about people like you. People online, they're not always who they claim to be.'

He offered her the Mage's sunglasses. 'I can see your real details. You're in Cardiff. You're logged in as Egg Magnet, but your user ID is *m.tegg@ caerdyddnet.net*.'

She took the sunglasses from him cautiously. Peered through them. 'What's an IP address?' she asked. She could obviously see more information about him through the sunglasses. 'And what's Torchwood?'

'IP address is like the phone number of your computer. That's how it knows where you are. And Torchwood…' He paused to consider this. 'There's so much more to tell you about Torchwood.'

Megan handed the sunglasses back to him. 'Hey,' she said, 'that's weird. The picture on my screen just got a whole heap better. How'd you do that, mate?'

'All part of the service.' Owen didn't know how, but wasn't going to tell her. An unexpected bonus by sharing the sunglasses through the Torchwood system, probably.

'The detail in the graphics is fantastic. Look at that! You can see chips in the brickwork. And your outfit, mate... wow! Hey, mine isn't too shabby either!' She stood up and twirled around. Owen's heart fluttered for a moment, because spinning around was the method by which players left the game. But Megan's avatar gave a little bow, and then sat down next to him again. 'It's my day off work,' Megan explained, 'I'm back on duty this evening and then overnight. Thought I'd spend Sunday morning bumming around in here. Shouldn't really be playing the game, I suppose, but it's a bit addictive isn't it? Mind you, I was pissed off when I got banished to the Sin Bin. I was about to log off. But now... well, here we are.'

Owen wondered if she was going to log out of the game after all. He blurted out, 'Can we meet up?'

'We are meeting up.'

'No, I mean in Cardiff. I'm in Cardiff, too. Now. I want to discuss something with you. In person. Make you an offer, sort of.'

Megan laughed, and nudged him with her shoulder. 'I remember that from the night we first slept together.'

'At the college ball,' he smiled.

'It really is you, isn't it, Owen?'

'It's not that kind of offer,' he said.

'Yeah, that's what you said then, too.'

Time to be more assertive, Owen. Take the initiative, if you want her to understand Torchwood. That's what Jack Harkness would do in this situation.

No, screw Jack Harkness. It's what Owen Harper would do.

'I'll prove it, Megan. If you want to. You can ring me. Now, on my mobile.' He gave her the number. Got her to read it back to him, to make sure she'd written it down.

Then he logged out of the game.

He eased his head out of the helmet-mounted display. The games room came back into focus around him. He got up from his terminal and had a big stretch.

The large window to one side looked down onto the lower floors of the Hub. He could see lights on in the Boardroom, where Toshiko had been working earlier. She'd looped the sponge thing on a thread around his neck, and then left him to do his own thing while he ran through the decontamination. She had phoned up to him a couple of times, and he'd abruptly told her to leave him alone. He examined the Geiger counter now, and saw that the reading had improved but was still too high.

Owen sat quietly at a table by the pinball machine, and thought about *Second Reality*. The initial excitement of it, then the disappointment when he found out who the participants really were, and their humdrum reality. They had to go back to that when they logged out of the game, back to their drab personal first realities. He at least could come back to this, to Torchwood. Even if he couldn't be more like his avatar in the game.

Owen pulled his shirt collar away from his neck with a couple of fingers, and studied his pectoral muscles through the gap in the material.

His contemplation was interrupted by the sound of his mobile phone. The display told him: 'Unknown Caller', and a phone number he didn't recognise.

Megan was calling him.

He was back in the game.

SIXTEEN

They drove through the pouring rain. A chain-link fence topped with barbed wire stretched off into distance as far as Gwen could see. Warning signs on the enclosure flashed past at regular intervals: 'Ministry of Defence Property'. After she'd seen a dozen of them, she'd worked out that the rest of the wording on them was the stilted formality of the Official Secrets Act describing the risk of arrest and prosecution for 'unauthorised persons'.

Eventually, Jack pulled the SUV over onto a grass verge. A painted notice on stout poles indicated they'd reached Caregan Barracks, home to *Y Cymry Deheuol*, the Southern Welsh Regiment. Parked under this sign, also angled up on the verge, was Gwen's black Saab.

Toshiko got out of the Saab and walked towards them, clutching a plastic bag under one arm. Gwen wound down her window so that they could talk.

'Only just got here myself,' said Toshiko. She held out the keys to the Saab. 'Want to swap?' Gwen accepted the keys and got out.

Toshiko took the passenger seat, next to Jack. 'Here's your shirt,' she told him, and passed him a tissue-paper parcel from the plastic bag. 'I chose you a blue one. You know, for a change.'

Jack wriggled about in the driver's seat as he started to remove his jacket and braces.

Gwen stood in the rain, feeling it soak into her hair, wondering how much longer he was going to take. She saw that Toshiko had demurely faced away from Jack as he pulled on the fresh shirt.

While he dressed, Jack leaned across the car a little so that Gwen could hear him through the window. 'Let's be cautious with the armed forces, OK?

In the face of alien weirdness, the military instinct is to involve UNIT at the first opportunity. We can do without that kind of hassle. Follow my lead.'

'Any other last-minute pearls of wisdom?' Gwen asked him. 'Only I'm getting drowned out here.'

'That's nothing,' said Toshiko. 'You should see it in Cardiff now. Much heavier than here, and still deteriorating. The worst seems to be confined to the Bay area. It's like a microclimate.'

'Microclimate as in "tiny amount of sun"?' retorted Jack, and put the SUV into gear again. 'We might as well be in Manchester.'

Gwen drove after them through the entrance. They showed their IDs and, after some further consultation, the sentries lifted the red-and-white-striped barrier to allow them in. A jeep with two armed soldiers escorted them past the crisp tramping of a drill practice, and into the visitors' parking area. One soldier was a stocky youngster with Slav features, the other was tall enough to look thin in comparison.

The army buildings were squat, low affairs. Grim and dreary in the afternoon's grey light, with wide and shallow-sloping roofs that glistened in the rain. Few had more than one storey, white stucco walls with aluminium-framed windows punched into them at regular intervals. One of the buildings had a second storey clad in stained dark timber, and it was towards this that the soldiers steered them.

The Torchwood team walked together between their escorts, Toshiko in the middle.

'What can you tell us about the base commander?' asked Jack.

Toshiko was able to read information off her PDA as they walked. 'Daniel Yorke. Lieutenant-Colonel. Queen's Gallantry Medal 1988. Played hockey for Combined Services. Graduate of Sandhurst. Did special duties in Afghanistan. Were you looking for anything in particular, Jack?'

'Just hoping to make polite conversation.'

There was a laminated notice affixed to the wall outside the base commander's office. It detailed, in brief, the expectations of soldiers at the barracks. The list started with 'Selfless Commitment – to put others before you', went through 'Courage', 'Discipline', 'Integrity', and 'Loyalty', and concluded with 'Respect for others – to treat others with decency at all times'.

After five minutes with Lieutenant-Colonel Daniel Yorke, Gwen wanted to drag him from his own office and press his nose up against the notice so that he could read the last one. Press it quite hard, in fact, pushing firmly on the back of his shiny bald head.

They had remained standing in his sparsely decorated office. He had not invited any of them to sit in either of the two chairs on the near side of his large, uncluttered desk. Nor had he risen to greet them or shake hands, remaining ramrod straight in his own chair.

Yorke's territorial hackles had already been raised by the authority that Torchwood assumed. But his mood had soured further when he learned that this Torchwood delegation was run by a Captain from the RAF, someone he would conventionally outrank. It was plainly as much as he could bear to take instructions from the shabby individual before him, who had his shirt tails hanging over the front of his trousers and a coat with a huge tear in the sleeve.

And worst of all, Gwen could tell from the lecture they were getting, was the fact that Jack was an American.

'British Army's held in the highest regard. All round the world. Respect that was hard-won over recent years.' Yorke spoke like he had to pay for every word in a telegram. 'Northern Island. Falklands. Bosnia and Kosovo. The Gulf, obviously. And countless peacekeeping ops throughout the world.'

'Yes, sir,' Jack said as Yorke took a rare pause to draw breath. 'We appreciate that.'

'We?'

'Torchwood,' said Jack calmly.

'Ah. I thought you meant the Americans.'

'My team are not American.'

'You're telling me that you're English, then,' said Yorke.

'Welsh,' Gwen told him, emphasizing her accent. 'And Doctor Sato here is Japanese. What's your point?' Jack nudged her with his elbow. 'Sir,' she added lamely, as though that might rescue the situation.

Yorke had barely met Jack's eye throughout the conversation. He preferred to keep looking back over his own shoulder, through the second-storey window and out over the grounds towards the assault course where distant figures struggled under nets and over walls. It also gave Gwen the impression that he was studying the crown and pip on his shoulder insignia. As the conversation continued, he was considering his position in more ways than one.

'Our professionalism in the British Army doesn't come through chance,'

Yorke continued. 'We attain it by constant, thorough and tough training. *Y Cymry Deheuol* produces the best here.'

Not good enough to pronounce Welsh properly, you English twerp, thought Gwen.

'Look at them out there,' said Yorke, nodding towards the assault course. He turned back to his desk and clasped his hands together on its buffed wooden surface. His lizard eyes flicked across his visitors, and the unspoken comparison was clearly 'and look at you in here'. But instead he said: 'Those youngsters out there started with reveille at 6 a.m. They've performed drill practice, map reading, first aid and rifle handling. A six-mile run and a drill test we call "passing off the square".'

'Busy morning,' said Gwen, and got another nudge from Jack.

'They are the best.' Yorke seemed to be addressing his comments now to the two soldier escorts who still stood at the back of the room behind them. 'And the best are taught by the best. So, no need to have dragged your team all the way out here on this lovely Sunday afternoon, Captain Harkness. We can conclude this investigation ourselves.'

'Was Sergeant Anthony Bee one of the best?' Jack said.

Yorke's fluent lecture stumbled to a halt. 'I really cannot comment at this stage of the investigation,' he said eventually. He'd stopped looking out of the window. Jack certainly had his attention now. He tried to rally again. 'It's "Anthony", by the way. With a hard "t".'

Jack ignored Yorke's attempt to reassert his superiority. He scattered six photographs carelessly onto the Lieutenant-Colonel's tidy desk. 'Recent brutal murders from the centre of Cardiff. Do they look familiar?'

Yorke gave the photos a cursory examination without touching them. 'You can't expect me to believe that these vagrants have any connection to Caregan.'

Jack shoved the photographs across the desk, closer to Yorke. 'Not the people. Their wounds.'

Yorke considered the evidence briefly before pushing it slowly back across his shiny desk. 'That's something you'd need to ask Doctor Death.'

'You're kidding me, right?'

'The MO. He's Doctor Robert De'Ath. It's a joke.' Yorke forced his thin lips into a tight, mirthless smile in an attempt to illustrate this.

'I'm sure Gwen will bear that in mind,' said Jack. He turned and said to her: 'You can start with the Medical Officer while Tosh and I finish up here.'

Yorke stood up, annoyed that Gwen was already moving towards the door. 'You may have jurisdiction here—'

'You know we do,' Jack interrupted him. 'You made three separate phone calls about it in the half hour after we told you we were on our way.'

'How could you…?' Yorke saw Toshiko's smug expression, and his bluster petered out at last. He sat back down in his chair. 'I didn't request any help from Torchwood, Captain,' he grumbled.

Jack sat down in the chair opposite him. 'Lieutenant-Colonel, I don't remember saying we were here to help you.'

Gwen leaned in to murmur in Jack's ear. 'Polite conversation,' she reminded him.

Jack was still telling Yorke what he expected from him as Gwen left the room with one of the soldier escorts and closed the door behind her.

Gwen's escort was the stocky lad, with Slav features. It didn't surprise her when he told her he was Private Wisniewski, but when she persuaded him to reveal his first name ('John-Paul… with a hyphen'), that was less expected. Private Wisniewski marched her briskly around the corners of several white stucco walls. The buildings were mostly indistinguishable, and laid out in a simple grid fashion that made it hard to keep track of the route. They eventually crossed a cracked expanse of grey tarmac, across which the wind blew directly at them. Wisniewski barely flinched as the gust whipped rain into their faces.

Over the noise of the rain Gwen could hear voices shouting a mixture of encouragement and abuse at the soldiers who were struggling through the assault course. They skirted another open expanse, this time a dirt and gravel rectangle traversed by wires on short red metal posts, around which trainees crawled, ran, or climbed, seemingly oblivious to the rainfall that soaked their uniforms, their weaponry and their huge backpacks. From further away came the crack of single gunshots on a distant firing range.

Major Robert De'Ath was a complete contrast to Yorke, and almost too eager to please. He took one look at Gwen as she entered his office and immediately asked her in his soft Scots accent to take a seat while he found her a towel to dry her hair. He dismissed Private Wisniewski, who said that he would wait outside. De'Ath then offered her a cup of coffee, apologising because he'd just run out of milk so it would have to be black, and would that be all right with her?

And yes, he'd heard all the jokes about his surname, thanks. 'My favourite is "De'Ath warmed up". Speaking of which, here's your coffee.'

Major Robert De'Ath was in his early forties, with close-cropped light brown hair that framed a freckled bald head. He was wearing fatigues, the standard green and grey battledress, so she assumed he was on duty.

'I need to know about Sergeant Anthony Bee,' Gwen said.

De'Ath settled into his own chair, and placed his hands on his knees. Gwen noticed that his desk was placed facing the window, so that the Major could talk to his visitors without having the furniture as a physical barrier. 'Terrible business.'

'Tell me more.'

De'Ath looked up at the ceiling, as though he was visualising something. His voice sounded further away somehow. 'Anthony Bee was a PT instructor here at Caregan. Well respected. Admired by the men. Some of the officers suspected that he was too familiar with the other soldiers.'

'In what way?'

De'Ath paused. 'Having a drink with them at the Feathers,' he said cagily, 'that sort of thing. Not the sort of fraternisation Lieutenant-Colonel Yorke really approves of.'

'I can imagine. Did you disapprove?'

De'Ath smiled at her. 'No. Though you'd expect a Medical Officer to say that, wouldn't you?'

'Why?'

'Soldiers don't just come to me for straightforward medical problems. They can turn to the MO for advice and counselling too. So I think the best MOs are those who wholeheartedly join in with the life of the community they serve. Sports. Social. You do a better job if you understand the daily routines of the soldiers in your care. Bee was like that, actually.'

Gwen finished her coffee, and cradled the mug in her hands. 'Did Bee come to you for advice and counselling?'

De'Ath gave her a mock frown. 'I'm sure you know I couldn't tell you if he had. But I can tell you that what led to his death was utterly out of character for him.'

He could see her expression encouraging him to continue.

'Sergeant Bee was shot dead while trying to steal an amphibious vehicle loaded with tools. I was also told earlier today that he had previously been suspected of stealing a jeep and some scuba equipment while supposedly on leave. So the authorities here kept an eye out for when he returned from his leave. They identified him as soon as he signed back into camp, and then tried to arrest him. He was shot dead while resisting arrest and threatening the sentries with a handgun.'

'No prior indication of this?'

'None,' said Major De'Ath. 'With anyone else, you'd suspect some extraordinary change in his personal circumstances or medical history. A trend of behaviour, unexpected absences. *Something*. But this was like some psychotic episode. And yet...' His voice trailed off in puzzlement.

Gwen pushed him to go further. 'And yet what?'

'I spoke to some of the soldiers who witnessed the shooting. The man who killed him was one of the same youngsters whom he'd been teaching earlier in their training. Now, that young man needed some advice and counselling, let me tell you. Put yourself in his boots – he killed a man who he admired and respected.' De'Ath looked straight at Gwen, and his cheerful eyes were cold and hard now. 'He shot Bee because the sergeant had just shot dead one of his own. Kandahal was just nineteen. Bee killed him rather than surrender. How do you think the young soldier reacted?'

Gwen considered what Lieutenant-Colonel Yorke had said earlier. 'Professionally?'

'Well, yes,' snapped De'Ath. 'But what about after that? You must know what I mean, surely? The consequences for him. Emotionally.'

'I'm sorry.'

'You know, Sergeant Bee said a bizarre thing just before they shot him.'

'Bizarre is my strong suit,' said Gwen. 'What was it?'

The Major shook his head, puzzled. 'He said "See you again soon". Foxton heard it cldearly. No one understands what he meant. But then, no one understands why he did what he did. The people he killed. And how...'

He put his face in his hands. It was as though he was trying to hide from something. Gwen just sat quietly, waiting for him to compose himself.

Eventually, he lifted his head again. Gwen didn't say anything. It was something a detective inspector had once told her – make the other person uncomfortable with the silence. They might say anything to fill the gap, and that anything might turn out to be something useful. So she resisted the urge to speak even a few words of reassurance or distraction.

'Lieutenant-Colonel Yorke briefed me ahead of your arrival,' admitted Major De'Ath. 'He told me you Torchwood people always take the extreme view. We have a saying in basic training: "If you hear hoof-beats, you look for horses, and not zebras".'

'You don't know the half of it,' Gwen said. 'In my job, if I hear hoof-beats, I expect to see unicorns.'

'I'm starting to understand that now.' De'Ath took in a deep breath, and exhaled it slowly. 'What Bee said though. That wasn't the only strange thing. We've had two other deaths here recently. Two more young soldiers. They had… savage injuries to the backs of their necks. At first we thought they were animal wounds…'

'… but the tooth-marks were clearly human,' Gwen continued.

De'Ath's reaction told her she was right.

'And from your post-mortem on Sergeant Bee, you concluded it was him that had bitten them. Murdered them.'

The Major was plainly astonished. 'We've told no one. We hardly know how to describe what happened, never mind anything else. How can you possibly know about it?'

Gwen smiled apologetically. 'Bizarre is my strong suit.'

SEVENTEEN

It was surprising how long Jack had managed to keep his temper, reflected Toshiko. The Lieutenant-Colonel had been unable to get him even to raise his voice, despite his continued evasions and obstructions. Jack had just nodded a curt agreement when told that he and Toshiko would be accompanied around the barracks at all times by an armed guard. Faced with a walk across the parade ground in the pelting rain, Jack had merely rolled his eyes, pulled up his collar, and stalked off at a brisk pace with his hands thrust deep into his pockets. What had made him blow his top was the sight of the barracks garage.

It was spotless.

'You'd better explain what the hell happened here,' Jack raged at Private Foxton, their unfortunate escort.

The tall blond soldier didn't flinch. 'Corporal Schilling was found over there,' Foxton began politely, 'by the Pinzgauer...'

'Not my point,' yelled Jack. He'd moved so close to the soldier that Toshiko began to wonder whether Jack might strike him. Which would have been a mistake. Jack was taller and broader than Foxton, but the young soldier held his rifle with a calm ease that told her he was not going to be intimidated, especially by an eccentric senior officer from another service. Toshiko didn't want to be carrying Jack's body out from the camp with a bullet through his head.

'What is your point, Jack?' Toshiko asked quietly. She placed her hand softly on Jack's arm, not sure whether she was restraining him or reassuring him.

Jack wheeled around, with an exasperated gesture that encompassed the whole room. 'Look at this place.'

Toshiko looked. In the corner opposite them, two mechanics worked on the carcass of a flatbed six-wheeler. Apart from the equipment around them, tools were neatly stacked in racks against the wall and locked behind cages. An orderly row of vehicle wheels were arranged by size and aligned on parallel rails. She could see two Land-Rovers and half a dozen trucks, all in the grim khaki of army vehicles. The screed concrete floor was swept clean. 'They keep the place tidy,' she joked.

'Exactly!' To her surprise, Jack was pleased with her observation. 'After all that polite chit-chat with the base commander, we learn that one of his maintenance engineers was slaughtered by one of his training instructors. In this room. Now we're here, and the scene's not even secured. The first responders are long gone or buried on other duties. Look at it. And smell it.'

Jack filled his lungs with a deep breath in. Toshiko did the same, more tentatively at first. Amid the smell of engine oil and stale sweat was a chemical scent in the background. It was the chlorine tang of bleach.

'Yorke sent his clean-up crew in here early,' continued Jack. 'No hope of getting any trace evidence here now. No impressions, no hair or fibres. Do you see evidence of a struggle? Blood spray? Anything?'

Toshiko shook her head. 'And a luminol trace for blood is no use, because the bleach will overwhelm it.'

'Shoulda known,' muttered Jack. 'Shoulda known as soon as he told us the body had been transferred offsite. Better hope that Gwen's getting more cooperation from the MO.'

Toshiko walked over to look at the oblong shape of the six-wheel truck, the Pinzgauer, that Foxton had indicated earlier. The bleach smell was stronger here. The unnaturally clean grey white of the concrete beneath the Pinzgauer showed little evidence of recent oil spills, mud or tyre tracks. Evidence of absence, she thought. The scene had been scrubbed clean.

'Private Foxton,' she said. 'What else do you know about Corporal Schilling's murder?'

Foxton looked less comfortable now. 'Nothing but what I was told, ma'am. Sergeant Bee smashed Schilling's skull in because Schilling caught him stealing a truck full of equipment.'

'How do you know what happened here?'

'It was what Lieutenant-Colonel Yorke told us. Told those of us who caught up with Spadey.'

'Spadey?' asked Toshiko gently, trying to contrast her mood with Jack, who was still pacing up and down the garage as though working off his anger.

'Sergeant Bee, ma'am. Big hands. Like shovels.'

'Was the dead man a friend of yours?'

'I didn't know Corporal Schilling.'

'I meant Sergeant Bee,' Toshiko said. 'Was Spadey your friend?'

There was a flicker of something across Foxton's face. Then he stiffened, and the moment had passed. 'I saw Sergeant Bee shoot dead one of my friends.' Foxton shuffled his feet. 'I shot Sergeant Bee, ma'am. In the line of duty.'

It seemed that Jack had concluded that stamping around the garage was getting him nowhere. Toshiko felt a little surge of irritation when he barged into her polite questioning of Private Foxton. 'Nothing to see here any more,' he snapped. 'You'd better take us to Sergeant Bee's quarters.'

They made another series of short dashes through the open, skirting close to walls wherever they could in an attempt to obtain some shelter from the continuous rain. As they sprinted between two squat buildings, Toshiko looked up and saw towering thunderheads looming in the distance over Cardiff, dark and menacing.

Private Foxton ushered them into one of the sleeping blocks, and firmly pulled the outer door closed. Apart from the three of them, the building was empty and silent, which made the contrast with the hiss of rain outside all the more marked. The occasional gust rattled rain against the windows like handfuls of thrown gravel.

'This is the single living accommodation,' Foxton explained. 'Trainees plus some of the staff.'

Toshiko had imagined the place would be set out as two rows of beds in a barn-like space, with a sergeant-major pacing between them while squaddies in vests stood to ramrod attention beside their neatly folded grey blankets. There would be grim communal showers, large dank rooms with wide expanses of mouldy tiles and a dozen corroded shower heads poking out of the walls.

Instead, there was a series of smaller rooms, containing no more than four beds each, sometimes only two. Each was tidy and organised, though with none of the formality of an old-fashioned barracks. The narrow single beds had plain white headboards and neutral covers. Toshiko was pleased to find at least one stereotype was true, because the beds were all perfect: their crisp white sheets covered by grey blankets with hospital corners and pulled so tight you could practically bounce a coin off them. Next to each bed were either fitted cupboards or cheap but sturdy chests of drawers. There were bedside lamps and small family photos, sometimes of parents sitting on sofas or in gardens, while others showed young women grinning at the camera, their complexions bleached and flattened by flash photography. Shower rooms contained single cubicles in a row, and a separate room housed washing machines and dryers.

'I didn't think the facilities would be like this,' she told their escort. 'It's less… well, less regimented than I'd expected.'

Talking with Toshiko rather than Jack seemed to have relaxed Foxton again. 'It's not the institutional stuff that civilians expect,' he agreed. 'It's a modern training site. For example, newcomers get their first taste of shooting a weapon on a computer-simulated firing range.'

'Owen would love that,' Toshiko smiled at Jack, who was still looking sullenly at their surroundings.

'I'd still whip his ass,' Jack growled back.

'We've got the obvious stuff like a sports hall,' continued Foxton. 'But there's also a cinema and a bowling alley.'

'A regular holiday camp,' interrupted Jack. 'Where's Sergeant Bee's room?'

Private Foxton showed them to the end of another corridor. 'As an instructor, Sergeant Bee had a single room. I think the door may be locked.'

Jack stepped back, raised his right leg, and kicked out savagely just above the handle. The door crashed open, taking a splintered chunk of the lintel with it.

Toshiko followed him into the room. 'You could have tried the handle first.'

'I'm not a try-the-handle kinda guy.'

Inside was a compact, square space. Set into the far wall was a window behind two short, half-closed curtains. Toshiko made her way across to open them fully. Greyish-white light filtered into the room through a screen of rainwater. Drawing the thin blue material back revealed a thermostatically controlled radiator beneath the sill and, in the corner, a freestanding basin on a metal frame. The bed was stripped bare, revealing a mottled mattress on which fresh blankets and sheets had been piled. Presumably, these had been delivered to Bee's room for his return from leave, but he was never going to put them on his bed now.

A plain, bare desk and armless wooden chair stood against one wall. Beside the desk were piled three stout cardboard boxes, one much larger than the others. One of the smaller boxes was so overfilled that it would not close, and papers jutted out of the top.

'Looks like the door wasn't locked,' said Foxton. It was an observation, not a reproof. The soldier seemed unfazed by Jack's violent method of entry. He held his rifle in one hand and was examining the doorframe with the other, cautious not to get splinters.

Toshiko indicated the boxes by the desk. 'He was all packed and ready to go?'

'No,' explained Foxton. 'We packed those up to make space for when the new instructor moves in. Tomorrow, I think.'

'You don't waste much time around here, do ya?' Jack flipped open the top of another box. 'Door unlocked, no guard on the premises. New guy practically installed. It's like Bee was never here.'

Foxton looked at Toshiko to see what her reaction was. He seemed to be judging Jack's reaction from her own.

'You're not even curious, are ya?' Jack hefted the smallest box onto the desk, sat next to it, and then turned to consider the soldier. 'You seen any battlefield action, soldier?'

'Not yet, sir.'

'So,' continued Jack. 'Soldiers at Caregan Barracks. Expendable, huh? Replaceable.'

'Not my place to say, sir.'

Toshiko studied Jack thoughtfully. 'They're trainees. In and out all the time.'

The largest box contained a mesh duffel bag, black with red details and the word 'Edge' printed on one side. It was almost empty. Toshiko pulled out three items. She found a yellow and white snorkel with reflective tape at the surface end. Beside that, still in its packaging, was an SL951 close-up lens for a SeaLife Reefmaster camera. The third thing was a squarish, zippered bag that contained a circular black and silver device that Toshiko did not recognise.

'It's a diving regulator,' Jack told her.

'Spadey was a sub-aqua enthusiast,' explained Foxton.

'Where's the rest of the equipment?' asked Toshiko. 'No wetsuit, for example?' She explored the wardrobes, but the rails were bare, empty except for a handful of jangling metal hangers. 'Do you mean snorkelling?'

'No, I mean scuba,' said Foxton. His voice was pensive as he started to recall something 'Spadey was always telling us about his latest trip. Loved to take pictures of the fish.'

'That would explain the lens,' said Jack. He continued to rummage in the other boxes, and located a clutch of film negatives. 'A bit old-school, don'tcha think? Thirty-five millimetre, not digital. So I wonder what happened to the rest of the photos? Ah, here we go.'

Jack had found a shoebox, labelled 'SGWBA' in neat capitals, and filled with glossy prints. Jack started to spread them out on the desk. They had not been sorted, so out-of-focus shots were mixed with other, clearer pictures of exotically coloured marine life. Some included divers, anonymous in their dive masks, exploring underwater.

Toshiko realised the difference between these pictures and the photos she had seen earlier in the soldier's quarters. 'No pictures of his family.'

'Didn't have any immediate family,' Foxton said. 'No known next of kin. But he went on dives with a regular group of friends.'

'I've seen this somewhere before,' Jack said. He passed one of the photographs to Toshiko. It showed three people suited up for a dive, all masked. The vivid colours in their wetsuits echoed the images of divers in the other photos.

With the pile of glossies scattered over the desk, Jack eventually found a handful of pictures that included some shots of the divers without their masks on.

'Well, hey!' Jack slid one of the photographs across the desk so that it was in front of Toshiko. 'Recognise this guy?'

He had the defined torso that a well-fitted wetsuit gives to any man who isn't very overweight. The figure's wet hair was plastered to his head, darker than its usual grey. It took her a moment, and then Toshiko remembered.

The last time she'd seen him, he hadn't looked much like this. There hadn't been that much of his face to recognise after it had hit the pavement. She only knew what he should look like from seeing the identity pass photo she'd obtained from the Blaidd Drwg security database. 'It's Guy Wildman.'

They rummaged around in the pile for more photos.

'Have you been making a mess?' said a familiar voice from the door.

Toshiko looked up to see Gwen coming in, accompanied by her escort, the dark-eyed soldier from earlier who looked like he might be Russian. Private Foxton had jumped into a more alert mode as he heard Gwen arriving. He now relaxed a little and nodded a greeting to the other soldier.

Gwen kicked at some of the splinters of wood from the broken door. 'I didn't need John-Paul's help to find you. I could have just followed the trail of debris.'

'John-Paul?' asked Toshiko.

'Private Wisniewski,' said Gwen. She glanced at him, and his polite smile told her that she'd got the pronunciation correct.

Toshiko passed some of the glossy photos to Gwen. 'We made a connection with Guy Wildman.'

'There were underwater photos at his apartment. Not to mention some wildlife in his bathroom.' Gwen was rummaging in her pocket, and brought out a small Geiger counter. She switched it on, and it clicked reassuringly at the lowest end of the scale. The two soldiers had stiffened, their eyes showing their alarm. Before they could say anything, Gwen spoke reassuringly to them. 'Nothing to worry about. Entirely routine.' She showed them the readings. Toshiko noticed that they didn't seem much more reassured.

'Here's another of the three divers,' noted Jack.

Gwen and Toshiko looked at the photo he had held out. A trio of divers on a boat, ready to drop into the blue water behind them, their masks on and their thumbs raised. 'We saw that picture at Wildman's apartment,' agreed Gwen.

'Wildman, Bee, and another one,' mused Toshiko. 'And this could be the third. She's quite a looker. Girlfriend?'

'I don't think "quite a looker" is likely for Wildman, do you?' laughed Gwen.

'That's one of the other instructors,' said Private Foxton. Toshiko had been unaware that the two soldiers behind them had been looking at the photographs too. 'That's Sergeant Applegate. She was another sub-aqua enthusiast. *Hwntw*, the two of them.'

'They were what?' asked Toshiko.

'South Waleans,' explained Gwen. 'Perhaps she was having a thing with Bee, though. The MO wasn't very forthcoming, but he said that some of the officers thought Bee was too familiar with the other soldiers. Do you think that's code for "shagging the staff"?'

Toshiko passed her the photograph. 'I don't know. What do you reckon – would you?'

At first, she thought Gwen might have been offended by her teasing question. As soon as she saw the photograph, Gwen's expression had hardened. She twisted the photograph so that Jack could see it more clearly.

'I would,' said Jack, but there was little humour in his voice. 'But then I have a thing about blondes with legs that go all the way up to their ears.'

'It's Betty Jenkins!' Gwen said.

Toshiko laughed. 'The pensioner at Wildman's apartment?'

'No,' replied Gwen. 'The woman who claimed to be Betty Jenkins.'

Jack leaped from the table and made for the door. He paused in the shattered doorframe and snapped a question at Foxton. 'Where is this Sergeant Applegate? We need to see her now.'

Foxton looked flustered for the first time. 'I don't know sir. Sorry.'

'What kind of outfit is this?'

'No, sir. I mean, no one knows. She's been absent without leave for three weeks.'

Jack screwed up his eyes tight and bellowed at the ceiling in frustration. He slammed at the open door with his clenched fist, and winced. 'I wish I had time to go and slap the Lieutenant-Colonel in his stiff upper lip. He knew this and told us nothing when we got here. It's obstruction, pure and simple.'

'It's trust,' Gwen told him quietly. 'It's not right, but it's understandable.'

'No time for polite conversation,' Jack decided. 'Well, we know Applegate wasn't at Wildman's flat to feed his plants.'

'Unless she was feeding them to that disgusting starfish thing in the bath,' Gwen agreed. 'And all that squeaky nervous behaviour? That was a routine. She's a trained soldier, she wouldn't be scared of guns or violence.'

Toshiko saw that Jack was picking slivers of wood from a cut in the side of his hand. He had slammed his fist into a broken section of the door, and caught a bunch of splinters. 'Maybe you were right, Tosh. I should have used the handle.'

'Not locked,' she agreed. 'No guard.'

Jack stared at her, astounded. 'No guard!' he yelled. 'That's right. But there *was* a guard at Wildman's apartment. Wasn't there, Gwen?'

'Applegate?'

'No! The thing in the bathroom! We know that Wildman could puke up those things. He musta barfed one into the tub to guard whatever he'd hidden there. C'mon, we gotta get back. Whatever it was guarding… it could still be there!'

EIGHTEEN

The rain squalled around them during their sprint across the barracks, so the front of their clothing was swiftly soaked. Privates Foxton and Wisniewski trotted behind them, keeping pace and not trying to overtake. It must have looked to the troops marching on the parade ground that a bedraggled trio of visitors was being casually chased off the Caregan grounds by two soldiers.

They reached the visitors' car park, skittering to a halt in the puddles by their vehicles. Jack ignored Foxton's request to sign out, slipped into the SUV driving seat, and started the engine. Gwen tossed her Saab keys back to Toshiko. She knew what to expect back at Wildman's apartment, and planned to travel back there with Jack.

The SUV slewed backwards across the rain-soaked gravel of the car park, crunched into gear and skidded forward, off and out of the barracks.

Gwen watched the blur of the chain-link fence as the car speeded up. The vehicle's suspension was superb. The main evidence that it was scudding over the rutted roadway were the sprayed sheets of water, like blankets cast out to the side of the car, as the wheels plunged into frequent rain-filled potholes.

The front wipers swished on fast setting, and through the windscreen ahead of them Gwen could see the bruise-black sky that lowered over their destination. A huge swathe of boiling cloud that was turning the afternoon dark. A monstrous presence awaiting their return.

'Insufficient information,' said the navigation system. 'Attempting to locate fourth satellite.'

Jack switched it off. 'I think we know the way back.' He punched the phone's speed dial, and it connected with a rapid series of beeps.

Gwen didn't see which number he'd dialled. 'Are you calling the police? We should warn them about the apartment, so they know to stay out of it. And they can put a call out for Sandra Applegate. Then we can listen in on their frequencies—'

'They already know to stay out of the place. So what are they gonna do, flood the area with cops? That's not gonna happen. We don't want it to happen, for sure. They'll get in our way, and we haven't got the time. Ah…' The line connected with a chirruping sound. He had dialled the Hub. 'How's it going, Owen?' The line was distorted, and Gwen thought Owen said, 'What do you care?'

'Sounds like the storm's wiping out the phone network, too,' Jack said. 'So, listen up. Are you still irradiated, Owen?'

'Yeah, I'm lit up like a novelty lamp.'

'OK, well you can still make yourself useful. Need you to do a search on Sergeant Sandra Applegate. Training instructor at Caregan Barracks, Southern Welsh Regiment. Lives at the barracks, but spends time on scuba-diving activities off of it. Find out known associates – we already connect her with Wildman and Bee, so skip those, she ain't gonna be visiting them much now. So, who else? Where she hangs out. Clubs she's a member of. Whether she has a Tesco Clubcard. How many library books she has overdue. You know the score.'

There was a pause in which Gwen thought she could make out swearing. 'Can't Tosh do that?' Owen moaned.

'Not while she's driving the other car,' explained Jack.

'I thought she had hands-free.'

'What were you planning to do in the meantime,' snapped Jack, 'work on those pecs, maybe?'

'Oh, come on Jack. I'm not your data guy, I'm not your gadgets guy either. I'm a doctor. I was born a doctor, I live every day a doctor. I will die a doctor.'

'Sooner than you think, Owen. Get on with it.'

By the time they arrived back in Cardiff, thick dark clouds had blotted out every scrap of sky. It was more like late evening than late afternoon. The drainage system in the centre had collapsed, and the SUV had to surf a filthy stream of debris that washed down the angled streets that led into Splott. Fast-food cartons bobbed and jostled with shreds of paper, discarded cans, empty bottles, all the floating detritus from dozens of overturned bins and ripped garbage sacks.

No point in subterfuge now, they decided, especially as Wildman's place would be guarded by a uniformed officer when they got there. Jack pulled the car up outside the apartment block, with the wheels propped up on the pavement to get them out of the torrent that coursed along the gutter. A flare of lights from behind them showed that Toshiko had arrived too. It was a wonder she'd been able to keep up, the speed that Jack had been doing on the journey in, though Gwen knew the Saab handled well. Or it did in normal conditions, so perhaps the low-profile driving position had been more of a struggle for Toshiko when trailing the SUV all this way.

Gwen scrambled over the driver's seat to follow Jack out and avoid the stream that was running along the road on her side of the vehicle. When she'd clambered out and shut the door, she found Jack stooped over something by the main entrance. Toshiko was standing beside him, her face pallid after seeing what Jack had found.

It was the police officer who had been stationed by the doorway. The body lay in a stream of water that spilled from a broken gutter far above. Gwen could tell he was dead from the crazy angle of his neck, and the way that Jack was standing and not helping. She clicked on her pocket torch and examined the body, flicking the light over the face. At first she worried about who she would find, and then she immediately felt ashamed at the relief she felt when it was not someone she knew from her old station. That would be nothing to the guilt she'd feel later, once Toshiko had concocted some Torchwood cover-up story – probably about how the officer had wandered off during his duty period and fallen into the river. It would have to be a big distraction to hide this massive and fatal attack.

Something had ripped into the back of the young officer's neck. Or rather, someone had. Brain and bone was visible in the maw of the wound, washed clean continuously by the downpour. There was very little blood visible, and it was even washing out of the young lad's shirt collar. He lay crumpled in the shrubs. A young lad, Gwen thought bitterly. A young lad they could have rescued with a phone call.

'We could have stopped this,' she told Jack coldly. 'One call and we could have saved this boy.'

'We don't know that,' Toshiko told her.

'He wouldn't warn them. On the journey here. It would have been one phone call.'

Toshiko put a hand on the sodden shoulder of her jacket. 'We still can't know for sure.'

Jack was already moving away. Gwen jumped back to her feet, half wanting to argue the point with him. But when he turned, maybe it was just the rain running down his face that made his blue eyes seem so watery as he stared back at her.

He jerked his head in the direction of the street, a contemptuous gesture that seemed to accuse the whole neighbourhood. 'What's happened to your curtain-twitchers now?'

Gwen couldn't hold his gaze. 'Staying away from their windows because of the rain, I imagine.' And she knew there would have been no witnesses to the attack in this weather, either. The young officer had died alone.

Jack shoulder-charged the doors to the apartment. On the third attempt, the lock burst apart and they were able to dash into the dingy hallway and out of the rain.

'No shopping bags this time,' Gwen said.

'Yeah, well, I'm not great at queuing.'

The three of them hared up the stairs, several at a time. On the upper landing, the real Betty Jenkins was poking her head out from behind her door with an angry look. Toshiko ushered her back into her apartment, and told her to keep her door closed while the environmental health team conducted a fumigation of the stairwell.

'This place has gone...' muttered Miss Jenkins as she retreated and closed her door.

On the next landing, they found the sprawled body of another policeman. There was no rain to wash away the blood. It had spurted out of a main artery in his neck, spraying up the nearest wall before running down and creating a congealed pool of dark reddish-brown liquid. Again Gwen felt that electric tingle of fear, relief, and shame as she examined the officer and found she did not recognise him.

'She's right,' murmured Gwen. 'This place has gone to hell. Completely gone to hell.'

Wildman's apartment door stood ajar. Gwen rose from examining the dead policeman, and hesitated.

'Come on!' hissed Jack. He drew his Webley, kicked open the front door, and angled his weapon into the hallway.

The way seemed clear, so Toshiko charged in, her weapon at the ready. She was barely into the main room when Sandra Applegate sprang at her from beyond the living-room door. Applegate knocked Toshiko to the floor, and loomed over her. Even from the front entrance, Gwen could see Applegate was a mess. Her face was bloodied, and her chest was stained.

Jack threw himself down the short hallway with thundering steps, and cuffed Applegate behind the head with the butt of his revolver. Applegate spun away into the room, tipping over a table and collapsing by an armchair.

Gwen rushed in and covered the fallen woman with her gun, a double-handed grip just like Jack had taught her in the Torchwood firing range. The weapon was recoilless, a neat feat of alien engineering applied to a standard-issue army weapon, but a two-handed grip made aiming truer. In the corner of her eye, she could see that Toshiko had fallen awkwardly against a sideboard and was slumped against the wall. Jack hunkered down next to her, checking that she was all right. And, for a moment, Gwen was distracted.

Applegate sat up abruptly next to the armchair and made a deep gurgling sound from somewhere in the pit of her stomach. Gwen's gaze snapped back to Applegate. The woman clutched at her stomach and made a profound retching noise. In horrified fascination, Gwen saw her mouth open wide, so wide that she could see Applegate's lips stretched tight in a circle around her bared teeth. At which point, Applegate heaved again, and spat a spongy yellow mass across the room at Gwen.

It hit Gwen's trigger hand, and she instinctively ducked and fired. The shot went wide. Applegate was on her feet at once, charging for the door. She shouldered Jack aside, surprising him so that she was able to get past. He recovered swiftly, stepped briskly into the hallway after her, and loosed off two shots in quick succession.

Gwen thought she heard a cry and then a great crash of glass. But then the pain in her hand hit her.

The spongy yellow mass was a small starfish-shaped creature. Its main body and one of its four arms were firmly attached, and starting to burn her flesh. She heard another shrill cry, and was shocked to realise it was herself. She dropped her handgun, collapsed into the arm chair, and stared in revulsion at the thing that clung to her hand.

Beside her, Toshiko groaned as she began to recover. Jack rushed back into the room, looked at both of the women. Gwen stared at him beseechingly. 'It's burning. Get it off me!'

Jack looked wildly around the room. He spotted something on the sideboard by the doorway, snatched it up, and hurried over to Gwen.

'Hold still,' he told her.

Jack had seized a letter opener. With his free hand he pinched two of the revolting creature's legs between his fingers, and peeled them away from Gwen's hand. She could tell from the way this made him wince that the vile thing was burning his skin too. Now that its underside was exposed, Gwen could make out a central mouth that had been biting into the soft flesh of her hand. Jack plunged the letter opener into the centre of the creature, and pushed hard. There was a rubbery squeaking sound as the dull blade of the letter opener pierced the yellowy skin. The point burst from the upper side, and a greenish ichor sprayed across the room and onto the carpet.

Almost at once, the starfish released its grip on Gwen's hand. Jack leapt up, the creature still attached to the letter opener, and he plunged the blade into the wall above the sideboard. The point pierced the plasterboard wall, and when Jack let go of the handle the letter opener had skewered the starfish to the striped wallpaper. The creature spasmed for a moment and then went still.

Gwen ran into the kitchen area of the apartment, and ran water over her wounded hand. The tap slowly ran cold, and the smarting pain seemed to ease a little. Jack joined her at the sink, and stuck his burned fingers under the tap.

'Thanks,' Gwen told him. Their hands met briefly in the cold water, so she stroked the back of his hand with a light touch.

Toshiko gave a little groan from where she had been dumped on the horrid shag pile carpet. Jack pulled his hand away, took a towel and went over to check on Toshiko.

Gwen had to dry her hands on a stained tea towel. The back of her right hand was blotched with circles and small scratches, but the skin appeared to be unbroken.

Toshiko was dazed, but not injured. Jack helped her back to her feet. 'What happened to Applegate?' she asked him. 'Did you...? Eww!' Toshiko had spotted the starfish spiked into the wall, level with her head. It had shrivelled still further, and was dripping yellow-green gunk down the wallpaper and onto the sideboard. 'God, I thought the decor in this place was dismal, but that's just disgusting!'

Jack beckoned to Toshiko and Gwen to follow him out of the apartment. Out on the landing, rain was washing in through a fresh hole in the half-landing window. 'I shot her. Upper arm, I think. Maybe the shoulder. She was running down the stairs, so the momentum carried her on and through that window.'

He trotted down the half-flight of steps. He considered the rain and wind gusting in through the hole before twisting the latch and opening the shattered remains of the window. He took a swift look through the gap, pulled his head back in. He obviously couldn't believe what he'd seen, because he bravely took another look in the face of the storm.

'I can't see the body,' he said. 'C'mon, two floors down, who's gonna survive that?' He studied Toshiko and Gwen's reactions. 'OK, we should check on the way out.'

They returned to the apartment, and went into the bathroom. As soon as the door opened, an overpowering stench of rotting fish assailed them. It was enough to make Gwen's eyes water.

The remains of the larger starfish had dissolved into a slimy gloop in the bath. Gwen didn't argue when Jack said he would conduct the search. Hidden behind the side panel of the bath he found a heavy grey box. He pulled it out onto the bathroom rug, and slid it across the room. Gwen switched on her Geiger counter, which ticked quietly. Jack lifted the lid of the box, and the ticking abruptly became a machine-gun rattle of alarm.

Jack snapped the lid shut. 'OK,' he said calmly. 'We appear to have the missing fuel rods.'

They had to make two journeys down the stairwell. On the first they carried the lead-lined box, and pushed it into the boot of the SUV. Second time, they wrapped up the policeman's corpse in a blanket from Wildman's apartment, and hefted the body down the stairs. By the time they'd put the other copper's body in the boot, all three of them were drenched in what felt to Gwen like equal measures of sweat and rainwater.

Jack slammed the boot closed. 'You two go back to the Hub and get changed. Take the Saab. I'll deliver the fuel rods to Blaidd Drwg and join you later. Tosh, you can start working on the cover story for these two in the back.' He checked his watch. 'Difficult to tell when I'll get back in this weather.'

'I hope that's waterproof,' Toshiko said.

'It's the best,' Jack told her. 'American military watch, 1940s. Twenty-four-hour display, a nice piece.'

Toshiko peered at it in the rain. 'Where did you get it from?'

'That was a long time ago,' smiled Jack. He shot his cuffs so that the watch was out of the rain again. 'That was a whole other life.'

Jack closed the door and steered the SUV upstream and out of the street. Gwen got into the Saab and watched the wake that the SUV left behind. She sat for a while gripping the steering wheel, studying the marks on the back of her hand and thinking about the two young policemen. What creative thinking would Toshiko employ to explain away their absences? Their deaths. She hardly dared ask her, even though she was now sitting next to her.

It was while contemplating these things that Gwen was startled by the sound of her mobile going off. A quick glance at the display revealed that it was Rhys. Was she coming home for dinner tonight? Gwen smiled sheepishly at Toshiko. Not sure, she told her boyfriend. Rain's really terrible, so she'd need to take it steady. No, she was fine, being over-cautious probably. She'd call him when she knew.

He loved her, he said. She missed him, she replied.

When the call ended, Gwen sat silently for a few more moments in the car. Thinking again about the inventive excuse that Toshiko was going come up with to cover the policemen's absence. Pondering the excuse she herself was going to offer Rhys tonight when she'd missed dinner again.

Ianto found it surprisingly difficult to close the front door. There was a gale blowing straight across the Bay, and that meant straight at the entrance to the Hub from Mermaid Quay. He put his shoulder to the edge nearest the frame and, after a bit more effort, he was able to get the door to click into place. He shot the bolts securely across the top and bottom, and leaned back against the door, exhausted.

Jack had breezed in, but so had several gallons of water, and the reception floor was awash. 'We're gonna need some sandbags out there, Ianto, if this rain keeps up.'

'Yes, the neighbourhood's gone to pot,' said Ianto. 'Maybe we should move.'

'I don't think so,' said Jack. 'Imagine how many tea-chests we'd need to pack. That, plus we'd need to get the stationery reprinted.' He shook himself like a wet dog, and rainwater spattered across the room. His trousers were soaked up to the knee, and he decided it would be a good idea to grasp the material and squeeze water out of the legs right there and then.

Ianto resisted the strong temptation to tut loudly. Instead, he plucked a handful of tissues from a box and mopped the worst of the splashes off the paperwork at the desk. He was able to rescue the flyers for the Redflight Barcud event at the Millennium Centre, but a pile of Tredegar House information leaflets was as good as ruined.

They had disguised the Bayside entrance to the Torchwood Hub as a Tourist Information Centre. And not a particularly salubrious one at that because, obviously, they didn't want to encourage a steady stream of eager visitors asking for directions to the Pierhead Building or opening times for the Norwegian Church. Not that Ianto couldn't answer those questions, of course. He prided himself on his arcane local knowledge, whether Cardiff indie bands or the history of Tiger Bay. Mostly, though, they only wanted to know the reason why the word 'Brains' was stencilled on a city centre chimney stack. This had all proved useful cover on an awkward occasion when a film crew from a BBC Wales travel programme wouldn't take no for an answer when looking for an interview.

Ianto helped Jack out of his wet coat. 'You've got a big hole in your sleeve,' he said.

'Nothing escapes your eagle eye.'

'I see you've got a new watch, too.'

'I'm trying it out. Though it's an old watch. Antique.'

Ianto looked at it admiringly. 'Very nice. Perhaps you should have one for casual and one for best.'

'I don't think so.' Jack shucked off his sopping wet shoes and kicked them into the corner. 'A guy with a watch knows what time it is. A guy with two watches is never sure.' To Ianto's dismay, he proceeded to peel off his socks and wring them out into the waste bin. 'Are Tosh and Gwen back?'

'Waiting for you downstairs,' said Ianto.

'You're not wearing any socks,' Gwen told him.

'Nothing escapes your eagle eye,' replied Jack. 'Have you admired my watch yet?'

He plonked down into a Boardroom chair, and waited for Toshiko to complete her presentation materials. 'That flooding is getting critical. We're gonna have to seal the side entrance. Or put Ianto on a steroid regime, so he can get the door closed.'

Gwen pointed through the Boardroom's glass wall and into the main Hub area. She could see the water at the foot of the stainless steel tower was rippling. 'The basin is tidal, isn't it?'

Jack followed her directions. 'Yeah. And look how much higher that's got. Tosh, have we got a valve control on that thing to prevent it flooding the Hub?'

'Yes,' she told him, 'but I can't promise that the rest of the place is waterproof. There's a pool of water building up against the exterior window of the Autopsy Room. It would only take one careless accident for that to break.'

'Owen had better be careful then. He around?'

'I think Ianto knows where he is,' said Gwen.

Toshiko tapped the display screen to get their attention again. 'As for the rest of Cardiff, they're a lot worse off. Three hundred thousand people are staying at home to avoid getting their feet wet. We're supposed to have thirty-six inches of rain a year, and we've had twenty-four inches in as many hours.'

'The Oval Basin is starting to fill up with water,' agreed Gwen. 'It was like a river raging through there when we walked back from the car. If it carries on like this, by tomorrow morning only the people on the top floors of St David's Hotel will still be dry. And they probably won't notice until the caviar runs out.'

Toshiko showed a few more graphics on the display. 'They did a lot of groundwater modelling studies when they were proposing the barrage for the Bay. I'm going to tap into their instrumentation…'

Gwen laughed. 'Very good.' Toshiko didn't look pleased by this interruption. 'Sorry, I thought you were joking. You know, water… tap…'

'Tosh doesn't joke about her work.' Jack wagged a finger at Gwen in mock admonishment.

'They've got over two hundred boreholes recording groundwater levels every thirty minutes,' persisted Toshiko. 'And they measure other environmental parameters like rainfall, obviously, and atmospheric pressure. Tide and river levels. That lot should give us some idea what's going on.'

Jack leaned back in his chair, put his bare feet up on the table, and waggled his toes. 'There are some people round here who still talk about the Bristol Channel floods of 1607.'

'I imagine there may be some who are old enough to remember it,' muttered Gwen.

Toshiko was more impressed with the information, however. 'Thousands died. Houses and villages were swept away. Livestock got destroyed when farmland was inundated. The surrounding region was set back for more than a century. And there's a recent theory that it was a tsunami. If today's water levels continue to rise like this, it could do the same kind of damage.'

'But not as fast,' observed Gwen.

Toshiko switched off the display screen. 'A slow tsunami? Well, that would still cause devastation. Wreck the local economy. And kill tens of thousands this time.' She closed the lid of her laptop. 'If I'm right.'

Ianto came into the room to offer them coffee. He looked disapprovingly at Jack's bare feet, so Jack removed them from the table. 'OK, let's have your program run overnight Tosh, and see what it tells us tomorrow. Go home now, it's late. Have a lie-in tomorrow. You too, Gwen. Better take the scenic route, because I think Ianto here has welded the side door shut.'

Gwen knew better than to protest. She heaved herself out of her chair, and made her way to the exit platform with Toshiko.

'Doesn't your boyfriend mind you working this late?' asked Toshiko.

'He said he was going out to an all-night *Star Wars* marathon,' lied Gwen.

Toshiko looked unconvinced. 'In this weather?'

'They're *Star Wars* fans,' explained Gwen. 'They'd crawl over boiling lava to avoid missing their fifteenth viewing.'

'Ah,' said Toshiko, 'I understand. *Otaku.*' She smiled when Gwen frowned. 'Geek.'

'*Otaku,*' repeated Gwen.

The platform began to lift them upward.

'And *gemu otaku* is a video games geek,' Toshiko said.

'I think that's pronounced "Owen Harper".' Gwen looked up above them and sighed. 'You realise that we've forgotten the umbrellas again.'

The pavement slab opened up overhead, and the cold rain showered in on them.

Jack watched Ianto polish the table where his feet had been propped. Ianto could tell that his boss didn't really approve, but he thought that Jack would dislike it even more if the place got to be a mess. At the moment, he had other things to worry about though.

'Gwen tells me you know where Owen is, Ianto.'

Ianto stopped polishing. 'No. His radiation readings reached normal, and so he decided to go out. On a date, he said.'

'A date? What about the work I asked him to do?'

Ianto produced a buff folder of printouts. Balanced on the top of it was the radiation sponge. 'He asked me to give you these. He said that there's a lot of information about what a brave and resourceful soldier Sergeant Applegate is, fine service record. And she has 450 Nectar points, in case that's important.'

'I could kiss you, Ianto.'

'No you couldn't, sir.'

Jack flipped open the folder and stood up. 'I'm gonna take this down to my office.' They both walked out of the Boardroom and made their way down the spiral staircase to the main Hub.

Ianto noticed how the water in the centre had risen higher, and seemed to be slapping higher against the edge of the basin. The view through the portholes in the wall above them also seemed to be more turbulent, with fragments of weed whirling past in the dark water and fewer fish visible than usual.

Jack walked away towards his office. 'You can go home now.'

'Thank you. I have a bit more filing to do. In the basement. I'd like to finish it.'

Jack laughed. 'You may as well live here, Ianto,' he shouted before he closed his office door.

I could say the same thing about you, Ianto thought as he set off to the basement to continue his own work.

NINETEEN

The sodium glare from the streetlights cast a jaundiced pall across the sodden T-junction. Owen sat listening to the howl of the wind and the battering percussion of rain above the Boxter, and wondering if the roof latch would hold. No wonder he'd got a deal on the car. Too good to be true at 18K, even with 40,000 miles and schlepping all the way out to Colchester for it. He should have bought the Honda S2000, like he'd first thought. But he'd gone for style and speed, so now he found that the windstop on this 1997 model Boxter didn't hook properly and ended up rattling.

And windstop was what he needed right now. The storm outside buffeted the car, and rain lashed the windscreen until it was awash. Owen flicked on the wipers. They swiped the water aside so that he could peer through the glass at Megan's place across the road. Her maisonette was the top floor, up an L-shaped flight of steps at the gable-end of the house. Two windows were visible. One was unlit, with opaque glass. The other was much wider, bold red curtains illuminated. He thought he saw a shadow at one point, but through the downpour it was hard to be sure. The window was partly obscured by a large plane tree, that must have been planted by a pessimistic urban planner who'd not expected the houses to still be there once the tree had reached its final size.

He'd sat here for ten minutes already, kidding himself that he was just waiting for the rainstorm to ease off, just rehearsing what he was going to say, devising the best and most logical explanation for Megan. In reality he felt like he was a student again, the first time he'd arranged to meet her. Then, he'd stood outside the Angus halls of residence, uncertain, nervous.

She'd made all the running in the refectory earlier that day, and he'd hardly believed his luck in persuading her to go out that evening. Actually, she'd persuaded him to persuade her, he'd work out afterwards. And thus, his fresher insecurities fuelled, he'd worried about everything from then on – was he wearing the right T-shirt, was he heading for the right room in the hall, would he pronounce her name right, should he rehearse his line or would that sound *too* rehearsed, had he chosen the right film, was she allergic to Chinese food…

Another wild gust rocked the Porsche. The sallow glow of the streetlight revealed where he'd been tapping his fingertips. He noticed with a mixture of embarrassment and annoyance that it looked like he'd been doodling in the dust on the dashboard. Did that shape look like a heart? Not what he'd intended, at any rate. And what would Megan think if he ended up giving her a lift somewhere later and she saw it? He scuffed over the doodle with his palm. The result was a great smeared patch in the dust that somehow made the dashboard look even grubbier. Owen tugged a cuff up over the heel of his hand, and swiped over it. That looked better, at least. But now he'd got a tidemark of greyish dust over his left sleeve.

He blew an exasperated sigh, leaned back against the head restraint, and looked around the rest of the Porsche. Under his coat, the passenger seat had three old crisp packets on it, one only half-finished. Beside them was a bent plastic teaspoon with an uneaten raspberry yoghurt that he'd grabbed off his desk at the Hub thinking he might finish it on the way out. He slipped off his seat belt to look in the footwell, where he found bits of gravel, three Post-it notes containing grid references, plus a couple of forgotten AA batteries. Probably dead, but he stuffed them in his jacket pocket just in case.

He was experimenting with doing the same with the crisp packets when he thought: that's just stupid. He's arranged to see her for the first time in over five years, and he's bringing her a pocketful of empty crisp packets and a raspberry yoghurt. He should have stopped off to get her flowers. Roses, she liked roses, didn't she? Or was that too cheesy? A bottle of wine, at least. But he'd never been very good on vintages, always went for the third least expensive bottle in Threshers. Megan used to tease him about it, because she'd been to a wine appreciation group at Uni and could tell her Merlot from her Camembert. He recalled little about it now, except stuff about macerating the must, and how cross Megan got when he joked about 'length'.

Owen unlocked the glove compartment. The light flicked on, and he could see the dull sheen of the Bekaran tool. That was a better idea. Never mind the wine and roses. The alien device felt cool in his palm as he slipped it into his jacket pocket. He shoved the crisp packets and the plastic spoon into the compartment, and shut it.

He hadn't changed before leaving the Hub, and was still in his Torchwood standard: black jacket, dark trousers and shirt. Probably ideal for getting knocked down in the dark by a careless driver racing through Whitchurch on his way home to Cyncoed. Owen hadn't driven home for different clothes either, because that would have delayed him getting to Megan. So it seemed daft to sit here, just peering up at her room. He wasn't that uncertain undergraduate now, no way. He certainly hadn't been that awkward kid any more when he and Megan had split up. When he'd left her.

He struggled into his coat, determined not to get out of the car before putting it on because he knew he'd be drenched within seconds. The maisonette was thirty metres away. Owen popped the car door, levered himself out, double locked the Boxter with a flick of his wrist. The wind and rain formed an almost physical barrier as he ran for the cover of the tree. He huddled against the trunk, his feet straddling where the tree's roots had cracked the pavement. Then he scurried over to the L-shaped steps.

The house end offered protection from the worst of the storm, and so despite the rain he took the steps slowly, one by one. At the top, he pressed the doorbell, a button indicated by a small backlit circle. There was a 'ding', and then a prolonged hum as the button refused to pop back out. Owen pressed it again, to no effect. He slapped at it with his palm. He was whacking it with the heel of his clenched fist when the door opened, light spilled out all around him, and Megan stood in the doorway studying him. Appraising him.

'No dong,' he said to her apologetically. He pointed to the doorbell, which was still buzzing furiously.

She broke into her familiar chuckle. 'I hope you don't say that to all the girls.' She flicked at the doorbell with her fingernail, and the button popped back out again.

Owen looked at her for a few seconds that lasted forever. 'Are you going to invite me in?' he asked.

Megan stepped aside and held the door open. 'What are you, some kind of vampire?'

'Don't even joke about it,' said Owen as she beckoned him in. 'I mean it.'

Megan told him to remove his wet shoes and, when she saw his socks, those too. She peeled off his sopping coat to drape on a wall-hanging peg, before making him stand barefoot on the cold linoleum while she went to fetch him something to dry his hair.

He watched her disappear through the nearest doorway, her thin cardigan flapping behind her. Megan was still as slim as he remembered, accentuated by her Wrangler jeans. He discovered the raspberry yoghurt in his jacket pocket, so he set it down beside a pile of junk mail on a small table by the door.

Megan's voice echoed from the little bathroom, telling him how he would have to take her as he found her and that she'd barely had time to tidy up her paperwork, let alone run a Hoover around the place. Owen thought about how he'd been imagining her South Wales accent all the time they'd been talking in the *Second Reality* game, and now that he could hear it for real it was exactly as he remembered it. He closed his eyes, and imagined himself back in their Balham flat, calling from one side to the other as they caught up on the events of their day at the university.

When he opened them again, she was waggling a green crotchet-edged hand towel at him. 'Cleanest one I've got, I'm afraid.' She watched him towel his hair for a bit. 'I'll put the kettle on now you're here. Go on through. Thank you for the yoghurt.' She waved in the opposite direction as she disappeared into an unseen kitchen on the right.

Owen half-stepped into the bedroom. Big double bed with a pink paisley-patterned duvet, matching pillows. Picture of a piano in a sunlit room on the wall above. Piles of paperwork on one bedside table, just a simple lamp on another. A square wicker laundry basket stuffed so full that its hinged lid poked up.

He padded straight out again, barefoot, and into the room she'd meant. The lounge-diner was evidently the largest room in the maisonette, but felt cramped because of the amount of stuff crammed into it. He could smell the remains of a Chinese meal, not quite disguised by floral air freshener. A paper globe shade in the centre of the ceiling was unlit, but two art deco lamps on opposite walls cast a warm glow across the room

On the outer wall, pushed up near the window, a gate-leg dining table was unfolded and covered with a cream damask tablecloth. Four fabric-covered chairs, blue with no arms, were pressed up against three sides.

A small portable with a circular aerial sat in one corner. Owen noted that it made a little 'crack' noise that suggested the plastic case was cooling down because it had only just been switched off. The rest of the room was dominated by a battered leather sofa that dwarfed a tiny glass-topped wicker coffee table, and a crumpled green armchair so huge that he couldn't work out how it could originally have been brought into the room. He saw his own reflection wrinkling its nose in an octagonal mirror above the sofa.

He dropped into the green armchair. It faced the TV, and he wondered if it was Megan's regular seat. So he got up again and walked over to the dining table. In front of one of the blue chairs were perched a dusty flat-screen monitor, wireless keyboard and mouse. The computer itself was tucked under the table. 'This where you connect to the game?' Owen called over his shoulder into the room, in the expectation Megan would hear him in the kitchen. He couldn't make out her shouted reply. He flicked through a nearby magazine rack – *Radio Times*, *Guardian*, pages torn from the *BMJ*. 'Can't tell if you live here on your own or not,' he added in his normal voice.

'Mind your own bloody business,' Megan retorted mildly.

While he'd been looking at the magazines, she had walked into the room behind him. She carried a circular tray that held an opened bottle and two large wine glasses. She'd removed her thin cardigan, and the ribbed cream top she wore accentuated her slender arms and the roundness of her breasts. He pretended to look at her hair instead. 'You've cut it a lot shorter. Than I remember, I mean.'

'Easier for A&E.'

'And I like your necklace.'

'Do sit down, Owen, I don't charge people to use the furniture.'

He perched on the sofa. The leather cushion creaked. Megan set the tray down on the glass-topped table. She handed him a little white and yellow item that was also on the tray. 'Look what I have in my kitchen,' she said.

He examined the object. It was a fridge magnet in the shape of a fried egg, sunny side up. 'Egg magnet,' he grinned.

'I thought you'd come to talk about the online game,' Megan said. 'But all this interest in my living arrangements… I'm starting to think you're just after a shag for old times' sake. Don't get your hopes up, I changed my mind. About the tea. Thought you'd like a glass of wine, especially if you've had a hard day at the office. Assuming you're at an office. Are you at an office? Oh… but you're driving… I suppose one would be all right. I could pour you half a glass.' She was leaning over the table in front of him, watching him smile in recognition. 'I'm rambling on, aren't I? Sorry.'

Just as in the game earlier, he recognised her stream of consciousness explain-while-I'm-thinking-aloud manner. 'I haven't come for a sympathy shag, no. You and I were over a long time ago.'

'You count the days, I imagine.'

'Don't you?' he joked, and was a little surprised when her neck flushed. He recognised that reaction, too. 'I've had a very shitty day,' he continued quickly, 'and I'd love a glass of... whatever that is.'

She glugged out half a glass for him, more. 'Château La Fleur Chambeau 2004.'

'French.'

'Well done, Clouseau. It's a wine from Lussac Saint-Émilion. It's very similar to what you'd get from the more illustrious Saint-Emilion and Pomerol appellations. But it's cheaper, of course. Have you educated your palate since we...' She paused awkwardly. Poured herself a glass, and then breathed in the aroma. 'Are you more discriminating, or am I wasting this very fine bottle on you?'

Owen smiled. 'I remember how you tried to convince me to become an... oenophile? Was that the word?'

She sat beside him on the sofa. 'And I remember you thought that was a sexual practice.'

'There were a lot of wankers in your wine club.' He chinked his glass against hers.

'Bloody cheek. And don't just swig it down. Like this, remember?' Megan swirled the wine around her glass and inhaled the aroma. 'Don't think I haven't noticed that you came empty-handed tonight.' She narrowed her eyes, and studied him a bit more closely. 'Are those biscuit crumbs on your jacket sleeve? Or bits of old crisps? In fact, have you made *any* kind of effort this evening to...'

Her voice trailed off as she saw something else.

'Is that a gun in your pocket, Owen?'

Owen shifted awkwardly on the sofa, straightened his jacket and trousers. 'Yes, I'm afraid it is.'

Megan looked like she couldn't decide whether to get up or to remain seated. She fidgeted with her glass. She set it down on the glass table-top. Changed her mind and transferred it to the tray. Twisted her necklace between her long, pale fingers. 'Oh,' she said eventually. 'Oh God, you're a gangster. A gangster with a gun. In my living room.' She offered him a sort of desperate half-smile that seemed to beg him to contradict her. To reassure her. To say she was overreacting.

Owen listened to the sound of the rain battering the window for a while, thinking how best to go on. He took a gulp at the Château La Fleur.

'I work for Torchwood,' he began.

The second glass was better than the first, Owen decided. He'd helped himself, if only to punctuate his explanation with a pause to do something else.

He'd tried to explain, but his rehearsed routine from the car journey here had melted away into a mishmash of false starts and goings back and repetition. Megan had slowly relaxed into the sofa, bringing her legs up onto the cushion and cradling her glass lightly in both hands. He tried to decipher her expression, just as he had when they had lived together. In Balham, decoding her unspoken mood had been a different matter, the consequences less significant. In their kitchen as they cooked, could he escape some chore? In their hallway as he arrived back from university, had she caught him out in a small untruth? In their bedroom, was she expecting him to have noticed a change she'd made to the flat, her clothes, her hair? After making love, was she trying not to blurt out again that she loved him?

Here in her lonely, draughty maisonette, he watched her face for the familiar clues that he'd barely forgotten over the years. She couldn't quite hold his gaze, affecting to study his jacket, or picking at crumbs on his trouser leg. Finally, she said in a quiet, faintly mocking voice: 'So, you're like Customs and Excise for aliens. You're the space police?'

'Police?' Owen snorted, and immediately regretted the dismissive sound he'd made. 'I mean, all that process and procedure and paperwork just get in the way.'

'So you're *outside* the law.'

'You sound like Gwen. No, not that either. We're… tangential to it.' He rubbed pensively at his forehead. 'It all seemed so much easier when Jack explained it to me that first time.'

'Who's Gwen? Your girlfriend?'

Owen wanted to snort again, but decided not to. 'Hardly. Not my type. Think I'd need to be a bit desperate.' He thought about Jack gripping Gwen's waist as they'd risen towards the Hub exit. 'New girl at work. I'm sure she's not interested.'

'And Jack?'

'Guy who hired me.'

'Your boss?'

'We're more of a team…' The conversation was slipping away from him. 'Thing is, Megan, I think you'd be interested in Torchwood. I think you'd be right for us.' Megan was scratching idly at another crumb on his knee, so he grasped her hand. 'I *know* you would.'

'Is that the wine talking?'

'It's my instinct talking.'

Megan sat up straight, her eyes alive with anger. 'Oh, where have I heard *that* before? No, don't interrupt me, don't you dare interrupt!' She wasn't having any difficulty meeting his gaze now. 'It was your instinct that you couldn't stay in London, wasn't it? It was your *instinct* that you couldn't be cooped up, or tied down. You men, you young SHOs, you're all the fucking same. Fixing people up is like… like… building that coffee table. You follow the instructions, you put tab A into slot B, and they're done. The people in your life can't be put together so easily when they're broken. When you break them.' She was shouting now, enough to drown out the storm at the window.

He remembered. He hadn't known what he wanted back then. He'd only known what he *didn't* want. The weekly shop at Tesco. The visits to her sister in Penarth. The trips to Croydon Ikea, to buy furniture for the flat. Stuff that might do for when they got a bigger place together, she'd said. Flatpack furniture he could bear, just about. But he hadn't been ready for a follow-the-leaflet life with Megan. He'd escaped by making a feeble excuse, because he could. He was able to walk away from it, away from her. And he hadn't looked back as he left to see how much she was going to miss him.

'Your fucking *instinct* was a lot of good for us, wasn't it?' Megan concluded, more quietly. 'I thought you were joking when you first talked about how you'd always wanted to travel. Remember? You'd met a Kiwi at a gig in Battersea. That girl Esther that I said you were obsessed by, and oh no, you said, she was just so different, so *fascinating*. And we discussed whether New Zealand was as far away as you could get.'

Owen smiled. 'Australia. We were in Hyde Park, August Bank Holiday, and it was pissing down. And we decided that you can't get further away than Australia.'

She made an exasperated sound at him. 'You might as well have been in Australia after we split up. After you left.'

'I didn't think you'd want a postcard,' he replied. No, that sounded too hard, too dismissive. 'It was all bullshit, you're right. I didn't get as far as Sydney. Not much further than Sidcup, come to think of it.'

'Sidcup? So much for "I want to be the real me", Owen. Remember? That was your piss-poor excuse for running away.' Megan's started to chuckle at this, and her head bobbed up and down. Owen grinned too, until he saw that her face was starting to crumple. She was sucking in little sudden breaths, her eyes squeezed tight, and the laughter was turning into sobs. He set down his glass immediately, and reached for her. She mumbled an incoherent sound, and waved him away. He tried once more, and she gestured again. Got up and left Owen alone in the room.

After a few seconds, he followed her out. Off to his right, her bedroom door snapped shut with a final click. 'Oh, shit,' he muttered under his breath. Well, his recruitment effort was going right down the crapper. Which reminded him... the sound of the rain seemed to be having an effect on him.

He had a languorous pee in the little bathroom. He lifted the lid, tried not to splash around the edge of the ugly avocado-coloured bowl, and flushed. There was no soap on the basin, so he looked in the little mirror-fronted cabinet above. Found a fresh bar next to a packet of triphasic contraceptives

– a familiar combination of ethinyloestradiol and levonorgestrel. As he rinsed his hands, he noted there was just one bath towel. A solitary splayed toothbrush. No evidence of aftershave in the cabinet or on the windowsill.

The bedroom door was still shut when he came out. Owen half-considered knocking. He even put his ear to the jamb in case he could hear anything, but the noise of the rain from the front door drowned out anything else. So he was surprised to find Megan was sitting on the sofa again as he returned to the living room. She'd brought through a small box of tissues. Her eyes were still reddened, but she had stopped crying.

'I'm sorry,' he said, 'I didn't mean to upset you.'

'Just now?' she asked. 'Or back in Balham.'

He didn't reply.

'I heard you rummaging about in the bathroom cabinet,' she said. 'Maybe you are like the police, after all.'

Owen walked over to the dining table, aware that he didn't want to crowd her. 'This isn't an investigation, Megan. And before you say it again, it's not just an attempt to get a shag for old times' sake.'

'Not *just* an attempt..?' she asked.

'Be serious. I do want you to join us in Torchwood.' Her face was blank now, or wary at best. Owen tapped the computer screen with his finger. 'I recognised you in Second Reality after you used a few familiar phrases. You know, "safe of taxis", that kind of stuff. But even before that, I recognised something else. You just *loved* all those confrontations and crazy monsters and weird shit. Be honest, it's a hell of a lot more fun than A&E.'

He watched her reaction now. Moved across to the sofa and sat down beside her again. 'So imagine, Megan, having that excitement for *real*. Every day with Torchwood. That's what I did. That's what I do. Jack brought me in from my former life as an SHO. Rescued me.' He held out his hands in an open gesture. 'This is the real me.'

Megan stared right into his eyes, like she'd made a decision. 'Come on! I'm sitting here not sure whether to throw you out or call you a psychiatrist. What happened to you, Owen?'

'So why aren't you throwing me out then,' he insisted, 'right now? Or why aren't you making some excuse about how you've got another date to go to tonight, or you're due back on shift, or you have to feed the neighbour's cat…?'

'My shift does start soon. About an hour and a half…'

Owen leaned closer to her. 'And here I am. Still. Why? What are you thinking? What suddenly started to make sense?'

Megan pulled her hand away from him, uncertain. The window panes across the room rattled in the violence of the storm outside. 'Listen to that racket,' she said. 'Before you got here, they were saying on *Wales Today* that this is the worst flooding Cardiff's ever had. Since records began. But Ramsay, one of the other SHOs at the Royal, he comes in from near Bargoed. And they've had nothing up there. River's running a bit higher near him, that's all. Driving in, he said, it was like hitting a wall of water. How can that be?'

Owen said nothing. Urged her on with his eyes.

'That thing you said when you arrived,' she continued. 'The vampire thing. I thought you were joking. But you were serious, weren't you? I mean, really serious.'

He smiled, nodded at her.

She stared at him. 'No, this can't make sense! You're actually offering me a job with this Torchwood. "Save the world from alien infestation. Competitive salary, plus dental"?'

Now he grinned at her. He slipped the Bekaran tool from his pocket. By twisting the central section, he folded it out to display a screen as wide as a pocket calculator. 'State-of-the-art equipment. Look at this.'

He ran the scanner over her outstretched arm. The display showed the ribbed beige surface of her jumper.

'Digital camera, very nice,' she observed.

He shushed her, and adjusted the resolution. As they both watched, the ribbing pattern slowly faded away, and they could see Megan's pale, freckled forearm. Owen tugged her arm gently, getting her to stand, and then he turned them both to face the mirror above the sofa. He stood behind Megan so that they could see themselves reflected in the octagonal mirror. He moved the Bekaran device over her forearm again, up above her bicep, across her shoulder blade, and then over her breast. The material of her white bra showed in the display, reflected back to them. Owen thumbed the resolution further, and the bra melted away to reveal the skin of her breast and, comically flattened, one nipple surrounded by the pale brown areola.

'I can't believe it,' Megan said. 'Who made that? Where's it from?'

'It's Bekaran,' said Owen from behind her, his lips close to her ear. 'We don't know where they come from. Ugly things they are. But they have some pretty neat gadgets.'

In the display, Megan's nipple was now erect.

'Can it go further?' Megan giggled. 'I mean, can it scan deeper? Show the lactiferous ducts? Or as far as the pectoralis muscles?'

Owen thumbed the device and the skin disappeared as the scan displayed a subcutaneous layer, but quickly flicked it back again. 'I'd rather not.'

Megan turned to face him, eager to see the device for herself. He showed her how to adjust it, the touch-sensitive plates at its rear that looked and felt so unlike any human design. 'I can show you more,' he urged her. 'I can take you to Torchwood now, show you everything.'

'Steady on, Owen,' she told him, 'I'm on duty again in an hour. Let's see how this thing works, then…'

She ran the device over his jacket. Owen could see the display reflected in the mirror, over her shoulder. He helped her position her palm and fingers on the device, holding the back of her hand like a caress.

After a few false starts, Megan was able to adjust the scan. Owen watched his jacket dissolve in the display, then his crumpled shirt. She focused on his nipple with its little halo of short dark hairs. He felt her hand move down, until he could no longer see the display reflected. He could feel the device pressed lightly against his body. Slowly down his midriff. Over his navel. Below his belt now, pressing against his crotch.

Megan smiled as she studied the display. 'I see this thing has a zoom facility.'

Owen raised his eyebrows in surprise. 'I didn't know the scanner could do that.'

'I wasn't talking about the scanner,' said Megan.

Owen lifted up her hand and took the Bekaran device from her. 'When does your shift start?'

'About an hour,' said Megan, and took his free hand in hers. Guided it over her breast. 'So we still have time for a shag. For old times' sake.'

TWENTY

How did you come to be here? Everything recently seems to be a blur of noise and lights and the stink of early evening. Even at the best of times, no one in the city is going to stop to ask 'Are you OK?' or 'Are you lost?' or 'You seem hurt, is there anything I can do?' The usual crush of people on a Sunday has thinned anyway, and nobody gives you a second glance when they're already too busy hurrying past to get to their car or bus or train, to get away from the city, to get home to their family, to get out of this foul evening weather.

The gunshot wound throbs. You've never been shot before, though you've shot others on service in Kunduz Province. They told you it was nothing like you'd expect, and they were right. At the moment of impact, there had been no pain; it was instead as though you received a violent shove in the shoulder that spun you around. The landing's window had loomed in front of you as you turned, and you raised your arms in an instinctive survival gesture before the frame and glass gave way and you tumbled over and through and down, down.

A drop of that distance into the rubbish skip might have killed you. That would have been a definitive end, no respite, no escape, no one else to go to. And you couldn't allow that to happen, not now, not after getting this far. But the black bags of decaying waste were bloated, and cushioned your fall. The stench of rotting vegetables still clings to you now like some foul perfume. You could pass yourself off as one of the homeless vagrants who in the day clustered around the station steps for financial scraps, except that the rain has driven even them into deep cover.

Your first thought was to run for Caerdydd Canolog, the obvious escape route for a train out to Cefn Onn where your parents used to live. That childhood memory has brought you here as another kind of survival instinct. You can't really remember how you got here from Guy's apartment, the pain of your wound and the shock of the fall must have confused you up to this point. And now, faced with the stark reality of your impossible situation and the grey façade of Cardiff Central, you're able to compose yourself a bit, to reassess things.

You look up, half-blinded by the rain that tumbles at you ceaselessly. Huge capitals declare 'Great Western Railway', dwarfing the station's newer name. Above these carved letters, the station clock shows 8.30 p.m.

Now that you're here, you only know that there's no way out for you. The rain lashes down pitilessly, a stinging wash of sound all around. The noise and fury of this downpour outside hides everything – your smell, your small, muffled noises of pain, the blood that soaks your blouse and skirt. Inside the building you will have no money, no cards, no hope of getting into a train carriage unobserved. You need to get back to the Bay. If your body can survive that far.

You step away from the station and cross the road, staring enviously at the taxis that swirl away into the traffic. You stumble on, unwilling or unable to enter the Welcome Centre, and into St Mary Street. The shops have long emptied, and the rain is now like a curtain falling over the tall redbrick building. A stab of pain in your shoulder twists a stifled scream from you, and you slump awkwardly against a travel agency window. The grinning display of a holiday scene mocks you from beyond the plate glass, and light spills out around you and into the street. By your feet, a gurgling drain has failed, and larger puddles are lapping over the edges of the pavement.

The pain has spread over your whole upper back now. Pressing your hand against the wound hasn't staunched the blood, and you're beginning to feel dizzy. As you lie against the shop window, you consider how you're going to get medical attention.

You can't let it finish here. There must be someone to go to. But first, you have to survive this.

You stumble on past the glass and iron of the indoor market. Someone has piled sandbags across the entrance to stem the flow of rainwater. In the distance, the ululating wail of a police siren cuts across the noise of the rain storm. And you have your answer.

Your vision starts to blur as you stagger along the pedestrianised Queen Street. Its cafés and pubs and restaurants are either closed or forlornly empty under the storm, but you barely notice as you make your way, step by painful step. As a girl, you watched an 8mm film show of a school outing to Jodrell Bank, and the film had stuck in the projector. The image of waving children in front of the radio telescope had juddered, frozen and then burnt until the film snapped and the screen showed only white. The people hurrying past you through the rain seem to be slowing down, the sound of the rain and the traffic is merging into a background hiss, and your surroundings are fading... not to white, but black.

So you fight to stay awake. You heard that siren. There must still be a chance here, you tell yourself. There has to be something up towards the Millennium Stadium.

And there is. The startling blue flash of an ambulance is visible in the middle distance, back towards St Mary Street. The siren is not sounding, but the emergency vehicle is making swift progress towards you. It slows as it approaches the corner of North Road and Duke Street, and that is your opportunity.

To step out into the road in front of it.

There's a buzz of activity, a flurry of half-glimpsed movement and impressionistic images.

You were luckier than you knew. There was a doctor in the back of this ambulance. Pretty, short dark hair. She has given you morphine for the pain, and is conducting an inventory of your injuries with a paramedic beside her. No broken limbs. A gash to the side of the head. To start with, they think you are a drunk who has stumbled in front of their ambulance. Your erratic movements, the disgusting smell of you, and your inability to speak clearly have led them to this conclusion. But their demeanour changes now that they find the gunshot wound. Even in your haze of dizziness and pain, you can see the doctor is startled by her discovery. But she stays professional. Radios it ahead. Starts to treat it.

It was Guy Wildman who got you here, in more ways than one. He told you a joke, as you were setting out for the sub-aqua trip, about how he could always get hold of the police in any emergency. A story he said he'd read in the paper. Some bloke phoned them to say his shed was being burgled. Cops didn't wanna know, said they had no one available in his area.

155

So he rang them back five minutes later, told them not to bother because he'd gone and shot the intruders. Course, in another five minutes flat, his house is surrounded by armed cops. And they catch the bastards who were burgling the bloke's shed. Cops weren't too happy, of course. 'I thought you said you'd shot the burglars,' said the arresting officer. 'And I thought you said you had no one available in my area,' said the bloke.

So, the best way to get to hospital? Get knocked over by an ambulance.

The pain in your shoulder has eased. The other, old pain is coming back, though. The need. The hunger.

Can't do anything about that now. Not just at the moment.

You need to rest. Recuperate. Sleep.

For now.

TWENTY-ONE

Ianto wondered whether he should knock. He stood by the office door and listened for a moment, thinking that he might determine from the sound of Jack's breathing whether he was asleep. Maybe, like Owen yesterday, Jack had dozed off at his desk after a hard night. Maybe, but not likely, Ianto acknowledged. His knuckles hesitated beside the door jamb, while he balanced the tray of coffee things in the other hand.

The office was in semi-darkness, most of the light pooling from under the angled head of an old-fashioned gooseneck desk lamp. It eerily illuminated a creepy display of glass specimen jars that Jack had arranged on a low table. Two alien claws floated in formaldehyde; the scaled fingers seemed to beckon Ianto from across the room.

He studied Jack. Deep, regular and rhythmic would indicate sleep. In the unlikely event that the boss wasn't awake, Ianto thought he himself could sneak back to the kitchen for breakfast alone, plus maybe an extra quarter of an hour of his own research down in the basement. He'd come into the Hub early this morning, a 7 a.m. start. That was in part because he was worried that the unceasing rain might flood the local roads on his way in from Radyr, and in part because he didn't entirely trust the sandbags around the Hub entrance. Even Llan-Duffred hill was streaming as he drove in, and the way the rainwater was sluicing around the city centre he could well imagine it pouring into the underground Hub complex and wreaking havoc.

Jack was slumped down in his office chair, his back to Ianto, exactly as he'd left him the previous night. Maybe he'd fallen asleep working there. With his head on his chest, the back of Jack's neck showed above his blue shirt collar.

His greatcoat was neatly folded on top of a table beside a towering pile of pamphlets, printouts, scuffed old books, and a few leathery old apples. Jack's RAF cap still hung from a makeshift wall hook, its gold oak leaf motif faintly catching the lamp's light. Ianto had once made the mistake of asking if the hat was fancy dress, and Jack had teased him for a whole week about men in uniform. He'd eventually let Ianto try it on (further gentle mockery), but explained with what sounded like considerable pride that he'd had it custom-made by Tranter the Hatter in Jermyn Street, St James. It had been no more than a moment's Googling for Ianto to discover that this was more teasing – Tranter's had never reopened after a V1 had razed the business to the ground in 1944.

Ianto blinked in surprise. A hand was beckoning him, waggling its fingers. He worked out a fraction of a second later that it wasn't an alien claw, it was Jack's arm, the shirt sleeves rolled up to the elbow, waving him into the room. 'Excellent timing,' said Jack. There was no sound of tiredness in his voice, but he stretched both arms wide, shrugged his shoulders, as though starting to get the stiffness out. Even from the doorway, Ianto heard him breathe in deeply through his nose. 'That's a new blend, isn't it? What magic have you worked with those beans, Ianto?' Another deep inhalation. 'Same old aftershave, though.'

'Good morning.' Ianto moved forward into the office, his eyes growing accustomed to the lamp light. He didn't ask whether Jack had slept well. Jack frequently stayed overnight here in his office, and although there was a bed in the room, Ianto had never once found him asleep. Come to think of it, he'd never seen Jack dozing off in meetings either, or exhausted at the end of a long day.

Jack moved the formaldehyde jar into a deep desk drawer, scooped up a pile of papers from the desk, and locked those in the drawer with it. This made space for the coffee tray, which held a cafetière and two cups, plus a notebook with phone messages annotated neatly in Ianto's meticulous handwriting.

Ianto pressed the cafetière to pour one cup, 'I thought you'd like to try the *kopi luwak* today,' Ianto told him.

Jack sat up straight in his chair. 'You're kidding me! The stuff made from beans eaten by a civet and then pooped out?'

Ianto poured him a cup. 'Yes…'

'The stuff the Indonesians go wild for? The stuff that costs, like, a hundred pounds a kilo?' Jack sniffed his cup suspiciously. His lips hovered, uncertain, at the rim. 'You didn't get this from Waitrose. Boy, I never thought I'd be quaffing cat-shit coffee.'

'I meant "yes, I am kidding you".'

Jack clucked in disapproval, but he was smiling.

Ianto smiled back. 'They said they were fresh out of cat-shit coffee this week. Something to do with their trucks can't through in this weather. So it's the usual.' He leaned over the desk to pick the notepad off the tray.

Jack leaned back in the chair to appraise him. 'Such a pert ass, Ianto. Were you ever an Italian waiter?'

'I'm more of a French Press man myself.' He handed Jack the phone messages. 'That question may constitute work-based sexual harassment.'

'Only if you ask me real nice.' Jack waggled the notebook. 'What is this?'

'Bit short on detail. Said they had a problem, and would you please call him back at Blaidd Drwg.'

'What sort of problem?'

Ianto shook his head. 'Didn't want to give me any more details. He sounded a bit upset, but was still apologetic about calling. Bit strange, really.'

Jack drained his coffee. He jumped up from his chair, loped across the room and hit the main lights. Ianto blinked away the painful contrast as they flickered on overhead. Jack dragged a conference phone onto one table, and threw the notebook and then the phone handset at Ianto. 'Dial 'em in while I get changed. No, no,' he said as Ianto gestured that he could step outside, 'I'm not real shy.' From a nearby cupboard he pulled out one of half a dozen identical blue shirts, split the cellophane with his thumbnail, and discarded the packaging in the bin with the old shirt.

Ianto finished dialling. The phone's ringtone hummed briefly around the office, and then a voice: 'Hello? Jonathan Meadows.'

'Direct line?' Jack said quietly to Ianto as he buttoned his shirt. 'No secretarial shelter. Must be important.' He yelled into the air in the direction of the phone: 'Jonathan! It seems like we were talking only yesterday. So, early shift for you?'

'Under the circumstances…' Even in those brief words, it was clear that Meadows was trying to hold back some rebuke. The quality of the sound was good enough for Ianto to hear the scientist take a calming breath. 'Mr Harkness, we're most grateful…'

'Captain Harkness,' he interrupted. 'But call me Jack.'

Another calming breath. 'Captain Harkness. We are, of course, most grateful that you've returned those four fuel packs.'

'All part of the service, Jonathan. If we can't help our Blaidd Drwg colleagues recover their carelessly mislaid nuclear equipment, then what are we in business for?' Jack grinned hugely at Ianto.

Meadows persevered. 'Most grateful, yes. And we… well, we know that you Torchwood people like to lay claim to things you come across.'

'Let me assure you, Jonathan, we have no use for nuclear fuel. Everything here works off triple-A batteries, believe me.'

'Then what have you done with the other ones?' asked Meadow plaintively.

Jack looked at Ianto.

Ianto looked at the notebook as though the original message might contain a clue. It didn't.

'The other what?' asked Jack.

'The other two nuclear fuel packs,' Meadows replied in an exasperated tone. There was a long pause. 'You do realise, don't you, that Wildman took six of them?'

The thunder disturbed Gwen during the night, its rumbling a constant presence for most of the early hours. At first she did that childhood thing of counting between the flash and the boom, but it was quickly obvious that the lightning strikes were already very close. The susurration of rain on the roof wasn't soothing her to sleep as it had when she was a child. In the end she got out of bed and went to the bathroom, and then for a glass of water. Rhys had snored through the whole night's storm, of course, oblivious to its noise and her wakefulness. She found him sprawled across three-quarters of the bed by the time she got back.

The half-light of early morning was breaking through their bedroom curtain. She was starting to think she'd finally get some proper sleep when the phone rang and shattered that hope.

Rhys mumbled from underneath his pillow, and reached out blindly for the bedside phone. He misjudged the distance, and the phone clattered to the carpet in a jangling mess of coiled wire. He emerged from under the sheets, grumbling, scowling through his tangle of bed hair. 'Gwen, that's your mobile. Get your mobile.' He slumped back onto his pillow.

Gwen found her phone by their chest of drawers. It was plugged into the wall socket, recharging but still switched on. The display told her who was calling: 'Torchwood'.

'Ianto?' Gwen said. 'Hi. Oh God, look at the time. Yeah, sorry. What is it?'

'Problem,' Ianto told her. 'You're needed back here now.'

'On my way.' Gwen flipped the phone shut. She turned around, and Rhys was already sat up in bed, glowering myopically at her.

'I thought you had this morning off,' he told her. 'I thought we *both* had this morning off. I promised you breakfast. Mushrooms. Sausages. I was in the mood for eggy bread.'

'What an incentive. But honestly, I have to go in.' She pulled her nightie over her head, and started rummaging around for knickers. 'And don't give me that look. We haven't got time.'

'*You* haven't got time,' Rhys rebuked her. He closed his eyes and slunk back under the sheets. 'We don't even eat together much any more, Gwen. I'm starting to think you prefer your works canteen.'

'That's Gaz again.'

'Maybe he's got a point,' mumbled Rhys from within the bedclothes. 'I've seen more of him these past few weeks than I have of you, even with him on the road this past fortnight. And I bet he wouldn't turn down my mushrooms.'

'I'm not sure I've got a polite answer for that.'

She was dressed in only a few minutes. When she went to give him a kiss before she left, Gwen discovered that Rhys was clutching his pillow, already back asleep.

Toshiko leaned against the island unit in the middle of her kitchen and gazed out through the window. Rain bounced off the sill and splashed back up against the glass. In the downpour outside, next door's cat – Tinkle? Winkle? one of the Teletubbies anyway – made a run for cover across the street and vanished under the neighbour's car. Toshiko peered through her window, out into the torrent of rain, and smiled at the prospect of following a languorous breakfast with a warm bath.

She'd eaten only two spoonfuls of muesli before Ianto called her. 'Yeah, it's always a problem,' she told him. 'I'm on my way. And tell Jack that he is the guy who put the "lie" into "you can have a lie-in tomorrow, Tosh".'

* * *

Jack was stretched out across a chair in the Boardroom when Ianto found him. He had his boots up on the conference table, and his eyes were closed. Ianto knew better than to assume he was sleeping. 'Owen's not answering,' he told Jack.

Jack cracked open one eye. 'Location?'

'His mobile must be inactive. No signal.'

The eye closed again. 'Remind me to bang his head when he gets in.'

A thin-faced man tapped Owen twice on his shoulder, an imperious signal of authority. 'You can't use that thing in here.' He used the same finger to point at a plastic sign on the wall that stated: 'Please switch off mobile phones while in the Emergency Department. They can interfere with sensitive medical equipment.'

Owen held up his mobile, which was showing no lights. 'Switched it off as soon as I arrived.' He slipped it into the pocket of his white doctor's coat, and smiled ingratiatingly.

The man before him was mid-fifties, greying hair. His face was lightly pock-marked, like ravaged sandstone. Dark eyes peered over tortoiseshell frames, appraising Owen. The good-quality shirt and silk tie, the well-polished patent leather brogues and the easy authority marked him out as the man in charge, rather than another angry patient complaining about the four-hour waiting time. 'Who are you and what are you doing in my department?'

Megan appeared at Owen's side. 'Ah, hello. Haven't had chance to introduce you both yet.'

'A friend of yours?' the man asked her sharply.

Megan nodded. 'Mr Majunath, I'm sorry, I didn't have the chance to introduce you earlier. This is Dr Owen Harper. He's a former... um... colleague of mine. We were students together...'

'Another from St George's?' interrupted Majunath, his expansive tone a complete contrast to his previous suspicion. 'That makes, what, three in the department at the moment?' He stuck out his arm, and gave Owen a brief, firm handshake. 'Amit Majunath, senior consultant. Barts man myself. Worked there for fifteen years, until they lost A&E. Wasn't expecting you here, Dr Harper. All hands to the pumps tonight, though. Literally,' he added, looking around them at the corridor floor, which seemed to be covered in muddy puddles and footprints. He intercepted a nurse as she tried to bustle past on her way out to reception. Owen noticed that Majunath was doing his staring-over-the-specs business on her, too. 'Can we have one of the HCAs get this cleaned up. Now?'

'Sorry, Mr Majunath,' replied the nurse, completely unfazed. She was obviously used to being seized and stared at in the corridor by senior staff. 'I'll have Cerys sort it out. With this awful weather, people have been traipsing mud in all day. The auxiliaries seem to spend all their time with mops and buckets.' She disengaged her elbow from Majunath's grasp, and disappeared around the corner.

'Insurance nightmare,' muttered Majunath, squinting at the muddy floor. 'Lucky that we don't have the management skulking around tonight. Tucked up in bed with their spreadsheets for company, we can but hope. Onwards, eh?' He bestowed a big smile on Megan, as though it was a personal favour. 'We have a jumper about to arrive. Only this one chose to throw herself at one of our ambulances, on its way in with a suspected MI. Nearly gave the driver a heart attack, too!' Having delivered this special news with such relish, he stalked off towards cubicles.

Owen grinned at Megan. 'He's worse than you told me!'

Megan shushed him, but giggled too. 'He has spider-sense. He'll hear you. I think he's a bit on edge tonight because we're still waiting for them to appoint a Clinical Director for the ED. Majunath is the hot favourite, though he thinks they're going to hold it against him because he can't speak Welsh. Seven other languages, but not Welsh. The Board was supposed to meet yesterday, all hush-hush. But I'm not sure they all got in because of this rotten weather.'

'You know how it is,' Owen told her. 'The first sign will be when white smoke starts coming out of the hospital incinerator.' He stepped aside as a health care assistant appeared and started to mop the mess up around them.

Even this far into the hospital building, the storm outside was making its presence felt. The bass notes of thunder rumbled in the distance. Since he'd arrived, at the start of Megan's night shift, all the patients that Owen had seen had been soaked. The nursing staff had cut the outer clothing off a teenage boy, brought in with a suspected wrenched ligament after a fall at home, and he'd been soaked to the skin, even though he'd been in reception for two hours after triage. The emergency patients, trolleyed straight through to cubicles or resus by paramedics, were all drenched, even dripping as they were prepared for immediate treatment.

Megan stood back to allow the HCA more room, and leaned against the wall next to Owen. 'You must have switched off your mobile pretty quickly when Majunath caught you using it.'

Owen shook his head. 'My phone's been switched off since we left your place. He saw me using something else.'

'What?'

Owen slipped his hand from his white coat, and held out the Bekaran device for Megan to take from him. 'I palmed it for my mobile. Wouldn't do for him to get his hands on this scanner. You, on the other hand…'

Megan turned the device over in her hands, wondering. She checked to see that no one else was looking at them. The HCA was squeezing his mop into a bucket at the far end of the corridor. Megan stammered: 'I'm not sure that…'

'Why not?' Owen ushered her back towards the cubicles. 'Come on, it's been a long shift. You've seen the crowd out in reception, it's not getting any smaller. And besides, how do you think I spotted that emphysema case so quickly? The one brought in from the RTA? The one your colleague thought was an obvious pneumothorax?'

'Owen!' she hissed at him.

'Well, it wasn't by waiting for the portable X-ray,' said Owen, 'or getting him in the ever-growing queue for MRI.' He indicated the device with a movement of his head.

'You're not even supposed to be working here,' persisted Megan. 'You know the hospital's not insured for you. And even if it was, well, using this… alien thing…' She thrust it back at him.

Owen didn't accept it. He could see from the way her eyes moved that she was worried someone else would see the device. He waited. She tried to stick it in his coat pocket, but he shoved his own hands in them to prevent her. 'Come on, Megan. Isn't that why you let me come here? We could have met up afterwards. Or you could have made your own way to Torchwood. We'll go there later. I want you to see it.'

She relaxed her arm, and Owen moved in to hold her shoulders. 'Try it.'

'How can I explain it?' she protested. 'To Majunath? To any of them?'

'You don't have to. And if anyone asks, you can say it's a new pervasive device that you're trialling for me.'

They went into resus. Majunath and another doctor were attending to one of the other patients from the RTA, and waved away Megan's offer of assistance. 'Thank you, but no,' Majunath said. 'I think we may be on the final cycle here, anyway. One more, I think, Doctor Wilkins.'

Owen nudged Megan. On the opposite side of the room was the body of another road traffic accident victim, waiting to be portered away to the morgue. A blood-stained white sheet had been drawn up over the face. Megan was about to pull it away, but Owen indicated that she should leave it. He helped her position the scanner to one side of the corpse, and the photorealistic image of the sheet slowly melted away to reveal the hairy skin of the victim. 'Through the epidermis to the dermis.' Owen narrated the scan like a medical lecture. 'Look at that, you can make out the individual blood vessels, the nerves... he's a bit of a bear, isn't he, so look at those hair follicles... and through the subcutaneous adipose layer... and now that we're through the basement membrane, we can see the muscle and bone...

'Look there!' Megan pointed excitedly, trying to keep her voice down and avoid alerting the doctors working on the other side of the room. 'The sternal end of the fifth rib is split.'

'Sternum bifidum, very good,' breathed Owen. 'That's quite a rare neuroskeletal anomaly. If this poor bloke was still alive, we might be able to explain why he sometimes got respiratory difficulty. Bit late for him now.' He studied her reaction. 'Not too late for some of the others.'

'I think we should stop, if everyone agrees?' Across the room, Majunath had abandoned the resuscitation. 'Time of death, 8.46 a.m. Thank you everyone.'

Outside resus, a young nurse hurried up to Megan. She was a short, thin girl, and her neatly pressed uniform and eager manner marked her out as a new starter, late teens at most. Her badge told Owen she was Roberta Nottingham. 'Can you come through to eight, Megan? Mrs Boothe is a bit distressed.'

'OK, Bobbie, I'm right with you.' She moved off after her, explaining to Owen as they walked: 'Pregnant woman, mid-twenties, also in that RTA. Date of confinement is next Thursday.' She paused before Owen pulled back the curtain, and whispered to him: 'That was the driver we just saw in resus. Her husband.'

In cubicle eight, a small woman in a blue surgical smock watched them with frightened eyes. 'I can't feel him moving, doctor. Is he going to be all right?' Her fingers splayed out protectively over her pregnant bump.

'OK, Leanne.' Megan moved across to hold her hand and smooth the hair from her pasty white forehead. 'We'll see. They're going to have a bed for you in maternity really, really soon.' From Megan's expression, a pleading look at Nottingham over the top of the pregnant woman's head, Owen could tell this was unlikely to be true. Nurse Nottingham frowned discouragingly, with the smallest of head shakes.

'Non-stress test?' Owen asked.

'This is Dr Harper, Leanne. He's come to offer a second opinion.'

Nurse Nottingham said to Owen: 'Excellent fœtal heart rate. Two accelerations in twenty minutes, both at least fifteen beats above the baseline heart rate, and both lasted for least fifteen seconds.'

Leanne looked panicked. 'What's wrong? Was the baby hurt in the accident? And where's Barry? What's happened to my husband?'

'The ultrasound showed no sign of any problems with the baby, Leanne. Let's concentrate on you and the baby for the moment. Don't worry, try to stay calm.'

Owen said to the nurse: 'Can you go and check on that maternity bed please, Bobbie? Thanks.'

The nurse stepped out of the cubicle, pulling the curtain back into place as she left.

Owen took the Bekaran device from Megan's pocket. He ran it over the pregnant woman, without removing or lifting her smock. He indicated to Megan that she should study the scanner image. The blue-patterned smock material vanished, then the mother's skin, muscle, and suddenly the baby was visible.

By adjusting the resolution, Owen was able to show the position of the baby's limbs, the head, the placenta, the mother's bones. He gave the mother a running commentary of reassurance as he did so, while all the time checking for Megan's reaction to what he was showing her.

'That's just amazing.'

'I've been so worried,' Leanne told them, unable to see the image on the scanner. 'I could hardly go in a car since the last accident, and now I've gone and got in another one.'

'The last accident?' asked Megan. 'When was that?'

Leanne heaved a great sniff, and then an equally large sigh. 'About ten years ago. I was only about thirteen or fourteen. My mum's car got rearended on the M4.'

'That's a long time ago, Leanne. Were you or your mum hurt?'

'She was all right. I was in the back, where the truck smacked into us.

Broke my pelvis. I was off school for a month.'

Owen indicated the scanner image. 'There's where the pelvic fracture was, can you see? It's healed completely. And now look at the baby's head…'

He stood up, and gestured to Megan to come with him. 'Should be fine, Leanne,' he said as they stepped through the curtain. 'Back in a minute.'

The staff-room was empty. Owen sat down at the coffee table, and played back the scan images on the Bekaran device. 'Can you see the distortion in the pelvic bones? Not something you might have picked up before the birth.'

Megan stared. 'What do you mean?'

'Cephalo-pelvic disproportion,' said Owen. 'I don't think her pelvis is big enough to let the baby through the birth canal.' He switched off the image. 'As if she hasn't got enough to cope with, after losing her husband tonight.'

Megan took the Bekaran device from him. 'This is just astonishing.'

'I told you.'

'This could speed up diagnosis for the whole department. Owen, they're stacked up in rows out there in reception, a night like this. We could get them through twice as fast. No, *faster*, I bet! Just by having these for triage. And the whole idea of waiting forever to get an MRI or an X-ray…'

'You're missing the point,' sighed Owen. She looked at him, baffled, and he continued: 'It's not this technology that's important. It's where it comes from. What it implies about other alien tech. This is the good stuff, right? This is what can make things better. Us having this is like a group of chimpanzees having a digital camera. If they work out what the buttons do, even by accident, well they can take nice pictures and look at them. They might not be David Bailey, but it's better than scratching shapes in the dirt with a stick. Thing is, it's not going to do them any harm if all they want to do with this thing they've found is to wipe their arses on it.'

He could see from Megan's widening eyes that she was beginning to understand. She'd stood up and walked to the window now.

'What if the chimps found a hand grenade?' she said.

Owen nodded. 'What if they found a grenade launcher? What if they found a flamethrower? What if they were given a box full of anthrax spores?' He leaned forward. 'And what if they weren't just chimps?'

Megan shivered, as though there was a draught at the window.

'Torchwood's not just about potential benefits,' said Owen. 'It's about real and present danger.'

Megan stared out of the staff-room window, into the storm. After a very long pause, she faced him again. 'I want to see the rest.'

Owen didn't have time to reply. The staff-room door opened, and in walked Nurse Nottingham. 'There's a bed on maternity, Megan.'

'Excellent,' Megan replied, shooing her from the room as she followed her out. 'Keep it, even if you have to get in it yourself. I'll write up the notes, but tell them it's CPD and they should prepare for a Cæsarean. Don't mess her about with a trial of labour, she's been through enough already. They can explain to her. But someone's going to have to tell her about her husband.'

They were at the registration board now. Megan started to write up notes in Leanne's file, explaining to Mr Majunath about a 'suspected CPD', so that she didn't have to oversell her diagnostic brilliance. Owen, however, had seen something on the whiteboard, scribbled in blue marker pen against cubicle six.

'Sandra Applegate,' said Owen.

Majunath looked up. 'Yes. She's the jumper I mentioned earlier. Threw herself in front of one of our ambulances.' The senior consultant shook his head slowly in disbelief at the madness of the world. He picked up the phone with one hand, and his other hand raced down a list of numbers pinned to the wall. 'At least, we *assume* she jumped. She has had a fall, obviously. But she appears also to have a gunshot wound. We're going to have to inform the police…'

Owen had already peeled off his white doctor's coat, and dropped it on a nearby trolley. He reached into his jacket pocket, and brandished his Torchwood ID at the astonished senior consultant.

'Don't bother with that phone call,' he told Majunath. 'I *am* the police.'

TWENTY-TWO

'Where's Owen?' asked Toshiko Sato's voice

Gwen turned from her desk to see Toshiko standing by the entrance to the Hub's main area, bedraggled and dripping rainwater on to the floor. 'Couldn't he drag himself in here like the rest of us?' She brandished something in Jack's direction. Her apparent intention to look intimidating was spoiled by the bedraggled newspaper that she'd been using as an improvised umbrella.

Ianto managed to sound as though Owen's absence was his fault. 'We couldn't reach him this morning. I haven't seen him since yesterday afternoon. He wasn't irradiated any more, and said he was going out to celebrate. Didn't say where. He was a bit grumpy.'

'What are you, his mother?' asked Jack.

Toshiko peeled off her wet coat to reveal wet jacket and trousers. They looked almost as wet as the coat. 'The radiation has changed him.' She affected an American accent, ignoring Jack's mocking look. '"Doctor Owen Harper, physician, scientist. An accidental dose of radiation alters his body chemistry. And now, a startling metamorphosis occurs. Owen Harper is… the Incredible Sulk."'

Gwen laughed along with her. '"Captain Harkness, don't make me grumpy! You wouldn't like me when I'm grumpy!"'

'Thank you, ladies,' said Jack firmly. 'Owen going AWOL is not our only problem right now. Doesn't help, but let's save the ass-kicking for when he's in range.' Gwen watched his reaction. Behind his cheerful sarcasm, he was keeping something from them. Not information, she was sure. He'd not keep that from them. More likely to be his own worries about Owen, things that she knew he felt but that wouldn't help them at the moment, stuff that would only get in the way. That would be typical of Jack – reassuring, supporting, keeping them focused. In the police, she'd seen several teams deteriorate into helplessness when the head of the investigation had lost it in front of them. Their guv'nor, raging at a briefing meeting. Or cursing over a pint at the local pub. Revealing his own frustration, his own powerlessness – and, by implication, theirs. Not Jack. This guv'nor wasn't like that. He gestured towards the Boardroom: 'Shall we?'

Within minutes, they had been succinctly briefed by Jack. 'So, it turns out that we still have two more fuel rods to locate. And our missing soldier, Sandra Applegate, is probably hunting them down as we sit here.'

'You think she could have survived that fall?'

'Gwen, she did survive that fall. Unless someone was waiting for her to drop from the window.' Jack paused, as though he was considering the likelihood of this. 'So how can she be so resilient? Did she know she could make it? No, that shot merely carried her forward and she couldn't stop herself.' Another pause for contemplation. 'The other soldier, Bee, faced his death like there was nothing to fear. And Wildman… could he really have thought he might survive that drop from the eighth floor? Maybe there's something else that could survive a drop like that, but the autopsies showed that Bee and Wildman were human… What are we missing?'

His statement was punctuated by a roll of thunder from outside.

'Whoa,' Jack laughed. 'Timing, huh? And that must be some kinda storm, if we can hear it all the way down here. Ianto, run upstairs and close the bathroom window.'

Ianto looked for a moment as though he might take this request seriously.

'The weather has deteriorated dramatically,' Toshiko told them.

'Oh, you think?' smiled Jack helpfully. 'Are you dried out yet?'

Toshiko ignored him, and punched up some images on the meeting room main display. 'Here are some views from around the Bay area… the city centre…' More images. 'The wetlands… out into the Bristol Channel…'

The views came from traffic cameras, security cameras, CCTV. The images varied between grainy monochrome in half-lit areas through to higher quality colour shots of well-illuminated buildings. What they all had in common was that they showed chaos and devastation. In the shopping areas of the city, the pedestrianised streets were awash with streams of water carrying scraps of newspaper and discarded fast food containers. Shop awnings were ripped from their metal structures, and flapped madly in rage. In one road, cars crawled through a torrent of water that reached their sills. In another, a white van had slewed off the carriageway and into a post box. A park bandstand was whipped by the trees and bushes that bordered it. The foliage was thrashing about as though it was alive.

It was Monday morning, the start of the rush hour, but nowhere were there crowds of people. The few individuals Gwen could make out were struggling along, leaning into the rain and the wind like adventurers struggling against a foreign climate. The selection of images continued with a security camera on a boat in the Bay. She watched with growing incredulity as the camera surreally kept the seats and railings of the boat steady in the frame. Behind the boat, Bay water churned. Passengers were flung around like discarded dolls in a toy-box.

'It's getting worse,' Toshiko observed.

They were looking at an apparently endless queue of traffic on the motorway. Gwen thought it looked like a shivering snake made up of flickering headlights. Windscreen wipers madly, fruitlessly swiped away at the water. In the grey daylight and the endless deluge of rain, it was impossible to tell the colours of cars, and only the sodium orange of the motorway lights gave any indication that this was a colour image. 'Could it be worse?'

'You'd be surprised,' replied Toshiko in a tone that suggested the exact opposite. Her fingers danced over the keyboard again, and a different picture emerged on the main screen. A long queue of traffic still, but this time bright sunshine sparkled off the metal trims of the motionless cars, and their vibrant colours were clearly visible.

Gwen wondered if Toshiko had switched to the same stretch of motorway at an earlier point, but the timecode on the image showed it was a live feed. 'Where's that?'

'Eight miles further up the M4,' Toshiko explained. 'The end of the same queue. But look at the weather.'

Jack looked as amazed as Gwen felt. 'How?'

'The effect is localised.' More keystrokes. 'Here's the most recent satellite pass, about twenty-three minutes ago. It's like a typhoon, but restricted within an eight-kilometre radius.'

'Radius means a circle,' said Jack. 'So where's the centre?'

Toshiko overlaid a pattern of lines on the satellite image. 'From an analysis of the variables, it's out in the Bay. And you can see from the Bay cameras that there's nothing out there except for plenty of churning water and a crowd of seasick sailors.'

Gwen studied the composite image. 'It's underwater.'

'It's underwater,' confirmed Toshiko. 'Something must be coming through the Rift, below the surface. My projections show that if it continues then it will create tidal waves across the Bay. Maybe out into the Bristol Channel, too. The Wetlands Nature Reserve is flooding already—'

Jack laughed humourlessly. 'Aptly named.'

'And you saw what's happening out there above the water. A couple of water taxis were sunk by freak waves. They're struggling to prevent damage in the Roath Basin – the lightship berthed there has already smashed into the quayside.'

'Yeah, great place for a lightship.'

Gwen laughed at Jack's sarcasm. 'You'll never become a Blue Badge Guide with that attitude.'

'The tourists wouldn't like the stories I could tell them about Cardiff.'

'Hello?' interrupted Toshiko. 'Do you want to see these data and schematics?'

'Data,' Jack said. 'That's like information, right?'

Toshiko gave him a freezing look. 'Or I could just stop now. Go and do some more correlations of the variables on my own.' She paused, as though to let this sink in. Jack affected to look contrite, and Gwen stifled further laughter. Toshiko continued: 'The telemetry from the boreholes is so confusing, it's as though water is flowing uphill. Thing is, even though there have been unexpected tidal surges way up the Rivers Taff and Ely, it's all caused by this localised weather system.'

Gwen tried to put the information together in her head, and could see a flaw. 'If it's localised, then where is all this rain coming from?'

'Think of it like a localised typhoon. It's sucking water from the Bay. Dropping it back over the local area in this huge thunderstorm.'

'So why's the Bay not emptying?'

Toshiko looked at her, surprised. Gwen was started to feel like a slow pupil in the GCSE Geography class. 'Where do you suppose the water there came from in the first place? Out in the Bristol Channel. And beyond that, the Celtic Sea and the Atlantic Ocean. Imagine that lot dumped all over the vale of Glamorgan.'

Gwen's head was starting to spin. 'But a *typhoon*? A tropical storm, in Cardiff?'

'And I estimate that it's only Category 2 at the moment. The only good thing I can see is that the eye isn't moving. It's still out in the Bay. Or at least...' Toshiko checked some more figures. 'It's encroaching very slowly. But whatever is coming through, it's still coming.'

'And there's nothing to say that it won't suddenly get a shift on,' said Gwen. She thought about what Toshiko had explained to them the previous evening. The slow tsunami. Suddenly, it didn't seem so slow after all.

Jack slapped his hands on the table, an unexpected sound that startled Gwen. He was no longer pensive, he'd reached his decision.

'So, no Owen. We'll have to work without him. Ianto, keep trying his number and locator. Gwen and Tosh, you're gonna have to get out there into the Bay, find out what this thing is. Take the mini-sub, that needs two. And I'm going back to Wildman's apartment. I'm gonna find those missing power packs if I have to tear the place apart. Hey, I may tear it apart anyway, it already needs a makeover. Apart from that, who can tell? There are too many variables at the moment.' He thought about this briefly. 'D'you see what you've done to me, Tosh? You've got me using the word "variables". Now I *know* I've been sitting here too long.' He picked up his greatcoat from a nearby chair where he'd draped it earlier, and prepared to leave.

Gwen watched Toshiko for a reaction. She was shutting down the various programs on her computer, getting ready to follow her latest instructions from Jack. But Gwen hesitated. Despite her police training. Despite that instinct to obey orders without questioning every detail. Despite the copper's belief that the guv'nor assigns the jobs, picks the people, and doesn't have to say why. Somehow, in Torchwood, that was different now. After handling the stuff that she had – that they all had – in the past couple of months, she'd begun to believe that asking the obvious questions was what kept you alive.

'What about Sandra Applegate?'

Jack was shrugging his greatcoat over his shoulders. 'What about her?'

'D'you think she's human?'

Jack gave them a wave as he left. 'Enjoy your dive, ladies.'

Gwen wasn't any more reassured as the door closed behind him.

* * *

Owen knew it wasn't like brushing aside the local pointy-heads when he and the Torchwood team cruised into a scene of crime. When they knew that their reputation, their previous contacts, the whole *look* of them as they swept through the existing security cordon, was all the authority that they needed to operate unchallenged. The staff here would know nothing of Torchwood. There would be no scare stories, whispered among the staff as cautionary tales, of petty bureaucrats peremptorily brushed aside, or their careers stalled because they stepped in Torchwood's way and got trampled.

'I don't understand, Dr Harper,' said Majunath. 'I thought you said you were the relief SHO for this evening's shift?' Was Majunath going to question his police credentials, now? Owen knew from his own former career in A&E that doctors relished the opportunity to put the police in their place when it came to clinical priorities. Majunath had his personal authority at stake from the moment that ID card appeared under his nose. And Owen needed Megan to see him in control, to show her how Torchwood was an organisation that could get things done, take control. An organisation that she would want to join.

It was the storm that saved him from Majunath's suspicion. A fresh gurney stretcher crashed through the doors at the far end of the ED, with paramedics clinging to it as though they were launching a bobsled. It finally careered to a slippery stop beside Majunath. Both paramedics were drenched, water still cascading off their fluorescent jackets. The taller one exhaled upwards to blow the rain off his face and out of his floppy ginger hair. 'Four more on the way,' he explained to Majunath breathlessly. More water flicked onto the floor as he nodded at the unfortunate victim on the gurney. Owen noted quickly that the boy was probably early teens, unconscious, intubated, very cyanosed.

'Water taxi capsized in the Bay,' the paramedic was saying. He twisted the gurney through ninety degrees, and pushed it on through the doors of resus, all the while rattling off his diagnosis and the treatment he'd already given.

'I thought we were trying to divert patients to Royal Gwent?' Majunath snapped at the new arrivals.

'Storm's heading that way, too' explained Megan.

Majunath groaned. 'Swansea, then? St David's?'

'Well, this little lad is here *now*,' muttered the red-haired paramedic.

Majunath reacted immediately, professional once more. 'I'll take this one,' he told Megan. 'You and Doctor Harper take the next as they arrive.'

He snapped a swift glanced at his wristwatch. 'You may need to extend your shift, I'm afraid.' He bellowed into the air: 'Auxiliary? There's more water to mop up here.' And then he was gone, the doors into resus flapping behind him.

Owen seized Megan's hand. 'Come on. We need to check out Sergeant Applegate first.'

'Sergeant Applegate? You mean you *know* this woman?' Megan allowed him to lead her further down from the curtained cubicles, to the first of several small examination rooms. Just before they stepped in, Owen felt Megan hold back. She didn't let go of his hand, but she stared at him warily. 'She has a gunshot wound, Owen. And you had a gun…'

He squeezed her hand in reassurance. 'I don't know how she got shot. I do know that it wasn't me.' He pulled her into the cubicle and closed the door.

Sandra Applegate lay on the trolley, pale and still, her breath shallow but regular. Owen could see from the monitors that she was stable. He briefly examined the saline drip that was attached to Applegate by a long, clear tube, and then checked the other attachment, a bag of group O blood.

Megan was considering the patient notes, and looking surprised. 'She's not bad for someone who's lost a lot of blood. She has a gunshot wound to the lateral portion of her upper arm. Proximal humerus fracture, with the bullet retained beneath the scapula. They anticipated removing the bullet arthroscopically.'

Owen came around the bed and read the notes over her shoulder. 'That'll avoid a traditional exposure. Good thing too, it means not complicating her fracture care.' He was close behind Megan, so near that he could breathe in deeply and smell her short, dark hair. The antiseptic tang of the Emergency Room faded away around him. He closed his eyes, inhaled again, and the scents of her room came back to him. The sweet, chocolate fragrance of Angel Innocent, an indulgence almost as surprising as finding himself in bed with Megan. The lingering notes of the Château La Fleur on her hot breath. The musky warmth of post-coital cotton sheets. The fusty familiarity of an old-fashioned woollen blanket, pulled up over his face.

'They *anticipated* the arthroscopy?' he asked, suddenly back in the room. 'Why did they change their minds?'

Megan indicated the small table beside the patient's bed. In a kidney-shaped metal bowl they could both see a bloodied bullet. 'The bullet was subsequently found on the bed-sheet. The examining doctor suggests it must have worked its way out.'

Owen was about to comment on how unlikely that was when the cubicle door opened behind them. He stepped back from Megan, his movement betraying his guilt, and almost collided with a rangy, long-haired man in a scruffy white coat. From his stooped posture, his five-o'clock shadow and the rings below his eyes, this was a junior doctor coming to the end both of his shift and of his patience. The new arrival surveyed Owen with barely concealed hostility. 'This isn't your patient.' A statement made as an accusation.

'She is now.' Owen bridled. He fumbled in his jacket for the ID, and waggled it dismissively under the guy's nose. He was unsure whether he was offended by this young doctor's manner or being interrupted with Megan or being found close to her.

Megan swivelled around to face this other doctor. 'Jonny,' she smiled smoothly. 'I was really curious about this bullet. How did you manage to extract it? The notes say you were all set for arthroscopic intervention.'

'Oh, Megan, hi…' Jonny considered this for a moment. 'Beats me. I was sure it was lodged in the subacromial space. Bugger of a job to extract, but it looked right up Freeman's street.'

'That's out in Newport, right?' observed Owen.

Megan elbowed him. 'Not helping,' she hissed. 'Mr Freeman's very keen on promoting the Trust's minimal invasive procedures.'

'I must have been mistaken,' admitted Jonny glumly. He thumbed both his eyes in a reflex gesture, tiredness seeming to overwhelm his anger. 'Unless the bullet worked its way out on its own. Or the pressure dressing I applied is like a really powerful magnesium sulphate. Ha, ha!' His mirthless laughter at his own medical joke was cut short by the start of a huge, unstifled yawn.

Owen saw his opportunity. 'They're bringing more in from that capsized water taxi. Mr Majunath said we should remind you that he's asking everyone to extend their shifts—'

Jonny let out a groan to rival the noisy thunderstorm outside.

'—and we've already extended. So if you crack on with the new arrivals, we can finish off with this patient.' He studied Jonny's wary reaction, and added slyly: 'No need to make a big fuss about the thing with the bullet.'

The junior doctor's tired eyes lit up briefly at this exit strategy. 'OK. And you'll want these. Radiology finally sent her second set down.' He passed over a broad brown folder, and slipped out before Owen could change his mind.

Owen activated the light-box on the wall, and the fluorescent tubes stuttered into life. He slotted the films into place, and pointed out a detail to Megan.

'Another bullet,' Megan breathed. 'But there's no visible damage to the mid-thoracic vertebral bodies. No bone fragments. Little or no tissue damage.'

'Think it through,' Owen said. 'A gunshot wound to the spine would cause further nerve and tissue injury, even further from the bullet's path.'

'Nothing in the notes here.'

'She jumped in front of the ambulance, remember that? She was mobile. So unless one of the paramedics shot her in the ambulance, that thing was already there.' Owen took the folder from her and closed it. 'It's not a bullet. And I've seen it before, in an autopsy.'

Megan was astonished. 'What is all this, mate? You knew about this patient before you came here. What makes her so special?'

'Apart from that thing in her spine, you mean?' Owen checked Applegate's monitors again, satisfied himself that she was stable, before he sat down on one of the visitors' chairs. 'We've been looking for her all day.'

'We? Oh, Torchwood, right.' She sat down next to him. 'Why *is* she so important?'

Owen looked into Megan's hazel eyes. She wasn't questioning his motives any more. She wasn't quizzing him about Torchwood. Megan wanted to know about this mysterious woman; she looked to him for the answers. She wanted in, he could sense it now, and he had control. So it grated that he didn't know.

Why *did* Torchwood need to locate Applegate so urgently?

When Jack had phoned in to the Hub earlier, Owen had felt trapped and powerless. He wanted to be out there with them, with Jack and Toshiko. Not leaving it to them and the *new girl*. He hadn't felt those emotions, not like that, since way back when he first joined Torchwood. Those first few days, when he'd been overwhelmed by the newness and the strangeness and the *alien-ness* of everything he'd been asked to do. When he'd driven home and thrown up in the sink, every night for eight days. So to feel that familiar sick impotence in his stomach when Jack had phoned in to demand that he stay put, to do the research, to leave the rest of them to it... That had fermented into a kind of bitterness, an anger. He'd grudgingly accepted his research role earlier. Finished it with his usual efficiency, if not his usual diligence, and then left.

At least he could tell Megan what he'd found.

'Why *is* she so important?'

Owen watched Applegate's chest rise and fall rhythmically under the hospital gown. Her short blonde hair stuck out awkwardly on the white pillow. 'She is a brave and resourceful soldier. And we think she's mixed up in something she can't control. Something that's got out of hand.' He turned away from the prone body of Applegate on the bed, and leaned in conspiratorially towards Megan's chair. 'Thirty-four years old, unmarried, only child, parents both deceased. Her army record is remarkable. Currently a respected trainer at Caregan, but she's got a string of awards and recognition, starting at only 21. Got a commendation for bravery and swift action after a shooting incident near her posting while she was off-duty. Most recently she has a QCVS and a QCB from separate tours of duty in Afghanistan. In Khost, she was injured in a sniper attack, but remained in position to neutralise the gunman's fire while the rest of the patrol drew back, and only then did she get her injuries seen to.'

'You sound impressed.'

'Wouldn't you be? For fun, she works with a charity for blind ex-Service personnel on hundred-metre dives at Dahab in the Red Sea.'

'I bet she's kind to animals, too,' said Megan. 'And you got all this by researching her Army records?'

'She has no significant financial commitments, sometimes rents a small place in Porthcawl because it's handy for scuba diving. Her credit record is OK. No overdraft. She pays off her Visa on time, in full, every month—'

'Hang on, Owen! You don't get that sort of information from a quick search on the Internet!'

'That's every month, without notable exceptions,' continued Owen relentlessly. 'And the Visa bill's rarely more than three hundred quid, except when she bought herself some specialist diving equipment. So it's got to have been something really unusual, something outside the control of this brave and resourceful and organised woman, to cause her to go AWOL twenty-three days ago, wouldn't you think?'

Megan had her head in her hands now. 'How can you know all this?' She considered Owen, perhaps seeing him differently yet again this evening. 'I don't even have to ask really, do I? And all that stuff about the sniper incident and her injuries… maybe that's why she's coped so well with her wounds tonight. But hang on, you're not shooting at her, Torchwood doesn't want to kill her. So who does?'

Owen pondered the question. In the ensuing silence, he could hear that Applegate's breathing had changed. She was snuffling, short staccato snorts that soon turned into coughing.

Megan moved swiftly to the bedside and calmed Applegate, who was struggling with the oxygen mask.

'Have you been awake for long?' Owen asked her from the foot of the bed.

Applegate peered at him, waiting for the cough to subside. 'For a few minutes. Just long enough to hear your very kind biography of me. Not to mention your routine as my new independent financial advisor.' She raised a wavering hand to dismiss Owen's attempt to explain. 'I don't need you to say where you got that information. Unlike your colleague here…?'

'Dr Tegg. I'm supervising your treatment. Please call me Megan.'

'Owen Harper. Dr Owen Harper, actually.'

Applegate had composed herself a little more now. 'Unlike Megan here, I do know about Torchwood. Because it *was* Torchwood who tried to kill me.' Her brown eyes glittered at him. 'So one way or another, Dr Harper, you've located me just in time.'

TWENTY-THREE

Now that Sandra Applegate was fully conscious, Owen and Megan raised the back of her hospital bed so that she could sit up more comfortably. Owen checked the monitors again, satisfying himself that their patient was stable. She was still very pale, though not the deathly grey colour he'd seen earlier. Her gestures were getting stronger, and her voice no longer wavered when she spoke.

'Your colleagues made a mistake, Dr Harper. They didn't know I needed Torchwood's help.'

'Guess how often we hear that, Sandra.' Owen scraped his chair nearer to the bed. 'So, what's your story?'

His tone was light, unthreatening. He watched the tension drain away from Sandra, and her face seemed to brighten. 'They made a mistake. Oh, I mean, I can understand it, don't get me wrong. I'd gone back to the flat for one last attempt to talk Guy out of his stupid plans... But he wasn't there, and they thought I was working with Tony and Guy.'

'The hairdressers?' frowned Owen.

Sandra rolled her eyes at him. 'Tony Bee and Guy Wildman. My diving buddies. So I don't blame your colleagues, it wasn't their fault, really.'

'You're very forgiving, for someone who we shot.'

'When I tell you what I've been through, you won't think that.'

Owen smiled reassuringly. 'I'm hard to surprise.'

Sandra's eyes flickered between Owen and Megan, as though quickly assessing their mood. Then she closed them, and drew in a deep and shuddering breath, before releasing it like a slowly deflating tyre.

'It started,' she began, 'when we took our scuba-diving trip out in the Bay. If we're diving locally, we usually take a boat out of Porthcawl, maybe get out as far as Lundy Island to see the puffins and grey seals. But Guy could only take a short weekend, so we decided to explore out into Cardiff Bay.

'Easy enough to charter a boat locally. Nice clear day, not far, nothing too adventurous we thought. Until we saw the hatch poking out of the sediment. First thought, of course, was that it must be discarded debris. When it wouldn't budge, then you start to think it's a wreck – but this clearly wasn't anything like the wreck of the *Louisa* out there. This had a dull shine, even that far down. Modern, not nineteenth-century. Not even twentieth-century. When we opened it up, it was an airlock. But what kind of modern submarine would be buried down there?

'One of us should have stayed outside. I'm the most experienced diver, I should have known that. But we all went in – it was an unbelievable space, more like a hallway than an airlock. And once we were in, the door shut behind us and the place started to fill with gas.

'Do you know what I mean when I say that the military instinct kicked in, Dr Harper? For me and Tony, I mean. Checking for exit options, areas of danger, ensuring our backs were covered. Even unarmed, we were ready. Guy was starting to panic, though – scraping at the exit door with his bare hands, tearing off his own mask. That's when we knew it was oxygen, and we could breathe. Our relief didn't last long, because when the inner door opened what we saw made us abandon all that hard-learned military training.

'It wasn't human, that much was obvious. I mean, like with the hatch, your first thought is to make it normal: it's a bloke in a mask; we've stumbled into a film set; it's a weird kind of scuba gear; it's a trick of the light.

'It wasn't. It was alien. Tony's a big guy, you know, six-three. But this thing dwarfed him. Easily strong enough to force me and Tony further through that inner door. Guy was curled up in a corner, whimpering, terrified. It picked him up with one of its claws and threw him after us into the ship. The alien ship.'

Sandra swallowed hard at this point.

'The next bit is all a bit hazy now. I prided myself before all this that nothing could faze me. But it's not like the uncertainties of a combat zone. My first commander told me that the more you sweat in peace, the less you bleed in war. Let me tell you, no amount of readiness training could have prepared us. Maybe I was starting to react like Guy had, I don't know. All I remember now is being surrounded by alien machinery, and an agonizing pain in my back, and then I must have passed out.'

Owen pointed up at the wall, where the light-box still displayed her X-ray images. 'That thing was inserted into you. I think it's a tracking device.'

Megan stared at them, incredulous. 'What is this, *The X Files*?'

Owen touched her lips gently with his finger, and encouraged Sandra to continue. 'What do you remember next?'

'When I came round, Tony was pulling me towards the exit. Guy was helping him. The pain was still intense, as though I'd been knifed in the middle of my back. Yet there was no blood. I was able to stumble out with them. Tony got us back through the airlock. Don't ask me how. There was a lot more of the ship visible around the airlock when we got out, as though the sediment had started to fall away around the prow of some dull grey rocket.

'I don't remember much of the journey home, Tony seemed to handle that. Maybe my mind blotted it out, maybe it was like post-traumatic stress – we've seen that in the services, of course. "The invisible injury", it's called. Not a mark on you physically. But PTSD isn't something the Army likes to admit to.

'We spent the rest of the weekend at Guy's apartment, out in Splott. Tony explained to us that we escaped because the alien ship was failing. Its crew was dying, and couldn't stop us from escaping. And that's when Guy Wildman had this crazy idea. That we could go back. Reactivate it, maybe. Or cannibalise it, at least.'

Owen was surprised to hear Megan laughing. 'And *that* was the crazy thing, was it?' She stared at Owen and Sandra, wide-eyed, mouth open, daring them to contradict her. 'You are talking about alien ships as though they're real. And you Owen, you're just encouraging her! I don't think she needs our medical attention, I think I should be calling the psychiatric nurse!'

'Listen to what Sandra has to say.'

'Going back there? Cannibalising this alien ship? Just popping back underwater to grab some extraterrestrial spare parts?'

There was a note of frustration in Sandra's voice now. 'With Guy Wildman's professional contacts in the international scientific community, who knows what he could do? He certainly knew all about Torchwood, and didn't want to involve them. He'd have found some way of selling the stuff on.'

'Well,' said Megan, 'it doesn't sound like the kind of thing you could stick on eBay, does it?'

'You'd be surprised,' muttered Owen, and waggled the Bekaran scanner at her. 'It was only because Tosh was checking online for a pair of shoes that we first came across this thing.'

Sandra had sunk back into her propped pillow, like she'd received a physical blow. Owen reached out to touch her arm, a human touch to restore her confidence. 'I understand, Sandra. Now trust me for a moment. I need to show Megan this. Lean forward, if you can.'

Sandra levered herself forward carefully. She started to part her hospital gown at the rear, but Owen stopped her. He beckoned Megan to watch while he passed the Bekaran scanner between Sandra's shoulder blades.

'Look at this.'

The screen image revealed the vertebrae in Sandra's spine. But it wasn't the grey murk of an X-ray that needed close study to properly decipher its contents. Not even the artificial colours of an enhanced MRI scan. This was eerily like a post-mortem image, but the vertebrae and discs were still moving naturally as Sandra stooped forward and breathed in and out. From the sides, the vertebrae looked like white cubes in the red surrounding flesh. From the rear, the bones resolved into the familiar saddle-shaped structures that straddled the off-white intervertebral discs. 'See,' urged Owen, 'between T3 and T4, just to one side. Attached to the spinal column, but not within it.'

It was almost shocking to see. A sphere of metal, like burnished chrome, with a soft inner light somehow pulsing within it.

'Not a bullet,' he said quietly. 'You've seen it for yourself, Megan. What is there not to believe any more?'

She looked like she might be about to cry. Seemed to shake herself a little, rolled her shoulders. Looked directly at him. 'What do I do, Owen? I don't know what to do any more. I don't think I even know how to feel.' She let him hold her close, and he felt her shiver against his chest. 'Shouldn't we take this to someone? Shouldn't *you* have gone to the authorities, Sandra?'

Sandra settled into her pillow again. 'You're the one who said I needed a psychiatric nurse. What do you think the army would have said? PTSD, combat neurosis. And then kept me out of the way. The end of my career, whatever happened.' She watched them both cautiously. 'So I've come to you. To Torchwood. And I know what happened to Guy and… and Tony…'

She covered her face with both hands, and began to weep silently. Dry sobs heaved her shoulders. Owen put a hand gently on her arm, calming her, while he quietly explained to Megan about the deaths of Bee and Wildman.

'So it's over, then,' Megan said. 'They won't be going back to this alien ship… I can hardly believe I'm just *saying* that…'

'Neither can I,' said Owen, jerking his head in the direction of Sandra, who he was still comforting as best he could. 'Bedside manner?' he hissed.

'We have to go back to that ship,' Sandra blurted out. There was a fresh urgency in her voice.

'Steady,' Megan warned her, and rose to check the monitors. 'I'm amazed by your resilience, Sandra. You've had a gunshot wound, you've been in a pedestrian RTA that would normally result in major trauma. I know you're a very fit soldier, but for anyone else I'd have been arranging a bed in ITU at best, and maybe a visit from the chaplain at worst.' She was considering the evidence of the monitors in wonder. 'Owen, could this thing in her spine be helping her, do you think?'

'That's why I have to go back,' Sandra interrupted. 'I want to get this tracer thing out of my back. And I can't do that with conventional surgery here in the hospital, I could be paralysed. But you're doctors. If you return with me to that ship, you could use the machine that inserted this thing to remove it again.'

Owen studied her thoughtfully. 'That's a thought.'

Megan was infuriated. 'She's still in no condition to travel. You heard how traumatic she said it was the last time.'

'I have nothing to fear from capture now. I'm a trained soldier, I've recced the area already. And besides the aliens are all dead.'

'And in this weather…?' protested Megan.

'It's the alien vessel that's causing these freakish weather conditions.' Sandra grasped at Owen's hand, the one that he had laid on her arm to reassure her. 'Surely you could stop the ship? Save the Bay? I can take Torchwood there! Dr Harper, I'm at your mercy in so many ways here. But I want to help. You should contact your Torchwood colleagues.'

'I think we can handle this.' Owen patted her hand and released it. He looked at Megan and grinned. That familiar adrenalin buzz was kicking in, it was like his head was fizzing with an exhilaration that he thought had been gone for too long. 'Megan, this is it. Your chance to see what Torchwood is all about. First-hand!'

'It's insane – crazy!' squealed Megan. But he saw she was laughing too.

'Crazy is what makes me feel *alive*! C'mon! What's keeping you here?' He made a wild gesture that encompassed the room, the department, the hospital. That implied her whole life. 'Why accept just this?'

'Look at the weather,' she protested feebly.

'That's my whole point. You've got to put up with the rain to get the rainbow.'

'Oh, that's lovely, Owen,' said Megan sarcastically. 'Now you're quoting poetry at me?'

'I'm quoting something I heard on *Trisha*, actually,' admitted Owen. 'But my point stands.' He stood and watched her intently, his eyes urging her to decide.

Sandra made a decision first. 'If you won't help me, then I'll have to do it for myself.' She started to pluck the sensors from her body. As each sharp tug removed another one, the ECG machine flatlined and began to ping a warning. 'I won't stay here,' insisted Sandra. 'And you can't make me. I'll take my chances on my own.'

'All right, all right.' Megan hurried to Sandra's side, trying to calm her at the same time as helping her with the sensors and wiping away the remaining conductive gel beneath them.

The examination-room door burst open as a nurse barged her way in. It was the short, thin girl, Roberta Nottingham. She was looking less eager now and more panicked. When she saw two doctors in the room, she slumped back against the wall in relief. 'Sorry, Dr Tegg,' she said to Megan. 'I heard the ECG alarm went off.'

'That's OK, Bobbie.' Megan switched off the ECG monitor and the alarm stopped at once. 'Here, sort out her drips.'

'So,' said Sandra brightly, 'how long will it take to get discharged from here?'

'How long is a piece of red tape?' smiled the young nurse.

Now that Sandra had stood up, she was pressing her forehead gently with one hand. Megan moved to the door. 'I'll sort out some portable analgesia.'

Sandra flexed her arm where the nurse had removed the saline drip and attached a plaster in the crook of her elbow. 'It may just be that I need a drink, and I haven't eaten for a while. Owen, can you get my discharge papers sorted out while I get dressed here? I'll come and meet you out at reception.'

A soldier who protected her modesty, thought Owen. But he just said: 'Sure.'

'And I am absolutely famished,' Sandra told him as he was leaving the room. 'But don't worry. While you're gone, I'm sure Nurse Nottingham here can help me get a bite to eat.'

TWENTY-FOUR

There was no sign of the dead policeman outside Wildman's apartment building in Splott. The battering rain had scoured the pavement clean. Even the shrubs where the body had sprawled were flattened by the torrent from the broken gutter.

A half-hearted effort had been made by one of the residents to prop the front doors shut. It wasn't as if they'd be able to get a carpenter out to effect an urgent repair; there were quite enough other emergencies to attend to as the typhoon blew through the city. Only the two hallway tables and a couple of plastic brooms were holding the doors in place, and Jack was able to force them aside with no difficulty. The crash and clatter of falling furniture was masked by the howl of the wind.

Jack had brought a laser cutter and an axe. Up in Wildman's apartment, he pulled all of the furniture towards the centre of the room, and tossed pictures and wall hangings on top of them, so that he could methodically test the cavity walls. Where he found that the plasterboard sounded hollow, he applied the laser cutter to slice a hole through it.

Within half an hour, there were scorched gaps in every wall and in the backs of all the fitted cupboards. There was no sign of any lead boxes. A similar search of the small gap under the floorboards yielded nothing either.

By the time he had ransacked the small attic space, he was covered in cobwebs and plaster dust. He'd found boxes of musty novels in damp cardboard boxes, battered wicker baskets and Christmas decorations in supermarket shopping bags. But there was nothing that could contain the missing nuclear materials.

The last thing he did was examine the bathroom. The starfish creature had broken up into decomposed chunks of lumpy grey flesh, so that the bath was like a huge bowl of putrid mushroom soup. By poking at the plughole with the toilet brush he was able to drain most of the malodorous liquid, and satisfy himself that there was nothing concealed below the water line. The pungent stink of dead fish made him retch, even when he tried to breathe only through his mouth. He felt like the stench was overwhelming him, drowning him, and he was hugely relieved to finally abandon the search and close the bathroom door on the whole nauseating spectacle.

Jack sat amid the piled furniture in the middle of the living area. No nuclear materials here. Could Applegate have smuggled them out already, when they were last here? The Geiger counters hadn't recorded anything, but she'd been wearing a long coat and perhaps that had concealed a smaller lead-lined carrier. So, where could Applegate be now? Alone and wounded. Alone and wounded. He pondered this like a mantra, before deciding to call Toshiko at the Hub.

The call connected on the second attempt. Toshiko told him that she and Gwen were already mobile, and were en route for the Bay in Gwen's car.

'Any news from Owen?' Jack asked her. The signal was poor, and the line intermittent, so they both found they were shouting to make themselves understood. 'Has he called in?'

'He may have tried,' crackled Toshiko's voice from the mobile. 'But in these conditions, who can tell?' There was buzzing interruption and Jack had to get her to repeat what she'd said. 'I had an idea about checking his mobile phone records. Obviously we're piggybacking our own system securely on the service providers, and none of them log our calls. But I was able to...'

'Yeah, OK Tosh,' said Jack. 'Half of that's getting lost in the background noise, and the other half is leaking out of my brain. What have you found?'

There was a pause. Jack wondered whether the line had dropped or Toshiko was in a huff. Eventually she said, 'Owen received a call last night from a Megan Tegg. She's a Senior House Officer at the Cardiff Royal Infirmary. And a quick cross-reference shows she and Owen were at university together in London.'

'Good work, Tosh. I can look into that once I've tracked down Applegate. Thanks. Catch you later.'

Why was a doctor at the hospital contacting Owen on his Torchwood mobile? How could she know his number?

Jack sat for a while, surveying the wreckage of Wildman's apartment.

Applegate was wounded and alone.

Wounded and alone.

Of course. Where would a woman with a gunshot wound go for emergency treatment?

He barrelled down the stairs three at a time, out of the building through the torrent of rain. The SUV's engine revved and roared as Jack steered the car into the street and onwards towards Cardiff Royal Infirmary.

The Cardiff Bay Wetlands Reserve was well-named today, decided Owen. The wild storm seemed to rattle the whole frame of Megan's rusty old Skoda, and the windscreen wipers struggled to clear the water to let them see out. It was no time to go sightseeing, thought Owen sourly. Though he doubted that Sandra was going to be showing them much in the way of wildlife, because the animals had more sense than humans and would either have fled or be cowering in shelter somewhere.

He and an ex had been out here to the Reserve one weekend, and she'd been very excited at the prospect of seeing teal ducks and tufted lapwings and long-beaked snipe. At the time, Owen had been thinking more about the chicken he'd put in the oven for them to eat when they got back home.

Megan drove them out to the north-western shore of Cardiff Bay, between the stylish frame of St David's Hotel and the outlet of the River Taff. She was following directions from Sandra, who was hunched in the back. Owen tried to engage her in conversation, asking her how she'd been getting on since discovering that Wildman and Bee had died, and the circumstances in which she'd heard the news. But Sandra was too busy giving directions from the back seat, staring out of the car window and trying to make out landmarks made strange by the rain and the gloomy afternoon light.

Owen soon found himself distracted by Megan's hesitant driving. He hated being a passenger, and fidgeted in the front seat throughout the journey. His feet gave away his impatience as he involuntarily pressed a non-existent accelerator in the passenger footwell, or used an imaginary brake when Megan seemed not to notice some obstruction in the road. He had already regretted letting her drive him to the hospital earlier, eventually accepting with bad grace that her staff pass for the car park was for her Skoda and not his car. He imagined that his Boxter would now be up on bricks outside Megan's place. He tried to reassure himself that maybe it would be stolen outright, and he could use the insurance money towards that Honda S2000

GT he'd been eyeing up. Monocoque X-bone frame just like a Formula One car, two-litre VTEC engine…

Megan interrupted his thoughts as she slewed the Skoda to a halt and pulled the handbrake into position with a ratcheting noise that made his teeth grind.

'We need to walk from here,' Sandra told them. She popped open the rear passenger door and stepped out into the storm before they could protest.

'I must be insane,' Megan told Owen. 'What am I doing driving her out here on a night like this?'

He was going to show her the Bekaran device again as an encouragement, but found that it was no longer in his pocket. He felt his face and neck flush in a momentary panic at the thought of the alien tech turning up at the hospital, until he resigned himself to the impossibility of doing anything about it. So instead he said to Megan: 'Come on. You're not going to believe your eyes.'

'Assuming we can see anything in this howling gale,' she said.

They abandoned the Skoda in the St David's Hotel car park, and followed Sandra as she set off at a determined pace down a gravel walkway that led into the Reserve. In the open here, the storm seemed worse than ever. Owen started to worry that they would be blown clean off their feet. Last time he'd been here, on a date, his companion had pointed out the magnificent view across the Bay. Today, the towering clouds overhead let little sunlight through, and the wash of rain made it impossible to see across to the Penarth Headland. He could barely make out the barrage across the Bay.

What Owen remembered as a large reed-fringed reservoir was now a choppy lake edged with flattened grasses and snapped willows. Sandra led them along a network of flooded paths. Routes through the Reserve that had once been flat, hard-surfaced paths running around the wetland were now rapidly submerging below cold dark water. In places, it was deep enough that Owen could see fish shoaling beside the walkway as they broke the surface briefly and then vanished back into the dark.

Sandra was surging ahead of them. The howl of the wind made it impossible to speak, and even when he shouted Owen could barely make himself heard. He took hold of Megan's hand, to encourage her as much as to support her physically. She tagged along with him, her head bent against the oncoming storm. Owen muttered and cursed to himself as his shoes filled with water and his trousers got soaked up to the knees.

Eventually, Sandra navigated them over a precarious, wobbling boardwalk that stretched across the water. If the wooden structure had been secured, it would long ago have sunk beneath the swirling surface. Instead, they were able to make slow progress until Sandra gestured at something that was poking up through the nearby reeds.

It looked like a lump of burnished metal. The dark water lapped over it as the wind whipped up the waves. Sandra stooped down and lifted a concealed flap to reveal a curiously shaped panel of sparkling light. She activated one of the controls, and motioned for them to stand well back.

The water around the burnished metal surged and frothed. Within a minute, a tall wide cylinder had risen from the murky water.

The boardwalk bucked and twisted as the cylinder displaced a surge of water. Owen squatted, pulling Megan down gently as he did so, to lower their centre of gravity and avoid toppling off the wooden walkway. He glanced across at her. 'An escape pod!' he yelled. He could tell from her frown that she hadn't heard so he mouthed the words to her with exaggerated enunciation.

Megan leaned in close to him, hugging his shoulder, placing her lips near his ear. 'What happened to her boat? She said she'd used a boat.'

Owen pointed at the cylinder, which bobbed more calmly on the water now. His implication was: this must be what Sandra described.

Megan pushed against him again to speak again. Even in the biting cold rain, he could feel her hot breath against his skin. 'And where's her sub-aqua gear?'

He reluctantly allowed her to move her head away from his, so that she could see his reply. He pointed into the water, and nodded: down there somewhere.

Sandra opened a small doorway in the cylinder, and beckoned for them to follow her in. It was a cramped space, no wider than three telephone boxes stacked side by side. There were four moulded alcoves in the wall, oriented vertically. Owen noted that they appeared to be designed for a humanoid figure somewhat larger than the average man, and he remembered how Sandra had described the aliens earlier. At the far end of the craft he could see another softly flickering set of controls.

Once they were all in the cylinder, Sandra activated one of the controls and the entrance door slid shut. Owen felt his ears go pop as the air pressure inside changed. The raging noise of the storm outside was suddenly reduced to a dull murmur. The rocking motion of the craft started to disorient him.

'I think I might throw up,' said Megan.

'It'll be better once we are under the water.' Sandra slumped into the nearest of the alcoves, and struggled to strap herself in. It was as though she was afraid that she might fall down if she didn't somehow secure herself. Now that she was out of the rain, the blood from the wound in her shoulder was starting to seep down her sleeve and out over her hand. The frantic energy that had sustained her through the car journey and down the pathways into the Reserve had dissipated.

'I said you weren't well enough to travel,' insisted Megan. She checked Sandra's eyes, and took a pulse from her neck. Clearly not entirely happy with what she saw found, Megan slipped a boxed syringe from her jacket pocket and administered a painkiller. Then she checked the pulse in her neck again.

Sandra wriggled her head away from Megan, as far as the moulded restraint would let her. 'We have no time. We have to get to the ship and stop it. You must secure yourself in a harness for the journey.'

Owen helped Megan to slot her small frame into one of the alcoves. She gave a little squeal as he fixed one of the straps. 'Steady! That pinches. Ow! It's too tight.'

'Sorry. How's that now?'

'Better.'

'Now, hold on to these grips.' He moved her hands into position.

'Now what?

'This,' he said. He leaned his face in at an angle, and kissed her. She made a little noise of surprise. But then the tip of her tongue was pressing back against his. Her hands slid off the grips and around him until he could feel them squeezing his bum.

He heard a short groan from behind him, and broke the kiss. Megan pouted at him.

Owen shuffled around on the spot, and saw that Sandra's head was pressed back into her alcove. The rain had plastered her short blonde hair flat, and her skin was ashen. 'OK, we'd better get going,' he told her. 'I presume you know how this thing works?'

She nodded feebly. 'Terrific,' he said. 'Then you can explain it to me as we go. It is *so* my turn to drive.'

It was easy enough to operate the escape pod. It didn't have much speed, and the direction controls were simple. Owen was soon able to dispense with Sandra's explanations about the function of the pod's controls, and concentrate on her instructions about where to move the craft rather than how. The woman was a back-seat driver, no question about it.

Sandra directed Owen to manoeuvre the pod along the reen, a moat that ran the entire length of the reserve. The extensive flooding of the whole area had widened this out, and what had once been a series of lagoons separated by islands was now an expanse of water with shallows. He had to navigate carefully to avoid grounding the vessel or colliding with one of the floating bird refuges that, now untethered, drifted dangerously on or just below the surface.

To the south, still within the waters of the Bay, Owen steered a course past a large stone bund for several hundred metres. It was defunct, no longer able to protect the wetlands, as water-borne debris inundated the area with each fresh surge of water. But it was still high enough above the bed of the Bay to remain a danger to the escape pod.

Once clear of the bund, it was a straight run out across the Bay. There was no shipping to worry about, only the occasional surging cross-current to negotiate.

Eventually, Sandra heaved a huge sigh. For one dreadful moment, Owen feared that it was a death rattle, that distressing sound made by dying people as their level of consciousness decreased and they lost their ability to swallow properly. When he checked, he saw to his surprise that her eyes were more alive than ever. She was peering intently through the observation window, and delighted with what she saw. Owen followed her gaze, and had to gasp himself.

This wasn't what Sandra had described to them in the hospital. This was more than just a simple hatch poking out of the sea bed. It was a curving expanse of dull metal, glinting with a soft inner glow even at this depth in the cloudy water. The silt at the base of it, where the vessel emerged from the sediment, was vibrating as though the whole edifice was juddering its way into reality.

Slowly forcing its way through the Rift.

The escape pod jolted, and Owen felt the controls resist his hands. He relinquished his grip, and watched the controls continue to move without his assistance. The autopilot was in operation, and the escape pod was still in motion.

They were going in.

'I won't be best pleased if my car gets washed away,' Gwen told Toshiko. 'I've only had it three weeks. And imagine what the insurance claim would read like.'

'Relax. It's well up the causeway. And how else were we going to get the trailer out here?'

'Yeah, well you've seen how far up the water level is now.' Gwen indicated the view from the starboard porthole of the submersible. A hundred metres away, the lights of Mermaid Quay sparkled in the rain. The murky late afternoon was so dark that the light detectors on the streetlamps had already activated.

Toshiko peered out too, and together they watched the waves from the Bay surge up over the wooden walkway around the Quay. The boards in front of Torchwood's Tourist Information entrance were submerged by as much as a metre of water, completely covering Ianto's overly optimistic pile of sandbags.

'Look at that,' pointed Gwen. 'There's so much water running off the Oval Basin that I bet you could go whitewater-rafting down it. When we get back, what d'you reckon we'll only be to see the Pierhead clock tower poking out of the sea?'

'The tidal barrage has already been breached,' explained Toshiko. She was checking the computer display that fed her information from the local-authority computers she had hacked. 'The sluice gates failed about an hour ago. The Bay area's usually a couple of metres below spring tide. But even that can't account for this much flooding.'

'Why's that?'

'Well, it's not like the Bristol Channel has suddenly got a lot deeper. So how has the water level in the Bay risen by three metres? Or four metres in some places. It's like a localised bubble of water, angled out of the sea.'

'I didn't think water behaved like that,' said Gwen. 'I don't understand it, I'm…'

'All at sea?' suggested Toshiko. 'You're right, water isn't supposed to behave that way. So let's go and find out what's causing this, and put a stop to it.'

She settled herself in front of the controls and prepared to dive. The large hemispherical window in front of her afforded them a view of the

Bay's heaving water. The whole vessel lurched as another large wave surged beneath them.

Gwen watched nervously as the nose of their vessel started to sink down. Dirty green seawater began to lap higher and higher against the large front window. She didn't much enjoy confined spaces, and she wasn't a particularly strong swimmer, so this combination was making her particularly nervous. Was it her imagination, or was the air getting thicker in here? She closed her eyes, and took slow, deep breaths. 'What's this thing called, then?' she asked, hoping that conversation might divert her for a while. 'A diving ship, probably. Or a bathyscaphe?'

'What do you imagine?' Toshiko smiled as the water covered them completely. 'We call it the Torchwood sub, of course.'

It helped that he knew what to expect when the airlock opened. Owen remembered what Sandra had told them back in the A&E department. And it wasn't like he hadn't seen an alien spaceship before now, so he wasn't completely nonplussed by it.

For Megan, it would be a different matter. He'd expected to offer her a slow build-up, a gradual introduction to the wonders and astonishments and, yes, the horrors of the extraterrestrial. That's how Jack had made sure that Owen did not go bonkers. That he was open to the experience of things hitherto not imagined, not possible. That he wasn't totally overwhelmed with the utter *alien-ness* of the world he was entering in Torchwood. Jack had described it as 'inoculation'.

Owen had planned to do the same for Megan, his own protégée. Showing her the Bekaran device, to seed that thought in her mind. Introducing her to the grandeur of the Hub and its contents, a safe environment where she could face a Weevil safely from behind safety glass in the dungeon. And then a first simple foray in the field, for that adrenalin buzz you couldn't get anywhere else.

Sandra's unexpected arrival had put the mockers on that, hadn't it? So here was Megan, learning it the hard way, seeing first-hand an alien spaceship that had crashed on her very doorstep. Owen took her by the hand to help her out of the escape pod, and continued to hold it tightly as they ventured deeper into the unknown corridors.

In stark contrast to the ship's exterior, the inside was softly illuminated in a wide variety of green hues. It was as though the murky water of the Bay had been transformed into aquamarines and apple-green and viridian. Soft sage-coloured fronds dangled from a high, arched ceiling. Dark green walls pulsed with the arcane bright outlines of unknown symbols or images. A fizzing row of brilliance speared through the corridors at floor level, apparently steering them onwards. To either side, the corridor walls were punctuated by dark shafts leading downwards to who knew where, each hissing with the faintest wisp of steam.

Sandra shuffled ahead of them, as though drawn inexorably forward. When Owen asked her where the control room was, she merely beckoned him on with her hand without turning around.

After only a few minutes, they turned into large room. There was none of the brilliance of the corridors, only a subdued background illumination. Six scooped frames, each like an elongated letter J, were suspended by thick, olive-green tendrils from a darkened ceiling. They faced towards the centre of a circle. At its centre was a pale cylinder that might have been a table, and at the head of the circle was a closed cabinet fashioned from what looked like jade. Sandra staggered into the room, and slumped against the cylinder.

Owen took a quick look at Megan, who was still wide-eyed and speechless with amazement. He let go of her hand, and hurried across to Sandra. She shrugged him off, a feeble effort that seemed to wrack her with pain.

'No,' she insisted. 'You must take up positions in the control frames.'

He looked at her, uncertain.

'Hurry!' she hissed. 'Can't you tell that the ship's about to break through? It will…' Her body was wracked with a huge cough. 'It will destroy the Bay.'

She stepped awkwardly away from the cylinder, and indicated to Megan that she should use one of the scooped frames. Megan looked to Owen for confirmation. When he nodded to her, she leaned back and sat in the middle frame.

Owen took the one next to her. Sandra was already helping Megan to fasten the tendrils around her in the frame, like a seat belt. Next she did the same for Owen. The tendrils went taut, and he could feel them forcing him back against the hard frame.

'Ow!' shouted Megan. 'Oww!'

Owen laughed, and settled into his frame. 'Is it a bit tight again? Get Sandra to loosen it a bit.'

Then Megan began to scream.

Owen wasn't sure whether to call out something calming and reassuring, or to tell Sandra that she should release Megan for a few minutes. He craned his head forward to see what Sandra was doing.

Sandra was standing by the pale cylinder in the centre. Her whole posture made her look exhausted, like she was ready to drop down in front of him. But her eyes were different. They were alive, glittering with satisfaction, and in the soft green light of the room her grin was a startling rictus.

He didn't have time to say anything. The tendrils around him snapped tight, and pulled his head back hard against the frame. Megan's screaming abruptly stopped. By squinting sideways, Owen could see Megan's head slump forward like an abandoned rag doll.

'Let her go!' he yelled at Sandra. His voice seemed lost in the room.

Sandra limped over to him, still showing that terrible smile. 'We only just made it in time, Owen.' The effort of speaking racked her. 'This particular body's reached the end of its use. But I couldn't relinquish it until we got here.' She indicated the whole room. 'I'm not sure it will survive very much longer. But that's of no consequence now. See you again! Soon.'

The light in her eyes seemed to vanish, like an extinguished candle. Where previously there had been a kind of triumph in her expression, now there was only incomprehension, confusion, and pain. Sandra glanced around the room in bewilderment. She said one word: 'Oh.' And then her eyes rolled back into her head, and she dropped to the floor like she'd been poleaxed.

Owen struggled against his restraints, yelling and cursing and utterly failing to get free. His futile efforts were cut short by the buzzing noise and brightening light that engulfed the frame beside him. With a whipping sound, the tendrils around Megan withdrew and vanished.

Megan stepped out of her frame.

'Get me out of this thing, Megan!' called Owen. 'It hasn't released me.'

'It's not supposed to,' said Megan. Her voice was calm and secure. She walked slowly around the cylinder, with the confident gait of someone who knew she was safe.

Megan held her hands in front of her, turning them over, examining them as though they were a thing of wonder and novelty. When she looked at him, Owen could see there was no more terror in her eyes.

'Hello again,' she said to him.

He struggled vainly against his restraints once more. 'Not funny, Megan. C'mon, Sandra needs help. Get me out of this thing.'

Megan considered Sandra where she had fallen heavily against the pale cylinder. The blonde woman's eyes were closed, and she was taking frequent, shallow breaths.

'I think Sandra's beyond help now. And I certainly have no further use for her.'

Owen studied the woman he thought he knew, standing right in front of him. 'Who are you?'

Megan smiled brightly. 'Let me show you.'

She placed her palms on the top of the pale cylinder. Lights within it responded to her touch as she stroked the surface.

The jade cabinet at the front of the circle cracked from top to bottom as a pair of irregular, hinged doors opened up. Suspended inside, seated in a larger version of the scooped J-shaped frames, was a tall, ugly alien. Bipedal, broad-shouldered, with binocular vision. Its head lolled in the seat, and its skull was a carapace of etched bone. Its thin arms ended in long, thick, dirty claws. The whole of the creature's torso heaved as it took shallow breaths through the slit of its mouth.

Megan walked over to the cabinet, checking what must have been medical readings that played continuously on the inner edge of the jade cabinet. Satisfied with the results, she looked over her shoulder at Owen.

'*This* is the real me,' she said.

TWENTY-FIVE

You're tingling. It's a fantastic feeling, isn't it? You're not sure whether it's relief or worry or excitement or anticipation. Or is it that your lover's here with you, and he's hanging on your every word?

You met him at the university disco, what sort of a cliché is that? Or a 'cleesh', as he'd say. Owen was the thin-faced, nervous lad with the good cheekbones you'd seen in Anatomy, and joked with Amanda Trainor that you'd like to examine his Anatomy more closely, and did she know his name. Amanda had identified him as local boy Owen Harper, and declared him to be a rat-faced loser with a cruel mouth. You'd seen something else in him. And then, there he was, nursing his pint at the back of the disco, while his better-looking mate was hitting on your better-looking mate and eating her face off during some slow Alanis Morissette record (bloody hell! what were they *thinking*?). He was never going to make the first move, was he? Though you could see his hungry eyes following you around the dance floor, peering into the bright maelstrom of red and blue and green and white, surveying your every move. So you'd banged into his table and spilled his drink, and thus it began. The following morning was the first of many when you would wake first and see him sleeping beside you, admiring his long dark lashes above his freckled white cheeks.

Can you ever see yourself as others see you? Most recently, as Sandra Applegate, you caught sight of your face in the mirror at Wildman's apartment. Pale and tired, the blood smeared over your mouth and chin and staining your favourite coat. Before that, you watched your reflection in the shop windows as you ran for safety down the high street and into the building site. And, earlier still, you studied your nakedness in the mirror that hung over the corner sink in your room at the barracks. Amazed and amused that your pale pink body, with its curious musculature protected by a thin epidermis, was considered by humans as a peak of fitness.

Confusingly, you thought you were in peak condition, too. It's a curious double life to live.

And now here you are, facing yourself as you cling on in the life-support unit. This is a new perspective, indeed. Look at you there – the proud warrior, laid low by the accident. And yet also the inventive explorer who possesses the means of your own salvation.

You close the doors to the life-support unit, and seal your true self into the protective cocoon. When you turn around, you can see Owen in the restraint chair. He's not looking at you with hungry eyes now. His look is full of fear and fury. 'What are you talking about, Megan? What the hell is that thing in there?'

You shared everything with Owen when you were together in London. Your hopes, your aspirations, your dreams. You kept nothing from him, even when you knew he was never wholly open with you. It seems entirely natural to share your latest secrets with him now.

'I told you,' you tell him calmly. No need to shout. 'That thing is the real me. My body is in stasis, to protect me from the crash injuries. The rest of this warship's crew were killed during the collision that brought us to this strange place. I need to return to Bruydac for medical attention.'

Owen has stopped struggling against his bonds now. That's good. That will help. But he doesn't understand yet. 'What's happened to Sandra? We were supposed to be stopping this ship from coming through the Rift. And then removing that tracker from her spine.'

You prod Sandra's slumped body with your toe. 'Not exactly what I had planned, Owen. It's not a tracker, you see. It's a control box.'

'Oh God,' murmurs Owen.

'Though it's strange. As Sandra, I was able to control you without having to insert a control box in your spine. And now that I'm controlling Megan… now that I *am* Megan… I can understand why.'

'Let her go.' Owen is pleading. 'You don't need her. We're medics, we can help you – the real you I mean – to recover and get away from here,'

You place your fingers gently on his lips and silence him. 'See? That's what I mean. You need to be needed, Owen. Sandra recognised that. She convinced you by telling you what you wanted to hear – that she needed you. You're a rescuer; you're always looking for a victim to help. You think you have all the answers, and it makes you powerful, superior, the centre of attention. You want to be loved because you can protect people, you can salvage them, and they'll depend on you. Until they don't need you any more, and then you drop them.'

Owen is trying to shake his head furiously, but the restraint won't allow it. 'That's the alien using you. That's not you talking, Megan. That's not…'

'You want to be loved and needed, Owen. But you end up self-important, demanding, righteous. And in the end, contemptuous of others.' You're aware that you're smiling at him, but it's with sadness really. 'I loved you so much, you know. Megan loved you so much.'

He thinks he found something he can use, some tactic. You recognise that familiar look in his eyes from a dozen arguments in London. 'I loved you too, Megan. I still do. That's what last night was about, remember? I know you're still in there, Megan. You're a medic, come on! Don't get lost in this thing. Try to remember. You're an SHO. One of the best. We both are. We're good together, aren't we?'

And somewhere, you do recognise what he's saying. You think of his warm breath against your skin, his lips on your neck. His hand scooped in the small of your back. The heat of his body by your side. The feeling of him inside you.

'Come back to me, Megan. Come back. Look at Sandra there. She needs you.' He lowers his eyes. 'I need you.'

The way he drops his gaze, the crack in his voice, the well-timed appeal to your better nature. You remember his technique, now. His routine.

'I am a Bruydac Warrior!' you snap at him.

His eyes meet yours again, and you know that he sees he has lost you.

'I am not Megan any more,' you tell him brutally. 'The Bruydac stealth technology lets me use the captured inhabitants of the planets we invade. By possessing our prisoners in this way, we can infiltrate the native population in perfect disguise. And when I've finished with each person, I can release them wherever they are and return my consciousness back here to the ship – or to another prisoner.'

'The sub-aqua team.' He's as smart as you remember him. 'They stumbled upon your crashed warship, and you've used each of them in turn.'

'They were so feeble,' you explain.

'What do you mean? Bee and Applegate were trained soldiers. Literally fighting fit.'

Perhaps he's right. You think how easy it was for the soldiers to overpower other humans. 'The problem with you humans,' you tell Owen, 'is that the possession just burns up so much of your meagre supply of cerebrospinal fluid. Fortunately, it's easy enough to obtain more from other humans.'

You are surprised that Owen's reaction to this is one of such disgust.

You explain to him that you have discovered a lot from the humans you've possessed. From Bee and Applegate you learned about Earth's military structures. From Wildman, you discovered a way to refuel the ship with Earth's crude nuclear technology. 'And from all of them,' you conclude, 'I learned that they suspect and fear and despise Torchwood. So I was intrigued to discover that you work for Torchwood.'

His face is like stone.

'Now Megan…' you say to him. 'She has a depth of affection for you, Owen. That wasn't a shag for old times' sake, was it? Not for Megan. It was very different on that first night at university, do you remember? After the disco? That was a basic craving for sex. Shallow emotion. Straightforward physical contact. But good. She thought you were a cast-iron virgin she'd managed to jump in his first term, so you surprised her, you know.'

'I'm pleased to hear it.' He grates out the words like it's an ordeal.

'That's not always how it was though. For you, maybe. But not for her. She never told you before you left how she'd really felt. And that's why she wants to let you back into her life this week. Why she *trusts* you, despite all the craziness.'

'Stop it,' Owen says. This time the emotion in his voice is real. 'You said you could let her go. Well, let her go, then. Do it now. Let her speak for herself.'

'No, I think I need her now. She's a doctor, isn't she? She has a thorough understanding of the strengths and weaknesses of the human form. Physical. Emotional. And she's young and strong, too. She can get me back to the shore. She can retrieve the remaining nuclear packs that Wildman concealed. I still need those to refuel this warship.'

Not much more to do before you go now. If you concentrate, you can feel the creature growing within you. There is the bubbling stir of rising gas, a stirring in your stomach. With one brief heave, you regurgitate the tiny starfish creature and spit it out. It splays its four legs on the floor beside Sandra Applegate's shivering body.

Owen sees this, and his revulsion is clear.

You find yourself moving closer to him. He cannot move in the restraint, and you have to angle your head to kiss him softly on his lips. At first he resists, with his mouth set in a firm, hard line. And then his feelings begin to overwhelm him, and he softens.

That's when you activate the device. Owen's whole body stiffens as the restraint frame punches a control box into his spine. He can't stop himself screaming with the sudden, agonising pain. Now his eyes are staring into yours in horror and disbelief. Now they're glazing over. Now the head restraint relaxes, and his head slumps forward in the frame.

You will only return for him if you cannot complete your mission successfully as Megan. His eyes are closed now, and his long dark lashes flicker as he falls unconscious. You ponder your affection for him. You know how much this alien intervention means to him, how much he wants you to be a part of it. That's why you've enjoyed explaining it all to him.

But then you remember that it is Megan's affection, not yours. So you quit the room quickly, leaving him there helpless.

TWENTY-SIX

Jack was used to being able to enter anywhere and take charge at once. It didn't matter if it was a nightclub or a shopping mall or a dingy back alley or a church. By striding in with confidence – whether it was warranted or not – his appearance, his gait, his whole demeanour told people to back down and back off.

It wasn't like that in Cardiff Royal Infirmary A&E tonight. Jack had to squeeze his way into the building past a furious crowd who were being sent back into the thunderstorm by frustrated, irate hospital staff unable to cope with any more patients. A barrel-shaped security man didn't even want to look at Jack's Torchwood ID to begin with, but reluctantly allowed him through at the second attempt.

Despite the number of people turned away, the motion-activated sliding doors at the entrance were permanently jammed open as a constant stream of urgent patients staggered across the threshold or were rushed into the building on stretchers by ambulance staff. Three sodden floor mats, caked in mud, were evidence of a half-hearted attempt to prevent new arrivals treading dirt and water into the hospital. Sandbags piled by the entrance warned that they expected worse to come.

The waiting room ached with sullen frustration, and was filled to bursting with people who had already been allowed in. Two babies wailed, but the only other human voice was their mother comforting them. Everyone else was doing that British thing of sitting in sullen silence, not speaking to the person sitting right next to them, even if it was a friend or relative, but looking at crumpled copies of *AutoCar* and *OK!* as though they were the most fascinating read ever. Those without magazines checked their watches every thirty seconds. The whole place smelled of mud and sweat and anger.

Jack braved the hostile stares of the waiting room by making his way straight to the front. 'Do you mind?' insisted an elderly man who was clutching a bloodied rag to a cut on his temple.

'Not at all,' Jack told him. He kicked the outstretched foot of a seated teenager who was slumped behind an article on the Jaguar XKR he would never own. 'Get up, kid. This man needs your seat.'

Jack walked past the front desk. The pretty young redhead on reception was moaning to a nearby nurse that her boyfriend never noticed when she'd had her hair done, and why did she spend a fortune on it if he was never going to peel his eyes away from *Match of the Day*, the lazy, good-for-nothing sod? Even the sex wasn't what it was; she wasn't sure why she pretended any more. Hello, can I take your name, home address and GP details, please?

Beyond her, two tired doctors were discussing the latest batch of new patients. 'There's another capsized water taxi,' raged the younger of the two. 'Who the fuck is taking a water taxi out in this weather? We should just let the stupid bastards take themselves out of the gene pool if they insist on it.' His older counterpart put a comforting arm around his shoulder and led him calmly back into the cubicles.

Jack had located the staff picture board. He scanned its contents quickly to locate the guy in charge. The photographs told him that the red-haired receptionist was Kirsty Donald, the nearby nurse was Kai Mahasintunan. Megan Tegg was a Senior House Officer – slim face, elfin features, short dark hair, cute rather than pretty, definitely Owen's type. Terry Hartiman, the angry young doctor, looked a lot happier in his mug shot than in real life. Ah, there you go, the Clinical Director (Acting) was Amit Majunath – grey hair, thick glasses, slightly scarred face, best-dressed guy on the board.

Jack had already pissed off one consultant (Janette Brownlees, the photo told him) by abandoning the SUV across her reserved parking space. And within a few more minutes, here was another, refusing to answer any of Jack's questions.

'We'll get to you as fast as we can, honestly,' Majunath told him for the third time. The consultant peered over his tortoiseshell glasses at an LED display that repeatedly scrolled its mournful red warning above the reception desk: 'Estimated Waiting Time Five Hours'. 'So, Mr Harkness, please put your ID away. There's really no point you flaunting your credentials in here.'

'He can flaunt his credentials at me any time,' the red-haired receptionist muttered, and smirked at her friend the nurse, who was checking paperwork at her desk. Jack caught her eye and grinned. She hadn't thought that he could overhear her, and her pretty face blushed so deeply that her freckles almost disappeared. She picked up a manila folder and hid behind it.

'I'm gonna have to insist…' Jack began. He was interrupted by three trolleys being wheeled between him and the consultant, each bearing a soaking-wet victim in urgent need of treatment.

'Insist all you like, Mr Harkness,' Majunath replied wearily. 'Clinical need is what takes priority. God knows I'd prefer a break. Do you know that when the river burst its banks, a funeral home was flooded and bodies got washed out into the street? The ambulance crews spent an hour working out who were the fresh victims.' He turned to address the latest ambulance crew. 'Straight through to resus. I'm right behind you.' He held up his hands to forestall Jack's renewed remonstration. 'As soon as I can, I promise. We want to know who murdered Bobbie as much as you do. More so, I dare say. We've sealed off the crime scene, and you can use the Relatives Room as your base of operations if you wish. No doubt you'll need that when the rest of your team arrives. But you must see we're drowning tonight.'

'Wait a minute,' protested Jack. 'Murdered who?' This was an entirely unexpected piece of news. But Majunath was already off into resus.

Jack knew he didn't have much time. If they'd called the police, then chasing the consultant was not going to be fast enough to get what he wanted.

On the reception desk, the redhead was saying goodbye to the nurse. Jack sauntered up to the counter.

'Hi, Kirsty,' he told her. 'Cap'n Jack Harkness.'

She blushed again, and tried to hide it by facing her computer screen and typing. 'Can I have your address?'

'Fast work. I like that,' he grinned. 'Shouldn't we go for dinner or something first? Or a trip out. Not soccer, though. Not a big fan.'

She ducked her head down, grinning too. 'I'm sorry, I meant that I need your details to book you in.'

Jack showed his ID. 'I'm not a patient. I'm here to investigate the murder. Mr Majunath said you'd help.'

Kirsty's expression changed suddenly and completely. It was now one of deep concern, with the risk of tears. 'Are you here to find out who killed

Bobbie?' She blinked rapidly. 'I'm sorry, I mean Roberta Nottingham.'

He kept his reassuring smile going. 'Yeah. Need to see the scene.'

Jack let Kirsty lead him to a treatment room, but didn't allow her in with him. She returned to her desk, full of gratitude. The security guard posted on the treatment room door unlocked it and let him in.

Jack slipped in unaccompanied, and saw the body. The brutal gnawed hole in the back of the skull, exposing the spine and lower part of the brain. The casual disregard for the body, with no attempt to conceal it from discovery. The sticky mess on the smooth floor in which the corpse lay sprawled. The sprays of blood over the wall and nearby equipment. The body had been rolled over, presumably in a futile attempt to treat the victim.

In less than a minute he'd seen enough. Enough time to confirm that this was the same kind of killing as before. Enough to know it wasn't Owen. Enough time to find the Bekaran deep-tissue scanner casually abandoned beside a stainless-steel kidney dish on an instrument tray.

Jack asked the security guard to relock the room, and he returned to the front desk. Kirsty Donald was engaged in a frustrated conversation with a guy whose sharp suit was matched by his slick patter. His green eyes flicked lasciviously over the receptionist, and he kept smoothing his thin moustache with his fingers. He looked like a salesman who, by accident or design, had washed up in A&E this evening, and he was making every effort to get Kirsty to make him an appointment with the clinical director. His pinched features and over-earnest manner reminded Jack of Owen when he was trying too hard. While the sales guy held Kirsty's attention, Jack surreptitiously looked at the Admissions details on the desk beside her.

'Applegate, Susan' was near the top. Discharged an hour ago.

Jack cut straight across the sales guy's patter, as though he wasn't there. 'Kirsty, is Dr Tegg available for interview at the moment?'

'I think I was speaking, actually,' interjected the sales guy. His sharp green eyes flared with anger behind his strained but polite tone.

'I don't care, actually,' Jack told him. 'Can't you see these guys are real busy tonight? Why don'tcha take your briefcase and sit on it. Over there. Five hours waiting time.'

'Thanks.' Kirsty smiled at him with evident relief, though he was pleased to see there was a more appraising look returning to her eyes. 'I'm afraid Dr Tegg went off duty about an hour ago. Are you together? Only she left with another doctor. Good-looking guy, too.'

Jack laughed at Kirsty's transparent attempt to exaggerate Owen's appeal. Or perhaps he was her type, and he should convince her that this salesman was a better prospect tonight. There he was against the wall, sitting on his briefcase and looking resentfully over at them.

Briefcase, thought Jack.

Wildman had a briefcase when he chased him through town. But he didn't still have it when Jack caught up with him on the eighth floor of the building site. He must have concealed it somewhere in the partly constructed Levall-Mellon building. And his wasn't full of proprietary drugs, either; it would be where Wildman had concealed the remaining nuclear fuel packs.

Jack beckoned the sales guy over to the reception desk. The thin guy jumped off his case and scurried across. 'Mr Majunath will be free in an hour,' Jack told him. 'You should talk to Kirsty about setting up a meeting. And when you've got that sorted, she can get you to see the Clinical Director, too.' He pointed to the wall opposite. 'Don't lose your briefcase.'

Jack strode confidently through the exit of A&E, oblivious to the rain that pelted down around him, heading for the SUV. He had a briefcase of his own to collect downtown.

Another couple of minutes in the sub with Toshiko might have driven Gwen insane. Toshiko was going on about algal populations, and how they changed depending on the temperature in the Bay or the amount of sunlight or some nutrient or other. Gwen was a lot less interested in how blue-green algae formed a scum on the surface than in finding the scum who'd been killing innocent people back on shore.

It was almost possible to forget all of that when they got into the alien ship.

The alien ship. Gwen had to say it to herself over and over. The alien ship.

She'd never seen anything like it, never been inside an alien ship. There'd been the meteor strike and she'd seen fragments of the transportation shell they'd dug up in the foundations of a new supermarket. This was different.

While Toshiko was making sure that the sub was safely connected to the outer hull, and that there was air inside for them to breathe, Gwen had been wondering how it would look. She'd expected it to be like a film set. After all, she'd sat yawning through enough DVD special features with Rhys to know how the effects were done. That the sets were lit specially and then the post-production effects made the places look, literally, out of this world.

This was beyond anything Rhys could have imagined, spilling Doritos on the carpet because he was so engrossed in the film. The only thing Gwen recognised here was the smell of salt water in the air. The rest was – why was she surprised? – alien. She swallowed hard to release the pressure building in her ears.

The walkways were spongy beneath their feet as they stepped deeper into the ship. Soft green light dappled the undulating walls, rippling like a zoo's aquarium all around them. Frothy fingers of thin material wafted from an unseen ceiling, almost beckoning them to go further. Occasionally a sharp-edged symbol would fade into view on a wall and then just as slowly fade away. Gusts of brine-tasting air swirled gently as they proceeded.

'It's getting darker,' worried Toshiko. Her hand-held computer wasn't giving her any reassurance.

Gwen noticed that when they spoke there was no echo, even in what seemed to be a cavernous space. 'What's worrying you, Tosh?'

'There could be more of those starfish things you mentioned.'

Gwen brandished her torch. 'Use your flashlight.'

'Will that scare them off?'

'No,' admitted Gwen. 'But at least you'll see them waving their tentacles at you.'

The floor heaved beneath their feet, and a bass growl came from somewhere deep inside the ship. 'It's still lurching through the Rift,' explained Toshiko. 'It's shaking about like a stalling car. The ship could be tearing itself apart in the process.'

'There's a cheering thought,' Gwen told her. At a kind of T-junction, Toshiko took the left-hand fork, and Gwen hastened to join her.

They entered a wide expanse that contained a circle of suspended cages. They faced inwards towards a cylindrical block at the centre. Each cage had a curved back, and reminded Gwen of elongated versions of the enclosed retro chairs Rhys kept on about wanting them to buy. Probably because he'd been watching the DVDs of *The Prisoner* she'd bought for his birthday. One of the cages was enclosed at the front.

But that wasn't what had alarmed Toshiko. She was pointing mutely at the third cage along. Owen was slumped in it. Head drooped to one side, face pallid, eyes closed.

Gwen started forward to see if she could free him, but Toshiko held her back. 'Careful,' she hissed. 'On the floor in front of him…'

A short-haired blonde woman lay in an awkward heap in front of Owen's cage. In the half-light of the room, it seemed to Gwen at first that a large vein in the woman's neck was throbbing. Gwen stooped to take a closer look, gasped and immediately leapt away again. One of the starfish creatures was attached to the woman's neck, arching up and down like a hand pressing up against the woman's jaw.

Gwen reached for her gun. 'No! You can't fire that in here,' snapped Toshiko. 'The whole place is pressurised.'

'And I can hardly shoot it while it's on her face.' Gwen holstered her weapon, and took out her torch. She waited until the starfish creature was on one of its upward movements, and then prised it free with the lamp end of the torch. It rolled away from the woman's head, on its back, the four legs waggling pathetically as it struggled to regain a grip. Gwen pushed it further away with the torch, noting how the mouth section in the centre puckered in a foul parody of disappointment. The woman's neck and lower face were a raw mass of part-digested flesh. Her lips were eaten away at one side, revealing the teeth and lower jaw.

Gwen hefted the heavy torch and brought it down in a sharp blow in the centre of the creature. It squeaked, the sound of two rubber boots being kicked together. She slammed it with another blow, and another, and another, until its centre was pulped and two arms had detached. It wasn't twitching any more.

'OK, stop now.' Toshiko was holding her arm.

Gwen dropped the torch, and the light rolled around the room in a bright swirl until it came to a halt in the sticky remains.

Toshiko gave her arm a quick squeeze of reassurance and then stooped down over the blonde woman. By playing her own torch over the remaining half of the woman's face, she could identify her: 'Sandra Applegate.' She carefully felt for a pulse in the remaining half of her neck. 'Nothing we can do.'

Toshiko stood up again and examined Owen in his cage. His breathing was slow but regular. When she lifted his lids, his eyes were rolled right back into his head.

The ship heaved and shuddered more profoundly than before.

'Let's get him out of this thing,' Toshiko told Gwen. 'We need to get him back to the Hub.'

Once Toshiko had worked out how to release Owen from his confinement, his body dropped out of the contraption as a dead weight. Gwen caught him, her knees buckling under the weight. Toshiko grabbed his legs, and they half-carried, half-dragged him from the glowing circle of cages and out through the corridors towards the Torchwood sub.

The alien vessel bucked and warped around them. Gwen couldn't tell how much of that was supposed to happen and how much was the ship twisting dangerously out of shape as it struggled to fully breach the Rift. She was too busy dragging the profoundly unconscious Owen to worry about it too much.

Toshiko laid Owen down carefully at the rear of the sub. It wasn't designed as an ambulance, and he looked awkward and uncomfortable where he lay.

'We should bring the other body,' Gwen said.

'And put it where?'

Gwen looked at Toshiko coldly. She remembered the dead woman's partially digested face. 'We can't leave her.'

'Yes we can.'

'I can't leave her, Tosh.' Gwen stared at her until Toshiko couldn't keep eye contact any longer.

'Bring her if you want,' Toshiko said, and began to check the sub's systems. The whole vessel rocked on its axis. 'If it looks as though the ship's movement will compromise our departure, I will leave without you.'

Gwen didn't ask again. She ran back through the olive-coloured corridors, determined not to be distracted by the vine-like wiring or sudden splashes of emerald light. Although the rattling shudder of the vessel was increasing, she managed to drag the corpse of Sandra Applegate back to the sub. At every step she had to force herself to look away from the woman's ravaged face.

TWENTY-SEVEN

The SUV slewed and careened on the slick motorway. By activating the blue flashing lights at the base of the windscreen, Jack could scythe down the hard shoulder, and more quickly gain the A roads into the city centre.

The direction finder was useless, unable to get a signal in the continual downpour. The radio crackled and spat. Jack could just decipher some of the police reports and avoid the very worst of the congested roads. The emergency channel was alive with horror stories about the widespread flooding of Cardiff. The walls of one church in the centre had collapsed, and corpses were washed out through and beyond the graveyard into a tangled mess of bones and rotted clothing. At least, thought Jack, the rescuers could work out whether they'd been dead beforehand.

He tried to contact the emergency services to have them cordon off the Levall-Mellon building site. But his mobile signal fluctuated between poor and non-existent. In the brief time he did get through, it was obvious that there was no point deploying officers into an area of danger. Even looters weren't going into the city centre now, because the place was awash with storm water.

In the haze of rain and headlights straight ahead, it looked like traffic was gridlocked. Jack yanked the wheel, and the SUV swung into a residential area parallel to the main road. Halfway down this street, a shabby figure stepped out into the carriageway with barely a glance up. Jack was unable to swerve away, and hit the figure with a solid thump. He plunged his foot down on the brake, and the SUV slid to a halt twenty metres further on.

He couldn't just leave the poor guy there. And he couldn't risk reversing back and maybe driving over him. So Jack killed the engine, pulled his collar up, popped open the door and jogged down the street to where the guy was splayed across the road.

He could see the body more clearly now amid the dancing splashes of the hammering rainfall. A hunched, ugly humanoid peered back at him with deep-set angry eyes, and scowled through a ragged mouthful of needle-sharp teeth. It was a Weevil, dressed in the curious half-clothing that characterised the creatures when they had only recently come through the Rift. The creature lay, shivering uncontrollably in the roadway, its arms and legs spread clumsy and wide, jerking spasmodically beneath a weak streetlight.

There was no sign of movement from the nearest houses, and no pedestrians had been foolish enough to brave the storm. Should he put it out of its misery by reversing over it like road-kill? A bullet through its head? Or could it recover and be taken into custody?

As he watched, the Weevil gave one last heaving shudder, and then expired. The rattling sound of its final breath was audible even over the continuous battering of the rain on the asphalt.

At the far end of the road, a police vehicle had paused across the junction. Jack groaned. He'd not extinguished the flashing lights in the SUV. He hared back to his vehicle, switched them off and reversed swiftly back towards the Weevil. Wouldn't do to be caught reversing over it. Couldn't let the cops see the creature. The police car started to reverse back so that it could turn down the roadway. Jack popped the trunk of the SUV, and cursed. The two dead policemen were still in the back, and there was no more space for a third corpse. He slammed the trunk shut and opened the rear passenger door. By hunkering down in the street, he could get his arms under the Weevil's armpits, heft it up, and dump it in the rear passenger seat. It had a messy open wound that still leaked copiously from its forehead.

The police car drew up on the opposite side of the street. Jack fastened the safety belt across the dead Weevil's lap and chest, and shut the door before the young police officer could get her cap on and cross the road to see what was going on.

'He's overdone things,' Jack told her, 'I'll get him home.' He showed her his ID, and slid into the driver's seat to indicate that, as far as he was concerned, the conversation was over. He watched the policewoman look through the darkened glass of the Torchwood car. Not too close, not pressed up close to it, because she didn't need to check, she'd seen his ID. Plus, it was raining so heavily that she obviously wanted to get back to the warm shelter of her own car.

Jack steered away down the street. Before turning the next corner, he checked the rear-view mirror. The policewoman was not following, having chosen instead to execute a clumsy three-point turn in a huge puddle. Jack glimpsed the Weevil in the back seat, where it slumped backwards against the headrest with blood still seeping from its head wound.

'Ianto will be pissed,' Jack told the Weevil. 'That's never gonna come out of the upholstery.'

Ianto was not pleased. Not that he'd do anything so presumptuous as to say anything, Gwen knew. It was the absence of his usual cheery demeanour when she and Toshiko got him to carry Sandra Applegate's corpse into the Hub. She wondered if she'd disturbed him in the middle of something important, especially when he denied it with the same convincing tone that she recognised from when Rhys said he hadn't had more than a pint with Dutch Arthur at Dempsey's.

In any other weather, they'd have needed some extensive subterfuge to get an unconscious man and a dead woman across Roald Dahl Plass and into the Hub. This afternoon, though, the place was abandoned to the furious storm that continued to lash across the city centre. The Bay had already risen astonishingly high, flooding over the railings. The Oval Basin was starting to live up to its name as the Bay water began to lap over the wooden boardwalk and around the base of the first tall lamp towers. Ianto warned Gwen and Toshiko that they'd have to use the platform entrance, because the reception door was already underwater. Maybe that's why he was so tense – he was worried about his stock of tourist guides.

Ianto deposited Sandra Applegate's corpse in the pathology room, while Gwen helped Toshiko to carry Owen to the medical area. They so rarely needed to use it, and the last time Gwen had been in here had been when Owen was showing her around and showing off. The suite contained an examination room and three bedrooms, each an incongruous mix of stark medical white and Victorian brickwork.

Owen remained profoundly unconscious. As Gwen made him comfortable, she reflected that this was probably not how Owen would have imagined her helping him into bed. Toshiko switched on a dusty computer by the bedside, and connected up several monitors to Owen's body. Gwen had no idea what went where, and from Toshiko's look of concentration it seemed clear that it wasn't something she had done recently.

Ianto knocked politely at the door, and she beckoned him in. 'Have you been able to reach Jack?'

He looked apologetic, almost forlorn. 'No connection at all. The storm has wiped everything out.' He went over to the computer terminal by the bed. 'Meanwhile, I've done a quick scan of the corpse you brought back. It does appear to contain one of those spinal attachments. But it's completely burned out.' He tapped at the keyboard to call up the scan results.

Toshiko took the mouse, and arranged the computer image so that it showed a split screen. One half showed Ianto's scanned image. In the other, Toshiko displayed a second scan of Owen. Clearly visible below his neck was the stark outline of a new spinal attachment.

'He's alive,' Ianto said simply. It sounded like a plea.

Toshiko sat down on a chair, suddenly weary. 'He needs a doctor.'

'But he *is* our doctor.' Gwen folded her arms, unable to think what to do. 'We've heard him tell us often enough. Born a doctor, lives every day a doctor.'

'And he'll die a doctor,' concluded Toshiko. Her voice was hard now, more certain. 'But not today.'

TWENTY-EIGHT

'You're the strong, silent type,' said Jack. No response. 'Well, I respect that. But y'know, I can't see this going anywhere.' He took another quick look at the face in the mirror. 'I mean, this is never gonna work out. No matter how good an orthodontist you find.'

Jack surveyed the roadway ahead. He'd parked beneath a shattered streetlamp at the junction of a side street that looked out over the Levall-Mellon development. The street was pedestrianised, but there were no cops stupid enough to patrol in these monsoon conditions. The lamp was shattered because he'd shot it out, along with two others nearby. That way, the light didn't shine on the falling rain and turn it into a silvery opaque curtain through which he couldn't see. And he needed to see anyone approaching before they saw him.

Even over the endless drum of rain on the car roof he could hear the tarpaulin coverings around the building were slapping against the metalwork and making the scaffolding ring. The torrent of rain had emptied the city centre utterly. His Torchwood mobile had no signal. The Geiger counter clipped to his belt ticked quietly to itself.

There was no one else to talk to.

'Don't get upset. It's not you, it's me,' said Jack. He paused and grinned, and glanced again in the rear-view mirror. 'No, OK, it's you.'

The Weevil continued to stare sightlessly past him. It had stopped bleeding now. A red-brown stain had spread over its face and into the headrest. Its mouth was ajar, and drool had dried where it had spilled over its chin. 'Think about it. I mean, you're ugly and I'm cute. You're dressed in

Weevil rags, and I've got a sense of style. You're stone cold dead, and I'm…'

His words trailed off. A Mini was making slow progress down the road. It was the first car that Jack had seen for fifteen minutes. It continued past the T-junction and parked outside the Levall-Mellon building, offside to the pavement. From his position, Jack could only see a blurred shape rushing away from the car and into the building.

He sprang from the SUV and pelted across the street, throwing up huge splashes of water as he pounded through puddles on the way. In case this was some contractor or builder making an unexpected return to the site, Jack swiftly inspected the Mini. The passenger seat contained a dead woman. Almost certainly the original driver of the vehicle. The side and rear of her neck had been ripped open, exposing the spinal cord, and blood had spurted all over the driver's side of the car. The windscreen interior was smeared with blood where the killer had inexpertly wiped it away in order to see out.

The main reception area of the building smelled dank. The boarding and covers that surrounded it were hopelessly insufficient to keep the rainstorm from blowing through the shell of the unfinished building, and a wide expanse of water had pooled across the concrete floor. Four main stairwells led up into the body of the site. Jack tried to remember which one he had pursued Wildman up two days ago. It was the far corner. He hurried across, poked his head around the hole where the doorframe would go, and held his breath to listen. Jack heard the clattering footfall of someone who didn't know they should be keeping quiet.

He unholstered his gun, and started quietly up into the building. He hugged the breezeblocks that formed the sides of the stairwell. That kept him away from the sharp drop beyond the edge of the steps. It also enabled him to lean against the wall and stare up to where he could hear the footsteps.

The regular slap of shoe on stair had stopped, and now the sound was of feet sliding across concrete. The intruder was walking around, perhaps looking for something.

Looking for Wildman's briefcase.

He checked the Geiger counter at his belt. Nothing more than background radiation. Maybe he was wrong about the briefcase.

Jack slipped up the remaining stairs as quickly and silently as he could. On what he counted to be the eighth floor, he stepped out into the main floor area and covered the whole area with his gun.

Megan Tegg had the slim face he recognised from the photograph board at the hospital. But she didn't look cute any more. In the half-light of the room, she looked startled and then angry. Her jaw was smeared with the ichorous evidence of her attack on the car driver. She tried hopping across the finished floor, avoiding the concrete reinforcement wire and attempting to hide behind one of the central pillars. But Jack slid smartly to one side, and had her covered again.

A flash of lightning brilliantly illuminated the whole area and the ensuing peal of thunder demonstrated how close the strike was. Megan was clutching the briefcase tightly in her right hand, and her head flicked from side to side as she considered her exit routes.

'Give it up, Megan,' Jack called, his voice loud and clear despite the pounding of the rain and another crack of lightning. He hopped over a couple of girders to get nearer to her, and pointed at the briefcase. 'Thanks for finding that. I thought I'd let you lead me to it, rather than hunt for it myself.'

Megan considered the gap that yawned beneath them. Backed away carefully towards the exterior of the building. Felt for the floor with her feet all the way back. Never took her eyes off Jack's revolver.

He followed her carefully. She had reached the wooden platform outside. Wind and rain whipped around the edge and into the building, lashing the torn green exterior covering repeatedly against the metal scaffolding. The ladder to the next floor swung loose in the wind. A heavy-duty plastic debris chute clattered against the exterior brickwork.

Megan chanced a look behind her. Little was visible through the rain, except for the smeared outlines of the well-lit landmarks of the Millennium Centre and the St David's Hotel.

'Nowhere to run,' Jack told her.

Megan faced him again. Her anger had dissipated. He wasn't sure if she was unnaturally calm or trying to give him that impression.

'That's a Webley Mark IV,' she said. 'Point three-eight calibre, and a five-inch barrel. More than enough to pick me off where I stand.' Unexpectedly, she smiled at him. It was the last thing he'd expected. 'I wonder where you get your cartridges. Though I suppose I should worry more about where I might get one now.'

Jack frowned. 'What did you say?'

She was still smiling. 'You know, that's the Boer War model of that gun.

You should have asked for the Mark V. Bring you right into the twentieth century, with all the benefits of a nitrocellulose propellant-based cartridge.'

'Where did you hear that?'

'Tony Bee was a gun enthusiast,' said Megan. 'I learned a lot from him.'

'No,' said Jack. 'I meant the "pick you off where you stand" part. There's only one person I said that to. And he took a dive before he told anyone else.'

Megan reached out slowly with her left hand to clutch a scaffolding pole. In the next flash of lightning Jack saw her knuckles were white where she gripped the briefcase handle in her other hand. 'You're not from round here.'

'No,' said Jack.

'America.'

'Further.'

'New Zealand, then,' continued Megan unhurriedly. 'Or Australia.'

'Further,' Jack told her.

She laughed. 'You can't get further than Australia.'

'No,' grinned Jack. '*You* can't get further than Australia.'

'Oh, I might surprise you.' And now Megan's smile seemed different. More secretive, perhaps. Even facing a guy with a gun, she was confident. It reminded him worryingly of Wildman, and how he'd faced Jack in almost this exact spot.

Jack kept his eyes locked on Megan's. Not offering her an excuse to break this look between them, as though it physically bound them together.

'You didn't just hear all that from Anthony Bee, because you never met him. And you can't have heard about me from Guy Wildman, 'cause he didn't survive the fall. Somehow... you *are* them. And Sandra Applegate too, probably. And maybe others before that?'

'You're good, aren't you?' cooed Megan. Another flicker of lightning revealed that she was licking her lips. Nervous, or relishing the moment? 'I'm a warrior,' she said. There was pride in her voice now. She let go of the scaffolding, and it seemed to Jack that she was standing taller. 'I want to return home, to obtain urgent medical attention. If you'll let me.' Megan hefted the briefcase up, slowly so that she would not alarm him. It was heavy – he could see the strain in her arms. Jack's Geiger counter showed negligible radiation. Megan was showing him her means of escape. 'To do that, I must refuel and launch my ship.'

'Neat briefcase. Lead-lined?'

'Why don't you just let me get out of here?' asked Megan. 'I can be gone within the hour.'

She was watching him for a reaction. He knew it, and didn't give her one.

'You could even help me, Jack.'

Now that got a reaction, and she saw it at once.

'It is Jack, isn't it?'

He tightened his grip on the revolver. Made sure his stance on the concrete was steady, his feet solidly placed.

'Now how would you know that?' Jack considered the options. 'Right. Owen told you. Or he told Megan. Same difference, cos you're not Megan any more. Are ya?'

'I've only *borrowed* her,' pouted the alien. 'Think of it like… renting a car.'

'The price is too high,' Jack snapped back. 'Like it was for that woman in the Mini down there in the street. Some passer-by you let bleed to death in her own car, just so that you could get here?'

Jack could feel the anger building in his chest. His shoulders and arms tightening. His hands gripping the Webley.

Megan's smile faded. She backed away from him, moving further along the scaffolding.

'Stay where you are!' bellowed Jack. 'You're not borrowing anything. You're killing humans indiscriminately—'

'Humans?'

'You don't care what happens to them, they're just transport. Arms and legs.'

'I release them in the end.'

'Yeah, I've seen that,' retorted Jack. 'Just here. You'd remember that, right? You release them when they are incapacitated. No inconvenient loose ends, because you condemn them to death before you let go. By which point, it's too late for them to do anything but die. You take what you want, and you leave them with suffering and pain and ultimately death.'

'You're wrong about me,' she said. Her voice was calm but clear, even against the noise of the storm. 'I retain memories of the humans I've possessed. I learn what they learn, know what they know. Feel what they feel. Put the gun away, Jack. You don't need to hurt me to make me understand about human suffering and pain. I know how humans treat each other. I know how Bee and Applegate loved and respected one another. How Wildman craved the respect of his friends, and never knew that he'd earned it. I know how Owen Harper screwed up my life and broke me into pieces that I never put together again.'

'That's not you. You're not Megan.'

The alien used her eyes, her expression, her whole demeanour in a desperate entreaty. 'I am Megan, she's here. But so much more.'

A gust of rain buffeted them through the open side of the building. Megan shuffled aside and wrapped her arm around the nearest scaffolding post. She was in no rush to take a leap, Jack decided. 'Let her go,' he demanded. 'You know nothing of what it is to be human.'

'Don't get moralistic with me, Jack. I know enough. I know you talk a good story about human rights. But I know that some humans have more rights than others.'

Jack thought about Gwen earlier. 'You sound like a friend of mine,' he told Megan. 'Only she really means it.'

'Come on,' Megan taunted him. 'Why did no one care about a few dead vagrants? I took them for sustenance because Bee and Wildman and the others knew no one would miss them. Imagine the hue and cry if I'd killed a couple of stockbrokers, eh? Or a policeman.'

'You did kill a policeman. Policemen. And those soldiers.'

Megan shuffled uncomfortably. 'Not so many hobos around an army base. Needs must.'

'And a secretary, who only wanted to drive Wildman home. An A&E nurse who attended Applegate. People who wanted to help. So why should I help you now?'

'To put an end to it?' Megan's tone was hopeful, pleading.

The Webley was getting heavy in Jack's outstretched arm. 'You may have briefly lived these human lives. But you've learned nothing about being human.'

'I understand the human need to survive.'

'You've surrendered that right,' said Jack. 'Give me those fuel packs or I'll shoot you where you stand.'

Another crash of lightning. Jack saw that Megan was half-hidden by the scaffolding poles now.

'Get back out here,' he told her.

She slid further behind the scaffolding.

Jack lowered the muzzle of the revolver, squeezed the trigger, and shot Megan through her right foot.

The report from the weapon was shattering, echoing off the bare concrete walls. Megan shrieked in shock and anger and pain. She half-spun around the scaffolding pole, lunging for a cross-bar as the shot twisted her around. The briefcase dropped, bounced on one corner, and fell by the far edge of the platform.

'Get back out here,' Jack repeated slowly.

Megan had regained her balance. She shuffled reluctantly forward again, whimpering. Her right shoe was a ruined mess of leather and blood. She couldn't put weight on it, so she slid down and sat on the wooden planks of the external platform. It was a defensive posture, but Jack knew it made her more dangerous, because she knew she was completely cornered.

'I only want to refuel my ship and leave Earth,' she pleaded. 'Let me go.'

'Can't do that.' Jack moved closer, raising the gun to aim at her head again. 'Look at what's happening already. Your ship's causing this typhoon. Launching it would generate a tsunami that would barrel down the Bristol Channel and out into the Atlantic. On the bright side, I grant you, that would wipe out Bristol. But you know I won't let it happen.'

Megan stretched out a tentative hand, and tugged the briefcase towards her from where it balanced precariously at the edge of the platform. Even this small effort made her grimace in pain. She flicked the catches at the top, and lifted the lid.

Jack stepped towards her. But as the lid lifted, his Geiger counter started to crackle and spit its radiation warning. Jack hesitated briefly, and that was enough to allow Megan time to reach into the briefcase and bring out two foil-wrapped items. If the Geiger counter on his hip hadn't been rattling its warning sound, he could almost have believed that Megan was holding a couple of bars of chocolate.

Megan looked up at him. 'You're going to help me.'

'No, I'm not.'

'It wasn't a question. Give me the revolver, Jack. And then you're going to escort me back to my ship, or I'll throw these things into the street and contaminate the whole area.'

Jack peered down at her pityingly. He'd taken something out of his greatcoat pocket with his left hand. He held it up so that she could see it in the flashes of lightning. 'Radiation sponge. It's absorbing the stuff right now.'

Megan took a deep breath. Considered her options. Slowly raised her hands above her head. It wasn't a gesture of surrender.

'Then I'll slap these things together. The explosion will spread radioactive fragments so far across this city that you won't be able to mop it up with a thousand of those things. Ten thousand.'

'It'll kill you too.'

She was smiling again now. 'I have options.'

'And you'll have no fuel.'

'I'll start again. And I'd like to tell you that I'll see you again, Jack. Except that you won't survive the explosion.'

Her hands moved apart.

Jack fired as she brought them together. They never met.

The shot took her above the left eyebrow. Her head jerked back, and the movement threw her hands forward. The fuel packets spun from her grip, and hit the wooden walkway with a clunk.

Megan's upper body continued to fall back. The weight carried her over the edge. For a moment it seemed like the green netting behind her would hold her up. Until a gust of wind lifted it, and she slid off the platform and into the plastic debris chute.

A sequence of clanks and thuds slowly faded as Megan's body bounced and rattled down the chute. It tumbled down eight storeys and crashed into the skip at street level. Jack listened for further movement, but all he could hear was the steady drumbeat of the rain outside and the rumble of thunder.

In the medical suite at the Hub, Gwen was startled to see movement in the bed. Owen's eyes snapped open. He looked around wildly, struggling to rise from the pillow. His eyes widened as he took in his surroundings.

'Hey, hey.' She hurried over to the bedside to comfort him. The bedroom was calm, the silence broken only by the elevated bleeping of the monitors, and the hum of a vacuum cleaner from the corridor outside. 'It's OK. You probably weren't expecting to be here when you woke up, eh?'

'I'm in…' He struggled with his words and thoughts, as though he was coming back to full consciousness. 'I'm in the Torchwood Hub?'

'Yes. Hang on, I'll get you a fresh glass of water.' She went over to the basin to wash and refill his glass. 'How are you feeling?'

'Fine,' he said from behind her. 'So much better than I thought was possible.'

TWENTY-NINE

No one ever brought the Hoover up here, thought Ianto. How difficult could it be? The lift by the reception area had a stop on this floor, otherwise how would they get patients in and out. And OK, some of the layout in the Hub might be a bit idiosyncratic, based as it was on rebuilding existing underground vaults from Victorian times under the cover of the Tiger Bay redevelopment – if only the AMs in the Welsh Assembly knew why their Senedd building had *really* run so wildly over budget.

He'd have thought that everyone in Torchwood could agree that a medical suite should be spick and span, it was only hygienic. But it fell to Ianto, as usual, to lug the vacuum cleaner all the way up from the junk room in the basement and run it over the dusty carpets of the medical area. Not that any of them would thank him, mind. Nor was it likely that a single one of them would even notice. He might as well be invisible, for all the attention they gave him. Though that sometimes had its advantages.

He had just switched the vacuum cleaner off, in the middle of changing one of the attachments, when he heard a glass and metal crash from the nearest bedroom. Gwen's voice cried out in alarm.

Ianto shoved the vacuum cleaner aside with his foot and charged through the door. It wasn't locked, so he stumbled a couple of feet into the room before regaining his balance.

On the far side, by the basin, Owen was embracing Gwen. A broken glass and a scattered pile of toiletries lay on the floor at their feet. He had his arms wrapped around her from behind, and was trying to press his face into the back of her neck.

'Oh,' muttered Ianto, and started to back out. 'Sorry, I didn't realise.'

Gwen twisted, and managed to elbow Owen in the side. He doubled over sideways, and his grip on her loosened.

'Get him off me!' Gwen yelled at Ianto.

The back of her neck was scraped. Owen had been attempting to bite her.

Owen straightened up, and weighed his options. He feinted to the right, and then leaped at Gwen again, pushing her head over the basin and into the mirror above it. The glass splintered.

Ianto took two steps towards them, and swung the long metal Hoover attachment in a low arc that connected with the small of Owen's back. Owen whirled around, snarling. His eyes narrowed at Ianto. Focused on the Hoover attachment.

Ianto was considering delivering another blow, to Owen's head perhaps, when Owen took the initiative and shoulder-charged him. Although Owen was a lot smaller than him, the movement took Ianto by surprise and he crashed over a drugs trolley, rolling onto the floor. By the time he had regained his feet, Owen had fled the room and slammed the door behind him.

Gwen had slid down the wall by the broken mirror. She sat there, winded and shocked, looking at the chaos of the room. Ianto went over to her. She had a cut just above her hairline that, as scalp injuries do, was bleeding heavily, but was less serious than it looked. The gnawed mark on her neck had just broken the skin too, and her clothes were bloodied. Ianto hunted around for sterile wipes and some pressure dressings.

The sheets and blankets were rumpled where Owen must have leaped up. Ianto stripped them back completely, and got Gwen to come over to the bed where he could position the bedside light and examine her wounds. Gwen winced as he wiped the blood away.

Ianto sat beside her, one hand on her forehead and the other gently against her neck. When Toshiko came into the bedroom, she saw them on the bed together and backed out immediately. 'Sorry, I didn't realise,' she said, and closed the door.

Two seconds later, Toshiko had obviously thought a bit more about it. The door opened again. 'Wait a minute,' she said, 'where's Owen?'

Jack waded downhill to the phone box. For a moment, he thought he might struggle to find the right change to make a call. Would anyone accept the charge at Torchwood if he called collect?

With no signal from any mobile, he needed a landline to make urgent contact with the Hub. He'd spotted the box as he crested the hill of the side road. The SUV was still visible, clear of the water that was swirling around this lower-lying road. The cold water eddied around his knees and soaked through his trousers.

Ianto eventually answered the call.

'What kept ya?' asked Jack. 'OK, so the system wouldn't have recognised this number. I'm using a payphone. And I'm practically up to my ass in water.'

'Right,' said Ianto. 'The whole Bay area is flooding, too. The office is underwater.'

'I tracked Megan Tegg down to the Levall-Mellon building,' Jack explained. 'Jeez, if any more people are gonna fall off there, we should start selling tickets. Oh, and I had a messy passenger in the car, Ianto. Do you know a good valet service?'

Ianto wasn't responding to the banter as he usually did.

'What's wrong?' Jack asked. The pips started to sound on the phone line. Jack cursed – that was never three inutes, there had to be a fault somewhere. He grabbed for the spare change that he'd lined up on top of the payphone. Half of it slipped through his fingers and into the water. He managed to insert one coin just in time.

'Gwen and Toshiko found Owen, and brought him back. They thought he was injured, but he's woken up and attacked Gwen. Tried to bite her in the neck. We think he's being controlled by one of those devices inserted in his spine.'

So that's why Megan was so placid at the end. 'She had options,' remembered Jack.

'I don't understand.'

'Sorry, Ianto. Thinking aloud. You're right. Owen is not himself. He's being controlled by the same thing that took Guy Wildman and Anthony Bee. Are Gwen and Tosh OK?'

'Yes. They're tracking him down.'

Jack could hear a muttered conversation somewhere in the background.

'They've located his mobile signal in the basement. Our internal network's still up.'

'OK, Ianto. Our problem now is that the thing controlling Owen knows everything he knows. So it knows its way around the Hub. It won't need the fuel cells once it works out it can harvest the materials we've got down there.'

Jack thought he heard Ianto say, quietly but distinctly, 'Oh, God.'

No time for this, thought Jack. Need to make things safe. 'Stay with me, Ianto.' Steel in his voice now. 'Be careful. You got it cornered. It has nowhere else to go. No more lives left.'

A cold feeling ran right through Jack. Maybe it was the flickering intensity of the lightning that transformed the falling rain around the phone booth into strings of diamond brilliance. Maybe it was just the relentlessly increasing water around him, which had now risen up his thighs. He watched it slap against the glass insides of the phone box. From the outside of the phone booth, a passer-by might mistake this for a David Blaine trick. Would the magician escape the rising water in time?

'Hello? Are you still there, sir?'

'Yeah, sorry Ianto. I'm coming back in. You and Tosh, concentrate on finding Owen. Have Gwen meet me at the base of the water tower with scuba gear.'

'Scuba gear?'

'Yeah, coupla sets. And—'

The sound of the pips interrupted him again. Jack yelled urgently but clearly over them. 'Find Owen. You cannot let him outta the basement. Subdue him if you can. And Ianto…?'

'Yes?'

'Kill him if you can't.'

'Sir…?' He detected a note of incredulity in Ianto's voice.

But the line had gone dead.

You didn't expect to be so hungry, so badly, so soon. It clutches at your stomach, and your limbs ache. You've seen enough junkies sweating it out in the confines of an A&E to recognise addiction. The tremendous high. The hedonistic rush. But the brain develops a tolerance, and it demands more and more.

You thought about this when you were Megan. Now you've got another doctor's perspective on the matter and, better still, you're a doctor who has significantly more medical familiarity with alien organisms. Through Bee and Wildman, Applegate and Tegg, you've learned that the craving that wrenches your guts is now more than just a biochemical process in the brain, it's a dependency.

Your undergraduate tutor called it 'the interaction of opportunity and

227

vulnerability'. If she asked you now, you could make her proud by describing it as a function of the cortico-mesolimbic dopaminergic system. But nothing you said to her could convey the consuming, overpowering, blinding urge to kill and devour and satiate that animalistic need. To satisfy the yearning any way you can. And to indulge, too, the dark thrill of the chase.

Behind that is the sheer excitement of being here at all. You are starting to realise where you are, what the potential is. No wonder the others feared and hated Torchwood. With what you know now about the history of the organisation, the people who work here, the contents of the vaults, there is even more to strike terror into their hearts.

Gwen and Toshiko and Ianto are searching for you. You've covered your tracks well. Your mobile phone is concealed in the cells, because you know that will be standard procedure for tracking you through the building. So long as you can stave off that gnawing hunger, you can rifle the inventory in Jack's office for technology to power or repair the ship. Maybe even Bruydac technology, who knows. The others will be too busy in the cells to stop you.

Especially since you released the Weevil.

Whenever you've stared into that animal's eyes before, you've known that its one desire is to kill. Three weeks ago, you and Toshiko visited the cells and looked at the thing, apparently asleep on its cot in the far corner of its grubby enclosure. But when you both approached the security glass that encased it in the cell, the creature scented you both through the air holes. The nostrils twitched, and the arched, deep-set eyes flickered open in anticipation. 'This one puts the "evil" into "Weevil",' Toshiko told you then.

Well, when she locates your mobile down there, she'll have a chance to find out for herself how evil that animal really is.

The walk-in safe that dominates one side of Jack's office is sealed. Only Jack has the key. There's nothing of use below the hatch in the floor. There's a kind of daring to your actions. You'd never have attempted this kind of break-in before. Such a pity that all you've unearthed with your new-found bravery is a heap of confidential paperwork and two bowls of fresh fruit.

It's the fruit that sets you off again. Thinking of food. Your guts ache, and the familiar appetite reasserts itself. You slam your fist against a filing cabinet, but even the pain of that doesn't distract from the urge to feed once more.

You stagger out of the office, reeling with the longing. It's impossible to distract yourself with a calm medical analysis. No chance to dispassionately recall how there are modified ependymal cells in the choroids plexus, when your whole self is aching to sink your teeth into Gwen's spine and chew and grind until you've breached the final barrier of the meninges to drink down the salty dregs of her cerebrospinal fluid.

In the Autopsy Room, you're almost unable to control your drooling. Even the stained tray where you conducted Wildman's post-mortem is setting you off. On the instrument rack you find tools – a bone saw hangs beside the duralinium enterotome, the bulb-ended scissors that you use for cutting through intestines. There's a small box of curved flat-sided Hagedorn needles. And beside that, the hooked hammer with which you pull the calvarium from the lower portion of a severed skull. Why not take some of these with you? You can use the Stryker saw to cut through the skull, and get at the spinal fluid without the usual mess and fragments of bone in your mouth.

Convenience food. You could strike Gwen down, and then open her up like a packed lunch.

Suitably equipped, you set off for the lower levels.

Gwen didn't like sitting alone in the Hub, not at the best of times. This was worse, sitting by a computer terminal in the Hub while Ianto and Toshiko tracked Owen through the basement. At least she could guide them while she waited for Jack to return. She watched their identification icons slide silently across the computer schematic that showed the labyrinth of interconnecting tunnels that criss-crossed the Torchwood basement.

At first, the sound of their voices over an open channel made her feel less alone. Then she decided that Owen would also be able to hear them describing their progress. When Gwen brought this up, Toshiko considered restricting the broadcast to a point-to-point message between them and the headset at the terminal where Gwen sat, but on further reflection decided that Owen was just about smart enough to hack into that if he wanted.

'Doesn't that apply to these icons too?' Gwen asked. 'If I can track you on the schematic…'

There was a further silence from Toshiko. 'You're right,' she said eventually. 'He's a sneaky sod. Did I mention that he breached our firewall with that virtual reality game?'

'Only seven times.'

'I am so going to slap him when I find him. OK, Gwen, we'll reconnect if we need to. Ianto, you need to switch off your mobile. Now.' Toshiko's line cut out. The two identification icons on the schematic faded away into nothing.

Gwen listened to the hum of the computers, the drip of water, and the occasional rustle from the pterodactyl up in the rafters above the second floor.

The ping of an alarm drew her attention to a second display. It showed a high view of the surrounding area, seen from the top of the silver water tower. Only the humped outline of the Millennium Centre's entrance made the image recognisable. The evening light had faded dramatically under the leaden skies, and sheets of rain swept over an expanse of murky water. The Bay water flooded right up as far as the tower and completely obscured the paving stones.

The alarm detected changes in heat signals from the immediate area. At the top of the image, there was the imposing outline of Jack Harkness, making his way knee-deep through the water. He had his head down against the prevailing wind, and his greatcoat trailed in a wake through the storm water behind him. He splashed his way to the paving slab by the water tower, and activated the lift.

The relative calm of the Hub was disrupted at once. A square column of dirty water began to cascade from the ceiling as the paving slab began its descent.

Within seconds, Jack was visible above it, like a drenched statue on a tall, liquid plinth. 'Close it! Close it!' he spluttered down to her.

Gwen fumbled with an override control, and a replacement paving slab slotted into place and shut off the flow of water as abruptly as it had begun. She made her way over to the lift's hydraulic pole. The basin in the centre of the Hub was overflowing with water now, so she negotiated her way across by clinging to a higher walkway. A fish briefly broke the surface of the pool as Gwen shuffled tentatively across.

The slab reached floor level. Jack was soaked from head to toe. She helped him as he shrugged off his drenched coat. Gwen ruffled his hair, which was plastered flat to his forehead. He slicked it back with his hand, and she saw the watch on his wrist. 'It really is waterproof, isn't it?'

'Better believe it,' Jack told her. 'American craftsmanship.'

His soaked coat was heavy with rainwater. Gwen laid it over a railing. 'Take your brolly next time, eh?'

'Must be in the car,' he smiled. 'I left the SUV a coupla streets back, uphill.

Thought I could drive all the way back, but wasn't sure where to drop anchor.'

'Don't worry,' said Gwen. 'No traffic wardens out in that storm. It's not going to be towed away.'

'Hope not,' agreed Jack. 'Three dead bodies in it.'

'That's got to be worth at least twelve points on your licence.'

'If I had one. Never needed to.' Jack had sauntered over to the basin. He was sopping wet, so he didn't seem to care about wading across through the flood water. 'You got the scuba gear I asked for?'

Gwen indicated a pile of equipment on the other side of the basin.

'Suit up,' said Jack.

'Aren't we going to help Ianto and Tosh find Owen?'

Jack was already stripping off his outer clothes. 'No time. That ship you found, it's still coming through the Rift. You and me can best help Owen by getting back there.'

'Getting back there how?'

Jack pointed at the flooded basin that separated them across the Hub. 'This is a tidal pool. There are some valves and safeguards to negotiate on the way, but it's the fastest route. The ship will have come much further through the Rift now, because it's displaced a huge amount of water in the Bay. C'mon, get your gear on.'

Gwen considered the precarious railing to the side of the basin, and the flooded walkway. She was going to get wet anyway. She shrugged, and waded across the basin to join Jack.

'Did you bring a harpoon gun?' Jack asked her as she started to strip.

She paused and looked at him. 'You are joking, right?'

'Not at all,' he said as he adjusted the straps on his diving mask. 'You do remember the size of that starfish thing, don'tcha?'

THIRTY

The cell tunnels invariably smelled damp. Ianto could always tell if one of the team had been down there, because the clammy odour of mould clung to their clothes when they got back to the upper levels of the Hub. It was just like he'd been able to tell, back in London, when Lisa had been for a pub lunch with Trish, from the smell of cigarettes on her hair. Even though she didn't smoke. Doesn't smoke. That was a long time ago. Ianto looked nervously down the far corridor.

'All clear,' hissed Toshiko. She raised her gun and moved swiftly and quietly into the next corridor.

The lower basement was filthy. No point trying to keep it clean, Ianto knew. He wondered why Owen would choose to flee down here. The signal on Ianto's PDA told him that Owen was still in the middle of the three main cells. He hadn't moved from the area for fifteen minutes now. He seemed to be wandering between the different cells.

Was he waiting for them?

Toshiko pushed open the dungeon door. There were three glass-fronted cells to one side of a short corridor. Opposite were three more cells behind solid doors with tiny square windows. Once Ianto was in the corridor with her, Toshiko pulled a lever in the wall to seal the main door behind them.

The caged strip light hung above from the ceiling. It cast a pallid glow over the whole corridor. The three cells had their own internal lights, which showed up the grimy marks that smeared the glass fronts. Ianto knew that they had a Weevil secured in the middle cell, though the glass was angled up and so it was difficult to see where the creature was at the moment.

The nearest cell had been empty for ages now, and the far one hadn't been occupied since the incident last month with the Cyclops.

'Hang on.' Ianto put his hand on Toshiko's shoulder.

She was surprised by this unexpected contact. 'What?'

Ianto had worked out why light was sliding off the glass in the middle cell differently. Why he couldn't see the Weevil inside.

The cell was open.

He checked the PDA again. Owen's signal was behind him. He could smell the foul stench of something breathing close by. Something snorted in his ear. Belched and growled. He whirled round, shouldering Toshiko aside from the creature behind them.

The Weevil must have been lurking in one of the other cells, unseen behind the heavy studded door. She had stopped sniffing him now, and glared furiously. Though she always looked furious, thought Ianto. It was something about her deep-set eyes and the permanent furrow of lines in her forehead. That and the way her savage jaw seemed genetically incapable of smiling. It was snarling at him now.

Toshiko scurried aside as best she could, scuffling across the floor on her backside. The sound distracted the Weevil for a second. Just enough time for Ianto. He snatched the device he'd been carrying from his jacket pocket, and plunged it into the gap at the top of the Weevil's overalls. It connected with the leathery flesh of her neck, below the chin and her slavering fangs.

The Weevil barely had time to twist her head towards him before he slid the activation switch on the gadget. Her eyes stared into his briefly, and then squeezed closed in agony as the device sent a disabling jolt through her whole body. She slammed backwards, smashing into the fire-hose reel on the opposite wall. Ianto pressed forward, holding the thing against her neck as she slid down the slimy bricks.

The Weevil's eyes were closed now. Ianto stepped back, breathless, dazed, relieved. A bit incredulous at what he'd just done.

Toshiko clambered back to her feet and brushed the dirt from her trousers. 'Ianto. That was very impressive, but…'

'But what?'

Toshiko took the device from his hand. 'I've not seen this thing before.'

He took it back from her. 'Something we scavenged from the wreckage of Torchwood One. It doesn't last for long. Look, it's discharged already. Useless now.'

'It could be lethal.'

'I suppose,' Ianto said quietly. 'Better her than you and me, though, eh?'

'Not what I meant.' Toshiko's brow was furrowed almost as much as the Weevil's. 'You came equipped, Ianto. We didn't know the Weevil was loose. You brought it because you thought you might use it on Owen.'

Ianto stooped down to grab the Weevil's ankles, and dragged her back into her cell. Something tumbled from the pocket in the Weevil's overalls and clattered onto the floor. 'That explains a lot.' Ianto showed it to Toshiko. 'Owen's mobile phone.'

'He must have known we'd track him down with it,' groaned Toshiko. 'It's not as if he was going to need it to call any of us. And he opened the cell because he knew if anyone turned up that the Weevil might turn ugly.'

'She has a head start on the rest of us, that's for sure.' Ianto clicked the transparent front of the cell securely in place.

Toshiko was looking sadly at her expensive trousers. They were covered in slime from the dungeon floor. 'I think I may kill Owen anyway. Attacking Gwen. Releasing the Weevil on us. Plus what he did with the firewall security…'

Her voice had trailed off. She'd even stopped fussing about her trousers. Ianto recognised that distant, pensive look in her eyes. 'What is it?'

She grinned at him. 'I have an idea.'

The ship rattled and lurched. The corridors stretched into a misty haze ahead of them, just as Gwen remembered. The same green-tinged gloom interspersed by brilliant flashes, the same gusts of hot, sour steam from half-seen vents along their route. When she'd struggled out of here with Sandra Applegate's body, she'd hoped that was the last she'd ever see of this place. And good riddance to it, at that. There was a tight feeling in her chest now, and it wasn't because she'd chosen a wetsuit that was a size too small. It was the fear of not knowing the first thing about this place that was constricting her breathing. She shrugged her shoulders to detach the diving cylinder, and dropped her mask next to it.

Jack clearly had no such worries. He was already marching down the walkway, ducking to avoid catching his head on the bizarre fronds and tendrils that curled from up in the ceiling.

'This place is alive,' he called back to her.

'I know. I've never seen anything like it.'

'No,' he chided, 'I mean, you didn't turn it off when you were last here. We have to do that first. If we can find the controls.'

'First?' What else did he have in mind? He was already striding away again. Gwen hurried to catch up. Jack was taking this whole alien ship thing so calmly, as though he'd seen hundreds of them in his career. That couldn't be true, could it? He wasn't casual about it; she could tell that from the way he handled the harpoon gun as he made careful progress down the walkway. But he was measured, assured. His whole bearing told her that he considered a walk through an underwater alien vessel as routine as she would consider a uniformed search of a Butetown flat.

'C'mon!' called Jack from ahead of her.

She chased after him. The ship rocked and juddered erratically around them, and she struggled to keep her balance.

She caught up with Jack in the open expanse that contained the circle of suspended cages. He was still wearing his diving cylinder, with his mask dangled over his shoulder. He wriggled out of the scuba set, and placed the harpoon gun on the floor so that it was carefully pointed away from him and Gwen.

Jack studied the cylindrical block that squatted in the exact centre of the circle. Gwen didn't see how he did it but, with a few deft movements of his fingers, he activated the cylinder. The top spiralled apart like a time-lapse film of a flower head unfurling its petals. Two softly illuminated hemispherical panels unfolded from inside, and presented themselves like a remorseful supplicant offering his open palms to Jack.

Gwen could see a dark patch at the base of the cylinder. It was where Sandra Applegate had died, and the odd green light of the room made the blood-stain look black. Beside it, her original torch was half-immersed in the last gluey remains of the pulped starfish, which retained only the faintest outline of its original shape. She pointed it out to Jack. 'No need for your harpoon gun, after all.'

'We'll see,' he replied. He was intent on operating the two panels in front of him. He continued to manipulate them for several minutes, until he stood back and folded his arms. He grinned hugely. 'There ya go.' Even as he was speaking, the buffeting movements of the ship were dying down.

'What happened?'

'Put it into reverse gear,' he explained. 'Not enough power left for a secure return, so it'll tear itself apart as it heads back through the Rift. Still, the wreckage won't be littering the Bay. And it'll cause less damage around it than on its journey in.' He nodded at the harpoon gun on the floor. 'It's like the barbs on that spear. Goes through more easily in the right direction. At the moment, it's like the ship's trying to go the wrong way, and that's what's causing all this local trauma.'

Gwen looked more closely at the hemispherical panels that Jack had somehow manipulated to control the alien ship. She couldn't identify any switches or dials. All she could see were softly glowing areas of colour. 'And you can just control it? As easy as that.'

'It's a Bruydac battle cruiser,' he said. 'Nothing too tricky here.'

'Oh right,' she said sarcastically. 'Lucky for us that you passed your Bruydac driving test, eh? And that your licence is still valid.'

'Told ya before, I don't need a driving licence.' Jack began to examine one of the suspended cages, exploring its innards with his fingers. 'But I remember the lessons. Nice guy. Don't know what happened to him, but he wrote for a while. Aha!'

The largest of the suspended cages was sealed shut. The cage glowed softly with an inner radiance. Its rich, translucent blue-green surface had a glassy lustre that reminded Gwen of Chinese ornaments. Jack leaned towards it and manipulated the front with a series of hand and arm gestures that looked like t'ai chi moves. With the hissing sound of a vacuum release, the front of the cage split in two and peeled backwards.

'Now that is ugly,' Jack said.

The occupant was a large humanoid. If it had stood, it would have been more than seven feet tall. In the caged frame, it sat in a scooped position, its knees slightly lifted and its long, filthy claws clutched near its chest, so that it appeared like a monstrously large fœtus. Its bare skull had a ridge of bony protrusions that began at the bridge of its nose and continued over the back of the head. Its mouth was a gash in the bottom of its flat, cruel face, and it sucked in air with shallow breaths. Beneath its heavy, closed lids, the creature's eyes were moving, as though it was dreaming. Tubing and wires were connected from its scarred torso into flickering shapes of light in the side of the cage.

Gwen found that she'd wandered in front of the suspended creature. She was fascinated and repulsed by it in equal measure. A hand on her shoulder moved her to one side. She twisted her head to see that Jack was weighing the harpoon gun in his hands, aiming the wicked spike at the trapped alien.

Gwen considered the look in Jack's eye. 'You can't, Jack. It's helpless.'

'No it's not,' he told her coldly. 'I've spoken to it. You don't know it like I do.'

'I'm beginning to think I don't know you any more.'

Jack never took his eyes off the creature in front of him. It was almost as though he suspected he would falter if he met Gwen's searching, disbelieving gaze. 'It's controlling Owen. It's murdered others. It would have destroyed this whole area.'

'No, Jack. I can't let you.'

He hefted the harpoon gun higher. 'You can't stop me. It's surrendered the right to survive.'

The trigger clicked. The harpoon spear shot forward and penetrated the creature's chest, just above its folded claws. The barbed spike continued through the body and out the back of the cage. Jack braced his feet on the floor, took a grip of the unspooled wire that was still attached to the spear, and pulled back with all his weight. The reverse side of the barbed spike caught on the rear of the cage, until Jack tugged it one more time and the brittle casing shattered. The entire spear pulled back through the creature's chest. The Bruydac Warrior's eyes snapped open, red and wide and appalled. Its arms jerked out in an uncontrolled gesture, and for a fleeting moment Gwen imagined it begging, pleading. The spiked barb of the harpoon clattered to the floor in front of the cage, and the Bruydac Warrior slumped lifeless in its cage.

Jack concealed the remains of the ravaged body with the broken cage doors. The catch was broken and would not fasten, so he pulled the front pieces together as best he could. 'Nowhere to run,' he told the corpse quietly.

Gwen rounded on him. The initial sight of the creature had frightened her, revolted her even. But Jack's cold-blooded execution had nauseated her more. She rounded on him. 'You didn't have to do that.'

'No?' He stared her down. 'It's controlling Owen. It still is. I don't know any other way of helping him. You got a better idea, maybe?'

'I don't know,' she yelled angrily. 'What makes me the expert all of a sudden? You're the one who's had the Bruydac driving lessons.'

'Well, maybe that will make it easier for you to do this next thing for me.'

Gwen didn't want to listen any more. And she couldn't abandon Jack and retrace her steps down those corridors and find her way back to the Hub alone. Jack would know that, of course, and was able to make some further adjustments to the controls in the central cylinder while she scowled at him from the edge of the room. All the time, Jack continued talking, explaining what he was doing, what he was going to do, and the things he needed her to do. She didn't want to listen, but she found that she had to. And the more she did, the greater her dread became.

His work at the cylinder completed, Jack walked over to one of the hanging cages. It was the same one that they'd found Owen in. Without any hesitation, Jack sat in the chair of the cage.

'Strap me in,' he said to her. She hesitated. 'Do it.'

Gwen found her hands were trembling.

'Tighter,' Jack insisted.

She completed the final fastening. Jack was pinned into the cage. His hands were free, but he could not reach the straps that bound him around the neck, shoulder, and upper arms. He could move his head just enough to peer down his nose at his watch. 'Running out of time,' he told her. 'Listen, Gwen. If this doesn't work, you'll have to explain to the others.'

Gwen reached out to him. Placed her palm softly against his cheek.

He twisted his head as though her hand had burned him. 'Knock it off,' he snarled. 'Stay focused. Do not – I repeat do not – change the plan. You do exactly as we agreed. Understand?'

She nodded mutely.

'Say it!' he snapped. 'Understand?'

'I understand.'

'You must not let me change this plan,' he urged. 'No matter how much I may threaten you. No matter how much I plead with you or beg you.' Gwen could hardly bear to meet the blue intensity of his gaze. 'All right,' Jack said. 'Hit the button.'

Gwen reached behind the cage and activated the control Jack had shown her.

The cage quivered into life around him. With a brief cough, the mechanism punched a Bruydac device through the skin of his back and into his spine.

Jack bellowed in surprise, a roar that seemed to fill the whole cavernous room and that Gwen thought would never end. Eventually, Jack reverted to a series of anguished gasps.

'Not what I expected,' he told her, and slipped into unconsciousness.

THIRTY-ONE

Toshiko sat alone at her computer terminal in the main Hub area. Her desk was stacked high with half-repaired components, scribbled notes and an assortment of pens, half of which didn't work. Flat-panel screens flickered in front of her eyes, displaying the latest results of her search around the Hub for Owen's life signs.

At first, she'd worried about being too obviously exposed in the centre of the area. She reassured herself that Owen was not armed when he fled from the medical suite, and that she had now securely locked the armoury. He might be able to spot her by looking down from the gantry by the Boardroom, or from beside the cog-shaped entrance where the lift delivered people from the upper floors. But he would not be able to pick her off from either place. The idea was that it appeared she would have enough time to make a run for it if and when she heard his footsteps on the metal gantry, or detected the noise of the door opening behind her.

She was still in a state of some anxiety, though. That much was evident when the Tannoy system sounded, and she simply leaped out of her seat and practically whirled on the spot in panic as she realised that she had no idea where she was going to run. Her breathing was shallow, ragged, panicked. It felt like her heart was battering her ribcage.

'You're very difficult to reach,' said Gwen's voice over the Tannoy.

'That's the idea,' said Toshiko. 'Oh God, Gwen, you scared me to death.'

'Sorry,' Gwen said. 'I'm using some comms device that Jack brought along. He connected it to the Torchwood PA system. Just as well, because your mobile's still switched off.'

There was a clattering noise from the gallery. Toshiko looked up, momentarily distracted. Nothing to see.

'No sign of Owen yet,' she told Gwen. 'I think he may have gone to ground.'

'Thank God,' replied Gwen. 'Things seem to have gone completely tits-up here. We've managed to stop the ship coming through the Rift—'

'Well, that's great news!'

'—but Jack's got himself trapped in that place we found Owen. The place where he got that thing stuck in him. Oh, Tosh…'

Toshiko was torn between comforting Gwen and warning her. 'You have to be careful, Gwen. You're broadcasting on an open channel. Whatever I can hear, Owen can hear too.'

'I don't care!' There was a sob in Gwen's voice. She was starting to lose it, thought Toshiko. Her hand hovered over the disconnect button. 'Tosh, he's trapped in the machinery. It's all gone so horribly wrong. He's had one of those control devices injected into him. What am I gonna do?'

Toshiko didn't have time to answer. There was a clattering, clanking sound from the gallery beside the coffee machine. There was a blur of motion. The looped chain by the railing rattled and swayed. Owen had slid down it, and was plunging through the raised level of water in the basin, unstoppable, desperate to reach her. In his hand was an evil-looking surgical instrument. He made the near side of the basin before she had time to turn and flee.

He was right beside her.

She knew that surgical instrument from seeing Owen conduct autopsies. It was the hook-ended hammer that he used to prise the cap from the top of a severed skull. He'd joked about it being the inspiration for the Beatles' song 'Maxwell's Silver Hammer' that came down upon your head and made sure that you were dead. That gave her some clue about his immediate intentions.

She spun on her heel, ready to run.

Owen plunged forward, the hammer raised. He was on her. She could not escape.

The hammer came down onto her head.

Through her head.

Onto Toshiko's desk.

Two of the flat-panel screens burst into a bright shower of sparks and glass and shards of plastic. Owen recoiled from the explosion, and fell onto his back on the metal grating beside his own desk.

Within seconds, Ianto was on him, water spraying all around the area. Owen's eyes stretched wide, unbelieving, furious. Ianto took full advantage of his disorientation, and smashed him hard across the face with the back of his hand. Owen was no match for the bigger man, and Ianto was able to twist the hammer from his grasp and cast it aside. It bounced off under the nearby desk with the chime of metal on metal.

Ianto sat on Owen's chest, pinning him to the floor. He plucked a syringe from his pocket and, one-handed, popped the protective cap off the needle before plunging it into Owen.

Over by her desk, Toshiko flickered and faded and vanished. Owen saw this, and his head slumped against the floor in frustration. 'Second Reality,' he spat in disgust. 'Oh, very good, Tosh.' His tired eyes looked at Ianto, who was still pressing down on his chest. 'D'you mind getting off, mate. You're getting me all wet here.'

It was weird, decided Toshiko, to see yourself interacting with other people. The whole thing was quite different to seeing yourself on video, because you got the complete picture of the surroundings as it happened. Seeing the back of her own head made her want to get her hair cut as soon as possible. And did she really have that little bounce in her gait? Why had no one mentioned it before?

She had watched the whole sequence from her vantage point in the Boardroom on the first floor. She'd crouched there in the dark, waiting for Owen to locate the image of herself that she'd projected at her desk. There had been one nervous moment when Owen had made his way through the Boardroom and onto the balcony by the coffee machine, but he had been too fixated on the fake Toshiko at her desk below to notice the real thing lurking under the conference table, petrified and holding her breath.

Once Owen had committed himself to the attack, and fallen through the insubstantial image of Toshiko, Ianto had leaped up from his hiding place and injected the powerful sedative into him.

'Bit of an awkward moment there,' Ianto called across to Toshiko as she came down the gantry steps to join him. 'He almost trod on me in the basin as he charged through. Splashed water down my snorkel. Thought I was going to choke to death for a moment.'

Toshiko was beside him now. 'Nice work, Ianto.'

'You clever girl,' Owen slurred at her from beneath Ianto. 'Using the Second Reality software to make me think that was you.'

241

'I'll take that as a compliment,' she told him.

Owen grinned a wide, lazy grin. 'Don't be too pleased with yourself, Tosh. I heard that call from Gwen.'

'What do you mean?'

His eyes flickered on the edge of unconsciousness. 'I have another life left. Back in… back in my ship. Your friend Jack…' Owen swallowed hard, took a deep breath, exhaled it. 'Got a feeling he's going to be… the most useful of all.' He summoned up the strength to wink at Ianto. One last smile for Toshiko. 'See you again. Soon.'

After she'd contacted Toshiko, Gwen sat quietly in the cavernous room with her back to the central cylinder. The churning, lurching movements of the alien vessel had begun to subside now, and the flicker of green lights in the unseen ceiling was settling into a regular, uninterrupted illumination of the area around her.

She studied Jack from a distance. His breathing was regular, but he remained deeply unconscious. Gwen mentally rehearsed the sequence of events that Jack had explained earlier. But now he was trapped in the cage, nothing seemed clear any more. Everything seemed wrong, impossible.

Jack took a sudden, shuddering breath, like a man surfacing from water and gratefully gulping at the air. His eyes widened, accustomed themselves to the light. Focused on Gwen. 'Hey,' he said cheerfully. 'I was beginning to think things weren't working out.'

Gwen forced herself up from the floor. Turned her back on him. Began to operate the panels that sprouted from the top of the control cylinder, just the way Jack had shown her. The urge was to rely on what she knew from Earth technology – to feel the reassuring click of a light switch or hear the firm clunk that a car door makes that tells you it's closed. Her short training session at these controls with Jack earlier had made her nervous and frustrated. It was more a mental contact than a physical one. She began to doubt that she'd manipulated them correctly, until she heard the sound of running water in the distance.

She panicked for a moment, realising that her scuba gear was a long way from her down the corridors. Until she saw Jack's mask and diving cylinder on the floor. She snatched it up, and tried to remain calm as she slipped the harness on her back, strapped it across her midriff, fitted the mask over her eyes and nose.

The water began to gush into the chamber. It swilled across the floor, and swirled against the central cylinder and around her feet. In his cage, still clear of the incoming water, Jack's eyes registered his alarm.

'OK.' He had raised his voice to make himself heard over the sound of the water. 'You can let me outta here now, Gwen.'

She continued to check that her scuba set was working.

'Gwen? Gwen!'

The cylinder was half-full, and open. The air-hoses were securely attached and not kinked.

'C'mon Gwen. You can let me out now.'

She adjusted her mask, getting it comfortable. Not time yet to put the mouthpiece in.

The cramped cage couldn't be comfortable for Jack, but he was showing her his biggest, cheesiest, most reassuring grin. 'Tosh did it, y'know. She trapped Owen. He's locked in the cells. Right next to the Weevil, imagine that! So it's OK to undo these straps now, Gwen. We did it! We can get outta here!'

'You mean, I can get out of here,' she told him.

No, that was a mistake. Jack had told her not to talk to him. Not to get drawn into a conversation. She bit her bottom lip in frustration and annoyance. Jack saw it. Knew he was getting through. The incoming water was splashing up against the bottom of the cages now. Gwen leaned back against the cylinder and looked at Jack. She thought she saw a calculating glance, a transitory look that was gone almost as soon as she spotted it.

He winked at her. 'Time to go, Gwen. Place is flooding.'

'You warned me not to listen to you.'

'That was then, and this is now.' A note of studied exasperation in his voice. 'You said it yourself, my plan's gone so horribly wrong. Completely tits-up.' He could evidently see from her reaction that what he'd said had surprised her.

'How very interesting, Jack. Now, how would you know I'd said that?' His eagerness was evolving into worry, and then anger, as she continued to speak. 'Because you were unconscious when I called Tosh. So either you were faking it, which wouldn't be good. Or you heard it when you were possessing Owen. Which would be even worse.'

'Please, Gwen. This really isn't what I planned.' The level had reached his waist now. He wriggled impotently as the cold grey water lapped around him in the cage. 'Please Gwen. I'm begging you.'

'Pleading?' she asked him. 'That's so not Jack.'

'God dammit!' he flared, shaking the cage as he struggled against his restraints. 'That is me now! Up to my ass in seawater, you think I'm gonna *reason* with you, Police Constable Cooper? Think I'm gonna conduct a debate with you? Observe the niceties of reasoned argument? *Get me the hell outta here!*'

The water had reached her chest now. No more time to talk with Jack. Gwen inserted the mouthpiece. She ensured that there was a watertight seal between the breathing set and her lips.

Water slopped around her face and ears. She could hear her own breathing as she tried to inhale through her mouth regularly, calmly. Still she watched Jack in the cage as the churning seawater eddied around him, splashing in his face, making him splutter. He was shouting at her still, his bound hands thrashing and scratching at the bars in a futile effort to release them.

Jack wailed and pleaded and screamed at her. The last thing she could hear before the water rose over her ears were his threats.

'If you don't release these clasps for me, I will get outta here once the water has short-circuited the system. And then I am gonna bust your ass. You will regret this, lady. I will make you regret this…'

The water continued to rise over her face mask.

You're unable to keep your temper. The anger and desolation and anguish consume you. It's not like the hunger this time, not the exquisite agony of physical want. It's the knowledge that you are no longer in control. Not of your body. Not of the elements. Not of the woman who has trapped you here to face this alone.

The sea has reached your chin now. It's cold and dark and there is no comfort for you in its chill embrace. With your mouth clamped shut, you can just angle your head a little higher, keeping your nose and eyes above the water. Staring at the top of the cage. The last thing you expected to see, and the last thing you will see.

You consider what's inside yourself now. What there will be next. And it is so dark and lonely and empty. You knew that Sandra Applegate believed in everlasting life and a better place to go. Guy Wildman's unreasoned agnosticism allowed for something beyond death. But when you explore your heart now, there is nothing inside you. Nothing. Blankness, blackness.

Close your eyes now. How long can you hold your breath?

Your lungs burn. They ache for air. Every fibre of your being is telling you to open your mouth and your eyes.

You so want somewhere to go from here, but you don't remotely believe there is anywhere left. You are not Bee or Wildman or Tegg. You are not like them. You know there is nothing more.

You are—

Jack's face was underwater now, angled up to the last pocket of air in the cage. With her head underwater too, everything seemed closer to Gwen. Images were magnified, even in the greyish sea water. The sound of her own breathing, the noise of exhaled air, was loud and close.

She wasn't sure she could bear to watch this, but knew somehow she wouldn't look away. Think of how he had killed the Bruydac Warrior. He had told her that she should imagine him as that man, who showed no mercy to a defeated enemy. He was someone who should suffer the same fate, if it came down to it. He should be allowed to die, helpless and alone.

That wasn't Jack in the cage any more, cajoling and begging and threatening. Thrashing at the restraints in fury and desperation. It was the Bruydac Warrior. So wasn't she just doing the same thing that Jack did earlier?

Didn't that make her the same? Or, knowing that about herself, didn't it make her worse?

The bubbles from Jack's upturned face slowed to a trickle and stopped. His eyelids opened. His mouth gaped abruptly as the breathing reflex overcame him. His chest convulsed as he sucked cold grey water into his lungs in a final, choking rush.

Cold, grey seawater surrounded Gwen, so she couldn't feel the hot salt tears on her face. She forced herself to watch Jack until his seizures subsided.

Once he hadn't moved for ten minutes, she knew for certain that Jack was dead.

THIRTY-TWO

The mesh grating tilted up and over and toppled with a clanging echo. Gwen emerged from beneath it, surging out of the water in the basin and sending waves slopping over the edges across the Hub floor. Through the mask, she could see that she had broken the surface. She tore it off and eagerly gasped down clean, fresh air. Or as fresh as it got in the Hub. Even the slightly damp atmosphere of the main level made her feel home and safe.

Behind her, Jack's body floated face down in the water of the Hub basin. She had released it from the bonds of the cage in the ship and desperately dragged it behind her through flooded corridors, along an open stretch of the Bay, and finally through the interlocking junctions of the Hub's underwater entrance.

She'd found Jack's body a dead weight while it was in the water. Now she tried to drag it from the basin. It was more of a struggle than she had anticipated. Her body was telling her to stop, to rest. Gwen's legs and arms throbbed with dull pain, and she had to fight for her breath.

Eventually, she got her hands under his armpits and half-dragged him, half-fell with him onto the Hub floor.

Jack's body was supine on the chill metal of the walkway by the basin. His staring eyes were glassy, empty. His skin showed as a ghastly pale blue, his full lips were dark, and there were rings of black beneath his eyes.

She slumped down on the grating beside him, and removed her diving cylinder. Sat watching him. Urging him.

Why wasn't he reviving? She'd seen him take a bullet in the forehead and return to life. But she didn't know for certain if anything could kill him. An illness, a devastating injury… or maybe the inability to recover immediately? He'd been dead for at least half an hour this time.

She rolled him over so that he was prone on the floor, and began to push beneath his shoulder blades. Water spurted from his mouth and through the grating into the basin.

Gwen pulled him onto his back again. Her mind raced, and she couldn't focus on what to do next. She'd so believed that Jack would spontaneously recover once he surfaced that she was now panicking about the right course of action. What had they taught her in that Basics of First Aid course? Was it safe to give him oxygen from her diving cylinder? Or was that too much pressure? Did she need to empty the lungs of water? Or was it CPR first? Oh God, she hadn't even checked for a pulse! There was something about having to give CPR within a quarter of an hour of someone collapsing. And how fast did brain death occur after they've stopped breathing?

Jack eyes stared up at her, glazed, sightless. They were unfocused, peaceful, unaccusing.

She pinched his nose, tilted his head back. You were supposed to do that, weren't you? To extend the airway, or something. She parted his lips, sealed hers around them, and exhaled.

There was no response.

Time to start chest compressions? No, she thought. One more breath. She positioned her mouth over his again.

'Gwen?' There was a clattering sound from the spiral staircase across from her. Toshiko was hurrying down it, two steps at a time. 'What's going on?'

Toshiko hurried across the basin to join her. Gwen hardly registered that the walkway had now re-emerged as the water subsided. She was too preoccupied in devising some excuse about what had happened to Jack, why she was pressing her face to his. But if he was dead, then what was the whole bloody point?

'Jack had to abandon his scuba gear halfway back from the ship,' she lied. 'Ran out of oxygen. Only for a short time.' She could barely speak now. 'Oh God, Toshiko, I think he's dead. But he can't be…'

Toshiko's look was grave. 'Gwen,' she began gently. 'How long has he been without air?'

Gwen didn't know what to say any more. Didn't know how to explain.

She gave a little shriek of surprise. Jack had abruptly rolled over towards her, and barfed sea water over her legs. Her shriek turned into a shout of elation and then to laughter. She threw herself on him and hugged him tight. Let him go almost immediately, as he began to choke in her embrace. Apologised when he slipped back and smacked his head on the floor. Laughed again. Laughed, and thought she'd never stop.

With Toshiko's help, Gwen got Jack into the medical suite and onto a bed.

Jack was making a remarkable recovery. He'd spent some time explaining to Gwen and Toshiko and Ianto about the Bruydac Warrior – too much time to be plausible for someone purportedly recovering from a near-drowning. 'Don't make a fuss, Jack,' Gwen hissed close to his ear while Toshiko was busily wrestling a couple of monitors into position on the other side of his room. 'You'll just draw attention to yourself. Lie down and try to look like you're at death's door, for God's sake.' She sat down on the bed beside him, and tried to look concerned.

Toshiko smoothed the electrodes onto Jack's chest, and adjusted the sensitivity of the monitor by his bedside. The machine began to make an encouraging ping sound. 'You're a better patient than Owen. You won't be surprised to hear that.'

'How's he doing?' Jack's voice was a rasp.

'How do you think?' smiled Toshiko. 'Doctors make the worst patients. At least we don't have to strap him down any more.'

'I bet he was glad when you released him,' said Gwen.

'I said we don't *need* to strap him down any more,' replied Toshiko. 'I didn't say we'd actually undone his restraints yet.'

A roar from the next bedroom confirmed that Owen was awake and probably listening. Toshiko grinned at them, and slipped out of the room.

Jack sat up in his own bed. He placed his hand over Gwen's on the cover, and squeezed it reassuringly. Ianto was sitting in a chair against the wall, pretending not to notice.

'Owen's gonna be fine,' said Jack. 'The Bruydac Warrior must have relinquished control a moment before the sedatives rendered him unconscious. Because it didn't want to be captured alive by Tosh and Ianto.'

'And it knew it had somewhere else to jump. It knew you were waiting.'

'Right.'

'And it tried to jump again when it thought you were dying.' Ianto was unusually animated, excited at his own cleverness in working out what had happened. 'You had it fooled there, eh?'

Jack exchanged a look with Gwen. 'Yeah.'

She squeezed his hand in acknowledgement.

'But it really had nowhere to go, because there were no more hosts. And its true form was dead.' Ianto scraped his chair nearer to the bed. 'It abandoned the victims when it had to escape. Which explains why that implant in Owen's spine has burnt out. Like the ones in the other... er... victims?'

'Yeah.' Jack leaned forward on the bed, and ran an exploratory hand up his own back. 'Y'know, I gotta have this thing removed. Otherwise I'm gonna set off the alarms every time I check in at the airport.'

He had leaned too far forward and dislodged one of the electrodes. The monitor beside him flatlined, and an alarm went off. Toshiko hurried in from the other room, her face full of worry until she saw Jack sitting on the bed and laughing at her.

Jack allowed Toshiko to fuss about him and reattach the electrodes.

Gwen's mobile began to buzz in her pocket. After such a long silence, it was a surprise to hear it again. She flipped it open and saw that it was Rhys calling.

Where the hell was she, he wanted to know. The cinema thing had been rained off, and Josie and Brendan had bunked off without him because they were like that, weren't they, it was all about them since the office party. And he'd been worrying all night about her in this storm, and couldn't get a signal. But now the storm seemed to be abating, and he'd finally got through.

Gwen huddled in the corner of the bedroom, smiling a wan apology at the others in the room.

'I'm sorry,' she told Rhys quietly. 'I'll not be long, I promise. Just finishing up here.' She looked down at herself, and saw that she was still wearing the wetsuit that was a size too small. 'I've got to change first. Be home soon.'

She returned to the bed and had a good look at Jack. Despite his recent ordeal, he appeared to be in implausibly good health. 'I should probably get home,' she told him.

'Life goes on,' smiled Jack. 'It must be getting late.' He checked his wrist, but Toshiko had removed his watch earlier.

Gwen pointed out where she had placed it on his bedside cabinet. 'It got smashed,' she told him in an apologetic tone. 'You must have bashed it against the side of that metal cage thing. When you were... well, you know.'

Jack inspected the broken watch. The cover glass over the twenty-four-hour dial had crazed.

Gwen indicated the hands on the watch, buckled and unmoving. She leaned close, so that only Jack would hear her speak. 'Time of death: 21.46.'

'Oh yeah,' Jack replied. 'Now *that* was a great year for me.'

THIRTY-THREE

The Casa Celi was almost deserted. No rowdy bankers or ladies-who-lunched had braved the bright afternoon sun. Rico Celi polished the table next to them for the tenth time since they'd arrived, as though that might encourage some passer-by to come in and order something.

There wasn't much likelihood of that, Gwen thought. The high street was largely empty of people, too. There was so much mud silt washed up along its length that it wasn't always clear where the pavement ended and the carriageway began. When the Torchwood team had walked down it earlier, she'd wished that she'd worn Wellington boots instead of her sensible shoes. The water from the Bay may have subsided as suddenly as it had risen over central Cardiff, but many of the shops and businesses remained closed. Through most streets, the residual sludge wasn't the only thing left behind by the retreating water. There was the human detritus of food scraps and fast-food cartons. Shredded paper and cans. A solitary, soggy, striped pillow. Postboxes had a ring around them, dirty tide marks that showed how far the water had reached. Against one bent lamp-post was a twisted bicycle, awkwardly cast up from who knew where and still with its chain attached to one buckled wheel.

The café doors were firmly closed, despite the warm afternoon sun. It kept the foul smell of the mud out in the street. Gwen and Toshiko sat at one small table by the window. Jack and Owen sat at the next one alone. They were positioned by the front window so that they could look out into the street, alert for any sign of Weevils. In the ashtray in front of Jack was the exact change for his and Owen's drinks. Jack had also placed the anti-Weevil spray on his table, in plain view next to his tall glass of water. Gwen thought it more prudent to conceal the hand-clamps beneath her table.

'Rico,' called Jack. 'You're gonna wear a hole in that thing.'

The café owner stopped scrubbing at the adjacent table. 'For a while this morning, I thought that I'd never get this place clean again. I was stuck in here during the flood, did I mention that?'

'Only a dozen times. How were you?'

'*Cachu planciau.*'

Gwen coughed in an attempt to stifle her laughter.

'Very demotic,' said Jack. His eyes never left the street. But Gwen could tell his attention was on Owen, beside him. Owen had barely spoken to any of them since Jack had discharged them both from the medical suite in the Hub. Jack had made some excuse about an increase in the number of free-roaming Weevils in the last forty-eight hours, and that many more of the creatures seemed to have been flushed out from the sewers by the recent flooding. When they'd arrived at Casa Celi half an hour ago, he'd made Gwen and Toshiko sit at a separate table. Gwen sipped her lemonade, listening in to Jack's sporadic, almost one-sided conversation with Owen.

When he eventually spoke, Owen's voice was barely a mumble. Didn't want her and Toshiko to overhear him, Gwen decided. Deep down, he probably didn't want Jack to hear it either. 'I feel that this has been a test,' Owen muttered.

'A test,' Jack repeated in a level tone.

'Like a test of me. One I botched. But the person who suffered for my failure was Megan.'

Jack took his eyes from the window for the first time since he'd sat down. He looked closely at Owen. 'You know that I recruited you all because you are the best. Don't you?'

Owen nodded dumbly.

'It's a gut thing,' Jack explained. 'An instinct. Not something you can pass or fail a test on. And it's not something I'm gonna judge you on, Owen. You each earn my respect every day.'

Owen couldn't hold Jack's gaze. He distracted himself by swirling his slice of lemon round in the bottom of his Coke glass.

'Hard as it may seem now,' Jack continued, 'Megan was a part of your life before Torchwood. You are doing more to save others now than you ever were back in A&E. That's the old world, that's gone now. She's gone.'

'Don't you think I know that?' snapped Owen. His angular face was pink now, suffused with barely contained fury.

'Not what I mean, Owen.' Jack kept his steady gaze on the angry man. He would not back down, would not apologise. 'Your whole existence in A&E, you can't return there. You're so way beyond that now. You can't go back to that time, that place, those people. You're living another life. It's the twenty-first century, we have to help them be ready for it.' He took Owen's hand, and placed something in his palm. It was the Bekaran deep-tissue scanner that he'd retrieved from the hospital room. 'And giving them alien technology helps no one in the long run.'

Owen looked like he was about to say something, but abruptly there was there was no time for more chat. They were all startled by a face at the window. Fuzzy pale hair, grizzled weather-beaten skin, and a permanent scowl of anger and bemusement. If they'd been shocked by the Weevil, Gwen thought, well that was nothing to what it must have felt when it saw four humans on the other side of the glass leap to their feet.

Jack grabbed for the spray in front of him, scattering half-finished drinks and loose change all over the table in the process. Gwen and Toshiko scrambled awkwardly beneath their table for the hand-clamps.

Owen, meanwhile, was already in hot pursuit of the Weevil. First through the café door and into the mud-caked street. Ahead of them all.

Acknowledgements

Stuart Cooper, for the initial opportunity.

Brian Minchin and Gary Russell, for production insights.

Mathew Clayton and Steve Tribe, for editorial expertise.

Dan Abnett and Andy Lane, for camaraderie.

Peter Ware and Matt Nichols, for logistics.

Russell T Davies and Steven Moffat, for bringing Captain Jack back to life in the first place.

Adam and Samuel Anghelides, for background noises.

Also available from BBC Books:

TORCHWOOD

BORDER PRINCES
Dan Abnett

ISBN 978 0 563 48654 1
UK £6.99 US$11.99/$14.99 CDN

The End of the World began on a Thursday night in October, just after eight in the evening…

The Amok is driving people out of their minds, turning them into zombies and causing riots in the streets. A solitary diner leaves a Cardiff restaurant, his mission to protect the Principal leading him to a secret base beneath a water tower. Everyone has a headache, there's something in Davey Morgan's shed, and the church of St Mary-in-the-Dust, demolished in 1840, has reappeared – though it's not due until 2011. Torchwood seem to be out of their depth. What will all this mean for the romance between Torchwood's newest members?

Captain Jack Harkness has something more to worry about: an alarm, an early warning, given to mankind and held – inert – by Torchwood for 108 years. And now it's flashing. Something is coming. Or something is already here.

Featuring Captain Jack Harkness as played by John Barrowman, with Gwen Cooper, Owen Harper, Toshiko Sato and Ianto Jones as played by Eve Myles, Burn Gorman, Naoki Mori and Gareth David-Lloyd, in the hit series created by Russell T Davies for BBC Television.

TORCHWOOD

SLOW DECAY
Andy Lane

ISBN 978 0 563 48655 8
UK £6.99 US$11.99/$14.99 CDN

When Torchwood track an energy surge to a Cardiff nightclub, the team finds the police are already at the scene. Five teenagers have died in a fight, and lying among the bodies is an unfamiliar device. Next morning, they discover the corpse of a Weevil, its face and neck eaten away, seemingly by human teeth. And on the streets of Cardiff, an ordinary woman with an extraordinary hunger is attacking people and eating her victims.

The job of a lifetime it might be, but working for Torchwood is putting big strains on Gwen's relationship with Rhys. While she decides to spice up their love life with the help of alien technology, Rhys decides it's time to sort himself out – better music, healthier food, lose some weight. Luckily, a friend has mentioned Doctor Scotus's weight-loss clinic…

Featuring Captain Jack Harkness as played by John Barrowman, with Gwen Cooper, Owen Harper, Toshiko Sato and Ianto Jones as played by Eve Myles, Burn Gorman, Naoki Mori and Gareth David-Lloyd, in the hit series created by Russell T Davies for BBC Television.